D1298142

THE DEAL BREAKER

A Novel

Suzanne J Warfield

Copyright © 2017 Suzanne J Warfield

All rights reserved. No part of this book may be reproduced or used in any manner without the express written permission of the publisher, except for the use of brief quotations in a book review.

ISBN: 9781542477970   title: 6852921

Cover design by Dar Albert

Print layout by booknook.biz

Contents

PART I

PART II

PART III

PART IV

PART V

PART I

"FIRE"

Chapter 1

"KITTY, GET UP, GET UP! The House is on fire!" Tommy begins shaking me so violently, it's as if the bedroom is being rocked by an earthquake.

Groggy, I glance around the room. Everything seems fine.

Mr. Bug, Tommy's little pug, looks up sleepily from the couch as his master kneels over me, grasping me by my shoulders. "Wake up!" he implores again as he lets go and pulls on his jeans and shirt.

I sit up and grab for him. He sometimes has flashbacks of Vietnam. "Tommy, it's just a dream. It's okay."

He rouses me again by my shoulders, his face horror-struck. "Listen to me, The House is on fire! We've got to go, now!"

"Oh, my God, not The House! How do you know this?" I hear myself say the words but my mind hasn't caught up with what's happening.

Tommy tells me in a rush of words, "Bruno had been calling me at The House, and he just remembered that we said we were staying here. He saw the sky glowing on the way home from the Brass Rail, where he was playing pool until two. The fire engines we heard earlier must have been going to our place."

I remember, through my sleepy haze, Mr. Bug's making a little "O' with his mouth as the wail of sirens carried through the town.

I jump up and put on my jeans and pajama top. Tommy grabs my coat and holds it for me as I slip my feet into my boots. In the next instant we're both out on the street. There's a cold drizzle falling, and the roadway is glazed over with ice.

"Oh, my sweet Jesus," I murmur. The sky is blazing in the direction of The Carriage House, the historic restaurant that has been home and employment for Tommy and me along with a few very close friends for the past eight years. Why we both decided to stay at my apartment instead of his on this particular night is just short of miraculous, since Tommy's second-floor apartment in The Carriage House has always been viewed as a deathtrap in the event of a fire.

As everything sinks in, I have no thoughts except for terror and horror—and questioning reality in one way or another.

"What time is it?" I ask Tommy.

"A little after three," he says, choking out his words.

We round a street corner near the restaurant and are immediately met by flashing lights and a fireman waving a flashlight. The road is closed and Tommy pulls his Mercedes to a sliding stop.

A young fireman comes up to the car and says, "Hey, Tommy. I'm sorry, but you can't go down there."

Everyone around these parts in upstate New York knows Tommy Defalco, the manager and co-owner of the area's finest dining establishment, where he also serves as its maître d', And for many years, before coming to The House, he managed The Country Club, which in its way is just as prominent.

Tommy possesses dark features and a wide, bright smile that coaxes people into liking him immediately. It also doesn't hurt that he's extremely smooth and graceful in whatever he does. But tonight Tommy is out of the car and on the move, not concerned with appearances. He grabs my hand as we run to the driveway leading to the main building. The House, as everyone has come to call it, stands cloaked in a hideous film of blazing glory. Brilliant orange flames lick from every crevice of her skin, like a serpent's tongue flicking and teasing us to try and do the impossible and stop the devastation.

We hear Bruno, The House's head chef, calling to us from behind, and we see him pushing past the fireman and running after us. The police hold all of us back as we reach the main parking lot.

Tommy reels as if the wind has been knocked out of him, his face glowering like a jack-o-lantern in the reflection from the fire.

Bruno comes up to us; his words are hesitant and his voice is choked. "I thought you guys were in there." He covers his eyes. "I called Troy and told him that you both were okay, that you spent the night at Kitty's place. Oh, Jesus God, you guys could have died in there!"

Tommy puts his arm around Bruno's shoulder and pulls him close. By now my world has turned into slow motion. I'm drifting between universes. I see and hear what's happening but it doesn't touch me. Standing in the cold rain, I'm just an observer watching a building burn amid the oddly comforting din of the immense diesel engines in the fire trucks.

I see Tommy reach out with his other arm to me, and I hear his words, "Kitty, come here."

It's not until he draws me in that I feel the heat, smell the stench, see our working lives swallowed by this now grinning monster. I start to spin into uncontrollable sobs. Tommy hugs me tight as he whispers, "Just hold on to me, sweetheart," his words most assuredly more for him than for me.

A firefighter drapes a blanket around our shoulders. He knows all our names.

We hear the words, "Sorry" and "Too bad" and "Tragedy." Someone else comes up and asks if we're okay. Everyone seems to know us. It soon occurs to me just how many people are around us, coming from other bars after their late shifts. This is monumental news for a small town, and the night people utilize a grapevine that races like quicksilver.

Tommy says, "Look at me, Baby. Was everything turned off when we left last night?" His face is drawn and pale as he searches my face for the answer.

"Yes, Tommy, I turned everything off. Like always, I checked my bar, the kitchen, and shut off the fireplace." I'm a little irritated he would question me, and then he persists.

"Are you sure?" He slowly adds, "Think carefully."

"Yes, I'm absolutely sure. Was anything left on in *your* apartment?"

He shakes his head, "No, nothing." He doesn't press any further—and I decide not to as well.

Bruno meets Tommy's partner, Troy Meitzer, coming down the walkway. Troy pushes him out of the way and gasps when he sees The House, appearing now like a defeated dragon with its head lowered in shame. "Oh, my God," he repeats several times and nothing else.

Firelight paints age lines across Troy's face, making him look well beyond his thirty-two years. Troy's father bought him this old relic of a building to fulfill his son's dream of owning his own restaurant. Troy was only twenty-four at the time, but his father, who planned to be around to help open what was to become an elegant eatery, passed away that same year. Troy's mother joined his father a few months later, the result of a long bout with cancer. But before she died she contacted Tommy, as they were close friends at The Country Club, and she arranged for him to help Troy open and get settled in the business. Tommy hired Bruno, a highly talented chef, who in turn brought in Victor as his sous chef. With the knowledge of a top wine steward, Phillip Fairchild, and a few polished fine-dining servers, The Carriage House thrived and in a few years became an award-winning restaurant and a landmark in the community.

Even during the business's formative years Troy partied hard, and although he was touted as the restaurant's successful young owner, he never grew into or accepted his responsibilities. Tommy was forced to discipline him as a father might, and he managed to hold a tight rein over the restaurant's books. However, during the past two years Tommy began to trust Troy more and he relaxed his authority. This allowed Troy to gain control over most everything. Rumors swelled as the staff noticed blatant signs of Troy's drug use. Tommy worried about the financial health of the establishment. Then it happened.

Tommy uncovered a massive misappropriation of funds, which he learned were used to feed Troy's cocaine habit. As a consequence, the business was now in the red. Tommy's patience with Troy had worn thin and conversations between them had a way of exploding into fiery exchanges. Tommy addressed Troy's drug use many times, only to drive Troy deeper into resenting Tommy's counsel in his personal life—as well as his advice regarding the business.

Troy catches sight of Tommy and rushes at him, pushing him nearly off his feet. Tommy's face registers his total surprise. Troy shoves him again, and Tommy falls back against a fire truck. Troy shouts, "You bastard! Where in hell were you? If you were here this would never have happened."

He starts to take a swing at Tommy but stops midway, as Tommy is instantly ready to fight. This Italian never needs much of an excuse to lose his temper. So I quickly duck away, searching for someone who might have the courage—and bulk—to intercede.

From seemingly out of nowhere Bruno comes at Troy and slams him away from Tommy, and against the fire truck. He yells at Troy while holding him back, "Tommy had nothing to do with this, you asshole. The man has lost every goddamn thing he owns, including his home—and he and Kitty could have lost their lives. So back off or deal with me." Troy knows he's no match for Bruno, who is built like a bull, so he shakes him off and steps away.

A fireman, standing nearby, pulls Troy aside. "Let me tell you something, Mr. Meitzer, the fire came up so damn fast that no one would have had a chance in hell of escaping. She went up like a skyrocket due to the Christmas tree and decorations. We had one hell of a time getting this blaze under control. It was just plain lucky that no one was in that house."

Tommy pushes past me and walks down the lane. When I reach out, he snatches his arm away. He's angry and hurt and Bruno tells me to let him go. The two of us stand there shivering in the cold gloom, watching countless memories ride the sparks into the night sky, forever gone now, our beautiful business and life as we've known it for so many years just a passing glimmer.

I imagine the flames consuming the beautiful lounge, licking their way around my gleaming bottles, dancing across the cushions of the sofa in what we called The Pit in front of the fireplace, and sliding down my beautifully polished bar like a massive spilled drink. The countless hours of laughter and fun I created there as The House's lead bartender, clad in my uniform of tuxedo tails and fishnet stockings that earned me the nickname Legs. All those nights that Tommy and I entertained the customers with our fake arguments and cocky byplay.

Many memories of past years surface, pushing Roy McGrath to the forefront and causing fresh tears to form in my eyes. Roy McGrath, who loved me, who never tired of asking me for a date or trying to steal a kiss. Sweet Roy, who delighted in seeing me nightly at work, who lived for our mutual banter with one another. Roy McGrath, for whom I was to the point of giving up the bar business—living with the guilt that it was I who almost caused his death.

Troy comes over to Bruno and apologizes as he shakes his head. He says he is just so overcome. They embrace and pat each other on the back.

"Tommy's the one you need to find and say you're sorry," Bruno says, craning his neck. "I don't know where he went."

No sooner are the words out of Bruno's mouth that Tommy appears and wraps his arms around me. I need this. He buries his face in my neck and hair.

Troy offers his apology but Tommy says nothing, meeting Troy's eyes briefly and nodding.

We walk over to the back of a fire truck and sit on the wide back bumper. The House is altogether down now. Only the two end stone walls remain standing. I can't stop looking at the one with the fireplace, where so many happy times were spent. Strangely, I wonder about the elk heads hanging atop the mantle and how they paid witness to Tommy's marriage proposal to me on a particularly busy night not that long ago.

10

The fire chief approaches us, nods to me and says to Tommy, "I told Troy this, so I'll tell you the same thing. Right now, this fire looks as if it was started at three locations, indicating arson. We did our best, but there was no saving this one. Whoever set this wanted the place to go up in a hurry." He shook his head and clasped Tommy by the shoulder. "I'm sorry for your loss. We're going to conduct a thorough investigation."

"Arson," Bruno whispers as if in a dream, and he looks at us with knotted brows. "What the hell…don't know what to say."

The rest of the staff gathers around us in shocked silence as the news of suspected arson spreads. One by one, like war victims, we cling to each other. We're all in tears. Soon we cluster in twos and threes within the blankets the firemen provide, like lost children.

Polly, our head waitress, wordlessly falls in with Tommy and me. She wipes her eyes and holds onto us while Bruno and Victor talk with the rest of employees who care enough to come out and hold hands in collective grief. We are all family here, not by blood but through our work. There has never been a more dedicated staff at any establishment. We are the closest of friends, and for most of us the only family we have are those standing around us at this very moment.

The night becomes dawn and the funeral begins in earnest. Early-morning mourners in car after car slowly file past to pay their respects to the beloved landmark, some stopping to say a few kind words to us as well. The local news teams come and go, with their sound and camera equipment. Holding dour expressions, reporters gaze into camera lenses as smoke still rises behind them. Some interviews are granted. Tommy waves any news person away from us.

We're embraced by familiar arms as sad comments come to us from cracked voices; people wiping their eyes and shaking their heads; saying how much they loved The House.

Mildred Vassar and her son, Mike, appear, and she rushes to where we are all standing. It's amazing to see her at such an early hour. Millie is my most cherished bar customer. Her husband is a renowned surgeon and president of The Country Club, where I also worked before coming to The Carriage House six years ago. She is enormously wealthy but treats everyone as an equal. Millie is as close to a mother as I could ever hope for, and she views me and the entire staff of The House as her children. She claims her age to be in the early sixties, and she looks it, although I have a suspicion she is closer to the mid seventies. Her blond hair is meticulously styled and her make-up is always flawlessly applied. She has an elegant aura about her; a lady of means and style even though night after night she succumbs with simple gratitude to three gin martinis.

"I thought you all would be out here," she says. "It's all over the local news." She stands with us, in her fur-lined gloves and expensive fur coat, her diamond jewelry sparkling in what is now a light rain. "You didn't lose anything. This tragedy heralds a new start. Now you rebuild a bigger and better place to call home. This is a new beginning for everyone. That's what life gives us when it takes things away—a second chance. Get rid of the old and start new all over. By summer, this will all be a bad dream not worth remembering, and you will be back together and things will be true.

True to Mildred's grace and hang-tough attitude, she offers us the first hopeful smile since we all came together. She tells us to go someplace warm, and that all the wishing in the world at this moment isn't going to bring The Carriage House back.

The rain is becoming heavier, and Polly suggests, "What do you say we go to my place? This is crazy standing out here in this damn freezing drizzle. We can be just as miserable there as here, and I need some hot coffee.

Tommy has said little in over an hour. When I ask him if he wants to go over to Polly's, he peers over my head and into the smoking mess, then back at me and says with a sigh, "I just want to go home." He stuffs his hands deep in his pockets and shrugs. I know what he means, and my eyes fill with tears for him. He whispers to no one, "Arson. Who would do this—and why?"

I tell our friends we will see them later. Maybe meet at a local diner we all frequent and talk this out.

Back at the apartment I start the coffee, and we take a shower together to warm up.

Our clothes smell so much of smoke that we throw our garments in the washer and then cuddle in bed, where it's warm and dry. Tommy has nothing to wear, and it suddenly dawns on me that this man came over last night with only the clothes on his back.

Now, as we lie together with Bug curled alongside us, listening to soft music, Tommy is painfully quiet. When it seems he's searching for an answer in his thoughts, he looks into the air around him and then meets my eyes with his for a moment as if to see if the answer is in them. Should the answer appear in my eyes, he slowly shuts his for a moment as if in thanks.

I reach over and take his hand and thank God we decided to spend the night here at my place. We wanted to get an early start moving my belongings to his apartment at The House. Last night was to be my swan song to my little digs in the tiny town of Bigley, New York, where I called home for the past eight years. Now it seems that I'll be meeting with my landlord to renew the lease.

I smile and say quietly, "You are a wealthy man, Mr. Defalco. You have this woman who is your best friend and forever lover beside you, your trusted Mr. Bug on your other side, and your baby blue Mercedes parked safely at the curb outside." I point to his photo albums. "And here are your memories that we took with us—just by chance, to look at this morning—all of which could have been destroyed last night. We have this roof over our heads, be it what it is, so we have a home for now. We have so many things to be grateful for. And Troy will rebuild The House, as Millie said, and it will be bigger and better."

"I know that, Kitten. I'm just so damn tired and confused." Slowly his eyes focus on me. I feel strange. "Who called last night just before we closed up the lounge? Remember, you ran to the bar to answer the phone?"

I had to think for a moment. "It was a hang-up. No one was there."

Tommy rolls out of bed and calls the phone company. After a long while he comes back and sits atop the covers, his face grave. He studies me then mentions one name: Lillian.

I sit up quickly "You don't think ... she could be capable ... of arson?"

"I have no idea. But why would she call after closing and not say anything?"

"What are you getting at? Oh, my god, do you think she wanted us to be caught in the fire? Oh, my God—"

Interrupting my own thoughts, I feel sick to my stomach. I gather myself and reach for Tommy. I've never seen him appear so troubled.

Chapter 2

WE SLEEP UNTIL LATE afternoon when the phone rings. It's Jeannie, one of the servers at The Carriage House.

"We're all so worried about you guys. Are you two okay?" Her voice is strong but I can tell she's been crying.

"Yeah, we're fine," I say. "But poor Tommy, he has no clothes. He has nothing really. Not even a razor." I manage a giggle. "He only brought his toothbrush with him last night."

"Well, we're all coming over."

"Maybe everyone should give him some time."

"Screw that shit," she hollers. "We'll be there in a few minutes."

I get Tommy's clothes out of the dryer and kiss him awake. I tell him the girls are coming over and he laughs. We expected them, knowing how close we all are. It would be unthinkable that we wouldn't be together now.

In no time they're banging on the door and swarming around us.

Jeannie says, "We've come to take Tommy shopping for some clothes, bring you some food, and we can all use a drink. We cried all morning over losing The House, but we still have each other, thank God, and a job waiting—at some point. So life goes on."

Evelyn, another server, starts unpacking bags they brought with them and says, "We got you guys some coffee, bread, butter, milk, soup, and some sticky buns, which was my idea. And here's an electric razor for Tommy. Not sure what you use, but it'll work in a pinch."

Tommy smiles, and Polly says in her sweet southern drawl, "Here's the deal, so listen up. We're family, and what happened affects each of us. We'll stay close until Troy rebuilds, and then life will go on for all of us. Together." She pauses and glances from face to face. "And when the going gets tough, the tough go shopping. So let's go to the mall, y'all."

Bruno and Victor come through the front door, looking at everyone as if they are intruding. Bruno says, "We just thought, since we were coming over today to move Kitty's stuff, we'd come by now and see if you're all okay."

They give sad smiles to the girls.

"You guys are just in time," Polly says. "We're here to get these poor kids back on their feet and go shopping, then get dinner, talk, plan where we go from here, and of course, have a stiff drink."

And so it is. We take two cars and walk around the mall like the crowds of teenagers who hang there. A few people stop us and offer a sad hello. I never would have thought so many strangers knew us. Tommy's spirits are better, so we walk with our arms around each other, watching our friends help gather incidentals for us. We depart, loaded down with clothes for all seasons.

We leave a message for our wine steward, Phillip, and his boyfriend, Barry, who is the town's florist, for both to meet us for dinner at another restaurant in the area that we all favor, the Brass Rail.

When we arrive, they greet us in front of a large sign at the doorway that reads: "In honor of the memory of the best fine-dining establishment in town—and of our friends in the business. All tips and donations tonight will go to the staff of The Carriage House. Thank you, the staff of the Brass Rail."

We stand transfixed in front of the sign.

Tommy catches my hand and pulls me to him. "I can't go in there," he says, choking up.

"They want to do this," Phillip says and smiles solemnly. "We have to go in."

"Oh, my God," Polly says and, "let's just get a table in the back so there's no fanfare." But when we open the doors to the restaurant a wave of applause greets us. We are again spellbound, and Phillip says, "Maybe we don't deserve this, but it sure is nice the way it feels right at this moment." I can only agree.

We walk through a dining room full of people standing and offering condolences. Our emotions hit us hard as many folks we don't even know are showering us with love. It's truly overwhelming, and these people soon have all of us smiling, even Tommy. We cry and laugh; we drink and eat. We all get pretty drunk, too, and leave late. Those of us who are too toasted to drive stay over at Polly's place, which is within walking, or should I say staggering, distance. The tips and other donations that night are enough to pay for all of Tommy's clothes and some of the incidentals he lost in the fire.

The next morning brings brilliant sunshine and bitter cold temperatures, and I lie there in bed snuggled up against Tommy, who snores quietly beside me.

My thoughts turn to arson. Who would do such a thing to that venerable old restaurant? I remember a conversation Tommy had with Troy six months ago when the three of us went out lunch after a game of racquetball at the gym. It wasn't long after sliding into the booth at the diner that Troy released a bombshell.

"The books are a mess," he told Tommy. "I guess I should have kept a closer eye on our accountant, but I figured it was his damn business to keep us in the black, and he knows what to do. I'm afraid we're not in the best of shape. Anyway, he's history."

Tommy sighed and narrowed his eyes at Troy and said, "You fired our accountant? Why didn't you come to me? You should have conferred with me first."

Troy avoided his eyes and shrugged. "The guy was a loser. Anyway, I'm the owner so I made the decision."

"How bad is it?" Tommy asked, not giving Troy the opportunity to catch his breath.

"It's pretty bad," he mumbled. "I should've let you take back the books and keep them like you did when we started. I tried keeping up with paying the bills, but some invoices didn't get paid on time. I thought the accountant would take care of anything I missed."

"The bill paying was always your responsibility, not his. The accountant just makes sense of it all." All Troy did was shrug his reply.

As I consider everything else the two of them had said to each other during that lunch meeting, I couldn't help but accept that Troy might have torched the place for the insurance. Tommy had never told me how much Troy had embezzled essentially to keep his drug habit going. Could this be enough to cause him to have his beloved restaurant burned to the ground? I could only guess.

Lillian crosses my mind as another suspect. Would her hatred of me push her to do such a thing? No, as crazy as Lillian appears to be at times, she wouldn't have hurt Troy and the staff just to get back at Tommy and me. She's a businesswoman, after all, and sole owner of The Country Club. And, as I recently found out from Millie, partners with her husband in one of his questionable business ventures. She has enough on her plate without burning down the competition. Even though Tommy broke off their engagement to be with me, I have to believe that Lillian would resign herself to the finality of the situation and move on.

Jimmy Stokes, whom Tommy threw out of the lounge last week, is an interesting suspect. That whole wild group he runs with would do something like this just for the hell of it.

I close my eyes. I'm tired of thinking about arson. I get up and put Bug out the back door and into a little fenced-in area and make coffee. Soon I'm assessing my apartment's space and trying to figure out how I can rearrange everything to accommodate two people. I also have to get with the apartment manager so I can reinstate my lease before he rents my unit to someone else.

Tommy is still sleeping. I change into my sweats, slide on my slippers, grab my coat, and step out into the cold, clear air. I take a deep, cleansing breath and remember what Millie said: "New beginnings. Embrace change."

I buy a paper from the dispenser at the corner and see The House making front-page news, so I read some of the story while walking slowly back to the apartment:

"Now you rebuild a bigger and better place to call home," Polly Dixon, from Peach Bottom, Georgia,_told reporters. She had worked at The Carriage House since its opening, eight years ago, as head server. "We are family when we're there, so we're all losing our homestead," she went on. "Most of the staff worked six days a week just because they loved being there. We had so many happy times at The House. Plus, our customers are some of our dearest friends."

Christine Heartz, a cocktail server, echoed the same sentiments: "When Troy rebuilds, we'll have a bigger and better establishment for the area to enjoy."

Owner Troy Meitzer was too distraught to comment. The fire apparently started in the basement and fire officials are not ruling out arson."

I stop reading when I get to my front door.

Tommy's awake, lying with his hands behind his head. He smiles at me when I come in.

"I don't like waking up without you here," he says, pouting.

"You looked as if you needed your sleep."

"Take off your clothes. I want to look at you."

"Hell, no, I'm not taking my clothes off," I snap at him. "It's cold in here, and I have to get Bug in and cook breakfast." I can see by his eyes that he knows I'm teasing.

"Get over here, right now." He flips the blankets back as I walk past the bed to the back door to let Bug inside. The little pug makes a flying leap onto the bed and dives under the covers, jumping all over Tommy's naked body.

"Damn!" Tommy shouts, laughing. "You little bastard, you're like an icicle. Well, that took the starch out of me." He rolls around and springs out of bed. I give him a soft chuckle as I turn on the TV for the morning news. He comes up behind me and nuzzles my neck. "We could take a shower—and see what comes up," he says. I poke him with my elbow and point to the TV.

We stand as one, watching the fire report. Tommy and I sigh at the same time.

"It's front page news this morning too," I say to him. "The paper is over there."

The scene on the TV switches and Lillian and John Vassar are being interviewed. Tommy's mouth falls open. I sit down hard on the bed. "Holy shit," I gulp. "What's this about?"

John Vassar tells the interviewer how devastated he is over the loss of The Carriage House and how concerned he is that the fire may be the work of an arsonist. He asks for everyone to be alert to the potential that an arsonist might be at large.

A teary Lillian stares into the camera and says, "I am saddened beyond words by the loss of The Carriage House, and my heart goes out to the staff. I want the community to know that we will do everything in our power to help apprehend this arsonist so that our businesses remain safe."

"What the hell!" I say in a loud whisper. "Why would they interview Lillian and John?"

"They *are* our closest competition, so I guess they would offer a comment," Tommy says. "If the roles were reversed, we'd do the same for them."

"Yes, but just a few weeks ago they were in your face to get rid of me and threatening you if you didn't go back to work for them. They are hardly what I would call friends."

"The Country Club business is different, Kit. Remember, the public doesn't know about John Vassar's illegal enterprise and the role Lillian plays in it. They're just coming off as concerned people in the food and beverage business. You worked for her at The Club for two years, don't forget."

"I think they burned The House down because they thought we'd be in it. They want to kill us. That's why Lillian called so late and hung up."

Tommy wraps his arms around me. "Now, stop this. Lillian is crazy —but not that crazy. She probably was calling to harass me some more and thought better of it. You let Lillian get to you. I'm amazed you still buy into her idle threats after so many years of dealing with her ramblings. And I'm sorry I told you about John Vassar's other business. I probably frightened you with my concerns, but, I can assure you, murder wasn't one of them." He kisses away my tears and holds me close. "You're getting paranoid about this. John could not care less about us. We're little fish. He's abroad most of the time, anyway. Come on, sweetheart. I'm safe. You're safe. We have our whole lives ahead of us."

"I'm sorry," I reply. "You're right. I'm over the top with all of this." I go to the kitchen and pour two cups of coffee. We watch the rest of the news when the phone rings. I pick it up as Tommy whispers to me that he's going to take a shower. I tell him I'm not concerned about the future, but I tremble as I say, "Hello."

Chapter 3

IT'S TROY. HE SAYS he wants to gather the immediate staff together: Chris, our newly hired manager, Bruno, Polly and Jeannie. We're to meet him in the back room of the diner in an hour. I ask if he's okay, but he hangs up before giving me an answer. I strip and take a shower with my steamy, soapy Italian man.

The diner has a room with a private entrance that opens out onto the back parking lot.

Picnic tables and a small playground are beyond that, in a small wooded area.

When Tommy and I get to the diner everyone is already gathered around the door to the meeting room, which is locked.

"It's okay," Troy says as Polly fails at one final try to open the door. "This will be a short meeting. We can go over to the picnic tables. It's not that cold out, and we'll talk there."

We sit and he starts by telling us how sorry he is that the fire happened. He says he looked forward to the new changes. He thanks Chris for his short time aboard and wishes things had worked out better. He's slurring his words and his face is bloated and red. We all look at each other because there's something in Troy's behavior that's wrong, all wrong.

He goes on as if he's fine. "I wanted to tell you guys in person ... so you can give it to the rest of the staff." He pauses then blurts, "The House will not be rebuilt. There's no insurance."

We all just sit there, not comprehending what he's saying. Chris repeats Troy's words and asks as if an automaton: "The ... House ... was ... not ... insured?"

We again look stupidly at each other. Tommy has a deep, concentrated frown that seems to go all the way inside his skull.

"The accountant missed the payment," Troy mumbles. "Insurance company cancelled us over a month ago."

"How can that ... that happen?" Bruno stammers.

Troy's revelation is sinking in slowly for everyone.

"We must have a dang grace period of some sort," Polly says, her voice a fever pitch. "This just doesn't happen."

Chris rubs his fingers over his eyes. "Some policies don't."

Tommy says to Troy in an even but tense tone, "When you said a while back that you found some unpaid bills and paid them, did you not think to look back over the past months and check for more?"

"That's the accountant's job," Troy says and sniffles. "I thought he was on top of things. And don't forget, Tommy boy, you hired the guy."

Tommy is on his feet and bellows, "But it's your fucking business, Troy. You're the owner. You pay the bills. You check the books. I assumed you had a handle on the finances. But now I can see that any profits went up your nose." Tommy's entire body was shaking. "Just how much coke have you been doing? And why didn't you tell me you were in trouble?"

"You seemed too busy keeping your whores in line to be concerned with me. And you know damn well how much coke I've been doing. Ain't we all in the same black kettle of fish, my good friend?"

Tommy clears the tables in one leap and nails Troy so hard that it sends them both flying through the air. Tommy is on him good but Troy is fighting back hard.

Bruno begins dancing around them like a referee, looking for a chance to grab one or the other. I call out to Tommy to stop but my plea is useless. He has hold of Troy like a pit bull. But Troy is young and strong and gives Tommy two good hits to his face.

Bruno spins Tommy off Troy in a quick bouncer technique. He tries

23

to apply what I know is called a sleeper hold, but Tommy breaks free from Bruno and goes for Troy again. Troy picks up a limb the size of a baseball bat and takes a powerful swing at Tommy. He catches him across the stomach. Tommy goes down, but an instant later he's on his feet. This time Bruno has him in another kind of hold and struggles with him to the far corner of the playground.

Their foreheads are together and Bruno shouts, "Damn it, Tommy, it's me, Bruno. Look at me. Stop it, goddamn it."

Tommy angrily snaps away from Bruno and walks into the surrounding woods. Bruno is shuffling back to us, dabbing blood from his nose with the back of his hand. He spits angrily but nods to me when I ask if Tommy is okay.

Polly has disappeared into the diner and comes back with wet towels. She throws some to me as I go to find Tommy. I hurry away but hear her tell Bruno that Troy's nose looks broken, and they'll need to take him to the hospital.

Jeannie calls after me that she's there to help if I need any. I wave my hand at her in appreciation.

Tommy sits on a large log, his back to me. He's breathing hard. He's thrown up, the mess beside him, and I approach him carefully and touch his shoulder.

"Sweetheart, please tell me that you're okay?" I ask in a gentle tone.

He reaches out and covers my hand with his. His knuckles are scraped and bleeding.

"I'm fine, Kit," he says and then laments, "How the hell did everything go to shit so fast?"

I wrap a towel around his hands and sit next to him. "Let me see you," I say, turning his face toward me. I grimace and blot his eye with the towel before he doubles over in pain.

"How's Troy?" he asks, struggling with his words. "How badly did I hurt him?"

"You broke his nose in a masterly fashion," I reply. "Polly and Chris are taking him to the hospital."

He turns away from me, retches and vomits some more. "Damn it, I hate to puke."

"Love, I don't think anyone enjoys it." I pretend to laugh. "How does your stomach feel? Tell me truthfully, does it hurt?"

"Hell, yes, it hurts!" But then he pats my knee and says softly, "I'll be okay. It was just an unlucky shot to my gut." His eyes glass over. "I'm so sorry it came to this. But this fight just had to go down between Troy and me. It was overdue."

"Hey, I'm Irish," I say. "Brawling is in our blood. For the record, that was a pretty hard thing Troy said, and I don't mean about the whores, which was stupid and cruel. He drops a bombshell and then lashes out at you in the process. You had a right to be shocked and angry— as we all are. He dropped the ball on this mess, not you. You were hired to manage the business, not to pay the bills." I pause and square up with Tommy. "What did Troy mean about you knowing how much coke he did?"

Tommy sighs and says, "Kit, please don't read things into that. Troy was cranked up. Yes, I do know about his habit. And it's been growing. I've talked to him about getting some help. He doesn't listen." Then, as if he's reading my mind, Tommy adds, "Baby, I told you so many times before, I don't do coke. I'm fine." His mood swings and occasional sniffling for seemingly no reason tell me otherwise, but I never saw him do a single line in all the years I've known him, so I have to believe he's being straight with me.

He spits some blood into the dry leaves.

I change the subject. "Are you sure you're okay?"

"Yes," He growls. "I bit my damn tongue, okay? How do I look?"

"You look pretty rough. Jeannie will be the only one left, if she's still there. So let's go."

"Shit. I don't want anyone seeing me like this." I start away but he clasps my arm. "I'm serious."

"If she's around, I'll tell her that she can go home. You come up in a few minutes." I stroke his hair. "Do you still feel sick? You don't think you damaged something like a spleen, do you?"

He manages a deep chuckle that causes him to wince. "I'm okay. Just help get me on my feet and then go see if Jeannie is still around."

"You gave poor Bruno a couple of tasty shots too," I tell him in parting.

"Damn it." He groans and totally looks deflated. "I never wanted that to happen. I get so fucking crazy when I get mad."

"You think?" I give him a disapproving glance. "You've to stop going off like a rocket when you get angry. Jesus, Tommy you're almost fifty years old. Yes, you're fit, but just how much more of this can you take?"

He stands unsteadily and rubs his gut, looking frightfully pale as he stumbles about.

"He hit you hard a couple of times," I say, stating the obvious. "If you're hurt, please don't bullshit me. I mean it."

He smiles and a soft crease mixes with his pained features. "Thank you, Kitty."

Once home, I make him as comfortable as I can, but he insists he has to keep moving so he doesn't stiffen up. I clean up the cuts on his face with peroxide and Neosporin, and I put a butterfly bandage, with his instruction, to close a rather gaping slice over his right eyebrow. I kiss his wounds and tell him how sad I am he damaged his beautiful face. He looks so apologetic that it raises me to different tears from those that have flowed during the past day. He says he's sorry, like a little kid, and that pulls at my heart even more. His gut is so sore he can hardly move, so we sit with bags of frozen veggies on his tummy and watch movies on TV.

That night, settled in bed, we talk about our options for employment.

"You know," I say, careful not to jostle him with any sudden movements, "I love you more than life itself. But, in truth, we don't know a thing about each other outside of what we do at work. We know some of our secrets, and events in our past lives, but you and I say 'Goodbye' at closing and 'Hi' at opening, and what goes on in-between and on our days off is a mystery to both of us. What makes us think we can survive a life outside The House? It's all we know, Tommy. We are people who provide service. Suppose we just have the two of us from now on. Can we survive like that?"

He kisses me gently because of his sore mouth. "Let's sleep on it. We have time to decide."

A lot of time, I decide.

I can't sleep. It hits me as hard as Tommy's or Troy's punches that the future looms before both of us—equally uncertain and ominous. I have no skills beyond that of a bartender. Oh, yes, Tommy did some other work for the Vassars, but I doubt it provides marketable skills. And there's something else. I'm lying beside a man I have been working closely with for eight years—yet we know virtually nothing about each other beyond the bedroom.

I close my eyes and drift to classical music piped into a spotless, glass-windowed dining room with sunshine sweeping over the glistening tabletops. I see Phillip, the wine steward, joking with Polly, Jeannie, and our other young server, Robert, as they ready the room for the coming evening of diners expecting nothing but the very best of food and service and conviviality. I hear Bruno and Victor, bickering and cursing under their breath to each other in the kitchen. I'm polishing the bar to a high sheen, and Tommy's smiling from the podium and proclaiming to one and all, "Welcome to the Carriage House. We are at your service."

PART II

"THE CARRIAGE HOUSE GLORY DAYS"

Chapter 4

THE LATE AFTERNOON SPRING sky is a dark swirl of angry clouds, and by the time I swing my 1980 Subaru into The Carriage House parking lot, its wipers are beating out a steady lament. I blast into my Reserved Bartender slot, next to Tommy Defalco's classic, devilishly sweet, ice-blue 1976 Mercedes 450 SL convertible, which is parked in his own space under the sign of Manager/Maître d'. God forbid if he finds another car parked there. His sweet ride has a name: Baby Blue.

"Damn this weather," I swear to myself as I swing open my car door. The wet fury of hard rain hammers cold needles into my shoulders as a strong gust of wind takes my red curls and whips them across my face. The cars in the parking tell me that a good many of my regular customers are already waiting for me at the bar. Tommy, who is also my manager, has likely served them—glancing impatiently at the clock the entire time. He's also probably pacing—he loves to pace when he's beyond annoyed.

I take the steps up to the restaurant two at a time, just as a crack of thunder shakes out of the clouds, blowing me through the entrance in a burst of raging wetness. I slip on the Italian tiles and slide ten feet before managing to brace myself against the wall. All eyes turn to me in what is now a state of surprised silence. Before I can regain my composure, the entire bar crowd is hooting me a welcome, and Tommy is trying hard not to laugh as he taps his watch.

"Sorry I'm late," I chirp.

My manager greets me at the end of my bar with a look of total annoyance. "It amazes me that night after night I put up with you rolling in late to work. What, in the name of God, do you do all day that would render you so incapacitated that you can't schedule your time better and be here on time?"

"Oh, stop stressing," I say as nearby patrons stare our way. "And you're using those big words again. Look at the furrows between your brows. You can't afford any more lines in your face." I tap his forehead. "I know how vain you are. And if you must know, my life is very busy." I start to put away new glasses a busboy brings to the bar.

"Is that so?" He folds his arms across his chest. "Tell me what you were you doing, let's say an hour ago for instance—when you should've been here?"

"I was meditating. I meditate and do yoga before I come in. It relaxes me and makes me work better. And then the time here just flies." I shrug.

He drops his arms to his side. "Kitty, that's the most ridiculous excuse I have ever heard."

"It's not an excuse. If I wanted to give you an excuse, I would've told you that I was held up in traffic. That's an excuse. But you didn't ask me for an excuse, you asked me what I was doing before I came in tonight. And you really should try meditation. You're way too tense. I don't want you to have a heart attack on my watch—and ruin my shift."

"Tense? Do you think I'm tense?" His dark skin is shining. "Actually, I'm beyond tense. You absolutely infuriate me; do you know that?"

I smile and shoo him away with my hands. "You've been reading the dictionary again. Infuriate? Good word. Now, vanish. I have a bar to tend, and you're a significant distraction."

"You say *I'm* a distraction? Keep this up, Kitty, and you're going to be significantly unemployed, do you hear me? I could fire your Irish be-hind just like that." He snaps his fingers with a dramatic flair.

I turn and bat my eyes, and I snap my fingers back at him. "And I could quit just that fast too." We look away from each other to hide our smiles.

Polly, our head food waitress, comes for a tray of drinks and stands at the service area of my bar, checking her order book. "Oh, my God, you two," she says and laughs. "The night hasn't even started yet, and you guys are at it already. Good Lord, is there no peace?"

Polly speaks with a sweet Georgia accent that makes one think of Scarlet herself. She's the most popular server because of her professionalism and discreet yet friendly banter, but when she's alone with the staff after hours she lets her hair down and is a hoot. I love her like a sister, and I tease her unmercifully now that she's just turned forty.

"The Carriage House presents Friday Night at the Fights," another of our servers croons as she sidles up to Polly for drinks for her dining-room patrons. Jeannie has been with The House since it opened, and her comments about Tommy and me draw chuckles from the bar crowd.

The barstools are soon occupied by familiar characters who throw their smiles at me like precious coins. Mini dramas unfold among a team of lawyers discussing their recent cases while sipping their options off the tops of their expensive scotches.

Couples start to nest at the cocktail tables overseen by Christine and Evelyn, my lounge servers. They are supremely talented at remembering names of even our newest customers and what these people drink, which is an art. We anticipate a lively crowd every Friday evening, and this night is certain to be no exception.

Tommy steps behind me to get to the cash register. He's holding a large stack of ones and begins arranging my cash drawer. His aftershave curls around me like a friendly embrace. Oh, how I wish we sometimes didn't have Deal Number Five to contend with.

I can't help it but tease him. "Mmm, you smell yummy. What is that, Italian Jasmine on the Nile?"

"The Nile doesn't run through Italy," he says, nonchalantly counting out the bills.

"Whatever." I sigh, rolling my eyes as if he has said something I didn't know.

He chuckles without looking up from my cash drawer, and when he turns to leave he gives my arm a little pinch.

"Okay, Kitty Kat, you're all set," he says. "Play well with others."

For fifteen years I've honed my craft of bartending into a form of entertainment, juggling bottles and glasses and practicing magic that astounds even the sober. Many afternoons, before we open, and sometimes at night after we close, I'd practice with water-filled bottles and rejected bar glasses, on the grass beside the back driveway of The Carriage House. Tommy and our chefs, Bruno and Victor, would watch from their perches on a pipe fence while bottle after bottle and glass after glass would shatter—and what I'd say next would reflect my frustration. With every new crash they would take another sip of their beers, shake their heads, and offer a weak but appreciated, "That was better, Kit."

Tommy would often turn painfully away and say as an aside to Bruno, "If she wasn't so goddamned pretty I'd just shoot her and put her out of her misery." Everyone would nod solemnly, except for Joey the dishwasher when he was in attendance, who would give a toothless smile and announce, "You're doing great, Kitty. Try one more."

I got pretty good—over time. And bartending for me is now like being on stage every night. Oh, and wonderful, sweet Joey can do no wrong in my book—ever.

The restaurant guests start to stream past the podium and ride in on Tommy's familiar greeting, returning to him his contagious smile. Tommy is one of those men who seem to be born in a tux. Even though he's the manager, he's also the perfect image of a maître d', handsome with lifelines that tell equally of the serious and the joyous. He's always impeccably groomed, with sparkling, deep golden eyes, and a wide, friendly smile full of glistening white teeth. Despite his appearance of being a little on the heavy side, he's tight and muscular and entirely at home in his skin, not bothered by his age—he just turned forty-eight last May—which has him slightly balding with licks of gray at his temples.

Considered *the* heterosexual single-male catch in our area, Tommy Defalco plays his role as the ladies' man to the hilt. He has a faithful following of middle-aged women who cluster at the bar after dinner hours and set their hooks in hope of landing him for the night. Although he delights in socializing, he keeps most of them an arm's distance away. When he does date, he sees Lillian Mondale, who owns a golf and tennis facility just outside town named The Country Club, where we both worked before coming here to The Carriage House.

Their relationship is a stormy romance spiced with volatile partings. When Tommy and Lillian go through one of their splits, it seems that everyone who knows Tommy is relieved. She sucks the life out of him, and we all wonder what on earth he sees in her. But then he always goes back to her. Lillian comes across as a sophisticated, savvy professional woman, but she doesn't fool me. She's so damn spacey most of the time, I would swear she does high-end drugs. But I have no proof.

When Tommy hired me as the bartender eight years ago at The Country Club, it didn't take long for Lillian and me to draw our lines in the sand. Because of Tommy's outgoing personality and my dry sense of humor, we became fast friends. This didn't sit well with Lillian, who already had her perfectly manicured nails dug deeply into his back. But I was good for business, and the bar did well under Tommy's management and my way with members and guests, so I continued to work there for the next two years. Tommy and I always kept our relationship professional and platonic, but so many nights after I closed the bar we would sit for hours and share stories over warmed snifters of Grand Marnier. Even though we developed a deep fondness for each other, I never considered a relationship deeper than friendship, mainly because he was my boss and I never wanted to jeopardize what we already had. And that's the way it is between us to this day.

The Carriage House owner, Troy Meitzer, was raised in a restaurant family. Troy's father helped his son purchase the old restaurant but was taken ill a few months later. The man was close friends with Lillian, so he asked if she would lend Tommy to Troy to help with The Carriage House's opening. When Troy's father died later that year, Tommy decided to stay at The House. It was not a decision that Lillian had anticipated, or that in a month's time he would steal me away from her bar as well. That and her obsession with the thought that Tommy and I are more than friends make her crazier that I already think she is.

Tonight, the bar conversation is an easy meld of topics. It's the spring of 1989, and headlines about new president George Bush and the Valdez tanker's releasing eleven million gallons of oil into Prince William Sound in Alaska are highlights. I set up my bar station with the expertise of an operating-room nurse. Everything has to be just so; it's the difference between a fast, effortless night and chaos.

"Hey, Kitty, you look beautiful, as always." This comment comes from one of my regular customers who arrives every Friday night with four of his friends. His buddies file in behind him and smile at me. They adjust the stools under a small TV, mounted high in the corner to the right of the fireplace, the sound of which is barely audible. I call them my "beer men" because they have ordered nothing but Budweiser in the four years I've known them.

"Did you hear that Sugar Ray Robinson died today?" one man says to me. "I think he was only sixty-eight. What a loss. He was undoubtedly the greatest prize fighter of all time."

"Agreed," I say, although I have no knowledge of boxing. But a good bartender has to have an interest in everything. "That's sad news," I add. "He was the best. Beers all around for you guys?" They all nod as one.

Taking stock of my bar patrons as I fiddle with some liquor bottles, I keep my ears open to pick up the mood of my customers. The sacred rule of thumb for bar communication is that there be no heated discussions about politics, religion, or race, and to defuse any such talk with humor and quick wit. I'm a master at defusing.

"How are you, Sweetie?" longtime customer Claire asks me. "What a freakin' day we had at work. Thank God it's Friday." She shakes out her raincoat and hangs it over the back of a barstool saved for her. Her five secretary friends shift for positions at the bar, each one calling out their drink orders that I already know by heart. They're all regular customers who stop in each night after work for a lively bitchfest. They stay for two drinks apiece and then blow away into the early evening like thistles in the wind.

The lounge at The Carriage House is done in deep red leather and old barn wood and exudes the flavor of a hunt club, with artifacts from the area's countryside hanging tastefully on the dark distressed walls.

A commanding stone fireplace guards one end of the room and runs from the ceiling to the floor. Three majestic elk heads stare at bar customers from the middle section of the wide chimney. Two steps on either side allow patrons access into a recessed area where a large red leather couch wraps around a thick glass table. We call it The Pit—a great place for couples who seek intimacy or for a small group of friends. One of the perks of this job is watching a server miss a step and fly in with a tray of drinks. Funnier yet, however, is watching some customers stumble their way out of The Pit, fortunately in most cases without any dire consequences other than their wounded pride.

The Pit is also where the staff gathers after hours for their one free drink a night, and it's usually a time balanced between counting tips, bitching, laughing, foot rubs and general debauchery.

My bar is richly polished—aided by my considerable efforts and seats fourteen people. The wall behind the bar, known as the back bar, gleams majestically with glistening bottles of every kind of expensive liqueur standing at attention on shelves of beautifully carved mahogany. In the middle of the back bar my cash register resides, centered under a large mirror with inserts of etched horses "thundering" from left to right.

The whole room is softly lit by antique-brass carriage lamps strategically positioned on the walls. Eight dark-wood cocktail tables, replete with brass candle holders, are situated around a small dance floor. At the other end of the lounge, diagonally across from the fireplace, sits an upright piano in the far corner. There's also a large picture window with a view into the kitchen, through which patrons are encouraged to watch our chefs, Bruno and Victor, cooking and sautéing at the massive brick and brass stove and oven for which we are famous. My hope has always been that those watching can't read lips.

Christine_calls to me, "I need two gin and tonics, one Long Island iced tea, and two flaming brandies, all for The Pit." I make her drinks quickly, pouring the flaming brandy from glass to glass in a showy display before placing them on her tray. I smile as she deftly glides across the room and down the two steps to The Pit.

I'm now firmly ensconced in my dance, a smooth balance of movement and conversation, a perfectly timed journey from bar to register and back again. It's a crazy foxtrot, keeping up with the clinking of expectant glasses and the equally eager peal of the cash register's mechanism.

I hear Troy's voice behind me as he taps on the bar. "How's everything at Miss Kitty's Saloon tonight?"

I don't have to turn around to know he's straightening the stack of bar napkins in front of him. Troy's a stickler for presentation. He drives the staff crazy, always tweaking the forks on the tables, measuring distances of plates to glasses, and having the napkins perfectly folded into doves.

"Everything's grand, boss. How's the dining room?" It has to be filling up because of the quantity of drinks I've made already, but I ask anyhow.

"It's a good night so far." I turn to catch his boyish smile.

Tommy joins Troy and both men adjust their bowties and tug mindlessly at the cuffs on their white shirts, which have to be exactly an inch and a quarter from their coat sleeves.

I can't help but show off for them a little, spinning and catching my bar glasses after tossing them high in the air and flipping a bottle into my other waiting hand, free-pouring a perfect ounce and a half of Irish whiskey. Troy rolls his eyes at me and glances away, but Tommy gives me a wink and smiles broadly. He's my biggest fan—and I know it.

Chapter 5

"AH! TOP OF THE evening to you, Miss Katherine Grace Cunningham! How's my wee Irish lassie tonight?" Roy McGrath takes off his cap and smoothes his light red hair before sliding onto the barstool in front of my work station. I often wish I had never told him my full name.

"Hardly 'wee,'" I laugh. "If I gain any more weight, I'll bust out of my satin britches right here before you and God."

He roars with delight. "I'll tell you, lass, God wouldn't be any more delighted than I if you did." He shoots out his hand. "Hey, Tommy," he says in greeting as my boss walks by. The two men shake as he leans over to whisper to Tommy, but I overhear.

"Tom, are ya puttin' in a good word for me wid Kitty? Do ya think she'll have me? You know her better than anyone."

"Well, Roy, you know how Kit is. Kitty dances to her own drum when it comes to relationships. No one guy lasts very long. She has an aversion to falling in love." I hear Tommy's classic chuckle. "Good luck in asking her out."

My back is turned to the two men but I am smiling. I put down Roy's bourbon and soda on a coaster in front of him, and he quickly grabs my hand.

"What say you, we have lunch together at the San Souci tomorrow?"

I smile and let my eyes warm him. "Thanks for the invite, but I have so little downtime, and my afternoons are precious to me. And I work every night but Monday."

He draws my hand closer to his chest and tilts his head. He's smiling and there's a devilish glint in his eyes. "Damn it, Kitty, I'd be good for you. You would never want for a thing. I'm so rich, I don't even know how much money I have, but it means nothing to me if I can't share it with someone." He raises his bushy eyebrows. "I can make you happy, Katherine. It all starts with a simple date."

"You're way too young for me," I kid him, knowing he is well into his sixties.

He laughs. "You forget I was at your birthday party last year. You're thirty-five. You're not too young for me. You deserve an old, rich sugar daddy to pamper and shower you with whatever your heart desires. Come on, Lassie, take a wee chance with me."

I give him a smile and take my hand from his. "You're hard to resist, Roy, so I'll keep what you said in mind. But now I have to get back to work." Outside of busily refilling his glass until he leaves, I basically ignore him the rest of time he's in the bar.

At eight o'clock, right on the dot, Mildred Vassar comes in. I smell her perfume before she appears at the bar. She waves to everyone seated at the cocktail tables, just like a celebrity coming off an airplane. Her charm bracelets clatter and her rings shoot sparks in the soft candlelight that illuminates the lounge. Millie is a cross between Gloria Swanson and Mae West of old. Bright blue eyes that miss nothing shine from under full natural lashes. Her lipstick is always of a color I can't describe but wish I had in my purse.

She's in her usual high spirits and takes her customary seat right in front of my work station. She reaches out and grabs my hands in hers, as if she has not seen me in years—even though she was here last night, and the night before, and the night before that.

"Oh, my dear, how are you this splendid, damp evening? Ah, it's marvelous to see you; wonderful to be here. Hello to all." She turns and blows kisses to the people seated at the tables. Everyone takes this in stride, all aware that there's not a phony bone in her body. She's just, well … Millie. She calls to the beer men, "Isn't she just a gem?"

They raise their beers in a salute without taking their eyes off the TV screen. "To the gem," they harmonize. I want to bean them but it's too funny.

I place a martini in front of her. "Ah, how fabulous! Cold, extra dry, three garlic-stuffed olives and a dash of olive juice. Kitty, you're the mistress of martinis. No one can make them the way you do." She reaches around her neck. "Check this little bauble out." She leans over the bar and delicately runs her fingers over a dazzling diamond necklace with large stones set in gold. "It's my latest gift from the unscrupulous Dr. John Vassar."

"Holy crap, Millie, what did he do now?"

"You mean besides his affairs and nefarious business dealings?" She laughs heartily. "Oh, my dear, the stories I could tell you." Narrowing her eyes, she whispers to me, "I caught him having what I'll call an intimate lunch with Lillian Mondale at the Sans Souci. Lately, he's been spending a lot of time with her. He says it's purely business, as he *is* the president of The Country Club, which as you know, she owns, but I suspect they've been lovers for years. She was all over him." Millie giggles and fondles the small fortune around her neck. "Anyway, I threatened to look into their business dealings and, presto, this arrived yesterday by courier."

"My God, Millie." I cannot hide my shock. "Does Tommy know about this?"

"Tommy? Why would he be interested?"

"He's been dating Lillian ever since he worked for her six years ago. Didn't you know that?'

She purses her lips and frowns into her martini. "No, I never knew that. She doesn't come in here. I assume mainly because I'm here nearly every night. And John drinks at The Club, for the obvious reason. I never see Tommy anywhere with women except the Brass Rail. But he's never been with Lillian when I was there." Her face blanches, and she takes a long sip of her drink." I hope Tommy's not too involved with her. Do

41

you know if he has any business with her since he left The Country Club?"

"He still works at the club part-time. He goes into the city once a month and drops off receipts or something at the accountant's office. Lillian travels with him most of the time, and they take in a show on occasion. That's all I've been told by Tommy."

She sighs heavily, and I'm concerned as well. If Lillian has business with Millie's husband, the famous plastic surgeon from New York City—who it's obvious to me has many dark secrets—that can't be a good thing for Tommy. I mix a couple of drinks, deep in thought, trying to shake off the cautionary feelings. Tommy is a man who knows his own mind, plus this is clearly none of my business even though I hold the belief that Lillian is an unstable, high-class bimbo who just happens to wear a business suit.

Millie drains her first martini and smiles at a handsome, older businessman who has taken the seat next to hers. She looks extraordinarily beautiful, her make-up perfect and her blond hair styled just so, everything reflecting wealth and comfort. She has class and in all ways is a lady—as well as in all ways a lady richly alone. Every night she comes in, and every night's the same. And every night, around eleven, she fades and is driven home by her son, Mike.

Millie is delighted that the businessman has bought her next drink, and she smiles at me from over the rim of her glass as she takes a sip. For a well-seasoned bar patron, this is heaven to her: a strong drink and an attractive man to keep her company.

Every so often the beer men explode into cheers, drawing everyone's attention to the score of a baseball game I've not followed—and can't wait to have end.

When the dinner rush is over I stroll continuously back and forth, replenishing drinks, lighting up smokes, washing glasses, and pausing here and there to chat or to tell a joke. Millie's new acquaintance has left, and she fumbles with putting her cigarette into a short black holder that she swears removes all the tar and nicotine. I wait patiently and then put the flame from a stick match onto the tip while she draws in deeply.

"How many years do I know you and Tommy?" she asks out of the blue.

I pop the cork from a champagne bottle as I answer her. "Ever since I tended bar at The Country Club."

"And in all those years, you and Tommy never got together. I don't understand that. You two are so damn perfect for each other. He should be with you, not Lillian. What in the name of God does he see in her? I thought Tommy had better taste in women."

I throw my head back and laugh. "Tom and me? No, that's definitely not in the cards. Besides, we fight all the time. And it's always been one of his deals that employees don't date each other. It's Deal Number Five, posted on the kitchen wall, underlined twice in black."

Polly runs up and stands right next to Millie and coos in her sweetest southern drawl, "What's hot, sugar?"

"Me, but no one's interested," Millie says and sighs. "Kitty and I were just talking about Tommy's rules that can't be broken if you want to stay employed here."

"You must mean the Defalco Ten Commandments that hang in the kitchen." Polly smirks and then mimics Tommy's voice: "'Okay, listen up, here's the deal,' and we all settle in because we know a law is being chiseled in stone. We love him, but he's a piece of work with some things." She winks at me. "I need two more champagne cocktails."

I make them for her, and she swishes into the dining room, balancing a seemingly impossible-to-control array of drinks while maneuvering amid the tables.

Millie laughs softly. "We all love Tommy. Hell, I love all of you here. You're all like my family—my own kids, for God's sake. I don't know what I'd do without you, Kitty."

I can see she's two-thirds to where her fade awaits. But she's a bit early tonight. She calls out to the bar patrons, "What would we all do without our Kit?" then again yelling over to the beer men, "Isn't she just a peeeach?"

They raise their beer glasses and in unison holler, "To the peeeach." I could kill her but all I can do is laugh and shake my head.

At nine-thirty, Pauley, the piano player, creeps like a shadow across the back wall. He's an unassuming man of retirement age with a pencil-thin moustache and steel-blue eyes that glint behind heavy glasses.

His totem reflects the chameleon as his mood changes for the public in a camera's flash. Pauley is an old-time musician playing all the old favorites and coaxing people to sing along. He's funny and outgoing when he's "on" but quiet and reserved otherwise. He gives me a weak smile and waves.

I run a double bourbon on the rocks over to him and place it, on a napkin, just left of the piano keys.

"Hello, sweetheart," he says to me, pinching my cheek. "How's my little bean blossom?"

I chuckle. "Well, according to Millie, I'm just 'peeachy.'" We both snicker as I turn and walk away. I hear Pauley say, with a chuckle, behind me, "Jesus, look at those legs. This old man is grateful he still has eyes to take in a woman like you."

Over my shoulder, I wrinkle my nose at him. "I'm glad I give you a rise, Pauley Doodle."

"Oh, if that were only but true." He laughs. "Anything you want to hear tonight?"

"'Pennies from Heaven'" I say to him, still looking back over my shoulder.

Holding his drink, he follows me to the bar, something he's never done before. "You always ask me for that song," he says, taking a long sip of his bourbon.

"It was my mom's favorite song, and she used to sing it all the time while playing our baby grand piano when I was a kid. Hearing it reminds me of growing up in Philadelphia." I take a moment to remember the smell of lilacs and furniture polish in a room embroidered with oriental rugs, overstuffed sofas, and expensive artifacts that I thought were just junk. My sister and I were raised with the finer things in life. However, she took the high road—and I got lost on the lower one.

"My mom was a hefty but elegant woman who was registered in the Blue Book of Philadelphia's finest families," I say but can't conceal my sadness. "She would have made a fabulous bartender with her sense of humor, but that of course would have toppled her from her social stand-ing." He chuckles and I continue, shaking up a margarita. "She would have loved the equine decor of this lounge. Mom was an avid fox hunter. I can still hear her words describing the hunt as 'The too, too divine unspeakably in pursuit of the uneatable.'"

Pauley smiles. "She was a horsewoman?"

"God, yes. Horses were her passion. We had stables on our property. My sister and I had a show pony, but she was the rider, and it was actual-ly her pony. The little bastard always gave me a hard time. My mom used to host cocktail parties and formal balls in the barn for fun. She had Irish mischief in her heart and an amazing sense of humor, both of which I'm proud to say I inherited. My father, on the other hand, drank like a man on fire and looked like one as well, with his flaming red hair and ruddy complexion. His temper rattled the banshees, but he never raised a hand to my mother or my sister. However, he used to often physically toss me out of the house, amid the political debris I insisted on bringing to the table.

"I brazenly thumbed my nose at capitalism and merrily championed the liberal road throughout my college years, where I protested every cause that caught my eye. After one too many foolish antics, my dad disowned me for good. He of course didn't know that it wouldn't be long before he and my mother would die in a car wreck. I was left poor as a church mouse. Sister got it all—and everything was perfectly legal. But I survived, and here I am."

Pauley gives me a pat on the hand and Millie taps her glass as a signal for another—just as Jimmy Stokes and his gang of hooligans come in. Now this pleasant night will surely change.

Chapter 6

JIMMY IS THE PROVERBIAL little prick of misery, being both confrontational and stubborn. I've had to flag him many times because of his raucous behavior. I wish he'd go to a neighborhood tavern to drink. He runs with a fast crowd, and it hardly seems this is their kind of place. Last Friday, Tommy and I gave him an ultimatum: One more disturbance and he and his bunch can count on being thrown out for good.

Pauley is playing happy songs and tonight he's buoyant and funny, and more than once has me in stitches.

Tommy has been lured to the far end of my bar by his latest little harem who buys his drinks and fawns over him. He orders me to buy a round on the house, but this applies to those seated only at the bar and who haven't had enough alcohol already.

As always, Jimmy and his group sit at the back of the room. His lackeys routinely come to my bar for a round of drinks for their table. They do this because of their impatience to be served, and it allows them to get out of tipping the girls. Tonight the group is loud, rude and itching for a fight. I hear them cursing, so I catch Tommy's eye and he glances over his shoulder toward Jimmy's group just as a glass shatters. Tommy straightens up, his jaw tightly set.

"Get Bruno," he calmly says to me so he doesn't alarm anyone. Then, smiling at his bevy of beauties, he excuses himself.

I quickly leave the bar and bursting through the kitchen doorway I find Bruno, as usual, at the stove. I holler above the normal din in the busy kitchen, "Tommy's getting ready to haul Jimmy's gang out to the parking lot. There are five of them tonight, so backup is needed."

Bruno chuckles but soon groans, "Goddamn it," as he bustles out the back door, with Victor close behind. When Bruno was between chef jobs before he came to work at The House, he was a bouncer at Ricky O's. His reputation as a not so gentle giant preceded him. He's a large, burly man in his late thirties with the physique of a wrestler, the dialog of a trucker, and the heart of a poet. Like most chefs I have known, he's temperamental and explosive, but he runs an award-winning kitchen and manages his staff with great care.

My heart is pounding when I get back to my bar, but I find that Tommy has successfully maneuvered the group into the lobby without much ado. People are unaware of the drama unfolding as they are dancing and singing their old favorites along with Pauley. After a moment, however, I hear a scuffle in the foyer and then the front door banging open.

I start my act behind the bar, tossing bottles and balancing drink glasses. The crowd cheers me on. I juggle flaming shots and do some fast sleight of hand to keep everyone focusing on me and not on what I can only imagine is happening in the parking lot. Pauley takes a cue from me and plays a little louder, stringing together some jazzy songs while Polly and Jeannie get everyone clapping along. Our clandestine efforts are successful, and no one is the wiser as to what's taking place outside.

After a few nervous minutes on my part, Tommy and Bruno come through the lobby. I see Tommy adjusting his cufflinks and brushing off his tux as he follows Bruno back to the kitchen. When I pop through the door I find him wiping his forehead with his handkerchief. Bruno and Victor are laughing as Tommy addresses me, "Thank everybody for me for keeping the ship afloat out there."

"Are you guys okay?"

"We're better off than they are," Bruno says and laughs." I bet they won't ever want to see Tommy that cranked up again."

Tommy snorts. "I've had my fill of those assholes. Every time they come in here, it seems those sonsabitches cause a disturbance of some sort. Why they come in here in the first place, I can't even guess. Anyway, they're not to be let back in."

"You didn't hit anyone, did you?" I ask Tommy.

"And ruin a new manicure on those little pissants. Hell, no, I didn't." Tommy snorts again, louder this time.

"He didn't have to hit anybody," Bruno says. "Tommy held Stokes off the ground—by his throat. He was pleading for his life."

Victor laughs. "Kitty, the fight was trying to hold Tommy back after he let the kid go." And then to Tommy, "You're a freaking nutcase when you go off, do you know that?"

Troy comes up to where we're all standing, appearing concerned and annoyed. "What the hell just happened out there?"

Tommy shrugs and grins slightly. "They pissed me off."

"No doubt," Troy says, giving everyone a glare that says get back to work.

Millie's fade has arrived, and she plops her chin into her hand and looks mournfully at her empty glass. It's almost midnight, and as is our custom, coffee and tea, as well as light sandwiches, are served from a rolling cart in the lobby.

"Would you like me to get you a sandwich?" I ask her.

"No, but thank you," she says, appearing to be about to fall asleep at any second. "I guess you can call my Michael, though I just hate to go."

I call Michael, whose number I know as well as my own. He laughs at my request, saying he will be right out to get her. He's her devoted, loving only son, who lives nearby. A confirmed bachelor, he drops her off and picks her up the nights that I don't call her a cab.

She leaves and finally the night winds down. I glance outside, and the asphalt on the wet parking lot is covered in red and white streaks from the lights of the departing cars. I wash my bar, turn up the lounge lights and count my empty bottles and write down the totals. Then with the last of the polish rubbed into my bar and the shine flawless, I pour myself a stiff gin and tonic and plop down on the red leather sofa in The Pit, warming myself by a fire that's still got some life left in it.

Tommy races in like a sudden, stiff breeze and takes my cash drawer up to his office for the count as Polly, Bruno, Victor, Jeannie and Phillip make themselves drinks and join me. Phillip slides down next to me and pinches my knee. "Hello, Kitty Cat. I didn't get a chance to see you all night. Anything special happen?"

"This was a highly eventful evening," Polly says before I can answer him. "True fine dining in the boonies of New York. Our illustrious maître d' was brawling in the parking lot with Jimmy Stokes's gang, our head chef was trying to stop them from killing each other, and all this time the band played on as if nothing's happening. You gotta love this place."

Phillip sips his wine and says, "Tommy loves to fight more than anyone I know. I just hope I'm never on the receiving end of his wrath,"

Bruno gives a loud yawn and stretches. "Tommy can be a real hard case around here. But I've known him a long time, and fundamentally he's a really sweet guy."

"I heard the word 'sweet,' so you guys must be talking about me," Tommy says as he comes around the corner of the lounge.

"No way," I say and start singing, "'You're so vain, you probably think this song is about you.'"

"Well, you *are* a sweet man," Phillip says with a shrug and a smile.

Tommy sighs and shakes his head. "You have no idea how weird that makes me feel to hear you say that, Phillip." He puts his drink on the table in The Pit and runs upstairs to answer his office phone, which just started ringing.

We settle in, and someone always brings up an old memory that gets us all telling stories about The House. Bruno laughs at something Polly says and asks, "Do you guys remember the skunk in the kitchen?" We all howl at the memory. "It wandered in through the open screen door and sat under my stove most of the night. We were afraid to breathe."

Phillip giggles as he opens the collar under his bowtie. "I remember that well. We all stopped what we were doing as we pondered the consequences of shooing it away. We collectively decided just to act normally, a risk that thankfully paid off as we propped the door open and it left on its own."

"At least he went away," Bruno says.

"Except it was a she and not a he," Polly says. "If y'all don't remember, she came back the next year and had her babies under the back steps. Tommy thought they were kittens." Everyone roars, and I spill my drink I laugh so loud.

Mr. Bug, Tommy's little pug dog, is scrambling down the stairs from the apartment on the second floor of The House. In one clean leap he's on Polly's lap and soon covering all of us with gurgling, snorting kisses. He has the run of the House after hours and delights in showing us how fast and often he can squeak his little rubber mouse, whenever he decides to bring it with him. Tonight he has left it somewhere.

Tommy comes into the lounge, talking on the portable phone that Troy just bought for the restaurant. It's the latest in the electronic gadgets that Troy loves. Two computers are hooked up in the office but Tommy doesn't spend much time learning how to use them, much to Troy's dismay. Tommy's technical expertise lies in Pac-Man and Pong. Shutting off the phone, he steps down into The Pit and whispers to me, "That was Lillian. We had another fight. She's history."

I don't know why, but I whisper back to him, "Did you know she has a thing for John Vassar? According to Millie, they're more than quite close."

Tommy's jaw tenses. I'm not a gossip, so why do I get into his personal life? I'm certain he's going to bite my head off in front of everyone, which I deserve, but he quietly says, "She's discussed him with me. He *is* president of The Club, so they often have business together. The fact that they see each other socially doesn't bother me. And, since it's nobody's business but mine—"

"Bug!" Jeannie shouts as the dog leaps into her arms and releases me from a dangerous moment I cannot believe I allowed myself to get into.

"Come on, Polly, dance with me," Tommy says as he smiles and pulls her to her feet.

"Ah, the disco king is at it again," I say, as if he and I had been discussing the lightest of issues. "There goes my foot massage." I watch Tommy swirl Polly around the dance floor. Tom Defalco is a fabulous dancer, proficient in every step it seems. And he never misses a chance to dance. A half-hour and four dance partners later, Tommy grabs me for the last jitterbug of the night just as Mr. Bug runs past us and barks excitedly at the front door.

It takes a moment for us to realize something's wrong in the parking lot, as the dog is even more animated than usual. Phillip says he thinks he hears something but isn't sure. He sprints to the front door and opens it just as a car screeches out of the lot.

"What the hell was that?" Bruno says as the men follow Phillip onto the wet blacktop. "Oh, shit, it's Tommy's car," Polly yells from the doorway.

Baby Blue, Tommy's classic Mercedes, sits amid a circle of shattered glass, looking as though it had been caught in a sleet storm.

Tommy explodes, shouting imprecations and vowing quick revenge for whoever did it. Polly says, "I bet it was Jimmy, coming back pissed off about being thrown out earlier."

Phillip frowns. "The problem is, I saw the car leaving, and it wasn't Jimmy's old Jeep that rounded the corner."

"Could you make out what kind it was?" Tommy asks, his voice shaking.

Phillip nods. "Looked like a Cadillac. Late model in a dark color."

"Lillian," Tommy says, and our group lets out a loud, collective sigh.

Chapter 7

SATURDAY MORNING BRINGS SUNSHINE, warm for mid-April, and I take a drive over to The House to see how Tommy is doing after last night's drama. I arrive just as he's telling the police he threw out Jimmy and his crew the previous night for creating a disturbance. They say they will check it out, but since there are no witnesses an arrest is doubtful. Tommy mentions that the car may have been a late-model Cadillac in a dark color, but he does not bring up Lillian's name as its possible owner —and neither do I.

I walk over to Baby Blue to survey the damage. The windshield is smashed, as well as the passenger-side window and both headlights. She looks regrettably sightless, but whoever did this was careful not to damage the paint or trim, not something I can imagine concerning either Lillian Mondale or Jimmy Stokes.

The police leave and I follow Tommy inside to the kitchen. He's stirring a large pot of tomato sauce cooking on Bruno's stove. The aroma in its own way blends well with the classical music he has coming through the speakers.

Tommy flashes me his equally classic smile. "Taste this and tell me what you think. I was working on this when the police came." He holds out a wooden spoon for me and I sample.

"Umm. Yummy, but maybe more oregano?"

He frowns. "You really think so?"

He looks so concerned that I backtrack. "On second thought, no. It's a suburb tomato sauce. Really, it is. It's perfect."

He smiles. "It's called gravy. I do make impressive gravy. This is my great-great-great-grandmother's recipe, from Naples."

"They had tomatoes back then?" I ask and smirk.

He leans against one of the prep tables and folds his arms across his chest. His low-slung bellbottom jeans hang precariously on his hips and the wide cuffs cover his feet completely. He's wearing an open blue shirt that exposes his broad chest and stomach. Soft dark-gray hairs cover his torso and disappear into the waistband of his jeans. His body takes my breath away. I can't help but stare at him.

"You've been working out," I manage to say. "Are you still playing racquetball with Troy?"

"Every Tuesday and Thursday afternoon, and I'm jogging too, when I can find the time." He studies me and grins, obviously enjoying the fact that I'm relishing the view. "I'm not too shabby for an old dog. I have some redeeming physical qualities left."

"I hadn't noticed." My own grin sells me out. "Tommy, I think Lillian trashed your car. You said that you had a fight with her last night, and Phillip said he saw a Caddy pulling away.

"Don't be ridiculous, Kit." He starts stirring the pot of sauce fever-ishly, then just as quickly slows the pace and lowers the flame. "Lillian is fifty-five years old and her idea of physical fitness is doing her nails. Do you think for a minute she could swing a club or a bat that hard? The cops think there had to be two guys to do that amount of damage in that short a time. My choice is Jimmy and one of the clowns who hang with him. They must have come in a buddy's car, since we all know he has a Jeep."

"It's just—"

"I'm going to ask you not be so hard on Lillian. She is a bit of a bitch at times, but she's a friend of mine." He groans. "When we're not fighting, that is."

"Actually, I was thinking about how much older she is than you."

"You say that like you can't believe that I'd date someone older than me. I'm forty-eight, so there's not that much difference."

"I'm just surprised. I always thought you'd be with some young chickadee you could show off, and not an older woman—and this has nothing to do with Lillian. You clean up well, but you're really just an old hippie. You love to laugh and have fun, but you're not getting any younger. Time is running out. You're old and getting older by the minute."

"Jesus, could we perhaps not talk about age anymore today?" He casts me a wary look but I can tell he's not serious. He looks at me thoughtfully and comes over and releases the barrette that holds up my hair. He fluffs the long red curls out over my shoulders and says quietly, "Don't ever cut your hair. Actually, you should wear it down all the time."

I feel my cheeks burning and realize I'm blushing. Sometimes Tommy stirs up feelings in me that I hold inside. I'm usually quick to dismiss them, but today I'm a bit overwhelmed by him. Regardless, I have no faith in lovers, especially at work. Experience has taught me that I always lose a friend when the line is crossed, and my friendship with Tommy is what makes me whole at this point in my life. And it's something I will not jeopardize—no matter how much I might want him at times.

"So," he says. "Are you planning to go out with your rich, eager admirer, Roy?" He winks and his coyness drives me crazy. "Isn't he Irish? You can discuss mutton stew and Irish potatoes all day long, and that's got to be exciting for a woman like you."

"He's not Irish, smart ass. He's a Scot. And, no, I would not consider going out with him. He's too old." With that we both laugh. "And Deal Five says we can't date people from work." I wander over to the far kitchen wall and look at the poster that lists "The Deals" and giggle at the wording. "The Deals" were written by Tommy with his dry, tongue-in-cheek sense of humor.

One: The customer is always right no matter how big an asshole he/she/it is or you may think he/she/it is.

Two: Anyone stealing so much as a shrimp will be fired immediately, no excuses. It's just downright rude.

Three: No one is to bring his or her drama to work, meaning leave it at the door before you come in and pick it up when you leave. Again, don't bring it inside.

Four: Anyone coming to work intoxicated or nipping on the job will be fired immediately. No weeping or wailing allowed.

Five: Don't screw with the bosses, or each other for that matter, physically or emotionally. There will be no romantic involvements at work. What you guys do at home is your business. Here, it's our business. We can all be as sexy as we want and have fun with that, but don't cross the line or you'll be neutered or spayed, whichever fits.

Six: Don't challenge the bosses' decisions. They're always right, so get over it.

Seven: If you don't like it here, leave. We don't even want to know why. Just don't let the door hit you in the ass on the way out.

Eight: We will gladly buy you an iron if you don't have one. Don't even think of coming to work looking like an unmade bed. You'll be sent home without supper or pay.

Nine: We're all family here. We genuinely like each other, If you can't play fairly, take each other's comments in good fun, accept constructive criticism (even if someone calls you a dickhead, which you probably deserve at the time) and respect each other's space, we don't need to adopt you. We're proud of you, and we hope you're proud to be here.

Ten: To be announced when the mood strikes us.

Signed: Troy Meitzer, Owner (and make no mistake about it) and Tom Defalco, Manager (and otherwise Czar)

Tommy chastises me, "They're not rules, they're deals. And Deal Five only applies to working relationships among the staff." He pauses and gives me a weird stare. "It would do you good to find someone to love and share things with. You're a hot, fun-loving woman who deserves a good man. Roy is rich and not bad-looking. He could give you kids and then die and leave you a wealthy widow. Isn't your biological clock ticking away? To use your own words, 'You're not getting any younger.'" Tommy laughs. "You turned thirty-five on your last birthday, as I recall?"

He's off by a few years, but I'm annoyed with the conversation for other reasons. "Damn it, Tommy, you know I don't want a permanent relationship, let alone kids. Who needs all that heartache? I'm happy being alone. And, besides, friends care more, love more, and they're way more predictable."

He sighs but I can't read him. "Your *life* is way too predictable, and you have a need to control everything. That's not a good recipe for a loving relationship. Playing it safe isolates you from any chance of being happy. My God, when was the last time you even got laid? Don't you miss the passion? It's not healthy to be so … I don't know … unapproachable."

Now I'm really miffed. "You say I'm predictable and controlling? My God, you just described Lillian." I snap back. "Who can be more controlling and unlovable than her? And she's predictably bad humored, not to mention completely paranoid and jealous of our friendship. She has the passion of a snail and she looks like an alien with her pale face and ruby lips."

Tommy laughs, but this time it's rife with sarcasm. "That's way below you to talk like that. Lillian can look any way she wants. She's powerful and rich. She gave me work and a position you don't know anything about. Granted, she's jealous of you, which isn't surprising. You're popular, beautiful, and she knows she lost her ace in the hole when you left her to work for me. You and I have a special connection she doesn't understand. She sees this the same as being intimate, and I guess it is to some extent. You're like my little sister." He reaches out and pinches me in the butt.

I smile and smack his hand away. "Is that any way for a big brother to behave? Let alone a boss?" I walk over to the simmering pot of tomato sauce/gravy and stir it a little. "There's something dark about her. My God, Tommy, you can have any woman you want. Is it her money?" His eyes are registering pain. "I'm sorry for what I just said, but I hate to see you so torn up every time the two of you break up, which is now almost like clockwork." I hold my breath for what he will say next.

"It's complicated, Kit. Our relationship is both personal and professional. I still work for her and John Vassar at The Country Club. I have a line to walk. My life isn't entirely my own. This is all I can or will say about it."

"Okay, and I'll stop meddling with your love life if you stop looking into mine. And I'll have you know that I have plenty of passion in my life. I date. I get laid. You don't know everything about me, Mr. Thomas Defalco."

"I know more about you than you think, Miss Katherine Cunningham. You should heed the advice of your elders."

I check the time. "I'll see you later, Gramps." I give him a smile and a wave over my shoulder. Mr. Bug follows me to the door, squeaking his toy madly for attention, so I take a moment to play with him.

Bright, warm sunshine pours through the dining-room windows as I walk through the main area, and House feels alive with a hominess that tugs at my heart. I do love this place. I open the lock on the front door to leave—and run into Lillian as she's climbing the steps.

Today, she's wearing a black pageboy wig with bangs. Her hair is normally raven black and cropped close enough to her head to resemble a bathing cap. Her eyes have a lavender twinge to them not unlike Liz Taylor's, but with an unnerving clarity. She even looks a bit like Liz in a certain light, but her mouth has harder lines and it's tight and lacking the softness for which the movie empress is known. She slowly removes her sunglasses when she sees me, piercing right through me with those ... those eyes.

"Well, well, Kitty Cunningham. It's a bit early in the morning to be visiting an old friend, isn't it? But I guess I should have known you'd be here. I'm sure he told you that we fought and separated last night. You certainly wasted no time crawling into his bed. By the way, where are you going? Did he send you out for the morning paper?" Her sarcasm gags me.

"Lillian, it's never too early to visit a friend, and as you well know Tommy and I are devoted friends, although you continually accuse us of being more than that. Honestly, your jealously makes you unattractive and a bore to be around. I might add that you have some nerve showing up here after last night's temper tantrum in which you trashed Baby Blue. Tommy says it wasn't you, but I'll bet you had a part in it." I toss back my head and my hair flies in all directions, and of my flowing locks I'm certain she's more than envious. "What he sees in you I will never know."

Lillian's eyes harden on mine. "I just came by to pick up my belongings. As for the other, I just saw his damaged car and have no idea how it got that way."

"I bet."

"It is a pity. It's a cute toy, and I know he loves it. As for what he sees in me, it's exactly what he will never see in you. And so you know, you will never have Tommy, and chasing after him as you enjoy doing will only be an embarrassment to both of you."

I take a step closer to her. She raises her head in defiance. "Lillian, for the last time, there is nothing between Tommy and me other than a very close friendship, but I will always be in his corner to see him safe and happy. You have cheated on him for years. I know all about you and John Vassar."

She laughs. "John and I are business associates, and, yes, we sometimes socialize together. So what?

I'm raging inside and can't help myself as I say, "His wife may see that differently, and you can try to peddle that business loyalty crap to someone else. I know better."

She gives me a look that can curl one's blood, and she puts her face inches from mine. "I'm warning you, Kitty. Back off or you will find yourself in very deep water. You would be wise to mind your own business and stay the hell away from Tommy. Do you understand me?"

She hisses the last words but I remain right where I am and even lean a smidgeon closer to her, so near that our noses almost touched.

"You don't scare me, Lillian," I manage to say without blinking.

She steps aside and opens the door to The Carriage House, but she stops and turns slowly back towards me. "Oh, and I can and will scare you someday, Kitty. You can bank on that."

Chapter 8

TO SAY THAT LILLIAN has me addled is an understatement, but I show up for work, smiling. I breeze through The House doors and find Tommy at the podium, checking the upcoming evening's reservations. His eyes widen when he sees me.

"Good God, You're on time. Hell must have frozen over."

I ignore his comment and ask, "How are you? I assume that Lillian told you I met her on the way out this morning."

He shakes his head disgustedly. "She came by to pick up her things, but after seeing you she pulled the pin out of the grenade. One odd thing she mentioned though. Said I deserved what happened to my car, and I didn't tell her about it. Did you??"

"Yeah, I did. I'm sorry." I hesitate. "I know I should stay out of your business."

Tommy sighs and raises his eyebrows.

"I accused her of having something to do with it, which of course she denied. But she didn't act surprised about the news nor did she ask what happened, which I thought kind of strange. She just puffed up and said she had no idea what I was talking about. I swear, if she didn't swing the bat I think she found someone who did. I guess you know she assumes I spent the night with you."

"You could do worse."

I roll my eyes at him. "Oh, please. I've made a decision. I told Lillian that she and I are through— and this time for good. I have to tie up loose ends at The Club. and after that I'm not working for John anymore, either. I'm breaking off everything." He looks tired and harassed.

"That's good news," is all that I say, but inside I'm dancing a happy jig. I start toward the lounge but Tommy catches my arm. "Oh, by the way, on Monday would you drive me into the city? I'm taking Baby Blue into the shop to have her repaired, as there's a little damage to the paint I didn't notice before, as well as the glass, and I have to drop off the monthly receipts from The Club to the accountant in Manhattan. And John just called and wants me to pick up a package for him afterwards."

"It's none of my business, but I thought I just heard you say you were done for good with both Lillian and John."

"These are the loose ends. And they are *the* end. I'll treat you to lunch and then we can shop for some bar glasses. I'm sure you could use a few more." His tone becomes even more conciliatory. "I have no other way in, now that Baby's in the shop."

"This Monday I'm to get my hair done, and I plan to take my camera and hike Logan's Trail in the afternoon. And I've told you many times that I hate to drive in New York City traffic."

"Come on, it'll be fun. I'll drive, so just pick me up at ten on Monday morning." A day spent with Tommy anywhere is always a great time, and I find myself smiling as I walk away, for some reason thinking of Lillian. I sigh and turn and agree to his request.

At ten on Monday morning I pick Tommy up at The House and we take off in my car with his Motown tapes blaring from the speakers. He's wearing jeans, and a sports jacket over a T-shirt. He honestly looks like he just stepped from the pages of GQ. Adding to this, he glances at me from behind Ray-Bans and looks more like twenty-five than in his late forties.

In less than a mile he has me laughing and singing along to the oldies. Tommy enjoys a broad range of music and has an extensive library of classical, rock, bluegrass, folk and Motown. In his life there's a sound for every mood. But opera is his favorite, and usually The House is vibrating to some Italian aria in its off hours.

By the time we enter the tunnel into Manhattan we're laughing easily and sharing stories. The day is cloudy, with a bit of a breeze that promises to keep this spring day cool. But it doesn't put a chill on my spirits. As long as I'm not driving, I love New York City and its many facets. I drink in the skyline and marvel at its burst of energy as we escape the dirty tiles and yellow lights of the Lincoln Tunnel.

Tommy expertly maneuvers through the streets, with blaring horns and vehicles careening within a hairsbreadth of each other. We dart down a side street lined with dark brick buildings. He double-parks at a corner and reaches into the back seat for a manila envelope.

"Sit tight. No one will ask you to move. I'll drop this off and be right out." Before I can protest he disappears around the corner. I try to look nonchalant as people from all walks of life file along in front of my car. If I'm asked to move the vehicle, I will panic. In just a few minutes I catch a glimpse Tommy sauntering toward me.

"So, where are we off to now?" I ask, thrilled he's back so soon.

"I'm not sure of this address but I think I know where it is. We'll find a parking garage and walk. I'm to pick up the package, and then we'll go have some lunch and find the glassware wholesaler, okay?"

"Lead on, Leon, I'm just here for the ride."

He drives us to Brooklyn and we find a garage and park. Standing on a sidewalk hemmed in by moving body parts, Tommy searches his pockets for a slip of paper with an address. He folds his hand around mine and pulls me into the mainstream of people crossing against the light. From out of nowhere an impatient taxi driver speeds around the corner and stops just inches from his legs. Startled, Tommy goes off in a tirade, just like a typical New Yorker, banging his fist on the hood and shouting at the driver. "What the fuck! Are you blind, you moron?"

When the driver raises his middle finger to him, Tommy runs to the side of the taxi, stopping another lane of traffic." You want a piece of me? Come on, you stupid piece of shit, I'll tear you apart.

Horns are blaring, and I'm standing at the opposite corner with a grin splitting my face. Tommy settles down and trots over to me, his face sweaty and flushed. I giggle. "Do you feel better?" I laugh again and look away from him.

"There's nothing better to vent your hostilities on than a cocky New York cabbie." He laughs. "Yeah, I feel cleansed. That was just what I needed." He throws his arm around me and gives me a squeeze. "I'm sorry if I embarrassed you."

"You're such a product of this city, I wouldn't expect anything else. Just try to behave for the rest of the day, okay?"

"Okay," he says, dropping his arm from my shoulder and stuffing his hands into the pockets of his jeans. We walk miles of city blocks, or so it seems, as we turn right and left a dozen times before arriving at a seedy-looking high rise in an equally seedy-looking neighborhood. He checks the address then looks around.

"This can't be right, this place is boarded up." He reads aloud the numbers stenciled on each side of the building and sighs. "Well, shit… what the hell. Wait here, I'll find out if this is the place."

I back up against the wall and watch the people walking past me. I love the faces of city people, who often remind me of my hippie youth, when street corners were not scary places but opportunities to meet and greet strangers with naive messages of peace and love. But this area is downright frightening, and I don't like the faces I'm seeing.

Tommy comes from the steps of a neighboring house and shrugs. "No one's home. Let's just go. I'll find a phone and call John. It's obviously the wrong address or a misunderstanding.

The loud, rapid popping of firecrackers makes me crouch with my hands over my ears. I hear a woman scream and I see people running and dashing for cover. It's not firecrackers I'm hearing. I see a dark-blue car swerving onto the sidewalk and spinning around, scattering people in all directions. It bounces off the curb and speeds toward us. With one powerful movement Tommy throws me down practically under a parked car. I feel his body heavy on top of my back. A moment later he pulls me up and into an entranceway, his face pale and panicky as he looks me over.

"Are you hurt?" he asks. "You're not hit anywhere, are you?" His words swirl around me but I answer no in breathless confusion.

I look at myself and notice a slight tear in my slacks, just above one knee. I feel a sting, and when I touch the hole it's moist. But other than this I'm fine. "I'm okay, but what about you?" I ask Tommy. I'm instinctively touching him all over and soon he's holding me tight against him.

"My God, we could have been killed," he says. "I should never have brought you here."

"You didn't know this was going to happen. We're fine now, so let's forget it." He hugs me tighter, almost to the point of cutting off my breathing. I find my sense of humor and I tell him, "If you hold me any closer, I'll be behind you."

"I am so sorry about this."

"What are you sorry for? This is New York City. People shoot at each other all the time'" He pulls away and looks at me like I'm a space alien.

"Kitty, we were just caught in a crossfire. We could both be dead."

"Well, we aren't, and life is walking on past us as if nothing happened, so let's get out of here."

"I didn't count on dodging bullets just now," he stammers. "It's a little unnerving, don't you think?"

"Gee, I thought you would find this exciting," I kid him. "You being a Marine in Nam and all."

"Jesus Christ, Kit. In Nam, I had a gun to fire back with. That's a big difference than being shot at like a fish in barrel from a speeding car." He sighs deeply then chuckles. "I can't believe you're so cool and collected over this. You're amazing. If Lillian had been here she'd be hysterical to the point of hospitalization. She doesn't share your sense of adventure. I find it pretty damn incredible that you are so blasé."

"It will probably hit me later, hopefully when I have a drink in my hand." I laugh.

"Do you want to go home?" he asks me.

"What, and miss the rest of this day? So far, we've been almost run over, damn near got into a fight with a New York cabbie, and shot at in a scene straight out of Mission Impossible. Hell, no, I don't want to go home. I can't wait to see what else New York City has to throw at us."

He looks at me as if I'm crazy and then smiles broadly. "Okay, but let's get the hell away from here." He finds a phone and calls John. When he doesn't answer Tommy says, "Screw it. I tried. I'm ready for lunch and then we can get the glasses and leave."

We catch a cab to take us to the garage where my car is parked. We go back to Manhattan and this time drive to Central Park. He pulls into a no-parking area close to a street vender who is doing a fast business through a curtain of steam. Getting out of the car, he calls to me, "How do you want your hot dog?"

"What? Are you kidding me? You're going to buy me a lousy hot dog for lunch? I thought we'd be dining at The Tavern on the Green or at The Plaza. Quiche, with a fine glass of expensive wine; Belgian chocolate for dessert."

He gestures emphatically. "This is a Gino hot dog. Best in the world. People come clear across the country to eat a Gino hot dog. Trust me, this is far better cuisine than your other choices."

He returns with a couple of foot-long hot dogs and two orders of French fries. Without a word, he reaches into the back seat and produces a brown paper bag and two paper cups." With his eyes smiling at me, he says, "Come. We're gonna have a picnic in the park."

"What about the car?"

"Nobody will bother it. The guy in the hot-dog stand knows what to do if a cop shows up."

My gross disappointment turns to delight as we find a stone bench and sit amid budding bushes. He opens a bottle of Merlot in the brown bag and pours the wine into the paper cups. We eat in comfortable silence, gazing at the lake and studying the humanity walking and running by. Down by the shoreline people are throwing Frisbees to their dogs or lying on sun-warmed grass with their children. Every so often a couple of horses sashay by with their formally clad riders.

I sigh contentedly. "I do love New York City. You were brought up here, weren't you?"

"Yep, then I left home and joined the Marines."

"Was your childhood happy? Tell me about your parents."

"I thought we covered all of this once."

"You told me you grew up in the city, that's all. Maybe you told me more, but I'm sorry if I've forgotten." I take a couple of French fries and can't gobble them down fast enough.

"I had a very happy childhood," he begins between bites of his hot dog and sips of his wine. "I had a few good friends, and we played like city kids do: stickball, basketball, whatever else we could hit or kick. We all went to Catholic school and dated good Catholic girls. We had a strict upbringing, but it wasn't bad. My friends' families were large and close, and I knew a lot of their people."

"What were your parents like?"

"My parents arrived from Naples a year before I was born. They hardly knew English, so we lived in Little Italy. My dad ran a funeral parlor there. He was a mortician and my mom was a seamstress. They were well liked in the neighborhood." Tommy's eyes turned sad and dark, as if the blinds were just pulled tight on a bright, sunny day. "They were murdered when I was nineteen."

I gasp. "Murdered? You never told me this or I would have remembered. Are you okay with telling me what happened?"

"It was made to look like an accident, but it wasn't." He sighs and swallows a bite of hot dog and takes a sip of wine. "My dad was an honorable man. He ran a legit business but he came into contact with many questionable types who became friends. Some of those friends did favors for him. Once, when they came to collect a favor back, they asked my father to bury someone with falsified papers. He was very ethical about his business and refused. He discussed it with my mother who threatened to go to the police. A week later my parents were both found dead on their way home from a funeral. Their car left the road and sank in the East River. The police said it was a weather-related accident, but I know they were forced off the road."

My heart aches with empathy for his grief. "That's beyond tragic. I'm so sorry."

"With them gone, and feeling some eyes on me, I decided the Marines were the best idea. I had so much anger that I became their star recruit. I was ready to kill anyone and everyone. I went to Nam in '65 and came out in '69, when I was twenty-four."

I take a full breath and release it slowly, filtering out all that he's said about his parents' deaths. I do this several times and close my eyes and bask in a feeling of peace and belonging. This is a perfect lunch in a perfect place with my perfect boss, who is my perfect best friend. I am completely calm and happy.

We gather up everything to leave. Tommy whispers to me, "And you wanted The Plaza."

I get up on my tiptoes and kiss him innocently on the cheek and coo, "Thanks for this. It could not have been better."

Tommy was right, as the hot-dog vender had kept a cop from giving us a ticket or, worse, having my car towed. Tommy gave the man two twenties. We drive to the garment district, where dirty warehouses crowd both sides of the street. The small driveways are buffered with double-parked trucks, leaving a mere trickle of road for us to follow.

Adding to the stifling effect, huge hanging racks of bagged clothing swing like sides of beef as they roll down sidewalks, led by people all chasing their deadlines. We miraculously find a place to park in a narrow alley and enter a nondescript building. A spooky rattletrap of a freight elevator jostles us up three floors and opens its door to a spacious area with row upon row of shelves holding of all kinds of plates, glasses and vases. Tommy calls out to one of the men closest to us, and they clasp each other in a brotherhood handshake.

"Defalco, my main man!" the fellow yells out. "What brings you to this fair city?"

"Fair city, my ass. I was just involved in a drive-by shooting, for Christ's sake." Tommy laughs but it's quick.

The two men chat as old friends, and I ask if can I wander up and down the aisles of sparkling samples. I'm told to go ahead but to be careful where I walk in case there's any broken glass. Tommy soon appears beside me as I pick up a stem of Austrian crystal designed for martinis and observe its many facets glimmering in the fluorescent light. He reads my mind.

"Forget it. Seventeen a glass. And that's wholesale—for a gross."

"Oh." I let my disappointment show as I walk away with my shoulders slouching.

"This is nice," he says, looking at a water goblet with a thin gold band around the rim. "I think I'll get a couple of cases of these, and matching wine goblets for the dining room. I feel like changing things up for the summer."

Tommy also buys new table toppers and napkins, and a case of small vases. I pick a weighted, pebble-bottomed rocks glass that he likes, so he adds a couple of dozens of them to the list as well. But when I look longingly at a delicately etched martini glass, he snaps, "And just how long do you think that will last in Joey's dishwater?" I laugh out loud and put it back on the shelf. And then my eyes light up like a kid on Christmas morning. In front of me is the most beautiful martini glass I have ever seen. It's wide and whisper thin, with a frosted, long, graceful stem seemingly embraced by an entwining vine of pure crystal. I get Tommy's attention and give him my best puppy-dog expression, topped off with a shy little "please" smile. It never fails. He studies me and then slowly nods without so much as a faint smile. Then he laughs loud—and I do too.

Soon my little Subaru wagon is crammed to its roofline with crates and boxes, and I'm bubbling with excitement over our purchases. I can't help throwing my arms around Tommy and comically covering him with kisses, just like a little girl with her father on her birthday. I squeal, "Thank you, thank you, and thank you. You're the best boss ever."

He grows quiet and removes my arms from around his neck. I try to recover from my exuberance, saying, "I know, how unprofessional of me, but I'm giddy with happiness. I was just kidding and acting silly." I give him a big smile that he doesn't return.

He is now stark serious as he says, "We have a long drive home. It's close to rush hour, and I'm already tired."

I'm crestfallen, and I wonder why the abrupt change in him. The ride home is quiet. There's some polite conversation but he's noticeably uncomfortable. I keep going over in my mind how bizarre the day has been, with its danger turning into euphoria, and then I try to figure out why it turned sour at the end. I'm sure he had a good time, but perhaps I crossed the line.

We arrive at The House and unload the crates by the kitchen door. I can't let the day end with me feeling as I do, so I dive into my apology.

"Tommy, I'm sorry if I did something I shouldn't have. It was a crazy day, but I had such a good time. Lunch was great, and I love what you bought for The House. But in the last couple of hours I felt something shift between us, and I don't know how to handle it."

His mouth pulls into a tight smile and says softly, "Don't worry about it. I'm just tired."

"We're good then?" I say quickly.

"We're good," he replies just as quickly.

I drive away not at all convinced.

Chapter 9

SPRING MELTS INTO SUMMER as we tuck away a late Easter at The House. Ever since our daytrip to New York, Tommy has been all business—and involved in more than solely the restaurant. He's reestablished his relationship at The Country Club, as he's back to working part time for Lillian and John, and she has once again entangled him in her viscous web.

Upon hearing this news from his own lips, I went into a long rant about his now obviously wishy-washy convictions, when he had said he was quitting both The Club and Lillian for good. He gave me his pat answer: "It's complicated, and please mind your own business."

Lillian's resurfacing this time, however, is decidedly different. She's friendlier and even apologetic when she speaks to me. But although the olive branch is being extended, her past behavior makes me cautious as hell at accepting her gestures of goodwill. There remains something unsettling about Lillian that I can't put my finger on. Regardless, she appears to be making a genuine effort to get along with me, and Tommy seems more relaxed than he's been with her in a long while.

As for her possible involvement with orchestrating the attack on Tommy's car, no complicity was ever discovered. And no evidence of the damage to Baby Blue was ever found when the police questioned Jimmy Stokes and examined his Jeep. Regardless, I continue to believe that the bar tab for him and his merry band of assholes was paid by Lillian so these misfits would show up every Friday night at The House. This would explain why they were there without fail when clearly they would be happier drinking someplace else. What she didn't count on was their always causing trouble. No matter, it would fit her style for spying on Tommy, and as revenge for his breaking up with her, I can see her ordering Jimmy Stokes to get her car and come back after hours and break out the windows in the Mercedes. Petty, but effective to be sure.

Every night during this month, my little family gathers in The Pit for a nightcap and to tickle me with their respective humor. On this evening we all enjoy an early quitting time, so we pay for our own libations and sit down for a gabfest about the events of the shift just ended. As always Mr. Bug is with us, enjoying the company that he has been denied while in Tommy's upstairs apartment.

"Unchained Melody" plays over our sound system in the lounge and Tommy springs to his feet. "I love this song," he announces as he grabs Polly, who barely has time to put down her drink.

He's in rare form tonight, in high spirits, more open, and funnier than usual. He should be all of this, since business is thriving and he seems more rested of late. Maybe, too, he has a new girlfriend besides staid old Lillian. I secretly wonder where he goes some nights after hours when he's not seeing her. As close as we are, there's still so much I don't know about him. But I'm not his keeper.

He guides Polly onto the dance floor, spins her away and then pulls her to him, holding her close and not letting go. We all watch intently, salting their performance with gentle barbs and soft laughter.

He dips her with a sexy grind, and Polly squeals in her southern drawl, "Oh, Thomas, where in the name of all that is good and holy did you learn to do *that*?"

She's laughing, and he smiles and does another sexy dance move. "High-school gymnasium, and I took ballroom dance lessons," he says so we all can hear.

When the song ends and they come back to The Pit, Phillip gasps,

"Ballroom dancing! Be still my heart. You always surprise me, Tom. You're almost fifty years old, ride a bicycle, have a little foofoo dog, wear a pink-diamond pinky ring, get facials and manicures, and drive a baby-blue convertible. You are a hot man-beast. Are you sure you're not gay?"

We all laugh and Polly asks Tommy, "Do you dance with Lillian this way?"

For a moment there's stark silence, which Tommy breaks with a laugh and says, "Lillian doesn't dance. Lillian hates to dance. Lillian is all about sex."

At Tommy's remark I damn near choke on my drink, but it's the start of my third so I'm loose enough to blurt, "I can't believe I heard what you just said. So *that's* the reason you stay with her." I huff. "I find it incredibly hard to accept that Lillian is a sex goddess."

Jeannie and Christine shriek with giggles. Jeannie says, "She must be into pain. An S&M queen. Shit, I don't even want to imagine this."

I rub my hands over my eyes and Tommy laughs.

"Okay, I may be lying," he says as he cocks an eyebrow at me.

"Well," Phillip says and smiles, "I guess Lillian has a new name: She Who Does Not Dance." We all laugh but I think it's fitting for such a joyless person.

"Oh, my Lord," Polly says and gulps her drink, "I do so love this place."

Tommy punches some song codes into the audio set, and I'm surprised when he comes over to me and elbows me gently in the side and says, "You're next. Get your dancing shoes on."

I laugh and push him away. "In your dreams, cowboy. You pull one of those sleazy moves on me, you'll be walking bowlegged for a week."

He smiles broadly. "I didn't know you ever noticed my moves."

"Oh, I notice all right. You're like a bad scene I can't get out of my mind!" I laugh and poke him with my finger.

"See? You do love me too."

I roll my eyes and look away, but I'm really delighted with the exchange. It's the first time since our venture into the City that he wants to play with me. And it feels great. Whatever clouded the trip home is gone, and I welcome Tommy back as my fun-loving sidekick. I do dance with him, and he's the perfect gentleman—much to my disappointment.

The nights fold into one another like well-shuffled cards in the hands of a professional dealer. It's soon early summer and my favorite time at The House, as the terrace deck is now open. Tommy and Troy look like matched bookends standing together at the podium, throwing the ambiance of The House like an expensive shawl around each patron who enters.

The doors to our dining room, with their large glass panes, open wide to present pink linen tablecloths, and red napkins are folded like roses to elegantly grace every tabletop. Gleaming gold-rimmed water goblets and matching wine glasses stand like sentinels to the upper right of the pale-green-with-gold-trim dinner plates. Small mint-green vases containing pink tea roses command the center point of each of the tables. The mixture of colors blends to create a seasonal painting that heralds both the time of year and The House's sophistication.

Adding to the overall scene, sunshine throws mottled patterns across the patio as it filters through the surrounding trees. An abundance of bright flowers rise in layers from large urns in each corner of the stone deck that joins seamlessly with the shining hardwood floor in the dining room. Light, fragrant breezes visit throughout The House, like playful spirits dismissing any stale or damp residue from wet spring months.

Summer always brings fresh energy to the food and beverage profession at many levels, as fine dining establishments receive new business in the form of proms, graduation parties and weddings. And because it's a time of intense competition as well, we put on additional help and double our quantities of many foodstuffs and general supplies.

Our now very packed kitchen is a virtual hive of frantic worker bees, the intensity of their activity sometimes mistaken for anger, as frustration often spews out as a result of precisely timed preparations gone awry. But it only takes a funny comment or a quirky glance to send a round of immediate smiles and giggles throughout the room. The kitchen banter, which often borders on debauchery, is in direct contrast to the dining-room decorum that's demanded of our floor professionals. If only the epicure biting into the chateaubriand knew what Chef Bruno had said that piece of prime beef reminded him of just sixty seconds earlier!

We're overbooked today, which is a Saturday, so Tommy called me at my apartment to let me know that I was needed to help out in the dining room. This means I must assist the servers on the floor as well as cover my own bar duties. Most times it works out well, but the pace can be grueling. He reminds me to wear my long tux slacks and vest and leave the tails and fishnet stockings at home.

The kitchen always amazes me, as there appears to be sheer bedlam going on in there at all times. Tonight is no exception. Servers fly through the swinging doors on feet that don't seem to touch the floor while balancing massive trays of meticulously prepared food on their shoulders. Inside, Madeline, who works the salad and dessert station, calls out, "Please, someone deliver these salads to table six." Then, urgently to her assistant, "Andy, I need more blue cheese." Before he can open the giant refrigerator door, she barks three more commands at him.

Polly rushes in and slides a plate toward Bruno. "This filet mignon is well done and it's supposed to be medium well."

"Damn it!" Bruno yells and throws another filet onto the leaping flames. He checks four other steaks cooking on his grill and some lamb chops. "Come back in ten, Polly, but take this order out now," he shouts across to her and points at two plates full of food. Then he calls out to Robert, who just walked in, "Bobby, your filet will be up in five."

Victor, for his part in this chaos, is sautéing, with an eye on the orders that bob across the stoves like lost ships at sea. He prepares and garnishes a plate and places it on an already full tray. "Jeannie is ready to roll to table two," Victor shouts in his thick Bronx accent. "I need a runner, right now. Pay attention, people!"

Cheryl hoists a heavy tray as if it's nothing and rushes through the door. I often wonder where this woman gets the strength. And she can't weigh a hundred pounds soaking wet!

The amazing part of this entire, frantic backstage circus is that the instant any one of us enters the dining room, everything slows down. Our servers majestically stroll with bulky, weighty trays to waiting tray butlers and with flair and a smile lovingly present each plate of dining delight. Troy and Tommy visit the tables to collect the nods from approving patrons while busboys saunter casually around the room after removing and then precisely replacing all the dinnerware, glasses, and setups, filling water glasses, changing napkins and completing the illusion of simple, relaxed service no matter the demands placed on them. We all strive to present the perfect picture of impeccable care at every table, while personally stressing over the progress of each aspect of the dining experience. It's an awesome ballet.

Tommy comes into the kitchen and inquires, "Has anyone seen Phillip?" No one answers. "I need a bottle of Louis Jadot Pouilly Fuissé for table eight, and the bin is empty. So if anyone sees him, tell him to go to that table right away. Also, there's a birthday at table one." He glances around the kitchen and spots another employee he's looking for. "Maddie, I need you to get a cake up from the fridge and detail it right away." He hands her a paper with the necessary information, then calls out, "Anyone need anything?"

"Yes, these salads have to go right now," Maddie says. "Table six."

"I'm on it," Tommy calls out. He swings the tray to his shoulder and picks up a waiting round of dressings as he goes by.

I pass Phillip—tripping up the steps from the wine cellar—with a bottle in his hand, so I tell him about the Pouilly Fuissé for table eight.

"Oh, shit," he says. "Be a sweetheart and serve this bottle to table four for me."

He grabs a wine list and rushes out to table eight. He apologizes, followed by a gentle bow, folding his hands in front of him in the most suppliant manner possible as he waits for the diners to make another selection. The show is indeed a lot of what people pay for, and we deliver Oscar-winning performances every night.

I snatch a freshly pressed linen bar towel and flip it over my arm and cradle the wine bottle in the crook of my elbow. I'm smiling as I approach table four. I make pleasant small talk as I present the bottle to a gentleman who's with a much younger woman. He makes a grand display of putting on his glasses to read the entire wine label, obviously to impress his date. I get it that he doesn't have a clue as to what the words imply, as he mixes up a meaning, but I smile and nod as he glances my way.

He studies some more, looks up at me, and says, "Very good."

I open the bottle and place the cork next to him on the table. If he knows anything about wine, he will confirm the stamp on the cork matches the winery on the bottle. But he sniffs it as if it would tell him something about the wine and I wait patiently as he fiddles with it. I pour a mouthful of a nice Cabernet into the glass for his approval. This confuses him, so I save him the embarrassment and ask him if he would like to taste the wine first.

"Of course I would." he says and looks a little annoyed that he almost blew his cover for snowing his lady friend. He takes a gulp as if it were beer and announces to me, "This wine has oxidized, please bring another." I smile.

"Certainly, sir," I coo. "It will be but a moment."

I meet Phillip, coming off the floor right along with me. "Table four says this wine has oxidized."

"No way," Phillip says as he takes a small silver spoon from his lapel pocket and tastes the wine. "He's out of his freaking mind. This wine is perfect for what it is. He has to be a first-class asshole to say that."

"You've such an eloquent way with words," I say and follow him, grinning all the while.

We round a corner and he hands me the bottle. "Take this to your bar and serve it by the glass later, for a buck more than our house."

Phillip shakes his head. "What a fucking moron. I'll take care of him. Thanks, Kitty Kat."

In two shakes Phillip is striding confidently over to table four with a new bottle. He bows apologetically and swiftly opens the bottle with flair. I hear him explaining that this particular wine is from a special region in France, and that seasonal weather changes permit the wine to do such and such, which results in a slightly more woodsy finish, and that the wine is simply marvelous as it settles on the tongue of a discerning connoisseur. He smoothly sells the bottle to table four, and I spot him smiling smugly as he walks away.

I love to watch Phillip more than anyone else on the floor. He moves with the smooth elegance of a swan and the determination of a stag. Gay men can do that, and I have no idea how. He has the command of both utmost importance and genteel humility, and each is interchangeable at a moment's notice. Phillip is the perfect image of a butler from a manor in turn-of-the-century England. I think he's been reincarnated.

Table four sends the shrimp cocktail back because it smells strong, and they claim the soup is too thick and spicy. Their meal is delayed, and Mr. Wine Expert is getting increasingly agitated even though Tommy has already been to his table twice to massage his ego. We're all aware of a potential situation brewing, and true to form the word "asshole" escapes from the mouth of every staff member who's walked near this guy at one point or another.

I dash back and forth from the dining room to my lounge, covering my lounge patrons as well as I can, but my servers are also helping out behind the bar, since all evening long I've been carrying out a steady stream of orders, helping to clear and reset tables, and even seating reservations. Then, as if I have spare time, I serve desserts and cordials.

Table six, directly behind disgruntled table four, orders a round of drinks: two whiskey sours, a brandy Alexander and a Jack and water, all of which I cheerfully make, as I'm happy to get behind my bar for a minute or two. I complete the drinks with fruit garnishes and place everything on my round cocktail tray.

I pass Tommy, who is briskly coming out of the dining room just as Polly is approaching me with an empty food tray. I trip and fall forward —careening like a drunken sailor toward table four.

Polly, with one swift ninjalike movement, grabs my tray of drinks as I hit the floor. She spins around with them, each glass tilting and rolling dramatically around on its base in a wild, crazy dance.

I go down fast and hard, like a penguin sliding off an iceberg, and scoot right under table four. Mr. Wine Expert and his young date leap to their feet, their eyes huge with surprise—as mine are as well.

Polly is still spinning with my tray of saved drinks, and every one of them settles down. Miraculously not one has spilled, but they have lost their garnishes. Poly feigns a bow and some patrons applaud. One man cheers and gives her a standing ovation. I hear lots of laughing and chatter.

I stand and graciously apologize to the couple from table four, who now look at me in sheer terror.

Tommy walks to my side, and in professional calm escorts me from the dining room.

When we get to the kitchen he asks me, "Are you all right?" I nod and he holds a look of astonishment, not unlike the one Mr. Bug sometimes displays. He squeezes my arm and exclaims under his breath, "What the *hell* did you do?"

I'm red with embarrassment and start to laugh. "I slipped. I'm sorry. How did Polly, in God's name, save that tray?" Tommy shakes his head and walks off.

Jeannie comes into the kitchen, her facial expression like a cat makes when it sees a mouse. "What the hell are these?" she asks, pointing to the orange slice that is pressed into my lapel and the two cherries that are dangling in my hair like Christmas ornaments. She bursts out laughing, which has everyone in the kitchen doing the same once they see me, only louder.

It's all too much for Tommy, who's come back and now explodes in laughter as well. He collapses against the wall and finally lies across the sideboard, breathless, and I honestly believe almost in tears.

Polly rushes in, trying to catch her breath as she chokes out, "Did you see the look on the faces at poor table four? Having a bath in those drinks would have really topped off their already terrible dining experience in fine style." She gets her voice back and squeals. "I *love* this place, y'all, I really do."

Tommy can only shake his head. "You're a class act, Kitty, sliding on your belly as if you were going for home plate and then standing there with fruit all over you and not knowing it. Is it any wonder why I love you?" Without warning he grabs me by the waist, draws me to him and plants a kiss on my lips. It was a quick, spontaneous act that no one would think unusual, as small shows of affection are common in our workplace. But it stopped my world for an instant and left me reeling.

Later that night, for those who missed it, my fall is reenacted and becomes an instant legend. Over and over I'm asked to demonstrate exactly what happened. I cover everything in great detail, including what went on in the kitchen with the staff. Everything, that is, except for Tommy's kiss.

Chapter 10

ALL OF MY WORKING nights are now breezing by, one right after the other. The Carriage House traffic is brisk, with parties and late dinners the rule rather than the exception. Lillian has started to pop in now and then to see Tommy, and she flaunts him like a prize won at the County Fair, catching my eye and smiling coyly as they share a drink together after the late-dinner rush. I'm often convinced she's high on something, as she paws him over like she's on catnip. For reasons I don't understand, Tommy acts deferentially toward her.

For obvious reasons, Millie is also uncomfortable with Lillian, and I have managed to keep a distance between her and She Who Does Not Dance. As far as Tommy and I are concerned, any attempt at our old banter at work falls flat and humor is strained, at best. The whole happy and contented feel of my bar is thwarted by Lillian's presence. Tonight is no exception, and I make small talk with her as I tend to her along with my regular customers.

She twirls the stem of her martini glass and grins at me. "Kitty," she says, her voice soft. "I really owe you an apology. I see now that my Tom has no desire to be with you. How could he? You may be a fabulous barmaid but you have nothing that could interest him. You should find someone, Kitty. You're not getting any younger." Tommy comes to her side and avoids my eyes. He hasn't heard the conversation so far.

"Actually, I am seriously seeing someone," I shoot back.

Tommy turns slowly and leans on the bar. "I didn't know that. Who is he?

"Well, you and I seldom talk anymore." I smile at him. "And you two lovebirds are always all over each other or on the move, so how could you know?"

He stiffens his posture and arches his eyebrows. "Again, if you don't mind my asking, who is this guy?"

As if on cue, Roy thunders into the lounge, announcing to everyone that he has, indeed, arrived. He sits next to Millie, who I can sense is grateful that he blocks her view of Lillian. I gaze affectionately at Roy, hoping he doesn't notice me, but say to Tommy, "Who do you think, Mr. Defalco? I took the advice you offered me not so long ago." I doubt my lie will work, but it's all I have available on such short notice.

I feel Tommy's eyes on me as I step over to Roy and make a big fuss over him while I pour his drink. Roy needs no encouragement to reach over the bar to give me a hug. Usually I pull back, but this time I move toward him. When I turn to Tommy and Lillian, they're leaving. Tommy never even offers to say goodbye.

On this night, Millie and Roy chat together for the longest time—on the topic of *me*, until Raymond, the businessman she'd met some time ago, comes in. Now Millie's in her glory, with a man on each side buying her drinks. She winks at me and sips her martini, as if it's the ultimate elixir. And I guess for her it is.

As the evening rolls on, the three of them get pretty toasty, so I cut them off and bring out coffee and sandwiches. Roy gets a little incensed that I've flagged him and remains somewhat belligerent, but I eventually charm him into calming down. I beg for his keys, which he will not relinquish, but when Mike arrives for Millie, he offers to give Roy a ride home. Roy assures me that he will go with Mike and Millie just as Raymond waves goodnight, telling me he's okay to drive. I'm not convinced, but Roy is my immediate concern. He's acting really plowed even after two cups of coffee, and I'm worried he might still get in his car. I should've stopped serving him and Raymond sooner. But it's not easy when Millie isn't driving so the amount she drinks doesn't have the same implications. The whole thing gnaws at me as the night winds down.

Tommy comes in just as Polly and I are closing up. He's disheveled and fairly drunk. Polly kids with him as he comes into the lounge, "Hey, Defalco, whatever you and She Who Does Not Dance are doing, you should stop."

He growls at her and grabs her arm. "Shut up, Polly." Then off to the side to me, "Are you sleeping with him?"

Polly looks incensed. "Who are you talking to?"

"Shut up, Polly," he says again.

I put my hand on my hip and swagger up to Tommy. "That is just about as none of your business as *none* can get. And poor Polly. Apologize to her. That was rude."

Polly laughs and stares at me. "So, *who are* you sleeping with?"

"Why, Roy, of course. Who else?"

Polly lets fly with one of her Dixie yells and says, "Roy? Y'all are lovers? Seriously? That must be like romping a boar hog. How come I didn't know this?" She turns to Tommy. "She's sleeping with Roy." Then to me she says, "You *are?*"

I give her a look that says no and then chastise Tommy, "You're drunk on your ass. Go to bed. You're ridiculous. Why on earth would you care about my sex life? Besides, you said it yourself, Roy's rich and he adores me. You were the one who suggested I go out with him. So get over it—and get over yourself and let me live my life."

Tommy climbs the stairs to his apartment and releases My Bug, who runs down the steps and sprints from room to room in the restaurant, acting beyond ecstatic to be free.

Polly and I finish locking up, and I fill her in on the short exchange between Lillian and me earlier that night. "I made it all up about Roy to ace Lillian. Tommy must have overheard me and probably can't understand, as close as he and I are, why I didn't tell him about Roy." I sigh. "I don't know why I said it. I've been depressed all day for some reason, and I didn't want to listen to her shit tonight."

We decide to go to the Brass Rail for a nightcap, but once I'm outside I notice that Roy's car is gone from the parking lot.

"Damn it, Polly, Roy must have refused Mike's ride home. He had way too much to drink and I didn't demand his keys."

"Don't be so hard on yourself. Roy's a veteran drinker if there is one. He can handle himself. Sometimes you just can't tell how booze affects a person. Someone can drink five manhattans one night and walk a straight line, and that same person at another time gets sloppy over a single glass of wine. You know that. You can't be responsible for everyone at your bar.

"That's not true anymore. There's a new law on the books that holds a bartender responsible if someone gets drunk and leaves the bar and something bad happens." My skin is cold in the hot night air. "I don't feel like going out now. I'll see you tomorrow." We hug goodnight, and as I'm driving home my mood sours even more.

I'm miserable about a lot of things. Worrying about Tommy with Lillian for one. But they seem to deserve each other. I also want to forget Millie, whom I watch fade from bright and happy to dull and depressed because of the poison I serve her every night. I'm also disgusted by a man like Roy, who has everything he could possible want, yet the more he drinks the more he clutches at me in desperation. And it's not me he desires; it's anyone to quell his fear of being alone.

As for me, I'm thirty-eight. How many more years can I continue being the darling of the saloon? I'm tired of babysitting drunks and policing those who abuse themselves with alcohol. I'm lonely and constantly living in fear that my life will never work out right for me. I worry about the bills that pile up on my dresser week after week and whether I'll always have enough tips to pay them. I'd like a day job with regular hours, benefits, and a guaranteed income. I'm so confused and alone at this moment that it brings me to tears. Yes, it's just a mood, and by tomorrow night I'll be back onstage and performing and laughing. That's show biz. But for now I just want to wallow in self-pity.

I fall into bed, exhausted from all my self-criticism. But sleep is hard to come by. Instead, my thoughts are all about the bar business and how it brings out the worst in people. I would be doing something else by now if it weren't for my friendship with Tommy. He's the one stable thing in my life. I only wish he'd drop Lillian and find someone else to romance. Like me. God, I can't believe I'm thinking this, but I wish he would find real love in his heart for me. However, no, Tommy would never love me. He says he's too old for me; he considers me more as a sister. And we're friends—but friends don't hurt each other like I'm hurting now.

Polly greets me at the door when I arrive for work. She hands me the evening newspaper. "You must be a freaking psychic. Did you see this yet?" I shake my head. "Roy had an accident last night." I rudely grab the paper from her and see a short article in the Police Reports section. She fills me in before I can read the column.

"He hit a utility pole on the way home, knocking out the power for hours. He was hospitalized for head injuries. Of course, DUI charges were leveled against him, and it says this is his third offense. He's in deep shit. I'm sayin' that, not the paper." My glare stifles her from trying to make some kind of joke about what happened.

"He could have been killed, or killed somebody else, all because of me."

"Don't be silly. It's not your fault. Anyway, he's fine. Paper says he's in stable condition."

"He got a DUI because I let him drink too much."

"Who hasn't got a DUI in these parts? The paper is full of them every night." She gives me a hug. "I love you, Sis. Lighten up. Shit happens. You can't take everyone home and tuck them into bed after a night of partying. Come on in. Tommy has called a quick meeting in The Pit."

Tommy nods at me from the steps of the fireplace, and in a few minutes everyone is sitting on or near the horseshoe sofa. He assumes the power stance we all recognize: legs shoulder-width apart and arms folded across his chest. He starts the meeting with his standard, "Okay, here's the deal." Whenever we hear this, we all know that a new Deal is about to be born.

"As most of you know by now," he begins, "we dodged a bullet last night when one of our patrons left here pretty inebriated and ran into a pole. The reports say he'll be okay, but it may not have turned out this way. The bartender and The House would have been held responsible if the outcome had been more serious. So we need to change some things, and here's what's going to happen." Tommy then goes into a long spiel about The House's and its bartenders' liability if a patron leaves drunk and has a wreck. I'm thoroughly versed on the new law and cannot wait for him to finish, as I have to think that most of what he's saying is aimed at me.

Tommy wraps it up and excuses everyone, but he catches my arm as I turn to leave. "I'm sorry about Roy. I had no idea you and he were, you know, *serious*. I apologize for prying last night."

"You were drunk," I say with disgust. "Which is so unlike you. You usually have more class than that. Lillian is turning you into a real ... I don't know what. But I can't handle her presence at the bar anymore. And, please, don't defend her. To be honest, I'm truly tired of the way both of you act around each other." I snatch my arm away from him, and we both walk off.

It's soon unusually busy for a Sunday evening. My mood is melancholy but I put on my happy-go-lucky bartender face and try to make the night hum. But Millie's in her customary place at the bar and sees through my façade.

"Darling, I know you're upset about Roy's accident. I hope you don't think it's your fault. I'm the voice of experience, and I'm here to tell you that you can't tell a drunk what to do. You can have their best interest at heart, but people who drink rarely take advice or accept help, no matter who offers it."

I change the subject. "Are you happy?" I ask Millie in an even voice.

Her chin comes up and she blinks slowly twice. "Frankly, I've found that few people are genuinely happy, Kitty. Most of us just exist from day to day, seeking out those little oases that give us comfort. I believe the only thing that brings true happiness into a person's life is to be of service in some way. To reach out and pull someone along who's struggling. And make no mistake about it, everyone struggles. But I'm fortunate to have known happiness from time to time. I'm far from bragging, but my money has helped a great many people, and the good feeling I get from making others happy is very powerful."

"But are you happy?" I want an answer and not doublespeak.

"Kitty, you're adroit enough to understand that at my age I get to ask the questions as I want them posed. Which means that I'm not very good at answering questions others ask me. Regardless, I meant what I said about giving service providing me with great joy. I have to believe you hold the same belief. You are a person of service. You bring me joy. You make me laugh, and you give me permission to forget. I will always be grateful for that. I've watched you work for a long time, and I admire the way you can lift people into your world and make them happy. You're a gift, Kitty."

"But what if the *service* I provide hurts people—and I know it?"

Millie takes my hands in hers. "Let me say this. If you're talking about what you do here, you heal far more than you harm. It's a lot more than dulling senses with alcohol. It's giving people a chance to understand things they otherwise wouldn't. In some cases, you enable them to make contact with their own selves in a very positive way. To answer your question about my being happy, there are times when I'm happy because of you and for no other reason."

I don't know what to think, but I thank her and step away to wait on a couple who just sat down at the end of the bar. The night soon comes to a crawl, as all I can think about is what Millie has said to me. After she leaves and the night dribbles out and the last customer waves goodbye, I check that the gas knobs are all turned off in the kitchen and that the refrigerator is locked. I start to flip off the lights and find that Tommy has come in behind me.

"What?" I ask.

"Nothing." He leans against the open doorway with his arms folded.

"What?" I ask again.

"I'm just looking at you." His bowtie hangs open around his neck and several buttons are open on his shirt, showing the bed of graying hair on his chest.

"Well, stop! You're creeping me out."

He chuckles. "Come on, Kitten. Don't be mad at me. Last night I was miffed that you never once mentioned you and Roy were seeing each other. I figured you'd confide in me, like we always do with each other, and I guess it hurt my feelings that you didn't."

"Whose fault is that? We never talk anymore. Or play. You and Lillian are nightly items. You don't need me around. You've got enough on your plate."

He frowns. "That's simply not true. You and I have something special that Lillian nor anyone else can hold a candle to. We're a team. You make me crazy sometimes with what you do and say, but I can't imagine life here without you." He gives me that smile that I can't help but return. However, I know his tone and feel a lecture coming. "Your mood tonight isn't like you. I hate seeing you so down. This has something to do with Roy's accident, doesn't it? I assume you went to the hospital to see him. Is he hurt worse than the paper said?"

"No, he's fine … I think." Oh, my God, I forgot about my *deep affection* for Roy. I'll have to make certain Polly doesn't tell Tommy that I didn't learn of the wreck until she showed me the paper when I came to work today. I hate to keep this lie going, but it comforts me in an odd way. It makes me appear less needy, and as long as Lillian continues to flaunt her control over Tommy, it helps balance the situation, at least in my mind. I don't foresee Roy coming in any time soon, so I'll keep the façade going until I find a delicate way out.

I've never lied to Tommy before about anything, and it feels terrible but the words tumble out of my mouth anyway: "We're just dating, so I don't know what I'm feeling, to be honest. But I'm having a really hard time with his accident. It's holding up a mirror to what I do here. I don't want to tend bar anymore. I need to move on. Do something worthwhile."

"You didn't cause what happened to Roy. I was told that Mike Vassar was driving him home. I went through the new Deal this afternoon so that everyone understood The House's responsibilities, not just you. You did everything right with Roy."

"I get that. It's just … Roy could be dead right now, or he could have killed someone else last night." My head begins to pound. "I can't control people and their actions, but I turn them into weapons to do harm to themselves or others." I sigh. "Millie talked to me tonight in a way that was different from ever before, and what she said was beautiful, so I don't know what to believe. All I know is that I'm very confused and I don't want to bartend anymore."

"Millie loves you, Kit."

The tears come too fast for me to catch them as I feel Tommy gently fold my body into his wide chest. He holds me steady, stroking my hair, not saying anything.

"Millie says I'm a gift, but I'm a thirty-eight-year-old woman who's afraid of losing her looks and needs to grow up and get involved with something meaningful for once in her life. I need to get away from this work, and you need someone young, cute, and sassy behind the bar, someone without a conscience, someone who can let what happens to the drunks of the world roll off her back."

He gently pushes me an arm's-length away and looks at me intently. "Are you insane? You're absolutely beautiful, and the older you get the more stunning you become. Don't ever think you're not important to The House—and to me. You play a huge role in holding this place together."

"You have to say that."

"Are you ever wrong. Bartending is one of the hardest jobs for anyone to do well. You have to be all things to all people: mother, sister, a little bit of a whore and a small dash of a nun, a business consultant, a doctor, a psychiatrist, and a confessor. You are all those things to all sorts of people. You absolve them of their sins and give them a reason to go on. You make them feel like someone cares. You listen to them, and you allow them to believe that they have a friend they can trust while they're here."

I wipe my eyes. "Millie sort of said something like that. Or I think she did."

Tommy laughs and steps back from me. "You bring out the best in people. You do that, not the booze. You show them that their lives are okay. Their problems, their angers and hates, their agendas are still there inside them, but you temper their anxieties with your own beautiful self in ways that allow them to relax. It's you and not the alcohol. In this lounge, bartending isn't about the booze, it's about you. Millie is right, you are a gift. We serve them meals; you, Kitty, serve them their souls. And I mean this. I'm not being dramatic."

My thoughts are still muddled. "I just don't feel it anymore. Does that make sense?"

"If you leave, it will break my heart. Hell, you're my best friend. This is your home." He comes forward and presses his lips to my forehead in a long kiss. "You're not really giving up the business, are you?"

I shrug. "I'll be here a while yet, but the time is coming. Right now, I've lost my mojo for it all. We'll just have to see how much longer I can go on."

I put my arms around him. I can feel his heart beating and his slow, deep breaths. He's right, I am home. And it's the only place I want to be. His arms tighten around me before he pulls back and searches my face, letting his gaze rest on mine for just a moment. I think he might kiss me, but Tommy only kisses me in earnest on New Year's Eve, and as always it's a colossal joke among the staff and an impromptu comedy routine for us. It's not officially New Year's until Tommy makes up for the fighting we do all year in a "wiping the slate clean" kiss.

"Look out, Kitty, here he comes," Polly will squeal in delight. And I tell him in mock sternness, "No tongue. Behave yourself."

"Okay, I promise," he always says, never listening to his own words. I wind up making a disgusted face when his sloppy, wet kiss ends and we part laughing. My comment, "Why are you such a pig?" kicks off a whole new year of war.

But now I remember how it felt away from all the banter. How deliberate he was in taking me into his arms, everything about him slow and passionate, his tongue filling my mouth with the taste of Grand Marnier, his breath quickening.

"Happy New Year, Kitten" he would whisper in my ear and then flash his great smile before turning away and leaving me with my legs feeling like jelly and my stomach in knots.

Tonight he doesn't kiss me but gives me a small smile as he delicately touches my face with his fingertips. "Come on," he whispers and takes my hand, "I'll walk you to your car. One day Roy will take you away from all this and make you a queen. Just know, you're the best in the business and many will miss you—but no one as much as me."

Chapter 11

As SUMMER MOVES ON and opens its sunny smiles to us, we enjoy a rash of graduations and prom parties at The House. The festivities are fun to host but present a challenge, as we have to keep an eye out for underage drinking. The happy news is that these student-oriented events are usually finished early in the evening, as the kids come in for a memorable dinner and then move on to other parties, where the real drinking occurs.

One particular evening, at a prominent family's request—and pocket-book—we close The House and host a pre-prom party for fifty kids, complete with a DJ and buffet dinner. It runs from 6 to 10 p.m., in the dining room and on the terrace, and it promises to be an early, easy night for all of us.

Tommy and Victor do the buffet, and I'm to take care of serving the soft beverages. I wear my long tux pants and vest, as I always do when I serve food. I usually have my hair pulled back from my face but tonight I let it fall down over my shoulders.

The afternoon, prior to the kid's bash, is picture-perfect, the weather bright and warm with air tinctured by the rich scent of lavender and lilacs. The grounds are green and lush and we're constantly serenaded by larks that flit from limb to limb on nearby hardwoods.

Black stretch limos arrive, and a parade of startlingly beautiful young girls and their wide-eyed, trying-to-be-cool dates file into the restaurant. The gowns are drop-dead gorgeous, and these young women look like starlets on the red carpet. Many parade around like seasoned movie legends, perhaps Harlow or Monroe with an occasional Bacall tossed in for good measure.

Tommy and I lean on my portable bar and watch the show. He sighs softly and remarks, "Jesus, look at these kids. Every year they seem to get younger and the girls more beautiful."

I laugh and tell him, "No, every year you get older—and more wishful."

The DJ is rocking, the food is fabulous, and the kids are having a great time. Tommy floats back and forth from the buffet to my bar. He's relaxed and happy and gets me giggling over sly comments about the kids. He pours us two Grand Mariners that he brings from the lounge, and I keep them behind my bar for discreet sipping. After the buffet slows down, there isn't much to do but chat with each other and watch the festivities. He reaches over and plays with one of my long curls. "I like your hair this way. You should wear it down more."

"Yes, you told me that before," I playfully inform him.

He's silent, continues to take in the crowd, then says, "I love doing these kinds of parties with you. We work well together. We have a lot of fun. I'm really glad we're friends."

"Me too," I say, matching his eyes with mine. We smile at each other for a long time. "Are we having a moment here or what?" I ask, feeling warm all over—and this has nothing to do with the temperature on the terrace.

He looks away and chuckles. "Funny, I was just thinking back to when I first hired you at The Country Club. I wanted a middle-aged guy with tons of bar experience, and in you waltzed like you owned the place and started to interview me instead of the other way around."

"Well, I didn't want to work for some schmuck."

"Glad I passed the interrogation," he says.

I laughed at this word choice. "What made you think you passed anything? I came for the money, honey."

He smuggles me another drink and we watch the kids tear up on the dance floor. Some of those dresses had to cost a thousand dollars, and now they're full of sweat and makeup, and I'm going to guess food. Tommy tells me, "Their dates don't care about the gowns, so long as the girls can remember how to get out of them." I tell him, "Men, that's all they think about."

We start talking about The House and the magnificent slide I made under Table Four, and we share tales about our craziest customers, as the party is now over and the busboys are cleaning the tables. Picking up my hands, he looks at the many rings I always wear and wants to know the stories behind each one. He rubs his thumb over every stone as if he can feel its life. Most I can tell him about—while some I won't. A woman has secrets that she never reveals.

"My mom gave me this amethyst when I was sixteen." I point to small opal next to it. "This one was my grandmother's, came from a broach, and this tiny sapphire I bought at a boutique in Vancouver, Washington. I spent a summer manicuring the lawn in the old town square and picking weeds in the flower beds. It was a beautiful place, but I swear it rained every day."

"Vancouver? That must have been one of your hippie adventures."

I nod and shake out my hair, most of which thankfully lands away from my eyes. "I was hitchhiking to Oregon and landed there. I was eighteen and needed a pre-college fling."

"Of course." He laughs heartily.

Tommy focuses on one of the rings and raises a questioning eyebrow. "Sam Morrissey?"

"You have a good memory, Defalco," I say to him. "I'm surprised."

"What surprises me, is that you are still wearing the ring he gave you."

I pause and touch the stone. "Well, it reminds me not to make the same mistake twice."

"Do you remember how you cried on my lap that night after work when that asshole broke your heart? I wanted to kill the sonofabitch and dump him back where he came from in New Jersey."

"I've always been grateful that you ran a background check on him, although I don't know why it was so important to you."

"I couldn't afford to lose a good bartender. I keep telling you that." He laughs. "And you were set on marrying him—" Tommy interrupts himself to tell Victor to come over and join us as soon as the kitchen is cleaned up.

"Yeah, and to think he hid it so well that he had a wife and two little kids." I frown at the memory. "You were such a comfort to me that night. You've been a wonderful big brother to me, Tommy."

"Well, the truth is, when that happened I didn't feel like a big brother at all. As I was holding you and feeling how shattered you were, my heart just swelled. I wanted so badly to be a part of you. My thoughts were anything but brotherly." He adds with a shy smile, "you know, I was almost ready that night to break Deal Five."

My eyes meet his, and my stomach does a little flip-flop and I have to turn away from a gleam in his eyes that goes beyond alluring. "Yeah, I felt that way too, but that was a long time ago. It's a good thing you didn't act on those feelings or we probably wouldn't be here now. You know how it is with work relationships, they never seem to pan out. I hate to admit it, but Deal Five is a good one—one deal that should definitely never be broken."

He shifts around and shrugs and looks over his shoulder, I assume to see if Victor is anywhere nearby. "I don't mean to keep poking around your personal life, but you've not said a word about Roy in a month. You two still together?"

"If you don't mean to poke, then don't." I laugh.

Tommy says, "Okay, so I don't know where you are in your relationship with Roy, but take you and me for instance. We're best friends, we're good together, and we care about each other, maybe if we—"

"Mr. Defalco?" one of our busboys, Cory, calls out, "Everything is done that I know of. You have anything else for Marty and me to do?"

"No, Cory, if something's missed, Joey can take care of it in the morning Thanks for your help tonight." He gives the kid a smile and a wink. The boy acts like God himself has just honored him. Tommy can have that effect on people.

Victor saunters over to us a few minutes later, and Tommy gets him a drink. The three of us stretch out on chairs we pull together on the terrace and watch the DJ pack up his equipment. The night soon has the feel of our own private little party, as Tommy goes inside to the sound system and soon Johnny Mathis is playing "Chances Are." over the outdoor speakers. Tommy extends his hand. "Come on, Kitten, dance with me."

"Ah, I don't know, Tommy." Then to Victor, "The last time I watched him dance with Polly, it was so obscene I couldn't sleep for a week." Victor laughs and finishes his drink and waves us off to the dance floor. We hear him call good night and I wave farewell to him response.

I do a little pirouette and turn into Tommy's arms. He smiles and moves me to the side to twirl under his arm. We dance together in perfect sync, covering the floor with his expert dance steps.

"Misty," another of my favorite Mathis songs, comes on. He must like it too, as he sings softly, his eyes burning occasionally into mine, and I get that he's completely mellowed out and enjoying the soft summer night. Smiling, he dips me back and does a little grind that sends a spark up my spine.

"Yikes, stop that," I tease, rolling my eyes. "You have some pretty dangerous moves there, Mister. You could find yourself in a heap of trouble."

"You're pretty dangerous yourself. Do you have any idea how beautiful you look tonight?"

"Pffst, I'm hardly dangerous with you." I laugh to try to ease the fire that's simmering inside me.

"I mean it, Kitty. Sometimes I get lost just looking at you."

"Gee, that's a very unprofessional comment for a boss to make to an underling. No more drinks for you, Mr. Defalco." His mouth tightens but his eyes have their familiar sparkle.

Emmylou Harris's "Too Far Gone" comes on, and I feel the song through his perfect dance movements, gliding with his rhythm more so than the music's. He draws back every so often and then slowly presses his cheek to mine. Everything is so damn romantic, and I smile to myself at how much fun this is—and how his body feels next to mine.

He quietly pulls me tighter against him as his hand curls mine to his chest. I have to admit I'm enjoying the closeness, the smell of his after-shave, the pressure of his body against mine. I start to relax in his arms, lost in the music and the warm glow from our drinks. I'm pleasantly aware of his breathing in my ear. This has to stop—but I don't want it to.

Soon I'm completely lost in the sensual atmosphere of this special night. He's gently rubbing the small of my back, so I allow my fingertips to lightly trace a path across the back of his neck. I feel him tense up, and he glances at me with that look of pure desire.

It makes my throat swell. I'm aware that my breathing has deepened. I look away, thinking I should not have touched him like that. The sensation of reckless abandon not tempered by my usual caution and control excites me. But it also makes me very nervous, as well.

The song is about to end, and he releases my hand and slowly brushes my hair away from my shoulders. I feel his lips press against my neck. "You smell marvelous," he murmurs. His breath is warm and sweet with liqueur. The music has stopped and now I'm aware of just how alone we are.

Tommy breathes into my ear and runs his tongue around the rim, biting the lobe. It awakens all of my senses even more, which I didn't think possible. His arms hold me so tight I can hardly breathe. He kisses my temple and lowers his lips to the corner of my mouth. But he pauses for a seemingly endless moment before kissing me full on my mouth. I return his ardor and he kisses me harder, biting my bottom lip until I feel it burn. He relaxes the pressure and I let his tongue tenderly play with mine. I know if I don't stop now I'm in sweet trouble, yet I don't want this to end. I suck his tongue deep into my mouth, and I feel his entire soul entering me.

I revel in the softness of his full lips and how perfectly they fit against mine. Running my hands down his broad back ignites our desires still further. He grinds against me, and I feel how aroused he has become, as his energy shifts and feels more driven, more determined. He kisses me deeper, harder, and longer, his passion rising above me like a huge, hot wave. For a moment all I want to do is to go under and drown in him. One easy, deep breath and I'm released from the struggle that's been consuming me. In one smooth move he unbuttons the collar of my shirt and kisses my neck and moves his lips lower. One hand goes to my breast as his other finds its way under the back of my shirt. We're on this runaway train. I want Tommy Defalco to hold me and devour me—and I never want him to let me go.

He's sweating slightly and pulls my hips tightly against his, making me gasp in short breaths. I'm mesmerized by his desire for me and equally surprised by how much I want him. My voice is low and trembling. "Tommy, I want this to happen between us. You know we've been headed for this for years. I don't want to stop wanting you tonight."

He pushes me back against the dining-room wall and presses against me. He brushes the hair back from my face and studies me. "Kitten, I've never wanted anyone as badly as I want you tonight." He reaches up and takes my arms from around his neck. "But we need to stop right now." He runs a hand over his forehead and steps back. "This simply can't happen. It's the booze, the music, this room, you with your damn long red hair. I'm sorry, Kit." His face is a mixture of passion and regret, and I've never seen anything like it. He turns and walks away. I fall dully against the wall, hearing only my heart pounding in my ears. I'm trembling all over as my body burns with unfulfilled desire. The room swirls around me as I bring my breathing back to normal.

I don't remember finding my purse or taking out my car keys. All I'm certain of is that I'm driving home and doing the best I can to gather my thoughts: What just happened? What was I thinking? What the hell was he thinking? Goddamnit. The cost of a night of pure pleasure between Tommy and me was way too much for either of us to risk. Everything would change between us. In a matter of weeks, if not days, we'd become as jealous and controlling as the disgusting couples I see every night. Nothing fades as fast as new love. I know this to be true; after all, I'm a pro at failed relationships.

I need to get to bed, but I take a long shower first, the hot steam raising the passion within me. Every cell in my body screams for his touch, begs for his lips on every part of me and mine on him. In my bed, I feel him pressing against me, entering me, filling me, making love to me with both tenderness and rage. All night long I obsess with the illusion of Tommy consuming me completely.

Over coffee the next morning I analyze what occurred. I convince myself that it wasn't as personal as it seemed. Instead, it was a power trip on Tommy's part. During the past month or so he'd lost control of me, and this pissed him off. That's all. He didn't mean the things that he said. So what if we both got turned on. Hell, I teased him; he seduced me. It's a perfectly natural development. We're not teenagers. We know shit happens. This level of physical attention was bound to happen at some point. But friends are better than lovers. Better to be friends and keep the space open and breezy between us—to love from afar so that whatever we have is always fresh and lasting. Best friends are forever, no matter what happens. Intimacy grows old and leaves just dried-up shells of people, clinging together in desperation because they believe there's nothing else.

I talk myself down and have a level head by the time I leave for work. I do, however, harbor a lot of trepidation about seeing him again. I shudder at the thought of just how it will play out. Will he be angry? Will he think it was funny? Maybe he won't even be there tonight, and all of this will just blow away with time. But perhaps he will want to fire me, saying we're getting too close. Then there's Lillian, whom I've somehow left out of the equation. All these thoughts ramble through my mind as I stand with my hand on the door handle to let myself into The Carriage House.

I timidly pull the door open and slip inside. I glance around the foyer. All's clear so far, and I walk quietly to the lounge. It's still safe. I'm by myself.

I go to the bar and open the register, cringing at the loud click as it springs open. I look around nervously and take a deep breath. I want to get my drawer in order, so I get my bank from Troy. I still don't see Tommy. This relaxes me a little. He's probably not even here.

"Oh, good, there you are." Tommy's baritone voice fills the room as he walks briskly across the floor to the bar and comes in behind me. He hands me a piece of paper. "I need you to call in this beer order today because they will be closed Monday due to the holiday. Also, you'll have to close out your register and do the bottle count tonight and leave the report on my desk. I'm driving Lillian up to the lake for a couple of days. I want to leave now to beat the traffic."

"The lake sounds like fun." The sound of my strong, happy voice floods me with my old confidence. "Maybe it will do you good to be with She Who Does Not Dance for a few days." I give him a smiling but condescending side glance and raise my eyebrows.

He comes around the bar to my side.

"I'm really sorry about last night. I was way out of line and just went over the edge." His voice drops and he opens his hands in an apologetic gesture. "Kitty, our friendship means a lot to me too. We were right to stop. I don't know what I was thinking. After all, I'm with Lillian, and, I guess, you're still dating Roy. I shouldn't have come on to you like that. Very foolish and all wrong. I apologize."

I feeling a burn returning to where it shouldn't. I'm hoping my eyes don't register how much I still want him. "It wasn't all about you. I let my guard down, Tommy. But you're right, we had to stop, and I respect you for it." *Hate you for it too.*

"You have no idea how much I wanted you, but it just can't happen. My life is too damn complicated."

"We're good," I say.

"Yeah, we're good," he replies, then adds, "Too good," and leaves.

I finish counting my drawer, but before I'm done he's skipping down the stairs from his apartment just as Lillian comes through the front door. He calls to me from the lobby "I'm leaving you and Polly in charge. Try to keep the place standing until I get back."

"Okay, Boss, have fun," I yell back. I'm amazed, and a little pissed off, that I'm so damn positive. But I refuse to let what happened last night carry any greater significance. It's over and done with, and life now goes on for both of us. Our friendship is intact—and this is what matters. We got past this fast and in perfect shape, although I'm a little puzzled at why I feel so damn hollow inside.

For the next few months none of us at The House see nearly as much of Tommy as we are accustomed to. He often leaves early from work, and he takes a lot of days off to spend with She Who Does Not Dance. According to Troy, who's not thrilled he's out so much, the lovebirds go to shows in New York City, to bed and breakfasts in New England, and to beaches on the Jersey Shore.

When Tommy is at The House, my working relationship with him is back to normal in many ways. We talk about the little things as we always have, batting topics back and forth like a game of table tennis. We joke with each other and make the customers and staff laugh. He doesn't ask me about Roy, and I don't volunteer details that I'd have to fabricate. Sometimes I think I see Tommy looking at me with deep sadness in his eyes, but maybe I just imagine it. One thing that has changed is his not calling me Kitten anymore, and he's stopped giving me foot massages and quick hugs like he always used to after work. In fact, he never touches me at all anymore, and I kind of miss that. No, that's not true. I miss it a lot.

Chapter 12

"Look at these old photos I found under the podium," Cheryl exclaims as she trots out onto the terrace where Christine, Polly, Jeannie and I lie on loungers, sunbathing in the now late-summer sun. It's a Monday, and we enjoy our day off relaxing at The House as if it were our private club. The picture album is all about our House baseball games we enjoyed for so many years here.

"Y'all, those were the best days," Polly says, "We played every Monday afternoon, all summer long. Laughing, drinking beer, eating BBQ and smoking weed. Sadly, I guess we all had to grow up and become adults."

"Not me, I'm never gonna grow up," Jeannie says as she thumbs through the snapshots. "These were great fun times. How we laughed. Speaking of something to cause laughter, look what I have, ladies." She produces a tightly rolled joint from her purse.

"Just what this afternoon requires," Polly says as she lights the end and inhales the hot, bittersweet smoke and coughs. "I keep saying how lucky are we to work here. We own our positions and have the freedom to do our jobs well without some overzealous manager asshole looking over our shoulders. I love the trust and ownership I feel here. We're family in the best of ways. The House is really our home. Where else do people love to come to work six days a week?"

"And then spend their day off here as well," Jeannie adds and tokes. "We're all nuts."

"Y'all, look at how great Tommy looked when we first opened here," Polly says, pointing to a photo of him. He's spectacular in his bell-bottom jeans and cut-off T-shirt and his tattoos: Marine insignia with Semper Fi on one arm and a lotus with the word Peace on the other.

Christine turns the page. Jeannie, hanging over her shoulder, says, "He must have been a hoot back in the sixties, but he's still a free spirit at heart. Now that he's always off with Lillian, I miss him. I don't like her. She acts like she's on drugs all the time. Someone told me she deals coke. Tommy seems a bit off too some days, if you ask me."

The comment regarding Lillian I expected, but certainly not Christine's assessment of Tommy. Just when I thought the remark was simply one person's misguided opinion, Jeannie says, "I don't know if you guys know this, and maybe I shouldn't say anything, but Bruno told me he came in here early one day last week to marinate some meats, and he thought Tommy was high."

I bristle at this. "He smokes a little pot now and then, like we all do, but Tommy hasn't touched heavy-duty drugs since he kicked them after he came home from Nam. He admits he had a problem then, but swears that he doesn't do anything outside weed. I asked him not too long ago. Remember when we had that flu thing going on? He got sick and I came over to see if he needed anything because he looked like hell for a few nights. I jokingly asked him if he was coked out. He got mad at me and said 'Kitty, you know I don't do hard drugs anymore.' Then he told me the flu meds were knocking him out. And I believe him. He bounced back and has been fine ever since."

"Maybe he and Lillian indulge in heavier drugs when they're together," Christine says. "Let's face it, none of us know what Tommy does when he's with She Who Does Not Dance."

"Well, I do," I say to no one in particular, unable to hold back my bias. "I know Tommy better than anyone here, and he wouldn't lie to me about doing drugs."

Jeannie says, "All I'm saying is that maybe he falls off the wagon now and then, especially when he's hanging out with Lillian. He has some really wicked mood swings, and sometimes he's just not himself even when he comes back around a day or so later. I know you two are tight, but over the past six months or so, not so much." She stops and refuses the roach in the clip that Christine tries to hand her. "Kitty, please don't be mad at me. We're all best of friends, but it's what I feel." She shakes her head and a bug flies off. "That's all I'm going to say about it."

The conversation annoys me. Maybe it's because I'm reminded that there's a legitimate distancing between Tommy and me that has been growing since *the* night, and neither Christine nor anyone else has to explain it to me. Maybe it's because I'm a bartender and can generally spot coke users a mile away. Maybe I'm blinded to Tommy, but I've always had my suspicions about Lillian, who claims allergies cause her chronic sniffling and red eyes. Maybe that's what Tommy means about staying with her because she needs him. Maybe he's trying to get her straight. Maybe I'm an idiot.

If I'm being honest with myself, this isn't the first time I've considered that Tommy might still do drugs stronger than weed. But I can't place him back in the hard-drug scene, even though he freely admits to being addicted to opiates and pills, which he swears he's kicked. He always appears clean to me, and has for the eight years I've known him. He's definitely "together" when I see him at work, even though he does have a hot temper. But so do a lot of people who don't touch even aspirin. And the mood swings Jeannie brought up, we all witness those from time to time in every one of us. I can only hope that I'm not overly defensive and naïve when it comes to Tommy. Cheryl, who always acts stoned when she even looks at a joint, changes the subject, for which I'm now happy to the point of tears.

She says, "Tommy was our Babe Ruth, although Troy and Bruno were good, too, and Victor could run like crazy. He chalked that up to a survival tactic from when he lived in the Bronx as a little kid." Cheryl laughs and snorts, which gets us all laughing with her.

"Phillip was the best player of all," I say, pointing to his picture. "He could run, hit, and pitch; the whole shebang. Of course, we would have to remind him that he was the straightest gay guy in baseball. We heckled him unmercifully about how butch he'd become when he picked up his glove."

Polly takes a hit from a fresh joint and passes it to me. Her southern drawl is now more pronounced than in all the years I've known her: "We had a flock of busboys back then too, who would show up mostly for the beer and food, but they rounded out the teams, so that was good We'd play to well after twilight, then sit around under the trees and get stoned on homegrown. Those was the great days, for sure, y'all."

"Remember how Tommy would have the music blaring on the outside speakers," I said. "It was clearly musical mayhem. Sinatra to the Beatles, from show tunes to bluegrass, Joni Mitchell to Janis Joplin, and The Doors to Motown. And right in the middle of everything he'd stop the game so he could listen to an opera aria by someone none of us had ever heard of—or ever wanted to hear again." We all laughed hard, but I had to turn to wipe away a tear that had nothing to do with joyful reminiscing.

Those were the nights Tommy and I really grew together. We'd talk into the early morning, sprawled out on oversized cushions under the pine trees, my legs across his lap. We were easy company for each other, probing the depths of each other's souls, enjoying the casual closeness without sexual agendas, and having the freedom to be entirely open. It was then that we learned to trust each other, never fearing attack or criticism when showing the soft underbelly of our emotions, hurts, or individual dreams for the future. I chill at the knowledge that now I'm deceiving him with a fake boyfriend. Lying to Tommy all these months makes me hate myself. As for Roy, I hear he has quit drinking, but he never comes to The Carriage House anymore. I assume he'll get in touch with me at some point, but he hasn't yet and all I can believe is that he's too embarrassed. Frankly, it's for the best, as it will make it easier for me to tell Tommy that Roy and I have "broken up."

Seemingly overnight, fall is in full brilliance, painting the mountains in splashes of yellow, red and golden green. The nights are chilly, and the parties that occupied the terrace have nodded off for another year. The once open doors are now closed, locking in the memories of summer and harkening to months of warm fireside chats.

The Carriage House closes for Thanksgiving and Christmas so the staff can enjoy the holidays with their families. This Thanksgiving, Phillip and Barry invite me over for dinner, and I'm grateful for someplace to go since I don't have family and usually spend the time alone. It's my saddest time of the year, and for some reason depresses me more than Christmas. But on this Thanksgiving I'm the happiest I can remember in years, as I'm finally meeting Barry, Phillip's partner.

He's much shorter than Phillip, and looks way younger, boyishly handsome, with short sandy hair and soft blue eyes. It's quite obvious that he and Phillip are devoted to each other, as their home reflects a shared joy in beautiful things. The house is immaculate and grand with decorations. Barry has cooked a fabulous dinner, and of course the best wine is served. They have invited two other couples, and they crown me "The Goddess" because I'm the only woman there. It would figure that their friends are funny and delightful, which they are, and I spend a blessed evening feeling the genuine warmth in everyone's heart.

We all agree that the only person missing is Tommy, since with his being single and having no family he's a holiday orphan as well. Except that I know he's somewhere with Lillian, and I feel a brief stomach cramp that has nothing to do with the aftermath of the meal. I finish off the wonderful time with Phillip and Barry and their friends by telling funny stories about The House. Of course my slide under Table Four tops the tales, and I say goodnight at around midnight, buzzing on wine, food, and friendship.

The morning brings a rare, warm day, odd for late November when most times we can expect snow flurries to arrive, if not a full-fledged storm. I pour myself a cup of coffee and stroll to the corner to buy a newspaper from a box under the traffic light. I'm still in my pajamas and haven't brushed my hair, but the neighborhood is dead quiet and just one lone car passes by. I could be naked and the elderly driver wouldn't have noticed, his face glued to the windshield of his old Dodge.

On the way back to my apartment, I drop my newspaper. I have good reason. Tommy is biking up the road. He's wearing a polo shirt, cut-offs and moccasins. He smiles as he rolls to a stop in front of me, and he reaches down and picks up the newspaper and hands it to me.

"Well, well," I say through a smirk. "How's my dimpled-kneed Mediterranean friend? And how do you keep your legs looking so tan and sexy? You look as if you've been spending all your days at the beach."

"I'm like this all over." He flashes his mischievous grin that always drives me crazy. "Italian, you know."

"Uh huh. No doubt and no comment." I take a sip of coffee and roll my eyes. "What are you doing here?"

"I was just rambling around and found myself over in your neck of the woods," he says, as if I'm supposed to believe him.

"Cool. Come in and have a cup of coffee. I have to tell about my dinner with Phillip, Barry and their cool friends. I had such a great time."

He follows me into my apartment, and I shuffle into the kitchen "Excuse the mess. Working girl, you know."

He sits opposite me at my kitchen table, and I fix his coffee, black with sugar. I tell him all about my Thanksgiving with the gay couples; how adorable Barry is and that he should meet him someday. He nods but says nothing.

"So? Where did you and Miss Lillian go for Thanksgiving dinner?" I ask to break the quiet moment.

He takes a deep breath and rolls his coffee mug between his palms. "We went to dinner at Sans Souci and had a little chat."

"Wow, that set you back a few bucks. What did you two chat about?"

He looks across at me and gives me a quick, nervous, little smile. He reaches over and takes my hands away from my coffee mug and holds them in his.

"Kitten," he begins. I'm surprised to hear him call me that. It has been a long time since I've heard him call me Kitten, and I've missed it.

"We talked about you and me. We have something extraordinarily special. We've developed and nurtured a friendship during these past eight years that I never thought would be possible for me to have with a female. It's way deeper than physical, and this is what sets it apart."

I'm puzzled about the way this conversation is going. He's not making much sense and he's holding tightly onto my hands which feels odd. I can't resist running my thumb over his knuckles in an under-standing gesture.

He takes a deep breath and swallows hard.

"Lillian and I are getting married. We're planning a wedding some-time after New Year's, and we'll be moving to Italy to live, probably near Florence. I wanted to tell you in person before I tell the others at The House. I think I owe you that."

I'm stunned and slowly take my hands away from him. He's uneasy and doesn't look up to meet my eyes.

I manage to find my voice. "Why would you do *that*? Are you out of your mind?"

"Well, Lillian and I have been together a long time, and we share the same business interests. She needs me, Kitty, and I suppose I love her." He shrugs and smiles stupidly, as if I'm supposed to say it's okay.

I'm numb and trying to figure out how on earth I'm to accept what he's told me. The silence that hangs around us is deafening until I cry out, "Lillian is a total bimbo, and you know how damn unstable she is. Why on earth are you really doing this?"

"Kitty, I expected you to be more accepting. You don't know her as I do. She may have her problems, but we're good together. It's time I moved on with my life. I know this is pretty hard news to take, but I just want you to know I will carry our friendship for—"

"For what? You know ... you can go screw yourself." The words came out before I knew I was saying them. They bring with them a rush of hot, angry tears.

"Come on, don't be like this. Be happy for me. I'm getting older. I need some stability in my life. We'll always be friends, you and me."

"Tommy, you're tearing my life apart. You know how I feel about Lillian, and that's never going to change. And how am I supposed to work at The House without you? How is anyone there going to do that? I was going to quit a year ago, but I stayed on for you." I can't look at him. I get up and walk to the sink. "You go marry Lillian, but don't tell me how I'm supposed to take it. How can you do this to me? To *us*?"

Tommy's fist comes down hard on the table, spilling what coffee was left in our cups. He shouts, "Do what to *us*? This has nothing to do with *us*. There *is* no *us*. You have pushed *us* away for years. Do not go there about *us*! You want *us* to be friends, goddamn it. Okay, so we are friends, or I thought so until now. Yes, we had fun for eight years, but now it's finished. It's done. Get over it."

I don't remember when I've felt such rage. "Get out of here! You have made your choice. And don't ask me to be happy for you, knowing that you're throwing your life away on a coked-up scorpion."

He rushes from the table and the door slams behind him.

Chapter 13

I ARRIVE AT WORK as Tommy has assembled the rest of the staff in the lounge and has just finished telling them the news. When I step into the room everyone becomes deathly quiet. All eyes are on me.

"It's okay, guys," Tommy announces. "She knows."

Polly comes rushing over and hugs me. She asks in her slow southern drawl, "Oh, Kitty, are you really okay with this?"

"Not really," I reply, loud enough for everyone in the room to hear me.

People stare at me but then gather around Tommy, congratulating him. Bruno is shaking Tommy's hand so hard I'm amazed he doesn't pull it loose. "Holy shit, Tom, this is fantastic news. You and Lillian. Wow!" Victor then says, "Way to go, my man. But we'll miss you." When it's Polly's turn, she says, "I wish you weren't going so far away." She starts to cry. "But I guess we all just have to be happy for you."

"No, we *all* don't," I say, strolling over to my register.

Tommy cringes. "She's not on board with all of this."

"Oh, she'll come around," Phillip says. "She'll be happy for you and Lillian ... just like the rest of us." His delivery's trailing off makes it clear he isn't so sure about any of us—including himself.

"Have you told Troy yet?" Jeannie asks Tommy.

"Yeah, he knows. We have a new manager coming in. We've been talking to him for a while now. He's got a lot of experience. You guys will love him."

So, Tommy's been looking for a manager for a long time and never said a word about it to me. I cut my fruit for the bar with a vengeance. The guys who always drink beer and watch the game walk into the lounge, offering their usual cheerful hellos. I bring them their tray of beers just as one of them turns on the TV. I say not one word, and it dawns on me that they don't seem concerned. All they want is their beer and some damn sporting event to occupy their time.

Tommy comes around the bar and stands close to me. He runs his hand through his hair and sighs deeply. "Look, we got a couple of months left to work together, so let's just get through this without attitude. I don't want any hard feelings. It breaks my heart that I hurt you. I'm sorry."

I turn and miraculously manage to smile at him. "It's okay, and I'm okay. It's just a huge shock, is all. I'm sorry I reacted like I did. Of course I'm happy for you. You're my best friend. How could I not be happy for you?"

He eyes me suspiciously. "So we're good then?"

I remember the last time he said that, after the "dance" on the terrace when we both wanted each other so damn bad. My chest starts to ache again.

"Yes," I reply, and he smiles hollowly and saunters off. I just couldn't add, "We're good," no matter how hard I tried.

The rest of the month is sheer hell to get through. The staff is edgy and unhappy, and I have a hard time putting on the constantly happy face that's so essential to my job. I've lost my appetite. Most nights I cry myself to sleep. I hardly know myself at times, and I no longer want to get together with the girls after work. I wear my depression like a wet woolen coat in the dead of winter, dragging me down, weighing on my every move, making everything a challenge.

While my discomfort continues unabated, Tom and Lillian's upcoming wedding is now old news to my bar patrons. Of greatest interest to them is whether The House will remain the same. They ask me questions about the newly hired manager, Chris Fuller. I did see his resumé photo and even though he's forty, and very good looking with youthful, clear features, he could easily pass for early thirties. Every woman will want to know if he's straight, something at this moment I could not care less about. Still. Wow.

During this past month, no matter how hard I tried to fake it, Mildred hasn't been fooled by my pseudo happiness as I work behind the bar and interact with patrons. She confides in me that she's devastated by the news of Tommy's marrying Lillian and leaving the area.

"Damn it," she says one dreary autumn night, taking the last sip of her second martini as I begin to make her another, "it should be you and not Lillian. Anyone with one good eye knows that you and Tommy belong together. Lillian's a viper, and she's swallowing our Tom. You have no idea how I've worried about his continuing to be involved with Lillian. I wish he'd washed his hands of her and The Country Club for good that last time he walked away."

I grumble, "Who are we to judge anyone else's relationship?"

"Well, no one can fault a woman my age for having a romantic heart. I'm sorry you two never got together. It would have been right."

"Right or wrong, it wasn't meant to be. I don't care that he's getting married. I want him to be happy. I just wish he wasn't going to Italy. It's so damn far away…." I'm overcome with emotion and excuse myself and go to the Ladies' Room, where my tears can flow unnoticed. Soon I hear the door open and I hear Millie's voice.

"It's time to go to school, Kitty. Sit down. let's talk." She pats the seat of the little sofa in the powder room and then takes my hand. "I can't let this happen without speaking my mind. That man loves you—and you love him. It's been obvious to me for years. I don't know for sure, but I can guess why Tommy is running away with Lillian. And running away is what he's doing. He doesn't love her any more than he loves having a toothache. You need to tell him how you feel or you will regret this for the rest of your life. Tell him you love him, Kitty."

"I can't tell him, Millie. I can't. I'm too afraid. And, anyway, he thinks that I'm in love with Roy."

Millie gasps. "Roy McGrath?" I nod. "Why in the name of God would you tell Tommy that?"

"Because he's in love with Lillian, and I can't risk losing his friendship if he thinks I'm in love with him, so I made up an imaginary romance." I sniffle. "I can never act on what you're suggesting. Relationships don't work for me. And love surely doesn't work for me." I start to sob again.

"Listen to me, Kitty, and listen well. This cockamamie belief of yours about relationships, it's a lie you tell yourself. That's not your truth. Your truth is that you are beautiful, talented, intelligent, loving and deserving of love. But if you believe you're unworthy long enough, you can become unworthy. This is a universal law of cause and effect. As you think, you so become. So start telling yourself, out loud, throughout every day, that you are worthy of love, that only good things happen through love, and that you can handle whatever life tosses your way because you are capable of embracing love. It will start to change you."

"As for Tommy, I think he's running away with Lillian because he thinks you don't want him. At the very least, tell him there is no Roy, or this lie will destroy you both."

"I can't. Millie. It's already too late. I let that lie go on for months. I love you and appreciate you wanting to help me. God knows, I want to believe all that you are telling me with all my heart." I get up and splash cold water on my face and daub at my smeared makeup. "But too much has happened for me to interfere with what Tommy thinks is his path to happiness. He wants to go to Italy. He wants to be with Lillian. I can't change that now."

"Well," she says softly. "I believe in miracles, Kitty, and I believe we're all in need of one right about now."

Jeannie rushes in and says I'm needed at the bar, so I hug Millie and kiss her on the cheek. I tell her I'll get through this, and when I return to my station no one is the wiser about my meltdown with Millie in the Ladies' Room.

I chat with my patrons, filling in those who don't already know about the new manager Tommy has selected for the job. I share that his name is Chris Fuller, he comes from a resort background in southern California, is highly proficient with numbers, and has an impressive management history. I tell those listening at the bar, "Chris will come in and begin learning our system anytime now. He'll take the reins before Christmas, and Tommy and Lillian will leave for Italy shortly after the first of the new year." Mildred remains impassive at first but shakes her head at my last remark. She has me call Mike to pick her up early.

Decorating The House for Christmas is always a big deal, and we happily work overtime to make each year more spectacular than its predecessor. The piano is moved into the dining room, just left of a towering Christmas tree in front of the wide double doors leading out to the terrace. For the next month, this fragrant balsam pine will command the immediate attention of anyone entering the dining room, as it rises amid the beautiful gold- and white-trimmed tables that have been arranged to accommodate it.

We always get a balsam tree because it's Troy's favorite, and every year the staff gets a kick out of saying, "For thee, I pine and bawl some," and every year Polly laments, "I don't get it, y'all."

Each table has a crème-colored cloth and a holly centerpiece adorned with red carnations and baby's breath. The napkins are deep green and fan open upon gold and white plates; the tables glistening with gold-leaf glassware.

My lounge is stunning as well, and thanks to Phillip—with Barry's silent help—it's literally buried in flowers. The whole room glows in warm candlelight. The large round table in The Pit is covered in holly, and the fireplace is decorated with pine boughs, holly, red and white poinsettias, and gold and crème ribbons. Tall leafless branches standing on either side of the mantel are fitted with tiny gold and white lights. In past years, "breathtakingly beautiful" are the words I hear uttered most often by House patrons, and I expect more of the same now.

Even though Tommy is working side by side with all of us, and trying to keep the mood light, we a carry a sense of dread because this will be our last Christmas with him. There's a quiet sadness at knowing, in little more than a month, Tommy Defalco will be just a memory trapped in a photo on the lobby wall.

When the last of the decorating is completed, Tommy tells us that he's taking off with She Who Does Not Dance for a few days because she wants to start planning their wedding, and there's a lot to deal with. He tells us he'll be back Tuesday week so he can start training Chris. I'm too exhausted to care anymore, and I wave him off without so much as a goodbye.

I'm grateful for the busy holiday nights to keep my mind off Tommy and Lillian, and I do keep up with the affirmations Millie set for me. In the mornings, looking in the mirror, I tell myself that I'm worthy of love, that I deserve to be loved, and that it's safe for me to give and accept love. I'm slowly convincing myself that there is someone for me—out there somewhere. I'm also realizing that friends don't last forever and missed opportunities for love and happiness don't often come with second chances.

It's now Monday, and, as with everyone who works at The House, my one day off each week. I'm busy all afternoon with laundry, grocery shopping, and cleaning my apartment. Pleased with myself that I haven't thought much about Tommy, I remember he's due back tomorrow to begin showing Chris the ropes. I turn off the vacuum and hear the phone ringing. It's four o'clock.

"Hello." Silence. "Hello?" I ask again.

"Hey." I recognize Tommy's voice on the other end of the line. I take a deep breath. "You're back," I say. "How was your trip?"

"It was fine. I … ah, was wondering if you'd go out to dinner with me tonight. Break the Deal, just for fun."

"That's not a good idea," I don't hesitate to reply.

"Come on, Kitten, we'll make it special, get dressed up and go top-shelf. Please?"

"Does Lillian know you will be taking me out tonight?"

"Yeah, she knows."

"Absolutely?"

"Absolutely. I give you my word."

I sigh. "Okay, what time?"

"How about seven?"

"All right. See you at seven." I hang up, feeling pangs in my stomach and a hot fire going up and down my back. Why did I agree to this?

At six I slowly start to get ready. Since this is the last time we'll ever go out, I want to leave him with a lasting impression, so I decide to wear my favorite dress, a deep-green velvet number that brings out my eyes. It's low-cut in the front and back and short enough that it shows off my legs too. I slip on my black three-inch heels and finish the look with a gold necklace, another gift from my grandmother. I'm not sure if my main goal is to please or hurt him; either way, as I examine myself in the mirror, I'm more than a little confident I can get him to take notice. This is his night to say goodbye to all I've ever been to him.

It's a few minutes before seven, and I shake my head, letting my hair cascade down my shoulders and over my back. Tommy said he likes my hair down, so I'm going to give him what he desires.

"Hello, Boss," I greet him when he arrives at my door. He looks dashing in a blue silk suit that he told me a long time ago was made for him by a top-end tailor using the finest Italian fabric. I chuckle inwardly. It looks as though each of us wore our favorite outfit to impress the other.

His holds a wide smile and says, "Oh, my God, Kitten. You're beyond beautiful." He helps me on with my coat and laces his fingers into mine and walks me out to Baby Blue.

Throughout the dinner, which is at San Souci, a ridiculously expensive eatery one town over from us, which can't hold a candle to The House, I keep up what's been an awkward conversation. Tommy's eyes cast a dreamy glint when he looks at me, which has unnerved me at times. He says he's "over the moon" to be out with me tonight, but I'm experiencing a brooding sorrow because of losing him forever. I'm wishing I'd refused to see him this one last time.

As the meal winds down, he orders a dessert wine I've never heard of, and I thought I knew them all. It's called Chateau d'Yquem and is divine, and as we sip it he wraps his smile around me and begins following everything I say with deep chuckles. It's only now that I'm relaxing for the first time all evening.

We talk about the "family" at The House. We talk about Chris, and Tommy tells me he's confident he's going to be a great manager. But we don't talk about Italy—and we don't talk about Lillian.

With a little of the dessert wine remaining in our glasses, he raises his and solemnly offers the simple toast: "To best friends, forever." His face registers an odd, wistful expression, and for a split second I think he's going to cry. Then he asks me to dance. At this point, I don't see any harm.

When dancing, he holds me almost politely, trembling slightly as he pulls me close to him as if I were too delicate to handle except with kid gloves.

It delights me to see a control freak like Tommy a little unnerved.

Then it hits me that this game is ending, that indeed we're in the last inning together, that I'm actually losing this man I've treasured for so many years.

Back at the table the silence drapes over us like a shroud, and there are no more words between us for several minutes. Then he says, "I needed this from you tonight," adding only, "Thank you." Our waiter asks if we'd like something more to drink. I shake my head and Tommy requests the check. When he's looking at the bill to figure the tip, one of the duplicate receipts falls from the leather pouch the waiter left at our table. I pick up the bill and I'm staggered by the total. I quickly pass the extra receipt to Tommy, but while doing so I see that part of the reason for the exorbitant tab was the dessert wine, which cost one hundred dollars a glass. I give myself a bittersweet laugh. That wine is another thing I'll certainly never enjoy again.

We sit a minute longer. Tommy acts serious and distant, as if he has something monumental on his mind. I'm told it's natural to be a little depressed before a wedding. Or maybe he's unhappy he'll never see The House again after just a few more weeks. Or he could be sad at knowing he'll not see me again. Whatever is behind his mood, I'll never know.

He opens my car door and I get in, assuming he's taking me home, but he insists that we drink one last Grand Marnier for old time's sake in The Pit at The House. I don't know what to think, but I don't object so we head in that direction.

Once we're inside The House, Tommy turns the lights in the lounge down low. He ignites the gas fireplace with a long matchstick but as I walk up to the bar to get our drinks he stops me halfway. "No, you don't. You're on a date, my little deal breaker. I'll get the drinks." I laugh and kick off my shoes, and I slide my feet up under me as he turns on the music and pours our liquor.

I allow the warm golden liquid to slip around my tongue before swallowing it. "Yum, I love this." I let out a long sigh and give him an impish grin. "You can rub my feet one last time, if you're so inclined."

He takes my foot and begins to massage it.

"Damn, that feels delicious! You may think I'll miss you, but in all honesty I'll miss this the most."

"Why does that not surprise me?" He gives me a sad smile.

I poke him with my free foot. "I'm kidding."

"I wonder—"

"What's wrong, Tommy Boy? You've been brooding all night."

He takes a deep breath and holds it before slowly releasing it through his teeth, making a soft whistling sound. He sits upright and places my feet away from his lap and says, "I have something I need to talk about, and I'm really struggling with it. A lot ... depends on how you respond to ... what I'm going to be telling you."

"It can't possibly be any worse than the news you sprang on me a month ago, so if you think you can top that now, fire away."

"I broke off my engagement with Lillian last night."

Chapter 14

IF A PERSON CAN BE shocked but oddly not surprised, I fall in this category, knowing his and Lillian's chronically shifting relationship as I do.

"That's interesting news," I say, "since the wedding is only few weeks away, you've hired a new manager for the House, and I'm sure you already bought tickets to Italy." I sarcastically tell him, "You know you could have told me this over dinner, don't you?"

"There's more." He takes a drink of his Grand Marnier and says, "I told Lillian I was in love with someone else."

I give him a dubious look. "Are you really in love with someone, and it's not Lillian?"

"Yes, Kitty, I am." He rolls the snifter between his palms.

I can't help but laugh. "Just when did *this* happen? I'm amazed I had time to see anyone else, you and Lillian are always together." He's looking at me with a cat-who-ate-the-canary grin. "What did Lillian have to say when you told her?"

He stares into the fire. "She asked me, 'Is it Kitty?'" He glances sideways at me.

"Oh, damn, this can't be a good thing. Of course she would assume this. What did you tell her?"

"I told her yes."

"You said *what*? I can't believe you used me to break up with Lillian." My voice goes an octave higher. "What in hell were you thinking? That must have put her right over the edge. Why didn't you tell her the truth, whatever it is?"

He settles into his place on the couch and says softly, "I did tell her the truth." His eyes glisten, and a single small tear traces a ridge on his left cheek.

"I'm confused. You said you were in love with—"

He cuts me off and whispers, "You. I'm in love with you, Kitty."

"I'm supposed to believe you broke up with Lillian because you're in love with me?"

"I love *you*, Kitten, and no one else. Deep in your heart of hearts, you must know this. It has always been, and it always will be, you. I've been in love with you for years, but I kept my true my feelings to myself for a lot of reasons. I used Deal Five as my main excuse, because if we were ever lovers our relationship at The House would end. I thought I could use Lillian as my way to escape. She was the only way out for me."

"I think you're drunk."

"I may be, but I know what I'm saying. I was running off with a woman I clearly did not love, to the farthest away place I could go, to try forget you and Roy.

"What about me and Roy? Am I also supposed to just leave someone I'm deeply involved with?"

"Kitten," he says and sighs. "I always had a hard time believing you and Roy were a couple but it also drove me crazy, because I really didn't know for sure. Recently, I asked Millie and she said simply, 'There is no Roy. Now, go and do the right thing.' What do you think she meant by that?"

I feel clammy and a little sick to my stomach like when I was little and caught at something naughty. "I'll be honest with you—" I get the words out of my mouth, but this last drink lets all of the wine and booze from the evening get to me—"Millie told you the truth. I'm so sorry I lied to you about him. It started out having nothing to do with you. Please believe me, I only made up the story about Roy to get Lillian off my case. As you know, she can be relentless. I reached a point where I wanted her sniping to stop. Roy was an option, so I used him to—"

Tommy holds up a hand to stop me. "So, I'm doing the right thing, aren't I?"

"I don't understand what you mean."

"I don't love Lillian, and never have, but I've been in a complicated business relationship with her that I don't know how to end. However, that's another story. Saturday night, while having dinner with her, the thought of never seeing you again hit me hard. I knew right then, all that matters in my life revolves around you. And I can't be just your friend. I've wanted you every damned day since we met eight years ago. Every night, watching you, laughing with you, touching you, but having always to draw the line. I've fantasized about you a thousand times. It's a beautiful hell to be in, but not anymore. I can't do it any longer, I love you so much. How good it feels finally to say this to you out loud after all these years. I want to say it over and over: I love you, I love you, I love you."

"Damn it, Tommy, don't do this." I'm breathless and not aware, until I reach up with my hand, that my face is wet with tears. "Don't say anything more." I shake my head slowly as my heart is hammering my chest. "I'm terrified to hear you say this."

His eyes are so full of love for me that I'm staggered. He continues "When I realized how upset you were over my engagement to Lillian and leaving for Italy, I understood how much you loved me, as well. It tore me up inside when you put on the brave front and told me you were happy for me. But I was a coward and didn't say anything. However, not anymore—"

"Please, stop while there's time. What you're saying can change everything between us."

"It *will* change everything. It'll make us complete. I know you have so much fear surrounding relationships: the anger, the tears, the fights, the separations and making up, all the hardships and—"

"I can't think about any of that now," I tell him in a harsh whisper.

"If I ever allow myself to think of loving you, I would have to face the pain of one day losing you. I couldn't bear that. So just stop all of this." I place my hands on his arms and push away from him, my eyes away from his eyes, my mind away from saying anything more.

He clutches me and gives me a shake, forcing me to look at him.

"Listen to me. We can do this. There's no way in hell that I'm ever letting you go. You love me, damn it. I know you do. Say it, Kitty. Tell me you love me. Say it. I need to hear you say it." I can't tell if it's more desperation or urgency in his voice. I gently push away.

"I need to think. I need some air…you need to give me some space." I tell him as I stand up. I honestly think I'm going to pass out. He reaches for me but I walk quickly to the front door and push it open, feeling the stab of cold night air. My mind is swirling around countless questions and anxious doubts. I take a few deep breaths as I go over Millie's words. Millie said I needed to face the truth about myself. Of course I love Tommy. But my big question is whether or not he really loves me. He's never said anything like this to me the past, so why should I believe him now? But as I'm thinking about it more, why *shouldn't* I believe him. Isn't this what I have always wanted? I bury my face in my hands and let my tears come. I hear him open the door and I turn to face him.

His expression is grim and he stuffs his hands into his trouser pockets. He starts slowly weighing his words.

"Kitty, I'm sorry. I clearly put you in a difficult position. I know you must be overwhelmed by all this information. I wrong to expect an answer from you now. Quite frankly, I have no idea what I expected from you. I can't possibly assume you feel about me as I feel about you. I'll take you home."

I look at him over my hands which half hide my tear stained face and the words come from my mouth like birds freed from captivity for the first time in their lives. "Tommy, you misunderstand. I love you too. I'm scared to death, but so help me God, I love you. I really do. I've always been in love with you. I—"

I stop talking as he grabs me and kisses the tears off of my cheeks. "Kitten, you can't believe how much I've wanted to hear you say those words, but if you need time."

I touch his lips with my fingertips and then kiss him hungrily. I'm afraid to open my eyes, realize this is just a fantasy, and that it will pass like clouds in front of the moon. But he is here and I smile "I've already had more than enough time to realize how much you mean to me. I've loved you for so long.

We stand together in silence for a few moments then Tommy pulls away and looks at me with a grin. "Sweetheart, unless you still need these frigid temperatures to help you think of something else, I'd like to suggest we go inside," We share a welcomed laugh and he leads me back inside and positions me in front of the fire. He lifts his brandy snifter to my lips and I savor its warmth. He takes a breath and draws me close, kissing my eyes, my nose, my mouth, my neck. He grabs a handful of my hair and buries his face in its scent. He groans, "I'm lost in you, Kitty Cunningham." I absorb into him as water does on sand; sinking to a depth I have never felt before. We quietly dance to our own song, which doesn't require any real music, yet I'm following Tommy as if an orchestra is playing all around us. He slides his hands down my back and over my behind. I respond to his movements and our passions rise together until he draws back, breathing heavily.

He says, "Eight years of longing for you is pent up inside me right now."

My words come on a breath, "Good. Then make love to me right here, right now."

He pulls my dress over my head, his eyes sweeping me with desire. He gasps, "Your body is even more incredible than I ever imagined."

He systematically kisses me from my forehead downward, gently lingering on those parts he begs to own. I shudder and moan, twisting his hair in my fists. There's not one part of me that is not explored and taken away with him. One powerful movement is all he needs to sweep me up and lay me down on the fire-warmed sofa in The Pit. While the firelight shifts and shapes the shadows across our bodies, he enters me with a tenderness I would not have thought possible of him.

The opposite of his gentle movements and mildly passionate comments, my aggressive, unrestrained passion seems to delight him. We laugh through grateful tears; friends now discovering each other as lovers. I've never come this close to experiencing such acceptance and peace with another man. Feeling Tommy's strong, naked body against mine awakens countless secret fantasies I harbored about him for so many years. Yes, I've wanted him desperately. And now he's my lover and my life—and I'm finally both to him as well.

Sometime during the night he carries me up to his bed in his apartment above The House, and I wake up to find I'm buried in crisp, clean sheets under an old goose-down comforter that I'm certain is a family heirloom. Rising up on one elbow, I manage a look around his apartment.

It's surprisingly clean for a man's place, and it's homey. His antique bed is massive, and a gigantic bearskin rug "sleeps" on the hardwood floor in front of it. Under a window rests a cluttered desk piled high with papers and, of all things, accounting journals. In one corner sits a large leather chair, with a little blanket on the seat where I assume Mr. Bug sleeps. To the right of that is an African-drum table, with a mixture of coffee-table books and trade magazines on it.

Nailed on the wall above the chair is a poster dated 1968, with the words "War No More" inside a flowered peace sign. Next to this is a black-light poster of The Doors. A dresser is positioned across the room, with many framed photographs atop it.

I clamber out of the deep tangle of covers and patter into the bathroom, which is to the left of the dresser. It's spotless and smells of English Leather and sandalwood. I chastise myself for questioning the cleanliness of the apartment. It's only natural since Tommy is such a stickler about The House that his apartment would be kept to the same standards.

I steal a little of his toothpaste and brush my teeth with my finger and rinse out my mouth. I look happy and radiant in his mirror, if I do say so myself. I tiptoe into another area, which is basking in sunshine. There's a small kitchen on one side of the room. A hammock stretches across the other end, next to sliding doors that open to a little veranda. Several pillows are scattered over a well-worn oriental rug, and a brocade sofa, tight up against a wall, is littered with partially opened newspapers.

I walk to the window and look down to where we have our House picnics, and I see Tommy out on the now dormant lawn, Mr. Bug at his side. It's a cold morning, and he stands hunched over, his arms folded, shivering in a T-shirt and black sweat pants.

I smile, shaking my head at the sight of him. I had no idea how I'd feel when I awoke this morning, as my life has now been changed forever. But I have never felt better, which surprises me as much as my willingness to give myself to Tommy, since just eight hours earlier this was far from something I considered possible.

I hear him coming up the stairs, saying to Bug. "Hurry up. Let's go wake her."

I scurry back and dive under the covers just as he opens the door.

Mr. Bug springs onto the bed and wrestles with covers before climbing under them. "You're cold," I squeal. "And your nose is freezing."

Tommy takes off his shoes and flops down on the bed beside me. Then he grabs me, playing rough the way I like it. He says, "I can't believe you're here. Is this really happening to us?" Even though I'm under the covers, I can see he's studying me. He strips off his clothes and snuggles in next to me.

I shriek and wiggle around. "You're like an ice cube."

"I am that, my Irish lass, but no doubt you will warm me up." He pulls me on top of him.

We make love all morning as if we were two unbridled teenagers, with a passion that leaves the bed destroyed and the two of us bathed in sweat and laughter. We take a long, steamy shower together and delight in our new explorations. He washes my hair and blow-dries it for me as I sit between his crossed legs on the bed. I watch him shave while I'm wrapped in one of his flannel shirts. At this time each moment between us is a brand-new experience, and I've never felt more enthusiastic about learning. I guess unfettered sex will encourage that in a person.

Blazing hot coffee and soft bagels with cream cheese make for a tasty breakfast. Afterwards, we cuddle together in the hammock, listening to folk legends Joni, Arlo, and Pete.

"Don't forget, I have to drive you home later so you can get ready for work tonight," Tommy says after the last song ends.

"Where are my clothes?" I ask as I glance around the apartment for what I *don't* see.

"I think I brought up everything. All but your shoes and coat. We'll pick them up on the way out." He kisses me on the neck.

I get off the hammock to go find my dress, but before I do I spin back to him. "I don't suppose you've given any thought to what you're going to tell everyone about this?" I receive a nonplussed look, which I expect. "I guess we have to take Deal Five off the list and tell the staff what happened before they suspect me as the other woman."

"You're the *only* woman now." He chuckles.

"You never told me how Lillian took the news?"

"I won't sugarcoat it; not well at all. But she's the last person I want to think about now. As for telling the staff, I'd like to wait a day or two. I want to revel in just you and me for a while."

"What about Chris, now that you're not leaving?"

"I'm going to talk Troy into keeping him on. I'll be happy just frittering around as maître d' and letting Chris have all the grief of order-ing, hiring, firing, running the kitchen, the bar, the reservations, doing the bookwork, and keeping the peace." He laughs. "And I'm making you bar manager so you can handle all your own ordering and inventory."

"You mean I get a promotion for sleeping with the boss? Shit, I should've slept with you years ago."

"I wish you had." He pushes my hair away from my face and whispers, "We wasted a lot of years together."

"Well, we have today and all of the tomorrows."

He kisses me and announces through his brilliant smile, "I've got a great idea. Let's go back to bed."

PART III

"LOVE—A WORK IN PROGRESS"

Chapter 15

WE BOTH DOZE OFF to find that the day has melted away like snow in a patch of sunlight. Tommy springs out of bed and hollers, "Holy shit!"

"What is it?" I ask sleepily.

"It's a quarter after four! We should be open over an hour ago."

I throw myself back on the pillows and laugh. "Tell me the entire staff is standing outside, waiting for you to unlock the doors? This is just too good." I laugh some more.

Tommy, however, is racing around, shaving and brushing his teeth, fumbling with the studs on his shirt and putting on a fresh tux. When he's fully dressed, he says, "I just hope Troy was here earlier and this place is open. Is this registering with you, Kitty? You're supposed to be downstairs, dressed and working, right now."

I bolt from bed. I search for my bra, which I put on, and look for my panties and pantyhose—both of which I can't find. I wiggle into my dress, which is the last sort of outfit for me to be caught wearing behind our bar. "My shoes and coat are downstairs," I remind Tommy.

"I'll get them." He runs down the stairs—and right into Troy.

"Whoa, big guy," I hear Troy say. "Where the hell you been? We've got a restaurant to run here, in case you've forgotten. Chris has been wandering around for an hour looking for you. Hell of an impression to make on him on his first day on the job, don't you think?"

"I'm sorry. I'm not going to lie, I fell asleep."

"People are already seated in the lounge, and Christine is bartending.

Where in the name of Christ is Kitty? Damn it, Tommy, you really need to get on her about this bullshit of being late every day."

"Yeah, ah … about Kitty. Actually, she called. Something about a funeral. Old friend. Not a problem, though. She'll be in later."

The exchange between Tommy and Troy ends, and I pace around his apartment barefooted, looking for my panties and pantyhose. The thought of them tucked between the cushions of the sofa in The Pit, only to be plucked out by some fine unsuspecting lady while drinking a mai tai, paralyses me.

While I'm pondering my embarrassment, the door to the apartment flies open. "Your coat and shoes aren't downstairs where I can find them," Tommy says, out of breath. "Someone must've picked them up."

"Great. Now what do I do?"

"I don't know yet. The lobby is open, people are coming in, and the lounge is filling up. Troy has fixed himself at the podium. So you can't go down there now or it will look bad." He glares at me. "Okay, very bad."

"Tell him I just called and can't make it after all. I'll just stay in here all night."

"It won't work. I can't spare a waitress to cover you. We have a ton of reservations tonight, and Robert called in sick."

"I need to find a way to get to your car. Then I can drive home, change, and with a little luck be back here in a half-hour."

"Except that my car is right out front parked under the street light where everyone can see it from the dining room." He runs his hand through his hair as he thinks. "Okay, here's the deal. You go down the fire escape." He points to it. "Get to the shed in back of the kitchen. It's unlocked. And take my bicycle."

It requires a moment to comprehend what he's just said, then my disbelief becomes violently apparent. "Have you lost your goddamn mind? May I remind you that it is winter, and I have no shoes and no coat. What's more, the fire escape goes right past the kitchen window. And, I live four miles from here. How am I going to pedal your bicycle four miles dressed like a hooker who's been turned out on the street without even her shoes?"

"I don't know, Kit, but I know you'll figure this out. You have to take the bar tonight, and that is all there is to it. No options. I have to go. I love you, I really do." He kisses me hard and quick and runs from the apartment, his hair flying out of control.

It's half-past four. I estimate it'll take me at least thirty minutes to get home on the bicycle, fifteen minutes to dress, and five minutes to drive back here in my car. But, in reality, likely a full hour altogether.

First, however, I need to deal with the issue of my bare feet. I rummage through a drawer and find a pair of Tom's heavy winter socks, the kind a fisherman or hunter might wear. They come almost to my knees, but I swim in them and they hardly stay on my feet. I locate a pair of Tommy's leather boots, but the only way I could wear them would be if I tied them onto my feet, and I decide there's just no way I could ride a bike this way. I find a peacoat, but the arms are so long I could never wear it and control the bike. So I settle for a sweatshirt and roll up the sleeves. So far I've done nothing to protect my underside, but I pad over to the patio door and look at the flimsy, rusted fire escape, just an arm's length away, atop the balcony. I'll have to climb over the railing to grab it and pull it down.

I curse under my breath, "Goddamnit, Tommy Defalco," and go outside. It's bitter cold and I start to mutter like the crazed person I am, "I cannot believe I'm insane enough to try this at my age. But, so there's no question about it, I'm about to prove I'm totally fucking nuts."

I climb onto the patio and steady myself against the house. I have to lean far over the railing to be able to swing onto the little metal platform. I nearly bite my tongue and spit out the words, "Holy crap."

I manage to plant myself on the cold metal platform, and the thing creaks loudly. It, with me on it, swings perilously away the house. Shit, shit. But I pull it back and begin my descent. Tommy's socks make for slippery going, so every step is calculated. I soon realize that the kitchen window is directly below me, and I'll have no choice but to step right past it. And the kitchen door is located just to right of where I need to jump off.

I take a few more steps, and I'm almost to the window. I bend down to peek inside the kitchen. Then, scaring me half to death, the kitchen door flies open and Bruno storms out, carrying a pan of hot grease. He pours it into a container, and if he so much as raises his head he will discover parts of me he's never seen before. However, to my relief, he flings open the screen and walks inside, the kitchen door slamming shut behind him. My heart seems like it's racing a thousand beats a minute as I take one more step toward the window.

Joey, the dishwasher, is bent over the sink. All he has to do is look up and I'm busted.

He's an older fellow who's been down on his luck, but he's honest and trustworthy. He takes so much pride in working with us and being a part of our family that there's nothing he will not do, from washing dishes, to general maintenance, to landscaping, to even cleaning bathrooms and attending to patron mishaps. We cherish him.

I sidle down the last two steps and quickly tiptoe just past the window and onto the small grid platform at the base of the fire escape. The kitchen door explodes open again, and I'm so surprised that I lose my balance. By one arm, I'm now hanging onto the bottom of the ladder.

Bruno bellows to his kitchen staff, "Jesus H. Christ, it's roasting in here. Keep this freaking door open."

I struggle to where I can stand up, and to my consternation I see that it's much farther to the ground than I first thought. I'll have to hang onto the ladder and swing myself onto the ground. The vision of my hanging there in full moon view without my panties isn't quite in line with the ambiance of the elegant dining experience for which The Carriage House is known.

It takes a while for me to figure out the best way to carry off what I need to do to extricate myself from this damn fire escape. Resigned to my fate, it's now or never, so I struggle to lower myself over the few remaining feet to the ground. What results is not pretty. My dress gets pushed up and twisted around my waist, exposing all that I am, but I land, I hope unnoticed, in front of the dishwasher's window. Sadly, one of my socks dangles from a rusty step, of course just beyond my reach.

I hobble across the frozen stone driveway, wearing only one sock. I'm in excruciating pain, but I make it to the shed. Fortunately, the door isn't locked, which is the only good thing that's happened thus far. I'm ready to scream from the cold but I immediately spot Tommy's bike and this takes my mind off the pain. At least I can now get the hell away.

The bike is one of those lightweight racing things, and I can just get my leg over the center section. But when I do the metal bar that runs its entire length becomes intimately friendly with me, so I hop off on one foot. I'm reminded with horror that the temperature is close to freezing, and this conjures up the image of what can happen to the human tongue when stuck to a metal flagpole. The mere thought of me stuck to this bike evokes such terror that I vow to avoid that possibility at all cost.

The only way for me to mount this thing and not make the news at eleven is to take a flying leap and land on the seat—and avoid all metal in the process. Once I get going, it will be a ridiculous ride, but I will consider myself in the same league with those who climb Everest or swim the English Channel.

I pull the bike closer to the post where it had been leaning and prepare my jump into infamy. I perch, like a frog, on an old oil drum, readying myself over the bike. It's dark in the shed, and I can barely see. But I focus on the deed at hand, jumping in one violent motion from the oil drum and onto the seat of the bike. What I didn't see, or count on, nor was I told it might be a possibility by the exalted, Thomas Defalco, is that his bike is chained and padlocked by its rearmost section to the post. I now hate him with the same degree of ardor as I declared for him an hour ago. I crash down, landing amid steel, chain, sawdust, wood, and oil.

The ruckus was enough to cause Victor to throw open the kitchen door and yell at the top of his lungs, "You fuckin' cats, get the hell outta there!"

I lie where I am, not moving, not wanting to breathe if I don't have to. I catch a break as the screen door to the kitchen shuts again. Gingerly, I stand up. I'm not physically hurt, but I'm a total mess and downright desperate as to what to do next. I'm toast, and I know it.

Then I hear, "Would you like a ride home?" and the words make me jump and grab my dress to pull it down to cover my pantyless self.

I peer through the gloomy darkness and see Joey, standing at the shed door. He shyly says, "My car is right over there, Kitty. I can have you home in a jiff."

A deeply gasped, "Thank you," is all I can manage.

We say nothing all the way to my apartment and he doesn't glance once in my direction but I can't help but notice a small smile on his lips. I slide off the car seat and shut the door and turn to him with a weak grin. "I have no words, Joey, except thank you so very, very much."

He rubs his hand over his mouth and says, "Ms. Kitty, your secret is safe with me.

I make it back to work in record time, and Tommy is at the podium as I storm through the lobby. He breaks into a wide smile at the sight of me, "Wow, Pussycat, that was fast."

There's no one around, so I pounce on his chest with both hands and grab his lapels. "Don't even go there! Don't even talk to me!"

"Why? What happened? Was it too cold?"

My face has to be as red as a baboon's ass, and I spit the words at him: "Was it cold? That was the least of my problems. Let's see, where do I begin? I had no panties, which, by the way, are probably still in the cushions in The Pit. And how about no shoes? Oh, that's right, we lost them too. How about a fire escape that doesn't work and left me hanging out there like someone's dirty laundry? And, yes, let me think, perhaps someone, whose name I dare not mention, could have told me that he padlocks his freaking bicycle to a freaking post?"

The natural color drains from his face. "Oh, shit. I forgot that."

"*Ya think?*" I jump at him, as if I my words don't adequately convey my anger.

"You went home without your panties?" he whispers, looking around like some lecher.

"Oh, how terribly male minded of you to focus only on *that* part of the disaster. Yes, I had to hang off the fire escape with my whole bare ass out there for God and the world to see, if you must know." I'm positive he wants to burst out laughing, but I give him such a fierce look that he clears his throat and frowns instead.

"So, how did you get home?" he asks as if it's a purely inconsequential question.

I give him my best "eat shit and die look" and snarl, "Joey. My new best friend, Joey, drove me home."

His hand goes to his mouth. "You're kidding. Really? Oh, that explains why your coat and shoes are in the coatroom. He must have found them this morning when he vacuumed."

Polly flies around the corner, and we both snap to attention and look at her. "Hey, Kitty, you're here. Where were you?" she croons.

"Funeral," Tommy says.

"Baby shower," I say.

She frowns. "What's wrong with you two?"

I smile and shrug. "I meant funeral."

Tommy says, "Baby shower."

We both smile at her like guilty children. She looks from me to Tommy and back again and shakes her head.

"You guys are downright scary," she says and walks away with a disgusted look on her face.

"That went well," I whisper to him.

Tommy's now laughing and wiping his eyes. "Baby, I'm so sorry."

I turn and give him a hard punch to the arm just as Phillip comes by with the wine list. "Will you children cut it out? By the way, Kitty, it's so very nice of you to show up today." He gives me a look and rolls his eyes, then breezes by.

Tommy reaches down and squeezes my hand. "Don't be mad at me. It wasn't my fault. Shit just happens sometimes."

I stroll toward my bar, believing that to be one statement, above all others, I can rely on.

Chapter 16

GUESTS COME THROUGH THE door, chatting merrily, and Tommy smiles at them as I turn in to the lounge.

Christine gives me a relieved smile and says, "You are more than welcome to all this mayhem. Give me a tray and keep me out there on the floor where I belong." She glances around the entire lounge. "I don't see him now, but Chris was just in here. Asked me if I was new behind the bar, which should give you an idea of the job he thought I was doing." She laughs and trots off.

Despite the frantic last couple of hours, I'm glowing inside. Every time I think of what Tommy and I shared last night, I instantly segue from being mad at him to loving him.

Millie squints at me while idly stirring her martini with an olive pick. "There's something very different about you tonight, Kitty. Something has happened." She sips her drink. "It's not too late to stop the wedding. Stranger things have happened."

I smile, certain her intuition is the force behind her comments. It was she, after all, who really brought Tommy and me together. And, clever as she is, she knows this all too well. As I'm chuckling to myself over Millie's maneuverings, the bored-looking businessman from a while back is now occupying a barstool next to her, as he often has recently. They share all kinds of stories and buy each other drinks. It makes me happy that Millie has someone she enjoys chatting with besides me.

When I get the bar caught up, I wander into the kitchen and walk up behind Joey, who is diligently scrubbing a pan.

"Joey, you literally saved my butt tonight. I want you to know, I am forever grateful." I give him a shy smile that can't begin to display my level of embarrassment and slip fifty bucks into his apron. He tries to return the bills and I gently push his hand away.

"No, no, Kitty, please take your money back. I don't want it." He gives me a wide toothless grin. "This is what friends do. I got you covered."

"Joey, you enjoy that money. It's the *least* I can do. Keeping Deal Five intact is very important. I don't want the staff to know that Tommy and I broke The Deal."

"I won't say a thing. You have my word." He smiles again.

"How on earth did you know I was out there?"

He chuckles. "Oh, that's easy. I saw you flip off the fire escape and head for the shed."

I consider everything and take a moment to study his face. He nods and blinks happily at me, as if reading my mind. What else can I say? I turn stiffly and walk through the swinging doors and retake my position behind the bar. Tommy and Chris soon materialize next to me.

Chris smiles and says to Tommy, "Let me guess. This must be Kitty?" I'm staggered at how good-looking he is up close. Tall, slim, with sandy blond hair and eyes the color of the Aegean Sea, he could never pass for a day over thirty-five. He smiles and takes my hands in his. His gaze seems to pass right through me, leaving a come-hither glow behind.

He says, "Kitty, this is indeed a great honor to meet you finally. Tommy has done nothing but sing your praises."

"I'm afraid he puts me on a pedestal that's highly unstable," I say, smiling at him and wondering what he's really thinking about me.

"Oh, I don't think so." He's still holding my hand, and I'm beginning to feel odd, as the entire bar can see what's going on. And many can hear as Chris says, "Tommy certainly was right about how attractive you are."

I get it that he's a well-polished and highly confident people-handling machine. But I pull my hand away and smile sweetly and glance at Tommy, who stands at Chris's shoulder and grins like a Cheshire cat. I narrow my eyes at him. There's something else going on here, and I haven't a clue what.

"I understand you're quite the entertainer behind the bar; all legs and talent too." Chris says, but his flirtatious smile makes it clear that my juggling of bottles and plying of magic are not his interest, since he slowly strips me from head to toe with a look that drips with lust. I take a small step back, hoping to catch a glimpse of someone tapping an empty glass so I can make a clean getaway. But, damn, no such luck.

"I've learned a few bar tricks in my time," I say, now looking for someone who might need a bar napkin, swizzle stick, toothpick. But it ain't happening. It's as though each and every one of my regulars is enjoying my discomfort.

"I'm really looking forward to a close working relationship with you," Chris says as I spy someone who genuinely needs a fresh drink. But as I pivot toward that person, Chris touches my arm and adds, "I'm sure we'll have a lot of fun keeping up The Carriage House's reputation for excellence." He slowly kisses my hand, and I feel a flush coming to my cheeks. Tommy winks at me and the two men drift off together. *What is going on? Tommy sweeps me off my feet less than twelve hours earlier, and now a guy who could be a movie star is fawning all over me. And Tommy seems to approve. What the hell…!*

Mildred motions me over. "Danger, danger," she says, taking a long sip of her martini and picking out a fresh Virginia Slim from her mauve eel-skin cigarette case. "Be very careful with that one, Kitty."

A half-hour later Tommy saunters in to see if I need change. He stands beside me at my open register as I estimate the drawer's contents. He blurts, "Chris is nice, isn't he?"

"Are you crazy? Did you see him coming on to me? What the hell." I give a quick laugh that's full of sarcasm. "My guess is, Deal Five will be the first to go around here."

"Sweetheart, we trashed that Deal last night in good form."

I pretend to brush off my arms. "He's certainly sweet on me. What did you tell him?"

"Nothing that wasn't true. And I handpicked him especially for you."

I defiantly stand back with my hand on my hip "What are you saying?"

"I'm saying, when I decided I was going off to Italy forever, I wanted to find someone for you and maybe give Roy some competition, just in case you changed your mind about Roy, and I wanted to mend your broken heart with someone. Chris was to be the perfect match for you." He peers at me under raised eyebrows.

"You mean to tell me that you handpicked Chris so he'd come on to me? Can you be any more arrogant?"

"It might not appear to be good idea now, but it seemed like a kind and sweet thing to do at the time."

"That is so degrading. This is like a father pawning off his daughter on the man he approves of."

Tommy snorts and flashes me a hard glare. "This was hardly that, and I hope I'm not a father figure."

"I can't believe you would do such a thing. You're a major jerk, you know that?"

"Baby, this was way before last night. I was distraught at the thought of leaving you alone, just in case you broke up with old Roy, whom I really couldn't fathom you with anyway, and thought I'd get you not only a fabulous manager but a companion as well." Again, he looks up from the register drawer at me through his lashes and adds," since you were losing your best friend."

"How *dare* you assume that *you* need to take care of *me*. I've always been remarkably good at taking care of myself, thank you. And I do exceedingly well alone. I *like* to be alone. You amaze me sometimes. Why would you ever think of doing something like … that?" I give him a punch in the arm—this time even harder than when we were at the podium. It's enough to make him wince, which pleases me.

"Do you have to be such a little bitch all the time?" he says, rubbing his arm, smiling. "Here I was doing the best possible thing for you in hiring a guy who is beyond handsome to replace me, and you don't thank me."

"Tommy, you are the most egotistical, manipulative, misinformed asshole I have ever met in my entire life. How dare you assume *anything* about me?"

He grins and turns to leave but I grab his cuff and roughly pull him around. "And another thing, did it ever occur to you, that you could have just driven your damn car around to the back so when I came off that godforsaken fire escape I could have driven home?" My anger has brought out a series if arm flings and gestures that choreographs my exasperation. I'm wearing an expression of pure amazement not only from what I just blurted out but that thought even existed at all.

Tommy has a look of total astonishment and simply said "*My God...I never thought of that.*" We stand there a moment contemplating the simple solution that neither of us even considered. Finally, Tommy laughs right out and I can't help but join him. He walks away wiping his eyes, obviously overcome with the humor of it all.

Polly is laughing at us from the service bar, where she's been standing and waiting for an order. "What in the name of God are y'all bickering over now? Lord have mercy, you two!"

Half of my bar patrons must have overheard us, since they're ogling us and laughing. Two couples toward the far end are pointing our way, and since they're not signaling me for a drink I have to believe my "half the bar" assessment is really *everyone*.

Polly delivers her order, returns to the service bar, and holds a puzzling look while asking Millie, "What the hell happened between those two last night?"

Millie leans toward Polly. "Do tell."

"Nothing happened," I snap before Millie can say anything. "You people are reading too much into nothing. It's just a private joke, is all." Then I bark orders like a traffic cop: "Move along. There's nothing to see here." I'm trying to be funny but I feel the color rising into my cheeks.

Polly knows enough about me to scoot out to the floor even if all her tables are in great shape. Her good sense is another reason I love her so.

My spirits are high all night, and every hour that passes makes me more anxious for closing. Later, when Mike comes for Millie, I dance up to her and slip a bar napkin into one of her coat pockets. I see her fumbling for her gloves in the lobby and in doing so discovering the napkin. I wrote on it: "Millie, I don't know whether to kill you or kiss you. You have a strange way of asking for miracles."

She turns my way. I just smile at her and nod. She clasps her hands together as if in prayer and then looks up like a little girl on Christmas morning. I put a finger to my lips and pantomime "quiet," and she wiggles around like a happy puppy.

A little after midnight Tommy locks the doors and turns out the dining-room lights, closing up the back of The House. I hear him walking the halls and checking the kitchen, and I wonder what he has planned for us tonight. I finish counting my empty bottles and hear him coming into the lounge. He has Johnny Mathis playing on the sound system and is quickly unfastening his shirt studs. "What are you up to?" I ask puckishly.

He pulls off his cuff links and shoves them in his breast pocket, his shirt now virtually falling from his body. His face sports a devilish grin.

I play dumb. "What now?" I ask.

"After all these years, I'm finally going to live out my wildest fantasy concerning you." He tosses aside his shirt and moves toward me as a cat might advance to its prey.

"You're not going to strip me naked, douse me with Bacardi 151, and set me afire, are you?"

"No, but that's not a bad idea, then licking off the blue flames."

He comes around to the back of the bar and unfastens the barrette that holds my hair up, letting the curls shake loose on their own.

"Well, that was predictable. Is that your big fantasy?"

I learn it's not, as he takes off my bowtie, opens my tux jacket and unbuttons my shirt, his eyes never leaving mine. I have to admit this is turning me on—and Ferrari fast; zero to sixty in three or less. While he's kissing my neck I say breathlessly, "I hope you're not entertaining the idea of making love to me on the bar. I just polished it."

"Then you might have to polish it again." Thirty minutes later we wind up on the far end of the bar, completely spent.

"How the hell did we get over here?" I ask, giggling my words.

He's trying to catch his breath. "In my fantasy, I make love to you on the bar, on the piano, the tables, out by the podium, in the dining room, and in the kitchen. But, tonight, this is as far as I got. In my younger days, I could have made the circuit."

"Thank God those days are gone." We laugh and hold each other like lovers are supposed to, an experience I never thought I'd have with Tommy.

A few minutes later we're snuggling before the fire in The Pit, drinking Grand Marnier.

"The bar will never be the same to me," I say and laugh. "If people only knew."

I change the subject and ask about the night's dining-room traffic, then Tommy wants to know all the details surrounding my glorious fire escape adventure. By the time I finish my ribs hurt, I've laughed so hard.

"And to think that whole disastrous scenario could have been avoided if we had only thought to move the car." He roars out with another side splitting laugh. "By the way," he says, "I took your coat and shoes upstairs. Your panties and stockings were in a coat pocket."

We both cringe at the same time and I say, "Joey? Oh, that's *sooo* very bad. I know he saw my bare butt when I came off that fire escape. I gave him fifty bucks as a thank-you—but also for hush money."

"He should have paid you!" Tommy laughs until his eyes well up. "You are a treasure." We're both naked, but as he takes my hand it's more intimate than the torrid sex we just had, and he says, "In all serious-ness, I want you to know I'm really sorry about our rocky start. I was just so freaked out about oversleeping that I wasn't thinking straight. I'm so used to putting my job first. I assure you, from the bottom of heart, something like that will never happen again."

"It won't happen again; I can assure you!"

"What do you mean?"

I kiss his nose. "You're going to start parking Baby Blue out back from now on."

He nods and lifts my hand to his lips in a soft kiss. "You got it, Sweetheart, but for now, we'll always have this great story to tell. And speaking of great stories to tell, how are we going to break the news about the two of us to everyone? It is kind of sudden."

"I vote we wait. We both need time to settle into the new 'us' for a while. You just can't jump off one woman and onto another, as impressive as that vision is to most men. And aren't you still involved with The Club and John Vassar, which brings you right in front of Lillian again, doesn't it? At some point, we need to talk about her."

He runs his hand over his face as if a cloud is covering his thoughts. "Yeah, about that. There's something you need to know now. Lillian appealed to me because I enjoyed being part of the jet set, staying in five-star hotels, gambling, dining at the finest restaurants, spending time in New York City and rubbing elbows with the beautiful people. It's not easy for me to say this, but I've been a kept man in many ways. She introduced me to John Vassar. He's a plastic surgeon and president of The Country Club—"

"I know who he is." I give him a condescending look.

"Sorry. What you might not know is that he owns a company that makes implants used in surgical reconstructions. This isn't public knowledge, and that's how he wants it. And before you ask, all I can say is that there are issues with some of the implants he exports and issues with taxes. But here's what you really need to know more than anything else: Lillian not only owns The Club, she and John are partners in the implant enterprise as well."

"Damn, the hits keep right on coming." I get up and start to gather my clothes.

"I wish it were funny, but it's not. John Vassar is a very powerful man, Kitty. I don't know how much more I can tell you, only that I want to caution you that my breakup with Lillian may have consequences, because it might seem to John that I'm walking away from him as well. The two of them are that close." *Jesus, what have I gotten myself into?* Before I can ask Tommy to be more specific, even if he doesn't want to discuss any of this further, he adds, "I want you to know that I never proposed to Lillian. The proposal was just a matter-of-fact business discussion over dinner between the two of us. I've learned a lot about accounting, and she convinced John to place me in the position of helping him with a medical supply distributorship he was setting up abroad. Lillian wanted to marry me so we could sail off into the Italian sunset, and I'd be her trophy. I know, how's that for a switch? I won't tell you I didn't enjoy Lillian, but I never remotely loved her. And I wasn't sure that the operation John was planning for me overseas was up my alley. That's all I'm going to say about that."

I come back with my clothes and start getting dressed. I pause and say, "This entire thing with John Vassar and Lillian seems odder and odder the more you tell me about it. What on earth made you decide that now was the time to tell me you love me?"

"When this wedding was coming down to the wire, I knew I had to face my truth. That truth is that I love you more than anything or anyone in my life. There's not enough money in the world to make me walk away from you. I'm sorry I let John and Lillian control so much of my life. But I've made my choice, thank God, and now all of that is over for good. I'm just worried that maybe I've put us in danger."

"From which one, John or Lillian?

"Both."

I figured a long time ago that Lillian had some hold over him that was well beyond that of a normal relationship. If money was the reason, well, who was I to judge? What I do find intriguing is John Vassar's business. For a man who has an obvious multimillion-dollar medical practice, the implant business, however sketchy my knowledge of it might be, must make him fabulously wealthy. But what the hell was Tommy doing for John and Lillian, and why was this so secretive? And most important at this moment, what danger could we both be in? After all, Tommy is just quitting a job. Regarding Lillian, however, my new lover did spurn one of the craziest bitches on the planet, a vixen who would desire nothing more than to tear off my fingernails one by one while I boiled in hot oil.

I mull over what he's said thus far and ask simply, "Is that all of it?"

"Isn't that enough?"

"As for John's potential wrath, is your quitting all I need to be concerned with? It isn't some drug-smuggling organization Vassar runs, is it?"

Tommy shrugs off my comment and takes my hand. "No, it's nothing like that, just complex medical issues he's able to scoot around and some taxes he's avoiding. It would take hours to explain, but essentially he's bringing products to market that no one else has, but before they've been fully tested. And he's hiding the profits from domestic sales in foreign accounts."

"Could the untested products kill people?"

"This isn't like a drug that's not been fully tested, but it's not totally clean either. And some of these implants make it back to the States under other names. Frankly, he wants to keep his involvement in this business low key for tax purposes more than anything else."

Somehow, I'm not believing everything Tommy is telling me. "I wonder what Millie would think about this *implant* business if she knew everything," I ask, needing another drink, which I get for both of us. When I come back, Tommy is dressed and standing by the fireplace. "It's not our place to discuss any of this with Millie," he warns me. "Let's just be our happy-go-lucky loving selves when we're around her. And I'm as serious as I can be when I say you cannot divulge anything I've said to you about John to her. She may know everything, and she might know nothing. Either way, you and I don't what to learn the extent of her knowledge."

For the first time in our entire discussion, Tommy has scared me, but there's one more issue I need to have cleared up, so I ask, "I want our relationship to be based on honesty from now on in everything we say to one another. So I want you to think before answering and tell me the absolute truth." He takes a sip of his drink and nods towards me "Okay, shoot."

"There has always been the suspicion among the staff that Lillian does drugs. And I don't mean toking on a joint now and then. She has that *look* sometimes, not to mention her constant 'allergies' that she says causes her sniffling and red eyes. I don't care about her, Tommy, but I need to know, are you using?"

He stares darkly at me and rubs the side of his snifter several times before saying, "Lillian uses, Kit. And sometimes she goes over the edge. That's what I meant when I told you in the past that she needed me. And, no, she doesn't have allergies, at least that I know of."

This might make our "lovefest forever" the shortest in history, but I have to press him. "Did you two ever do drugs together?"

He stands straight and stares at me. "I'm clean."

There's a moment, a blink in time really, when his eyes don't meet mine and his smile breaks. I have a doubt, but then he sweeps me away with his broad grin and shining eyes as he wraps me in his arms and makes me his loving captive. I chalk up my feeling to the seriousness of the conversation. He trusts me. He doesn't need to lie to me. Why should he?

Chapter 17

MILLIE IS EARLY, AND she rushes to her place at my bar and smacks both hands down on the surface that was recently polished to a special sheen by Tommy and me. The words gush from her: "Tell me everything. I want details galore." Her blue eyes glisten under her long, black lashes and her face is aglow with the radiance of an inquisitive teenager.

I lean across the bar and whisper to her, "For one thing, there is no more Lillian. I think Tommy had an epiphany that he was truly in love with me because of what you told him." My voice cracks, "He loves me, Millie."

She comes behind my bar and embraces me. "I can't tell you how happy I am to hear this news. You have no idea how this will change everything in all our lives."

I give her a puzzled look but she dismisses it with a wave of her hand.

"You must keep this under your hat for a while," I say as she makes her way back to her barstool. We don't want to give Tommy the opportunity to appear fickler than he already is." I shake her martini as she says, "He's not the only person who ever found love for someone else at the last minute. I'm so happy he's no longer with her. I'm so pleased for you and Tommy. All is right with the world now. This was meant to happen. When will Tom tell the staff of this news?"

"He'll tell them tonight that his relationship with Lillian is over and that he's not going anywhere."

"And tell everyone about you and him?"

"I imagine he'll wait a couple of days." She wrinkles her brow. "Oh, it's not that we're not sure about each other. He has some loose ends to tie up … around here. The new manager and all. He wants Troy to keep Chris, then he'll work mostly as maître d'."

"On that note," Millie says, raising her voice as she turns and addresses the twenty or so sitting in the lounge, "drinks for everyone on me, just because I love you all." Of course her generosity is met with cheers. The beer drinkers who are married to the TV offer a toast to her, singing out, "Here's to Millie. We love you too, Millie."

Polly puts her tray down on the service bar and drawls, "What in pea heaven is going on in here?"

I jokingly cringe. "Pea heaven? Do I dare ask what that is?"

"It's an old southern expression. I was born with a ton of 'em." She gives me her drink order and asks, "So what's all the celebrating about?"

I want to throw my arms around her and dance her all over the room, shouting, "Tommy is in love with me—and I'm not afraid to love him back!" Instead, I grab her arm and whisper, "Tommy's going to announce this to everyone later, but I'll tell you now. He broke up with Lillian. And it's for good this time. But best of all, he's staying."

"Well butter my butt and call me a biscuit. Kitty, you must be as happy as a tick on a fat hound dog. I can't ever see you two parting ways, especially over a snake like Lillian. My prayers are answered. The House is back together." She's smiling but now stops. "What's going to happen to poor Chris? He just landed this job."

I tell her what Tommy said about asking Troy to keep Chris. Polly nods but remains subdued. "I wondering how Lillian is handling all this?" she says as I place her drink order on her tray, which she hoists shoulder high. She usually walks off quickly, but she takes just one step before stopping and giving me a cautionary look over her shoulder. "Sweetie, I'd keep a low profile around her. She's crazy as a bessie bug, and I don't doubt she'll come up with some way to blame you for Tommy's change of heart."

Hearing the warning come from Polly dampens my euphoria and

sends a chill through me. I wonder just how far over the edge Tommy's decisions will ultimately push her. Tommy's concern for the danger that might be around the corner hits me full force, and I find myself struggling to concentrate, even fouling up one of Jeannie's orders.

Tommy comes up behind as I count out change. He stands close at my right shoulder and I wonder why he doesn't speak. I turn away from my counting to see that it's Chris instead.

"Hey, you," I say in my cheeriest voice. "How are you? How's the dining room doing? Full?

His smile knocks me out. He's just about the handsomest man I have ever seen. His eyes again strip me clean, inside and out. He feels like a familiar soul; someone I've known for many lifetimes. He's different from Tommy. Tommy sparkles in a crowd. He's present on every level in an open-faced way. Chris smolders like sand under a hot sun, shape-shifting shadows like a mirage. I can't seem to get a handle on who he is yet. Only that he's intriguing and attractive—very attractive. I'm chastising myself for even thinking about another man in a physical sense with all that's happening between Tommy and me, but this is definitely my version of Adam and the apple.

"I was looking forward to an opportunity to break away and come say hello to you," he says. "It seems ridiculous, because I just met you, but for some reason it's like I've known you for a long time. If you're going to hang around after work for a drink, I'd like to chat with you. Talk about old times we never had." He laughs and so do I. Wow, is he smooth.

I flip two bottles from the rack and pour perfect measures into two glasses. "I'm not sure about tonight. I think Tommy is calling a meeting after we close. Another time, okay?"

He adjusts his bowtie in the mirror on my back bar and clears his throat. "Then it will have to be another time. I'll see you later at the meeting."

I assume that Tommy has spoken to Troy, and I wonder if our new-est employee has an inkling about what's to transpire. I can imagine how awful it would be to lose a job before even getting started. And right before the holidays to boot. I hope Troy agrees to Tommy's request. It would give Tommy fewer responsibilities and more time with me. And, although I hate to admit it, I like Chris despite his not-so-subtle overtures. He might have devastating looks and say all the right things, but I've been to a lot of rodeos, and I'm not going to let anyone mess up what I want for Tommy and me.

Whenever I'm in the throes of high anticipation about something, an evening will click off one second at a time. This night is no different, and when the bar closes and the last customer is cheerfully shooed away, I feel like I've worked a double shift.

Soon, the entire staff is present for the meeting, armed with the beverage of their choice as Tommy takes his power stance in front of the fireplace, rocking back and forth with his legs wide apart and his arms folded tight against his chest.

It's no surprise that Chris squeezes in between Polly and me on the sofa. Polly gives me a look I have never seen from her before, and I give her a wink that says, "I know."

Troy, who usually leaves immediately after work, sits on the fireplace steps with Phillip and shares a bottle of pinot noir, one they're considering adding to our house wines. He and Phillip laugh together, and I can't help noticing that Troy looks thin and pale. It occurs to me that I don't see Troy often these days, as he's always working the dining room or taking reservations. It's odd that, in such a small place of business, some people can go about unobserved for virtually weeks at a time. In addition to his ashen face, his eyes are bloodshot. If he's fighting a flu bug, perhaps it's good if he stays away until he recovers. Tommy breaks my train of thought.

"Here's the Deal," Tommy begins, and we all laugh.

Polly yells out, "Oh, dear God, y'all, here comes another Deal. This place has more Deals than fleas on a bloodhound. Let me get my chisel and stone tablet, 'cause I think this will be a big one."

Tommy laughs along with the others and says, "Actually, this will be quick. Lillian and I broke off our engagement. I'll be staying on here at the House indefinitely." The room explodes with cheers and Tommy raises his hands to quiet everyone. "Troy and I have talked this all out, and we've decided that Chris will stay on as manager in the exact capacity he was hired for, except I'll handle all the maître d' work. So, officially, welcome aboard, Chris." Tommy starts the applause and Chris beams at all the smiling faces around him.

Tommy asks Chris to step up next to him. He does this but I can tell he doesn't like leaving the two women he's nestled between. Tommy shakes Chris's hand and says, "Troy and I are going to suggest to Chris that he continue to let Polly run the dining room, because she will anyway." Everyone laughs. "And Kitty can be the lounge manager, because she is anyway."

More laughs. "And, Chris, you will be Czar over it all. How do you feel about this?"

Chris is smiling and puts his hand over his heart in what I believe is genuine relief, as I get the impression this is the first he's heard about any of this, even from Polly on the q.t., regarding Tommy's staying. Always could trust that woman, and she's proved it again.

Chris says, "I'm very grateful. Thank you, Tommy, and thank you, Troy." He nods his appreciation to both men and there's another round of applause.

Tommy takes a deep breath, and I'm hoping he isn't going to spill the beans about us finally declaring our love for one another. Moving our relationship from friendship to intimacy is new and exciting to me, but I'm unprepared to share it with others right now, except of course for the instigator, Millie. But Tommy has another kind of blockbuster announcement.

He smiles so wide he's having trouble speaking. "Troy has just made me a part owner of this fine establishment, and it's with deep respect for him, and for all of you whom I love just like family, that I accept his trust and generosity. So I'll just settle in as maître d' and secretary of defense around here."

Anyone who was sitting is now standing and applauding and cheering along with everyone else. I'm so proud and happy for Tommy. This will give him the stability and purpose that he's been craving for years.

Tommy gives me a wink and continues, "Christmas Eve will again see our yearly Holiday Choral Night for the patrons, and our little Pollyanna Party for the staff will follow afterwards. That's it, my babies. Love you guys."

We spend the next hour laughing over our drinks and good-naturedly teasing Tommy and chatting with Troy, with whom none of us really get to spend much time. I really believe he's sick, and I purposely don't get too close. Chris makes a point of keeping me engaged in conversation. He's funny and extremely intelligent. I think he will make a wonderful addition to our House family.

Tommy then holds court with Troy, Bruno and Victor apparently over whether or not to do tableside Chateaubriand for the holidays. He interrupts Chris and my conversation to ask if Chris can carve and serve the meal and Chris nods enthusiastically and adds, "I can also do a mean tableside Caesar salad from scratch with the raw egg and anchovies. It's my specialty."

"Excellent!" Bruno roars. "I like him. He stays. There's hope for this god forsaken place yet." When Polly says goodnight, this leaves Chris, Tommy and me standing in the lobby. Chris offers to walk me to my car, and I wonder how I can avoid this so I can spend the night in the upstairs apartment, but Tommy comes to my rescue, and I hope his as well, saying he needs to see me in his office before I leave. Chris squeezes my hand as he says goodnight. I feel giddy with all the male attention.

As the front door closes, I smirk at Tommy and say, "You did such a good job selling me to him, I think he's got a huge crush on me. I blame you entirely for this."

"With your expertise at handling men in difficult situations, I have total faith that you can deal with Chris's amorous outpouring of adoration."

"I didn't know you were so eloquent."

"Neither did I." He laughs and pulls me to him and kisses me passionately.

I decide to make the night special and fill the tub with steaming water. I find two little candles and sprinkle a bit of his aftershave into the water. I strip off my clothes and sink into the fragrant soft atmosphere I've created. It's hot but I love it.

I hear Mr. Bug barking furiously at something but then he falls silent. Waiting for Tommy seems endless. The apartment is deathly quiet as I lie still, the water just above my mouth and below my nose. I blow little bubbles, watching them float briefly on the warm surface before dissipating.

I'm not sure how much time has passed, but the water is now cooling somewhat and I grow more concerned. Long ago I should have heard Tommy's footsteps, the deadbolt catching, the light switches clicking off, Mr. Bug scampering about. I sit up in the tub and strain to hear something, anything. But I'm met with listening to my own breathing. I step out of the tub and wrap myself in his bathrobe, which had lain like a lifeless wraith on the bathroom door.

"Tommy?" I call out time and again.

I start down the steps into the darkened rooms of The House. The silence is excruciating.

"Tommy?" I yell this time. But my voice sounds weak. I come off the bottom step and peer into the dining room, the black moonless night pressing against the windowed walls. A fearful chill fingers along my spine, and I draw his bathrobe tighter around me.

"Tommy?" Still no response. I accept the eeriness of the moment and look into the lounge, which is dark except for the little red and blue and green lights on my register, coffee maker, and mixer, respectively, and the tiny button lights that line the rises of the steps to The Pit.

I shout as loud as I can, "Damn it, Tommy, where are you?" Again, no reply. So I enter the kitchen from the dining-room hallway because the lounge now feels very strange to me. Of course I could turn on the lights, but for some reason I can't, the soft orange glow from the stovetop's pilot light providing the only illumination.

"Tommy?" I say quietly this time.

I'm answered only by the tinny din from our commercial refrigerator's noisy fan. I see the back door standing open, and a cold winter draft washes across the recently scrubbed red tile floor like a bog mist. My pulse is drumming in my ears and I'm barely breathing. I manage to get myself to the door and look outside. I can't bring myself to call his name again. I stand paralyzed at the realization that Tommy is gone and I'm totally alone—or am I?

I spin around, expecting to see a shadow coming my way. I let out a sigh of relief. No one is behind me. Yet I feel danger everywhere. My mind is flooded with options: Should I shut the door? Call 911? Call Bruno? Oh, God, is it a robbery, has Tommy been kidnapped? Maybe I should check around some more before jumping to conclusions. One thing is for certain, I am doing no good where I am, and I cannot run around outside barefoot. Been there, done that, and it doesn't work.

I race from the kitchen and into the dining room to look out of the windows that provide the best view of the front side of the restaurant. Through the inky night I see two men on the road, standing next to a parked car, talking to a third man, who I think is Tommy. Their wild gesticulations indicate a disagreement. I faintly hear one man say, "Defalco, this ain't gonna work and you know it. This is fair warning, you need to clean up your act."

I see the man turn angrily away. Tommy walks off, his hands in his pockets. I feel my emotions start to burn in my throat as he heads around to the back door. I meet him there. Mr. Bug barks and Tommy takes a step back at seeing me.

"Baby, what are you doing down here?"

"What am I doing here? You've got to be kidding." My next words are a mixture of anger and relief. "I made a bath and waited for you. I called and called and you didn't answer, so I came down here and searched everywhere. The back door was wide open—" I wring my hands but I refuse to cry—"I was afraid something had happened to you. It even crossed my mind that The House was robbed and you were—"

He rushes to me, stroking my hair, kissing me. "Oh, Kitten, I'm so sorry. Everything's okay. I didn't mean to scare you."

"Who were those men?"

He answers in-between kisses, "They're friends of mine from the restaurant business. They saw me from the road as I was out checking the shed, which I decided to lock, so I walked out to say, 'Hi.'"

"Friends just happened by at two in the morning and see you closing up? Why didn't they come to the door?"

Tommy gives me his smile and raises his eyebrows. "You of all people know that the night never sleeps for bar and restaurant people. Our night is other people's day. There's a whole bunch of people who stop in now and then after I close. These guys saw I had company, and that's why they didn't stay, which reminds me, it might be a good idea if I park your car in back just to keep us safe from gossip."

I'm too upset to let this pass so easily. "One guy sounded angry. I heard something that sounded very much like a threat."

"It was nothing, Baby. Those guys are jerks. They came to argue with me over a disagreement we had a while back. They were drunk and looking for a fight so I blew them off. Don't worry, it's not important." He slides his hands still cold from the outside weather around my waist and pulls me close. "You feel damp, and smell like me. How did that happen?"

I dab my nose on his robe sleeve and sniffle, "I put some of your aftershave into the bath water. I was waiting and waiting."

He laughs and drinks me in. "Oh God, how I love you, Kitty." The feel of his hands on my naked body makes me melt into his rising passion and we spontaneously make love right there in the kitchen. Afterwards, he chuckles breathlessly, "We better hope to God Bruno never finds out about this or he'll have us both under his meat cleaver." We fall together laughing.

"I suppose this is another one of your favorite fantasies," I chide him as I wrap his robe around me. "What's going to happen when you run out of these sorted scenarios?" He sighs and picks me up into his arms again and carries me up the stairs. "That, my dear, will never, ever happen. I'll never stop wanting you, in all ways, always."

We fall into bed and curl around each other. He says he's exhausted and I kiss him goodnight. After a few minutes, right before I drift off, I look over expecting to see him breathing in sleep, but instead he's staring at the ceiling, deep in thought and looking worried.

Chapter 18

THE NEXT TWO WEEKS are magical in many ways. Knowing that Tommy is staying, the peace we all feel has everyone in the holiday spirit. There are lots of laughs around my bar, and Tommy and I are back to our old comedy routines. Sometimes he's the straight person, sometime I am, and keeping our love a secret is a challenge we now enjoy.

Polly catches us once stepping outside the lines when we stole a moment in the small hallway between my bar and the kitchen. We were locked in a tight hug when she popped around the corner and asked, "Who died?"

"No one," I say as we quickly drop our arms. "Why?"

"The only time you two embrace is when you're grieving." She pauses and purses her lips. "Unless … unless y'all are breaking Deal Five." I'm positive we both look like guilty children as she brushes past us, but she adds, "Naaa, Hell would have frozen over, and I would've felt that." She swings through the kitchen doors and we smile through our relief.

Chris is the only stumbling block we have, as he's continually wooing me. I get sweet little notes on my register, he engages me in not-so-innocent double-entendre conversations, and he never misses an opportunity to touch me on the arm or shoulder. I honestly believe he's fallen for me. So I had a heart-to-heart with him, telling him that I am quite seriously dating someone and that he will have to stop pursuing me in a romantic way. Instead of accepting what I told him, he said things can change between people, and that he will gladly wait—however long it takes.

Then, three days ago, he buttonholed me and said, "I do understand that a boss romancing an employee may be coloring outside the lines, but it does happen. And I'm crazy about you, so I'm not going to give up. Anyway, when do you ever see this guy you're supposed to be so serious about? You're always here."

I finally had to get angry with him: "I'm flattered that you like me. But this has to stop. And I mean, right now. I don't want to get you fired, but make no mistake, I can do that. I'm aware that sexual harassment is very hard to prove in a bar, and I'm not accusing you of this. Yet. But you're getting close." I tugged on his coat sleeve. "Chris, I like you. Hell, everybody here likes you. But you're making me so uncomfortable that I'm almost to the point of not wanting to come to work."

He does something I do not expect. Instead of apologizing, he asks, "Are we still friends?"

It takes me a moment to say, "Of course we're friends. But we're also co-workers." I give him a playful slug in the shoulder. "So lighten up and just behave yourself. We don't do drama here at The House." He nodded, and since then everything between us has been fine.

The Christmas extravaganza this year is more beautiful than ever. Phillip and Barry have set out massive poinsettias and added gold and white ribbons everywhere. It's all presented by candlelight, and no doubt the fire marshal would have a seizure if he were to happen by. Many people who come for dinner remain at their tables afterwards and we bring extra chairs in for those just coming for the concert. The dining room is full and we busy ourselves setting up a dessert bar and making specialty coffees and teas for the gathering.

A choir from a local church arrives, the singers dressed in red and white gowns, their voices angelic and their music flawless in its delivery. A long table is spread out with a wide array of wines and holiday snacks.

The House's Christmas affair is the townsfolk's favorite and one of the top social events to attend of one wishes to be seen. After the concert we get to socialize a bit with our patrons and most hand Christmas envelopes to the staff as a thank you for a year of fine service and friendship.

After we close, Barry shows up to be with Phillip at our Pollyanna Party. We wheel in the spiced rum and mulled wine, and what is left of the Christmas goodies from the dining room.

Troy hands out our bonuses and has a little meeting with us about new things planned for The House for next year. He tells us there will be landscaping on the back lawn, with a fountain and a stone patio. Chris will introduce garden parties next summer, as well as outdoor dining.

"There goes the baseball diamond," Bruno says sadly as others nod in agreement.

Chris steps forward and says, "Here's a thought for everyone to consider. And I won't need an answer until March. I was thinking of a uniform change. Drop the stuffy tuxes and maybe go for an Old-English look with peasant shirts and long aprons. Still formal but more like a carriage house of old. Just a thought, mind you, so I don't want any long faces." A few laughs filter through the room. "There are some period clothing styles in a catalog I'll leave in the pantry. Any comments will be appreciated. And as long as I get my way in the end, we can take a vote." That remark brought some serious laughter; Tommy is obviously rubbing off on Chris already.

"I don't have to wear buckles on my shoes, do I?" Bruno moans.

"Oh, you need to live a little, Bruno," Phillip says, dragging out his words to sound even gayer, making everyone laugh.

"I for one will love looking like a scullery wench," Jeannie says. "I'm damn sure that's what I was in my past life."

"Can I wear one of those crisscross midriff things with lots of cleavage showing?" I ask, giving my head a flip and letting a few long curls stay on my face.

"Oh, yes, most definitely," Chris says and smiles wide, showing a dimple I'd never noticed before.

Tommy grumbles as he sets down his Grand Marnier, "No doubt that would boost bar traffic. But Kitty's showing cleavage along with her already famous legs would keep me busy throwing young bucks out the door, not to mention how obnoxious she'd become owning more power over us men. I may have to veto the bar wear." More laughs from everyone.

Troy's health seems to be improving during the past couple of weeks, but he stands rather wobbly as he says, "I think a new look is a great idea. The Carriage House will retain its ambiance but with the elegance of The Old Mill restaurant that's so famous in Massachusetts."

"Oh, I love The Old Mill," Polly says. "I get what you're thinking, and it's a cool idea."

Troy continues, "We're adding permanent wait staff in the spring. Also, a new accountant will be on board to help clean up some issues with the books. We're looking at growing the business, with each and every one of you a part of this. And I might add, as we grow all of you will make more money." Everyone applauds. "That's it. Merry Christmas to all, and tonight please don't drink up our profits for the year."

I don't remember Troy more upbeat. One thing he said, however, confuses me. Tommy told me a long time ago that he reviewed the books when we both first came to work here. I helped him pick up a ledger he dropped, and this is the only reason we had that discussion. But, according to Tommy, he was solely a second set of eyes, as Troy always utilized an outside accountant who was a respected C.P.A. Now Troy is bringing in a new accountant. Tommy hasn't said anything to me about the books in years, and it concerns me that perhaps this is the first he's heard of any problems, since I watched his eyebrows raise at Troy's announcement.

My serious thoughts soon end when we give Troy and Tommy their gifts of handmade fisherman-knit sweaters.

Troy is most gracious but excuses himself from the rest of the festivities, saying he's under the weather, the first time he's publicly discussed being ill. Tommy tells me Troy's fighting a lingering infection, but it's hard for me to ignore what I'm seeing, as it appears to be an infection caused by nose candy and not the result of a bacteria or a virus.

My Pollyanna—the person whose name I picked from a hat—is Joey, and I found the perfect item for him at a gag shop all of us at The House have visited at one time or another. It's a rocks glass covered in bikini bottoms, and Joey turns three shades of red when he opens the plain box it comes in and pulls out the glass. He laughs out loud, shaking his finger at me as Tommy leans over and shakes his hand and says, "Much obliged, buddy." No one seems to get the private joke shared among us nor does anyone care.

Tommy drew Phillip's name and got him a blue sequined male G-string, and it draws a raucous laugh. Tommy assures everyone, "I bought that just to prove I'm not homophobic. But, please, Phillip, I honestly don't even want to think about where you might wear that."

Phillip looks at it and says wistfully that he hopes it fits. More laughs. He adds, "If not, Barry can wear it. I'll let you all guess what I mean by that statement." Several of us raise our eyebrows and laugh even harder.

When all the gag gifts are given and most of the leftover punch and dainties are gone, everyone sits close together, basking in the love and friendship that surrounds us.

Tommy lifts me from my seat and asks me to dance to Johnny Ray's "Cry," a song I hadn't heard in years. He pulls me close. "We're a perfect fit, you know that?"

"In all ways," I answer, as I close my eyes and sink into the sway of his body. I'm thinking that this might be the night we tell everyone the truth about our secret love.

Just as Johnny hits "cry" in its final crescendo and the song ends, the room grows quiet and we hear Jeannie say, "Hi, Lillian, John. What a surprise."

Polly yells, "Merry Christmas, y'all. We're just having our Pollyanna Party." Her voice trails off as all eyes fall on us as we we're the only couple on the dance floor. Lillian glares at Tommy and me but stays quiet as a church mouse.

After a stifling silence, John Vassar says, "We don't want to interrupt your fun, but we need Tom for a minute." Dr. Vassar's eyes fix on Tommy. "Can we talk privately?"

For Lillian's part, she's shooting me a scorching stare, yet she manages what I think is an attempt at a smile that comes across more as a sneer The three of them leave the lounge and climb the stairs to the office, with Tommy leading the way.

I retake my place on the sofa in The Pit as Jeannie tries to pick up the conversation. I have a cold, steely taste in my mouth, but I finish Tommy's snifter of Grand Marnier in two gulps to try to cloak my anxiety. The appearance of both John and Lillian is bizarre and has me more than a little unnerved.

Polly doesn't help when she leans in and says, "I can see John coming to talk business with Tommy, but not at this hour and certainly not with Lillian tagging along. That's kind of strange, don't you think?"

I just nod and shrug, trying to appear nonchalant while my insides are in panic mode. My first thought is, who says Lillian is doing the "tagging"?

A half-hour later, everyone in our little family at The House has gone home, with Chris, Bruno and me the only ones remaining. Bruno says goodnight and stands to leave, and Chris says he'll walk me to my car. I have no choice but to go with him, as I can't think of an excuse to stay that wouldn't reveal our secret. It appears I'll be staying at my apartment tonight and not Tommy's. I didn't think I could become any more depressed, but now I feel worse, as I'll be spending the night alone.

The three of us walk across the parking lot and Bruno finds his car and waves as he pulls out of his parking spot. I always park under the light pole, as it's safer. At my car door, I turn to thank Chris. I get halfway through "See you tomorrow" when he grasps me in a way I can't escape from, as I'm up against my car's sheet metal, and he kisses me. It takes a moment, and requires considerable strength, before I can push him away. I'm speechless. He goes to say something, still holding me in his arms, when I see Tommy, Lillian and John standing on the top of The House steps—staring at us.

All three have seen Chris kissing me, and I gasp as I pull back from him, which to our onlookers can't appear as if I'm trying to get away at all. But, thank God, Chris is not persistent and says goodnight to me—as if this was expected—and I'm relieved with the result. Then to add insult to injury, when he spots John, Lillian and Tommy still on the steps, he waves to them.

Tommy pushes back his tuxedo jacket and buries his hands in his trouser pockets. John descends the steps but Lillian lingers, a wide smile filling the miserable wretch's face. "It looks as if you have competition, Tommy Boy," she says triumphantly. "Seems we don't have a problem now, do we? What goes around comes around. Now you know how it feels." She chucks him under the chin and he snaps his head away from her, his face grim.

Their car is parked right at the entrance, and a driver holds the limo door open for Lillian and then John. They are swallowed by the dark road as they leave, tires throwing off pebbles as the car speeds off.

Tommy and I are now alone, and he stands across the parking lot, glaring at me. I slowly walk toward him and say, "Tommy, I'm so sorry. Chris just caught me off guard and kissed me. It surprised me. I didn't kiss him back. I didn't want him to kiss me. I—"

"Don't say anything," he tells me as I stand next to him, his face expressionless, like stone. I'm ready to get on my knees and beg to make him understand what happened. "I'm so sorry. I promise, it's not—"

He breaks into a crazy laugh and swings me in his arms. "No need to be sorry, Kitten, you may have just saved our lives."

Chapter 19

"WHAT IN HELL IS going on?" I ask at Tommy, who is scratching the bridge of his nose and still laughing. "You just caught Chris kissing me and you think it's hilarious? I'm ready to prostrate myself and plead your forgiveness, and you think this is funny?"

"My sweet Kitty, go park your car out back and come inside. I'll explain everything." He starts to laugh again, which is really starting to annoy me. "You could not have planned a kiss any better. It was fated, and I mean it."

I park the car under a now familiar tree out back, trudge up the steps to his apartment, change out of my work clothes, and seat myself at the kitchen table. He pours out two cups of coffee he's just brewed. "First of all," he says, looking ridiculously upbeat, "I'm not the least bit worried about you and Chris. I know you love me, and I've watched you handle a hundred men over the years. I'm sure Chris will be shown the light in your good time." He laughs again. "You and I know that kiss was going to happen at some point. It just occurred at the most perfect possible moment."

"What is all this about, Tom? Why on earth were John and Lillian here together to talk to you?"

He stares at his coffee cup for a moment. "Here's the deal. I told you that breaking up with Lillian had a connection with Vassar, through the work I do for both of them. John came to make sure I was going to continue to work for him. Lillian came to threaten me to stop seeing you.

So they both had motivation." He smiles, but I don't find a thing funny about what he's saying. "They both want me to go through with John's plans for me in Italy. They're very concerned that I might share sensitive information regarding their enterprise with you, and they want to be assured this will never happen. So they want me to dump you and go to Italy as soon as possible."

"And if you refuse?"

"Well, let's just say they will try harder to convince me. And now he's offered me a lot of money if I take him up on his offer."

"Oh dear God," I half whisper. "This is insane. What do you do for John and Lillian? And I want the truth. All of it."

"I handle transactions."

"What's that supposed to mean?"

"I pick up and make deliveries."

"So, you're a drop guy for drugs," I say with disgust.

"That's called a mule, but I'm not one of those, I assure you. The packages are much too small to be drugs. But I honestly don't know what I'm carrying around, nor do I want to know. I just pick up and deliver papers now and then. I do what I'm told, and I don't peek. I'm convinced that Vassar believes I'm straight with him, and always have been, but Lillian wants you out of the picture and persuaded him somehow to play a little hard ball with me. I half expected this."

"What happened tonight?"

"I gave them three little words: 'Go fuck yourselves.'"

"Oh, shit, we could in big trouble. You said once that we could be in danger. I thought you were being dramatic, but now it seems I underestimated what you said. We could be killed."

"Take it easy, Kitten." Tommy stands and pulls me up to him and takes me in his arms. "I probably was being overly dramatic. Vassar doesn't want blood on his hands. A lot of people in New York City know I work for John. If it got out that he got rid of me, he'd have a hard time keeping his operation together because no one would work for him in the way I do. I might be wrong, but what happened tonight feels more like

Lillian's revenge over our breakup, and she got Vassar to come along to bolster her plan. Anyway, when they walked out and saw you in the arms of another man, that took care of the problem. She knows there's no way I could have set that up. She assumes the guy is someone you're cheating on me with. I love it."

"I'm still scared," I say in a small voice. "After all the time we spent together during those years at The Club and now here, I thought I knew you. But the truth is, I don't know shit about you. I'm not ready to play Mission Impossible. I already hung off a fire escape, and that's as far as I want to go with this adventure."

"Sweetheart, all of The Country Club business is behind me. I'm not at all rattled about this, and I don't want you to be either. I admit, I was worried in the very beginning, and the two goons he sent over here that night didn't exactly thrill me. But I'm convinced that Vassar is cool with my leaving. He just can't show that hand to Lillian, who is very controlling. He wants to placate her, that's all. Now that your infidelity has come to her attention, everything will settle down. I've assured John that his precious documents are safe, as I don't know anything about what I've been carrying back and forth. He believes me, I'm sure of it. However, this Italy thing is different, and I don't want any part of it. I told Lillian that at our breakup, and I told Vassar the same thing tonight. That should be the end of it."

"Those two men that were arguing with you were sent by John? I knew there was more to what you told me." I can't keep from crying. "I'm very confused."

Tommy holds me tighter. "I'm sorry I misled you about those two men, but I didn't want you to worry about something I couldn't begin to explain at that time. Look, Sweetheart, it's almost Christmas. The House is closed Christmas Day, and it's slow all week. What do you say we go away? It would put your mind at ease until all this passes. And this will pass, I assure you."

"When will we tell everyone about us?"

"I'll tell the staff tomorrow that I love my Katherine Cunningham and always have. We're going to spend all the Christmas holiday some-place away from The House as kind of a pre-honeymoon." This makes me smile and I feel my concerns vanishing. "So, who kisses better, me or Christopher Columbus?"

"A woman never kisses and tells, but I think you know the answer." I kiss him long and hard, certain I've left no doubt as to who I believe is superior.

We make flight reservations so we can visit my sister and her family, Christmas Day, in San Francisco. I haven't seen her in years and Tommy has never been to San Francisco, so we are both excited. I spend an hour on the phone with her and tell her all about Tommy and our love for each other, and she's over the moon with happiness for me. She's aware of the way I feel about relationships and is so relieved that I'm willing to give love another try. I can't wait for them to meet Tommy. However, I'm equally excited to finally let the cat out of the bag about Tommy and me for our House family. I keep imagining the looks on their faces.

Christmas Eve is busy from the moment the doors open and neither one of us has opportunity to say anything to anyone. Chris apologizes for embarrassing me but says he'll never be sorry for the kiss. I start to tell him that Tommy and I have been together secretly for weeks but get interrupted. I'm so rushed that I don't even have time to chat with Millie, but she is so taken with Ray, the businessman who has befriended her, that I make time to listen briefly.

The dinner rush is over and the lounge is settling down to a nice pace when Tommy comes in. He takes my hand and leads me out onto the little dance floor, and in a loud voice says he has an announcement. The room hushes. Polly and Jeannie come in and stand next to Millie, who has swiveled around on her barstool to face us. Bruno and Victor sense something happening and come side-by-side through the kitchen doors. I was hoping for not so much fanfare, and I tell Tommy this in a harsh whisper but he's not listening.

He takes the pink diamond dinner ring off his little finger and holds it up for everyone to see. "This ring was given to me by my mom when I was in high school. It's a coming of age thing, and we Italian men are big on wearing jewelry and the fact that it's a pink diamond made me defend my manhood in a hurry." There's light laughter through the room. "Over the years, I had the gold band enlarged to keep the ring growing with me. It means the world to me. But not as much as this woman standing here means to me." He gets down on one knee, and I'm quickly so flushed I'm ready to pass out.

"What the *hell* are you doing?" I say as I grit my teeth and snatch my hand away from him. *"Get up!"*

He takes my hand again, and I pull it away and say in a tense whisper, "Do you think this is wise under the recent circumstances?"

"So, I'm a risk taker. Sue me." He smiles up at me and I look sternly down at him. "Get up," I plead. "Please, get up. *Now.*"

The room is as quiet as the winter night. I see Chris across the room with one hand covering his mouth in an "Oh, no" expression. Polly and Jeannie are both a study in concentration, and Millie is stuck in mid-sip, which I'd thought only an earthquake would prevent her completing.

He places the ring on my finger. "No one will ever love you more than I. Will you marry me, Katherine Grace Cunningham?"

"*What?*" I squeal, ready to go into hysterics. "Have you completely gone over the edge? We can't get married. We're too…"

He looks at me under raised eyebrows, waiting for my thought to finish but loses his patience. "Too what?"

"Too married already. We fight and bicker all the time."

"Then we should be a natural fit. Anyway, it would put everything in perspective. Just think, it would stop Christopher Columbus, over there —" he jerks his head in Chris's direction—"from exploring your potential. Might be kind of fun being man and wife, don't you think?"

"Kind of fun? Do people get married because it might be 'kind of fun'?" I ask these questions rather amazed, as I'm reeling from embarrassment and anxiety.

He lowers his voice. "God knows, I can't possibly love you any more than I already do, Katherine. Say yes. Please say yes."

I've never heard him call me Katherine except for now and a moment ago. I start to shake all over. The long pause is starting to make the room rustle, and Polly calls out to me. "For Christ's sake, Kitty, stop looking like a mule chewing briars and tell him yes so we can all get back to running a restaurant."

Everyone laughs softly and I gaze lovingly at Tommy, putting aside all the issues I'm certain I'm going to be facing, and I say, "You're the single most important being in my life, so, yes, Thomas Anthony Defalco, I will marry you."

If there had been fireworks in the building the noise could not have been any more deafening. The few late diners get up to see who died or is in a fight. Millie is in tears and is hugging Ray. The staff is dancing around like young foals and the bar patrons are toasting up a storm. Tommy tells those who were eating to go back to enjoying their meal, as it will be comped because of the commotion he was responsible for creating. But when they are told the reason for the noise, they applaud and tell Tommy they wouldn't think of accepting his generosity, and one man says to buy the entire bar a round on him.

Chris sheepishly comes to Tommy with a hat-in-hand apology, and Tommy surprises him with a man hug. "No harm, no foul, Chris," he says and smiles my way.

I tell Chris I'm sorry if he thinks I led him on, but that I obviously had to keep the relationship a secret. He says he understands, but he hugs me and cups my chin in his hand so my eyes meet his and says, "Just know, Kitty, I will always be there for you if you ever need me. Always."

I didn't cry once when Tommy proposed or when I accepted, yet for some reason Chris's words bring tears to my eyes.

I'm relieved that we'll be far away when the news reaches Lillian, but I feel deep concern about the events that could transpire once we're home again. For right now, though, with the man I love holding me close and all The House family wishing Tommy and me well, I'm as happy, as Polly would say, "as a three-peckered goat."

Christmas morning is glorious. The sun streams into Tommy's apartment in wide golden rays and warms the chilly air. I lie in his bed, safe and snug, and admire his ring. I had to wrap the band with thin strips of adhesive tape in order for it to stay in one place, just like I did for my high-school sweetheart's in what now seems another lifetime. And, in truth, it was.

There's classical Christmas music playing, and the smell of bacon and coffee playfully tugs at my senses. I get up to find a little trail of cranberries running from the bed through the kitchen and out the door.

Mr. Bug comes in and dances around, excited that I'm awake, then bolts downstairs.

I throw on my bunny slippers, which I'd brought from my place, and Tommy's pajamas, and creep down the stairs, following the cranberry trail into the dining room. The entire area is brilliant with sunshine. How beautiful The House is at this hour, and we are the only ones who are here to witness it.

The Christmas tree is glowing. By the far window, in the brilliant sunlight, a table is set with The House's finest dinnerware. I casually stroll into the kitchen, where Tommy is cooking bacon on Bruno's stove.

"Well, Mr. Galloping Gourmet, the maid wants to know what you're cooking up for breakfast," I tease him.

"Aw, shucks, I wanted to surprise you and now you found out."

I wrap my arms around him. "How beautiful this morning is. And a cranberry trail. How very creative."

"Yes, and I better gather them up and get them back in the fridge or Bruno, in his exact words, 'will cut my balls off.'"

I cringe. "We wouldn't want that now, would we?"

We have a sensational breakfast of grapefruit, bacon, eggs and toast, with cinnamon thingies, as Jeannie calls them, left over from the night before. We make a plate for Mr. Bug and give him a Christmas stocking with all sorts of doggie toys. He takes off running through The House, squeaking a rubber candy cane.

"Look at this place, Tommy, what an exquisite private house this could be," I say and sigh. "Living here would be wonderful. We'd have a nice pool outside, and the lounge would be a great dining room off the kitchen, which could turn into a brass and brick showplace. This room would be a fabulous family room, sunny and warm. Since you're a part owner, maybe you and Troy will build on and expand the restaurant so we could have all of this. Who knows what the future will bring?"

He smiles at my vivid imagination and stretches. "What time is our flight again?"

I begin clearing the table. "Three thirty-five, so we've got plenty of time. But we'd better get a move on because the airport's a two-hour drive and I have to pack yet at my place."

In an hour Tommy has his suitcase ready and at the door. The phone rings just as we're leaving. Tommy is carrying his luggage and a bag of mine, so I cheerfully pick up the call.

As I answer, "Hello," I'm met with, "Hello, Kitty."

My blood virtually turns to ice water. I look at Tommy and mouth: "Lillian." I hit the speaker key and her voice slips like poison gas across the room to Tommy.

"It certainly didn't take you two long to kiss and make up. News travels fast in these parts."

My voice is flat. "What do you want, Lillian?"

"I know this is awkward, but I'm just calling to say congratulations to you and Tom. I know that some things are just supposed to happen in life. I've been behaving badly and John has me on the rack for it, so I'm calling to apologize to you both. I always knew you two were destined to be together. I want you to know that I harbor no hard feelings and wish you well."

I try to hide my surprise and say in an even tone "Thank you, Lillian. I appreciate that, and I know Tommy does too." Tommy's face is a mixture of shock and distrust. He stands frozen in the doorway.

"Is Tommy there? Do you think I could I speak with him?"

Tommy emphatically shakes his head no.

"He's outside, putting some bags in the car. I don't believe he's coming back up. We're going away for a few days. Actually, I was just out the door myself." Tommy sinks against the doorjamb, his relief evident. There's a strained silence on Lillian's end of the line that makes me uncomfortable.

"Then I won't keep you," she says after the long pause. "Have a good time. Oh, and Kitty, please tell Tommy that I'm still here for all his needs. He'll know what that means. It's not the first time we broke up, and he always comes back to me. I have something that holds him that you will never have."

My blood pressure spikes. "You passive/aggressive bitch," I yell into the receiver. "*You* are there for his needs? If anyone cares for Tommy's needs, it's me. How dare you even suppose that Tommy needs you for any reason? I'm disgusted with myself for giving you the benefit of the doubt. How could I be so gullible as to think you were actually wishing us well?"

"I told you before, you will never have him, and I meant it. Haven't you ever wondered why it is always me he returns to time after time?"

Tommy drops the bags and charges across the room, pressing off the speaker and grabbing the phone. His face is dark with rage. "Let's get one thing straight, Lillian, I'm through with you. Kitty is all I'll ever want and need now until the day I die. Now leave us the hell alone, and don't ever call here again. And, Lillian, don't ever underestimate me."

He hangs up the phone and matches the angry concern in my eyes.

"Shit!" he says, half under his breath. I see a hint of fear in his eyes that chills me. I'm having serious doubts about the assurance he gave me that this will all take care of itself.

I glare at him. "What's going on? What did she mean by her taking care of your needs?"

"Jesus, how the hell do I know. She's wounded, hurting, and talking crazy. She won't bother us again, I promise." He kisses me and then says sternly, "Kitten, when we close this apartment door, we close it on that phone call and any memory of Lillian, John Vassar and The Country Club business forever. Everything is okay with Vassar and me. Lillian is just all talk. We're starting the first day of the rest of our lives together, as corny as that sounds. But it's true, and I don't want anything to spoil this day. Now, we're leaving, and shut the door tight after me."

I do this and hear the lock catch, but I can't shake the feeling of Lillian's presence, as if she's right behind me.

Chapter 20

WE TELL MR. BUG that he's going to stay with Jeannie just as we approach her house, and he does his happy snuffle dance all the way to her door, racing up to her porch with his rubber Christmas candy cane present in his mouth. He unequivocally cherishes Jeannie. I honestly don't think he'll miss us at all.

We arrive early at the airport and spend time looking in the windows of the shops. We find a stained-glass panel in one of the gift shops with the Irish blessing on it and buy it for Molly and Dan. Tommy picks out a fairy costume for Shannon, my beautiful little niece I've told him about, and I buy her a set of Golden Books. I'm surprised there's someone in the store to wrap everything in holiday paper.

After a hearty lunch we find our gate and wait for our flight to be called. While waiting to board, two men, wearing identical dark-gray suits, stand near us. I smile at the one closest to me and wish him a Merry Christmas, and when he looks directly at me I wish I hadn't said anything. His eyes are like deep holes, he doesn't respond to my joyful greeting, and I am filled with the sort of fear a child might develop; the one that has no foundation, only that it's present. I don't want to bother Tommy with my juvenility, but I press closer to him and take hold of his hand.

"Are you okay?" he asks.

"It's nothing. Just always a little nervous before I get on a plane."

"You sure that's all? Your face is white as a sheet."

I look around and don't see the men anywhere.

"It's … there was a man who frightened me a little when he looked at me. It was weird. He gave me the creeps."

"You're in an airport. Half the people look weird." Tommy laughs and our line starts to move. When we hand the gate attendant our boarding passes, he runs them through a machine but then pulls us aside and smiles, handing us both new passes that indicate first class seating; a Christmas present from Molly and Dan, I presume. But as we're walking down the covered walkway to the plane, I become curious.

"Tommy, you didn't tell anyone where we are going, did you?" I ask as we board the plane and a flight attendant sees our boarding passes and asks to take our coats.

"No. No one knows. You must have." I tell him only Dan and Molly, and he kisses me.

I have the eerie feeling that I'm going to see that scary man and his "partner" again, but to my relief they are nowhere around and the plane is much too large for me to check up and down the aisles, as it a wide-body jet that I was told holds 300 or so passengers. As for First Class, I have a window, with Tommy next to me, and then an aisle. He stretches out and grins. "We *so* deserve this."

We're offered drinks, and of course we ask for Grand Marnier. We're told there's no Grand Marnier but would we settle for a Bailey's, and the flight attendant even offers to warm it for us. We sip it and snuggle together, enjoying the whoosh of the engines as we trundle down the tarmac.

"I love to fly." I tell him dreamily.

"Thought you were nervous?"

"Only in the airport before I get on the plane. I know, it's strange."

The flight attendant collects our glasses right before the big jet takes off, but she comes back once we reach cruising altitude with a bottle of champagne and asks if we'd like a glass. Of course we accept.

"To first class," I toast.

"How about to us forever?"

I nod and lean over and kiss him. "Merry Christmas, my love."

The champagne, a full meal I am not expecting or we certainly would not have eaten at the airport, the muted lighting, and the purring of the engines put us both to sleep. I don't awake until the announcement to put our tray tables and seatbacks in the locked, upright position, and I have to elbow Tommy hard to get him to wake up.

We are just entering the waiting area in the main terminal when I spy Molly jumping up and down and clapping her hands and waving, her thick red hair, which is lighter than mine, bouncing wildly on her shoulders. Dan is standing behind her, smiling, holding Shannon in his arms.

"Let me guess," Tommy says and throws his arm around my neck as we walk.

When we get closer, Molly flies at me and runs into my arms.

"Kath, I'm so excited to see you," she squeals. "It's been so many years. You look wonderful!"

"Molly, meet the love of my life, Tommy Defalco." She throws her arms around him. "I'm so glad to meet you, Tom. Welcome."

She introduces Dan to Tommy, and they shake hands heartily. I give Dan a giant hug.

"And this," Dan beams, "is our Shannon. Can you say 'Hello' to your Aunt Kathy and Uncle Tom?"

Tommy blushes and whispers to me, "I'm an uncle?"

"You are for now at least."

He approaches Shannon and says, "You are *amazingly* beautiful, do you know that?" Shannon hides her face in her father's neck and peeks out at Tommy.

"She's really shy with strangers," Molly tells him.

Tommy reaches into his pocket and produces a tiny stuffed pug dog and says to her, "I have a little dog just like this at home, named Mr. Bug. Would you like to have this one?"

Shannon's face lights up and she reaches immediately for the toy, giving it a wide strawberry-mouthed smile. Tommy flashes his signature grin and gently tousles her deep red hair. He's in love.

"When did you get that?" I ask.

"At the airport, before we left."

"How thoughtful. Gee, I didn't know you had this sweet side."

"You don't know everything about me."

You got that right. But right now I like this part—very much.

Dan says, "Tom, I think you have made a fast friend with our Shannon, and that's not an easy thing to do."

I tell Molly how much Shannon has grown since her last picture, and how pretty she is.

"She has your hair, Kath, thank God, and not my unruly carrot top." Molly giggles.

We walk together to Baggage Claim, Dan and Tommy ahead of us, sharing a laugh. My sister and I link arms and chat, falling fairly far behind on purpose. I'm positive Molly's dying to say something about Tommy he can't hear, and she doesn't disappoint: "He's drop dead gorgeous, Sis, and seems so easy to know. You said he was a Marine, and I can see that. He's got that marine roll when he walks. Such presence— and that smile. Look at him up there with Dan. Tsk, I'm so happy for you. You deserve a good man in your life."

"Finally?"

"Come on. I didn't say that. You know what I mean." She cracks a big smile. "Mom and Dad would pop a gut that he isn't Irish, but I think they would approve of anyone who could settle you down." She gives me a squeeze and a chuckle. "Is he Catholic?"

I give her a look. "Are you kidding? He's Italian. Aren't they all?" She nods as if everything is now well in the world.

It being Christmas, the Baggage Claim area is exceedingly crowded, with one announcement after another coming over the speakers. When there isn't a distinct voice telling someone to find this person or that item here or there, "Hey Jude" is playing softly. Tommy starts to bob his head and sway along to the music.

"If you start dancing in here, I'll kill you," I tell him.

Before he can reply, Shannon reaches out to Tommy to be held by him.

Dan gives his daughter an "Are you sure?" look, but hands her to Tommy, who starts to dance around and calmly sing to her.

"She has never done that before with anyone." Molly says.

"This is simply amazing!" Dan exclaims and chuckles.

By the end of the song, the "daaa, da da dadada da, Heyyyy Jude" part, Shannon is squealing with laughter and mouthing "da das" along with Tommy.

"Kath, is he always like this?" Molly asks, wide-eyed.

I burst out laughing. "You have no idea."

"They really have a connection," Molly says to me as Dan reclaims his daughter.

"Actually, I'm not surprised," I tell my sister. "He acts pretty much the same age as Shannon most of the time." She cracks up.

We wait on the curb with our luggage while Dan scouts out his car, and off to my left I spot the two men in suits that I saw before we boarded. They are no more than ten feet away, lurking it seems. They carry no bags, not even briefcases. I glance away before either man can catch me analyzing them, but the one man who scared me looks my way just as I turn away. He raises such fear in me that I get goose bumps. I try to position myself between Molly and Tommy so I can get a fresh look at both their faces, but there is always someone between us or they move around just enough so I can't see either man clearly. Dan arrives and we all pile into his car and he steers us out into traffic. I glance backwards, out the rear window, and the men are once again nowhere to be seen.

I wait until now to mention the upgrade to First-Class, and Molly says it was the least she could do for me and for Shannon's new uncle. I sigh a silent sigh of relief at learning for certain that it was Molly and not some smart-ass trick perpetrated by Lillian, which would mean she knew where we were traveling.

Molly and Dan have a beautiful two-story with a gable roof right in the heart of San Francisco, on one of those typically hilly streets the city is famous for. It's dark on the drive to their home, and Tommy is fascinated by the spectacle of the Golden Gate Bridge and its special lighting, which has been in full view on the latter part our ride from the airport.

Shannon, who's been sleeping, is now fully awake and insists on opening the presents we brought for her. Molly relents, and after some wild tearing of the wrapping she gives me a hug in thanks for the books, but when she opens Tommy's gift she squeals with delight and rushes to put on her fairy costume. We all melt as she models it, and she announces that she will never take it off. True to her word, she insists that she wear it to bed, without her wings, of course. She hugs Tommy tight around his neck and doesn't want to let go. I just smile at the two of them. Shannon and he are ridiculous fun.

After Shannon is settled down, Dan and Molly prepare a platter of cheese and fruit and open a bottle of wine. They explain that they don't often drink, but since this is a festive occasion they will share a glass with us to toast our happiness. We sit in their living room, in front of a picture-perfect fire Dan proudly lit and nursed along. A rather wide Christmas tree graces one corner of the spacious room, an assortment of Shannon-opened gifts spread beneath it. A very old grandfather clock, an obvious antique, stands guardian to the left of the tree. The room is filled with many other antiques, all elegant but user-friendly. A massive oriental rug pulls everything together in its homey embrace. It is a room that instantly bespeaks comfort, family, memories, and understated affluence.

Tomorrow, Dan will go off to work, but Molly and Shannon have promised us a marvelous tour of the city. We chat a short while longer when Tommy and I hit the wall at the same time. The wine, the food, the fire and the recent days of adrenaline-filled events have us doing a classic crash and burn. Dan gets to his feet, pulling Molly up with him.

"Come on, wife, you have all day tomorrow to talk their ears off. But right now these poor souls need to retire. It's nearly three in the morning, their time."

We're shown to our room and told where the extra towels can be found, as well as more bed covers should we need them. I hear Tommy snoring within two minutes of his crawling under the covers, and I'm soon following him into deep sleep.

Chapter 21

THE GUEST BEDROOM IS quite private, as it's right off the living room, while Dan and Molly's bedroom is upstairs and just down the hall from Shannon's nursery. Our room has its own full bath, so we don't need to venture outside for anything. Of course I assume the door is locked, as Tommy would have done this last night.

However, I awake in the morning to discover Shannon sitting on Tommy's chest, patting his face. He opens his eyes sleepily and blinks at her.

"Hi, fairy princess," he says groggily, creasing his brow to focus his bloodshot eyes on her.

"Uncle Tommy, where were you just now?" she asks as angelically as she looks.

"Just now, Sweetie?" He gives me a puzzled arch of his brow.

"Yes, when your eyes were closed and you were inside. Where did you go, Uncle Tommy?"

He puts a finger on her nose. "I was dancing with this beautiful little red-headed girl." They smile at each other.

She puts her hands to his cheeks and declares proudly, "That was me, silly." Then she proceeds to curl up next to him. He gives me a look that screams, "Now what?" I smother my laughter into a pillow.

Molly comes rushing in. "Oh, my. I am so sorry, you two. Jesus, Mary and Joseph! Shannon, you come right here, right now. Let Aunt Kathy and Uncle Tommy sleep a little bit longer. I already have cereal and berries in the bowl for you." Molly blushes a deep crimson. "Sorry, sorry … ah, go back to sleep."

Tommy says it's his fault for not locking the door. They leave and he admits what I'm keenly aware of, saying, "That could have been disastrous."

I nod. "She's an angel, isn't she?"

"She's beyond adorable." He reaches over and grasps me by the waist and turns me to him. "She looks as if she could belong to you. The hair, those eyes. I think she looks more like you than Molly."

"I assure you, she's not mine." I snuggle under his arm.

"Do you ever regret not getting married earlier and having kids that beautiful?" His question doesn't surprise me as much as the faraway gaze he's giving me. Most men would ask this lovingly but Tommy's interest seems purely informational, so I decide to give him just that.

"I've never been particularly maternal. I do love kids, but I just never thought I'd be patient enough to be good at raising them. Molly was always the motherly one. I wanted adventure on the high seas—to be a pirate wench, that was my idea of romance."

Tommy checks to make certain the door is locked, and we welcome in the day after Christmas in grand style.

Molly has prepared a huge breakfast for us. A mixture of classical music and Christmas songs plays throughout the home, as there are speakers hidden everywhere it seems. We were so tired last night we did not notice just how much Christmas is all around us.

Over my coffee cup I reminisce with my sister. "This brings back so many happy memories of our Christmases as kids. We had a great life, growing up."

"Yeah," Molly says after pausing for a moment, "a happy childhood until you were sixteen and decided to end the war and save the world. Then our war broke out around the house. I was so afraid when you and dad would fight. He would throw you out, and Mom would go and bring you back. Those were terrible days for me."

"They were terrible for a lot of people back then. But then my real hippie days began, and these were fun times. Love, music, gatherings, dancing in the streets, freedom fighting for a cause. The whole idea of countering hatred with love was a divine concept."

"Sure was," Molly says, shaking her head, "drugs and more drugs, people rioting, idiots staring at the sun and frying their eyeballs. LSD overdoses, kids living on the streets and getting raped and killed. I was worried about you all the time, Kath."

I smile sadly. "We all have to write our own book. Mine was *War and Peace* from a different perspective."

"And mine was *Rebecca of Sunnybrook Farm*, fair or not."

From my spot at the table in the kitchen, I watch Tommy and Shannon interact with each other in the living room. True to her word of *never* removing it, my niece is still dressed in her fairy costume, and she is conducting a tea party. Well, not quite. Tommy's acting as her private maître d', pouring ginger ale into a champagne flute that I have a suspicion is plastic.

"I thought we left work behind for a few days," I call out to him.

"Milady over here is at The Plaza with me, and she has an extremely important luncheon date with Sir Oliver, who's sitting over there." He gestures to a yellow bear placed across from them at a child's table. "She demands the utmost in service. And, besides, this is a lot better than being her pony." Tommy pretends to rub his back.

Molly props her chin up with on hand and says, "Oh, Kath, Tom is wonderful. Almost too good to be true."

"And sometimes it scares me greatly. As long as I have known him, he has always been kind, concerned, loving and fun. But he has a flipside that he can turn on in an instant. He has a horrible temper, likes to fight, and he's a mega control freak. He's also an impulsive dreamer with no eye toward the future."

My sister looks at me lovingly and takes my hand. "Gee, I know someone just like that Kath, your life together is going to be very interesting."

I help with the dishes, and Tommy and I set out with her and Shannon for our tour.

Tommy stares into the morning fog. "It's a shame it's not a better day," he complains gently. "This fog is pretty thick."

Molly laughs. "Welcome to 'The City.' That's what everyone calls San Francisco. The fog rolls in every morning like this. Then the sun breaks through, and most of the time a glorious day emerges. You get used to the daily weather routine."

My sister should have been a tour guide. From the moment we leave the house she expertly points out landmarks, tells their histories, shares stories about the places she loves the most, and fills us in on facts pertaining to The City that only a long-established resident knows.

We wander around the Japanese Tea Garden and visit Golden Gate Park across from the great bridge, which sparkles like a red ruby in the crisp winter sunshine. We go to Fisherman's Wharf, where Tommy buys us lunch at Scoma's, a restaurant my sister says is a must. She also informs us that we have to order the crab cocktail—there is no other option. Neither Tommy nor I can believe just how much crab is crammed into the large glasses this unbelievably fresh crab is served in, and we both agree it's the best appetizer we've ever eaten, going beyond even the specialty seafood appetizers we offer at The House. Of course, we don't have our own crab boat, as Tommy learns Scoma's sends out every day to guarantee the freshest possible catch. That night Dan and Molly take us to Powell Street, where we eat and party till the wee hours.

The next day, Molly takes us to more famous locations, including Mission Delores, Washington Square, and Alamos Square. Then we ride slowly down her personal favorite "tourist site," ogling "The Painted Ladies," the classic estate houses on incredibly elegant Steiner Street. Of course, I have to go to the Haight/Ashbury district, just because I remember it. But I'm disappointed, as it has changed unbelievably from just twenty years earlier. Instead of kids on every curb and street corner flashing peace signs and asking, "How's your head," the streets are clear and clean, with no cops on horseback, and the generally seedy storefronts are now replaced by expensive-looking condos. I didn't expect the mid-'70s, but I didn't expect the sanitized '90s either.

This is my only disappointment, if I can even call it that, during the entire time we're with Dan and Molly and Shannon. I hate to think about returning home, and when I broach the subject of our return flight, Molly says she'll pay for any fare change for our airline tickets if we can stay just a couple of days longer. She wants us to go off alone on the Silverado Trail and explore the famous wineries of the Napa Valley. She explains that it's an incredibly beautiful trip, and one that we'd have a natural interest in because of the restaurant business. Tommy needs no encouragement, but I harp about the hassle and cost of renting a car. Molly eliminates that issue, tossing Tommy the keys to her BMW and saying, "Go, have fun."

The next morning, we start off with a little map Tommy picks up at a souvenir kiosk, and before long we are rolling smoothly along the two-lane Silverado Trail. By noon I've been spinning my head from side-to-side so much that my neck hurts. I ask Tommy to pull over so I can take a picture of a particularly stunning scene. "Look how beautiful this is. All these vineyard-draped hills bathing in a sea of sunshine. Phillip and Barry would love this."

"We'll ship them back a case of wine. God, I miss our friends. It'd be a blast to have them along."

"They're more than our friends. They're parts of us that make us whole. I can't imagine life without them?"

We spend the day floating between well-known wineries and their vineyards, sampling the grapes and of course the finished products. For us, it's truly a celebrity tour. We call Molly and ask if we can keep her car for another day, as we'd like to do more "exploring." She tells us she fully expected us to stay at least one night somewhere in Napa, and she asks me where I'm calling from. I tell her, and she wants me to give her the phone number. I provide it, and she says to stay put and she'll call me back. Ten minutes later she gives me the address of a nearby B&B and informs me that the room is paid for. What can I say?

Soon, Tommy and I are nestled in a lovely room overlooking a vineyard as nice as any we've seen. The night is crisp, the best cuddling weather on the planet. We buy a great bottle of wine and a cheese plate from a local store, and we eat and tire ourselves out enjoying each other until the wee hours.

The next morning and through early afternoon we stop at several more wineries. A couple aren't open to visitors at this time of year, but we sample a great wine at one, buy a bottle for dinner that night, and start back to The City. Before leaving, however, true to his word, Tommy buys a case of a lovely cabernet we tasted and has it shipped to The House, clearly earmarked for Phillip and Barry only and not for the public.

I call Molly to tell her we're coming "home," and she laughs and says for us to stay at least one more day in the Napa Valley. I thank her for her suggestion, but we've had enough driving around and Tommy says he needs to get back to the restaurant. I assure her we'll be back before dark, and we pull into her parking space in front of her house just as the sun is going down.

Before she opens the front door, the aroma of fresh-baked cookies, pies, and roast turkey fills my senses with reminders of the happiest of times when we were both little kids.

"Hi, you guys," she calls merrily from the kitchen. "Did you have fun?"

"It was fabulous," I say and hug her. "Even though we continuously embarrassed ourselves acting like gawking tourists, which we are."

Shannon runs to Tommy, who scoops her up and spins around with her.

"I thought we'd have an old-fashioned Christmas dinner for your last night here," Molly says. "After what you said, I figured I couldn't talk you into staying for another day, so I started on this right after I talked with you." Molly looks like she's about to burst into tears. "I wish you were staying, Kath. I miss you so much, and you aren't even gone." She wipes her eyes on her apron and composes herself. "Dan will be home soon, and we'll eat in about an hour, okay?"

Dan comes home, asks us to tell him all about our trip into wine country, which I thought a bit odd since he's not a drinker, and we sit around and chat until dinner. It's during the conversation that Dan lets it slip that he had been a heavy drinker, and now it all makes sense. With the Christmas meal spread out before us on a gorgeously laid-out table, we join hands. Molly then drops a bomb by asking Tommy if he would do the honor of saying Grace.

I freeze and glance over at Tommy, who appears somewhat panicked. I come to his rescue. "I can say Grace if you'd like."

"No, I'll gladly say it," Tommy says rather proudly. Now I don't know what to think, as he's made it clear to me that he's not a fan of religion. But he throws out his classic smile, albeit briefly, and bows his head.

I hold my breath, squeezing my eyes shut. I'm saying my own prayers when I hear in a resonant, even delivery: "Heavenly Father, we come together to give gratitude for this food and for the love that surrounds us on this precious day. Thank You, for Your protection and for our freedom from want. May this family always experience peace, health, abundance and joy in all ways, always. We ask this through your Son, Jesus Christ, Our Lord, in the name of the Father and the Son and the Holy Spirit. Amen."

We break hands and Molly bubbles, "That was beautiful, Tom."

"Yes, it was, thank you," says Dan.

Shannon squeals, "Let's eat!" and I give Tommy a look that screams, "Where in the world did *that* come from?" But I say instead, "That was amazing."

"I was an altar boy growing up in New York. I was quite angelic as a kid." He gives his head a little shake, which I don't know how to read.

"Really?" Molly asks. "What I mean is, did you ever consider the priesthood? You said Grace with such power and feeling. You'd have made a good priest."

My eyebrows deceive me and shoot up practically to my hairline, but Tommy surprises me further. "What Italian kid doesn't want to become a

190

priest?" He shrugs gently. "Even looked into the seminary while I was in high school."

"You did?" I question him, really blowing my cover now.

Tommy chuckles at me and says, "See, Katherine, you don't know everything about me."

"That's twice you have said those very words to me in three days," I say as the food's being passed around. "How many more surprises do you have in store for me?"

"What stopped you, Tom?" Dan asks as he's handed the biscuits. "It's a gift to be called."

"Girls." Tommy flashes a broad grin, reaches under the table and pinches me gently on the thigh. "Like my happily retired flower child here, who spent months singing and dancing with bells on at airports. Hare Krishna, Kitty."

Everyone laughs, and I'm realizing with each passing day how little I really know about this man. Eight years, and we've talked about virtually nothing of substance when I thought all of our discussions revealed something of the inner self of the other. Tommy's speeches were all window dressing.

I dismiss this one nettling issue, and the meal is simply wonderful, topped off with delectable desserts. I now fear gaining ten pounds on this trip. We all settle down with coffee, in front of the fire. Shannon, of course, sits close to Tommy. I'll have fond memories of everything about this visit—forever.

Our flight is at midmorning. Molly has to take Shannon in for a routine checkup at ten with the little girl's pediatrician, so we plan to take a taxi to the airport. Molly says she'll arrange this before she retires for the night, as she and Dan often use a particular service they've found reliable.

Tonight we say our final goodbyes, so it's a bittersweet evening. Shannon is especially sad—because Tommy is leaving—and she's asking him a hundred questions about where he's going and when he'll be back. She wants to sing and dance with him again, like at the airport. He assures her that the next time he sees her, this is the first thing they'll do no matter where they are.

"Okay, sweet Shannon, here's the deal."

"What's a deal?" she asks, studying his face.

"A deal is a sacred agreement between two people never to be broken. It's like a two-way promise that takes two people to uphold. Got it?" She nods happily. "So, the deal is, whenever we are together, and there's music playing, no matter where we are, or what we are doing at the time, we will dance. Deal?" He holds up his hand for a high five slap." Now, you say deal."

"Deal!" Shannon squeals and slaps his hand hard. He pretends it hurts and she takes his hand and presses it to her lips. "All better."

"Come Shannon, time for bed," Dan says.

She slides off Tommy's lap and gives him a pleading look.

"I'll be there shortly and we'll tell the moon goodnight." He softly tells her.

My eyes fill with tears. Maybe it was the compassion in his voice, or the love I feel for him, or being with my sister and what we did these past few days and realizing that all this will soon be a just fond memory.

Tommy holds out his arms to me, and I fall against him. With Molly at my other side, we sit huddled together on the sofa. Dan joins us and we chat for a while, then it's time to get up and say our heartfelt good-byes. Tommy runs upstairs to kiss Shannon goodnight and to tuck her in, and I pack away the last few items before getting ready for bed. We forgot to drink the bottle of wine Tommy brought so I leave it on the dresser with a note: "Many thanks. Enjoy this good wine, and a sister doesn't have to come for a visit to make for the right occasion. Love you both, Katherine."

Tommy comes in and shuts the door behind him. He looks entirely spent, so I ask if he's okay. He kicks off his shoes and says, "I have a headache, is all. Christ, I've never felt so tired."

Soon we fall onto the bed as one, and a few minutes later I'm fast asleep. I don't know what time it is when I roll over and find him not next to me. I get up on one elbow and look around the dark room. Only the nightlight is on in the bathroom, and its faint yellow hue offers little help with the shadows.

"Tommy?" I flip on the lamp in the nightstand to find Tommy wearing only his jeans, pacing the floor. I slip out of bed and pull the comforter around me.

I ask, "Sweetheart, what's wrong?" He's breathing heavily and pacing, hands on his hips, like a runner after a long a race. He paces continuously, his agony apparent. I see his wide smooth back glistening with sweat.

"Tommy, are you sick?" I reach out, touching him lightly. With the reflexes of a cat, he spins and slams me hard against the wall, his hand tight on my throat, I've never seen facial features as intense as his. I can't breathe. My eyes are bulging from their sockets. Then, as if returning from some other world, his expression softens into sorrow and he holds me to him and sobs. "Oh, Kitty, Oh, my dear Kitty. Oh, Baby, I'm so sorry."

We sink to our knees, and he grips my arms gently. He leans forward and buries his head in my lap and cries through his words, "Forgive me, I'm so sorry. I'm so sorry." I kiss the back of his head, which is soaked with perspiration.

Despite his violence, I'm filled with love and compassion. "What's happening? What can I do? You're shivering and you're soaked with sweat. Let me help you. I want to help you, Tommy. Just tell me what to do."

He says, "I'm okay now. It's all okay." He sits up and with trembling hands wipes his face. "Kit, there are three plastic pill bottles in my bag. Would you get me three of the white pills from the one?" I start to ask but he beats me to my question. "The bottles are clear and you'll see the whites."

I don't hesitate and find the three pill bottles, one containing only white pills. I get three and draw him a glass of water. He swallows the pills, ignoring the water. He remains on the floor, with his head on his knees, then his breathing slows and he stops shivering. I cover him with a blanket and gently stroke his back.

"I didn't mean to frighten you," he says after a few minutes of silence by both of us.

I look for medication information on each of the bottles. But no labels are affixed, not even each drug's name. "What are those pills for?"

"They help me forget." He reaches for me "I haven't had a dream like that in a long time. I can generally deal with those times in Nam without a problem, but when the memories come back with the smells and sounds and screams as if they're real, I can't handle that." The lines in his face are the deepest I've ever seen them.

"You've been under tremendous stress lately. You're emotionally exhausted. I know that and you know that." I take his face in my hands. "Tom, I love you. There's no road you can go down that I won't be traveling right there with you. But you've got to let me help you."

"This is what I love about you. You're tough—unflappable, even. There's nothing you can't handle. I never see you come unglued. Not when it mattered." He sighs, caressing my arms, his face knotted in deep thought. "I've told you many times, I was pretty fucked up when I came back from Nam. I spent some time shaking out the drugs in rehab. But that's not all of why I was in rehab. There's more. A lot more."

"You told me many things about Nam, so I probably know most of it. We're both exhausted. Let's get some sleep and talk about it tomorrow."

"No, not tomorrow. Now." His tone is remarkably calm. "There are some things you need to know about me that I haven't told you."

I can see I have no choice but to listen to what he wants to say. "Okay, tell me."

"The Marines train us to become highly efficient killing machines. That's what we are when they send us out. It's what makes Marines different. Some of us handle it while others can't. And a few of us revel in that freedom."

"Freedom to do what?"

"My division was known as one of the toughest units, and we saw a lot of combat. Usually guys were rotated in and out so they didn't get a steady diet of action, but our unit just sort of fell through the cracks. It wasn't long before we had no feelings one way or the other about life or death. We were proficient at killing. Killing was a game for us—and we loved it. We killed for the adrenalin rush. And we had no fear of getting killed." He took a sip of the water I brought him earlier.

"We didn't have a clear picture of the enemy. Everyone looked the same, and we never knew who were the bad guys. And as time went by, we didn't care, because children, old women, the very people we helped in villages, would ambush us. We believed the enemy was everyone and everywhere."

"How awful." I whisper, knowing this was one of the reasons I protested this war so many years ago.

"When you kill so many people, they cease to be human beings and, after a while, they just become things. I had no compassion for anyone. Those dreams I still have at times won't let me forget the bad things I did." He faces me. "Kit, here's what you don't know. I spent a year in a mental hospital while the government tried to straighten out my head and get me back into the mainstream. But I was so angry that I had trouble distinguishing between right and wrong. It was a very strange time. They had me on so many pills that I couldn't function, so after I was released I quit the drugs and started to heal on my own. I had a need to connect with the rhythm of life and the beauty of movement, so I learned to dance. Believe it or not, I firmly believe it was music and dance that brought me back."

"Except I can see that the anger has never left you completely."

"No, the anger has never entirely left me, and that's why I'm a loose cannon sometimes." He kisses my temple. "I need to know what you are thinking."

I start slowly. "All I know is that wars change the people who fight in them. Wars push people to do the unthinkable. Bravery doesn't describe those facing combat. It defines those who try and regain their sanity when they come home. I protested the war because I didn't think that people should ever be subjected to what you had to deal with. I wish I had something more to say that would make it all better, but all I can offer is my complete support so you get through these flashbacks. I just hope they are few and far between, because you could have killed me tonight."

We sit in silence for a short while. Tommy then sighs and says, "I hardly ever think of Vietnam now, or about what happened there or who I was then. It seemed as if my life belonged to someone else. I'm not that person anymore. But every so often a vision will pop up that takes me back." He shakes his head hard. "I love you so much, Kitty. And I will never let what happened tonight ever take over my mind and body again. Please forgive me."

I study his handsome face, his kind eyes, and his soft lips. It is so hard for me to imagine him as the man he described. Yet I'm learning this is how it is with Tommy. I've sat up with him so many nights, sharing all sorts of trivia about our lives in the past eight years, but I have no clue as to what really makes him tick. And it is trivia, as nothing that really matters was ever discussed. There's a dark side of Tommy that simmers under the funny, kind man that I love, and I'm open to discovering all I can.

I remember the pictures I saw of him from Nam, this cocky young man sitting on a tank, smiling with his buddies, all armed with various weapons, all of them looking as relaxed as if they were sitting poolside without the slightest concern that the rice fields around them were littered with the bodies of whoever was caught in their line of fire.

But one picture of Tommy stands out foremost in my mind. It's a tattered Polaroid of him glancing over his shoulder. He's wearing that wide, immutable, captivating smile of his, but I notice his eyes, deep and compelling, dangerously intense and vivid, with restless fire and craziness in them, the same eyes I saw a half-hour ago and never want to see again.

Chapter 22

THE HOUSE IS QUIET as dawn peeks in the windows and washes the walls in faint watercolor tints of rose and gray. I kiss my sleeping bear awake, pushing last evening's disaster from my mind.

"I brought you coffee." I push the cup and saucer in his direction and he manages to grasp it without spilling. "You have forty-five minutes to shave and get it together. How are you feeling?"

"Tired, but well," he mutters. "I'm sorry about last night. Do you still love me?"

"More than ever." I kiss him. "I mean it, and you need never ask me that again. Now get up and drink your coffee."

Molly called last night for a private airport shuttle service to pick us up at seven, and I start to leave a note for her in the kitchen as I'm waiting for Tommy, but she swishes in behind me for a last goodbye.

I hear a vehicle stop in front, and Molly looks out the window and says it's our shuttle. I want to cry, as seeing her standing in her plaid bathrobe and waving from the front door is exactly the way she looked when we were little girls. Sometimes I hate that time has passed, and this is one of those instances. I wish we were eight and six again. I stop before boarding the limo-style bus, while the driver is loading our bags in back, and blow her a kiss. My cheeks are already streaked with tears. I pantomime to her, "I miss you already," and she does the same.

The driver asks what airline we're flying out on. He nods and says it'll be a quick trip because he has just one more stop on the way.

The shuttle is empty except for three men. One man, in athletic wear of sorts, sits directly behind the driver, while two businessmen sit opposite each other in the middle section of the bus, which by my count could seat eleven. We choose seats at the very rear so our conversation won't bother anyone—and vice versa.

I look out the window at the shops and homes we pass by. The city streets seem sleepy. There's some movement, but almost everything appears sluggish at this early hour. The bus makes a series of turns and growls up and down ridiculously hilly streets as it grinds its way to the final pickup. The man in the front gets up and walks toward us. He's tall and dark, his face half-hidden inside his hooded sweatshirt. The two businessmen open newspapers, but each turns in our direction and I see them looking over the top of the pages. The air is suddenly charged with high anxiety. I clutch Tommy's hand but he doesn't respond. We sit still, and I'm trying to keep from breathing too loud. Something is happening or is going to happen, and I sense it revolves around us.

Everything that unfolds next takes place within a few seconds. I see the faces of the two businessmen, and I'm terrified to recognize the one with the black bottomless eyes.

He fixes a stare on me and stands, reaching around the back of his jacket. Fear grips my throat, and I am paralyzed. Tommy slowly positions his feet and tightens his hold on my hand. Up ahead, as if a miracle, I see flashing lights. A traffic accident at the corner forces the driver to slow the bus almost to a stop. With lightning speed, Tommy lifts the latch to the emergency exit, which is right next to him. It swings open just as the bus makes a sharp turn up a side street. It's enough to throw the hooded man slightly off balance, but he's able to reach into a pouch in the front of his sweatshirt. We don't wait around to find out what for.

We bolt from the bus and run to the accident scene, surprising the first officer we come upon. We tell him what happened and he radios his dispatcher. The bus is not in sight. My adrenaline is causing me to want to scream. I have no idea what just happened, and my first tangible thought is that we've lost our luggage.

In less than a minute a police cruiser literally flies to a stop in front of us. Tommy tells two policemen what happened, that we felt we were the target of impending danger, and fled the shuttle. I'm more practical, saying we have a flight to catch and have now lost our bags with our tickets and boarding passes. One officer gets on his radio and soon assures us that the police are tracking the vehicle. He could not be nicer, and Tommy finds out that he lived for a time in Queens and had been a rookie cop there. This policeman's light conversation helps settle me down. He gets a call on his car radio and walks over to his vehicle.

"Okay, you guys," he begins as he comes back to us. "We found the shuttle. The driver stopped not long after you opened the door and split. We have a report that a man was taken into custody, but I don't know why, and that's all I can tell you. I need a full description of everyone who was there, and exactly what happened. I'll file a report since you don't have time to go to the precinct. One of my guys will be here to take you to your flight, and he has your bags with him. Welcome to San Francisco." He guffaws. "You think New York City is bad? Stay here another week and see. It's just plain lucky this little fender bender happened when and where it did. Might have saved your lives."

I say out of the side of my mouth, "I don't mean to be inquisitive, officer, but I thought you said you didn't know why the guy was arrested?"

He says nothing more, just gives me an "I said more than I should have" shrug.

Tommy and I spend fifteen minutes answering questions and telling him every detail, right down to those terrible dark eyes, and soon we are zooming along in the back of a police car toward the San Francisco Airport. We buzz through the airport and make our plane with plenty of time to spare. No early drinks this time, and only when the plane finally levels off do Tommy and I start to talk.

He says over and over that we actually didn't see anything, no intent, no weapon, just a man changing seats. The other men were reading the paper and one got up to stretch. He contends that maybe my imagination got the best of me regarding the guy with the hideous eyes, as I called them, and I protest strongly.

"That man with those eyes was on that shuttle with us. And I saw both men up and moving the instant before we jumped off that bus. Something was definitely going on, and that guy coming toward us wasn't going to ask for the time. They were all out to get us. I'm sure of it."

"Kitty, stop it. Those two guys were probably catching the same early flight. It's a wild coincidence, I know, but it could be. And when we flew off that shuttle like we did, they were understandably alarmed and instinctively stood up. That's how I see it. Granted, I do think that hooded guy was maybe going to try to roll us. With only two other people on the bus, at that hour of the morning, he figured he'd hit us then go out that same door we exited from. Hell, in New York City people get robbed and even raped in crowded subways."

"You think I'm hallucinating or something?" I shift away from him, closer to the window.

"No, I don't think anything of the sort. But you are unnerved. Hell, so am I. But the main thing is, we're okay. It would have been the hassle of a lifetime if we lost our bags and missed this flight, not to mention spending all morning at the precinct picking men out of a lineup. All in all, it was pretty damn lucky the cops were in that area at that particular time." He gives me his look and I snuggle up next to him. He strokes my hair and comforts me, then tries to cheer me up.

"Do you realize, seemingly every time we're together in a big city, something like this happens? Maybe we're missing our calling. We should be super spies."

"Or stunt doubles."

This makes Tommy laugh, and I quiet down and look out at the clouds far below us. The vision of that man with the black eyes continues to haunt me. There is something about him that scares the crap out of me. My whole body prickles with fear when I think of him, as I see pure evil in his face.

* * *

We arrive to pick up Mr. Bug at Jeannie's in the afternoon, and she bounces around just as much as the little dog did at the sight of us. I laugh and tell her, "My God, we weren't even gone a week!"

"So, did everything go smoothly?" Tommy asks. "We ended up staying two days longer than we'd initially planned, but I called Troy and he said there was no problem. I got it that I could have stayed out for a month."

"Maybe *you* could have, but not Miss Kitty."

"That's what I thought," Tommy says and shakes his head.

"Victor and Bruno got into it Wednesday night, their normal 'Fuck you' fest." She laughs. "The bar backed up a little last night when Christine got into the weeds, but Chris jumped in and baled her out. They got it together, and all was soon okay in the kingdom."

"Chris is working out well, I take it?" Tommy says.

"Chris is working out well, especially with Polly." She giggles.

"Why does that not surprise me?" I say, giving Tommy a poke.

We stop at my place so I can change into my tux for tonight, and Tommy flops down on my bed to talk about the New Year's Eve party at the House, which is just two days away. New Year's Eve is always a frantic night, and a late one. We don't host a formal party, but all of the regulars stay and make their own fun. We supply hats and noisemakers, and of course, Pauley, the piano player is doing his thing until one o'clock.

The staff at The House exchanges their bow ties and cummerbunds for silver-sparkled ones, and we provide free splits of champagne to every table. We also have cabs at the door to take people home. Nobody drinking so much as a drop we believe is too much will be allowed car keys, and that's a Deal that will not be broken. Roy's incident chiseled that in stone—and then some.

Tonight I'm welcomed back with all sorts of fanfare. The staff is already there, and after brief hellos and hugs Tommy takes his bags upstairs and dresses for work. I fill everyone in on our trip, especially about the excitement that morning on the airport shuttle. I tell Phillip about the wineries and vineyards and to expect a case of wine soon. What I of course don't tell him is that's it's just for him and Barry to enjoy.

I wander into the kitchen, where Bruno is trimming the meats and fish and Victor is doing the seasoning. I need to gather my fruit for the night, so I say to them as I open the refrigerator, "A little birdie told me that you children had a fight in the sandbox the other day."

Bruno, who's holding a meat cleaver, points with his chin at Victor. "He's an asshole."

"Up yours, Bruno." Victor says, not looking up from his garnish tray.

I laugh as I'm opening the cooler doors. "It's good to be back. I so missed these little intellectual conversations."

Tommy comes into the kitchen, and I have to stop what I'm doing and admire him. He's so handsome in his tux, and the first glance at him in that jacket always takes my breath away. He adjusts his sleeves as the swinging doors shut behind him. His eyes are riveted on me, and he's walking toward me like a man with a purpose. He grabs me and bends me back, kissing me passionately. My fruit goes flying.

"Jesus H. Christ Almighty," Bruno barks. "That's why we've had Deal Five all these years. Get out of my freakin' kitchen, you perverts, before I throw cold water on you both."

Victor is laughing so hard he has to turn from his tray and cover his mouth.

"Just working on another fantasy I've harbored inside me all these years," Tommy informs the two of them.

"Well, you just keep your damn fuck fantasies the hell out of my kitchen. I don't even want to think of the possibilities you two could get into around here. But, make no mistake about it, I will cut your balls if I find out about it."

"It's so good to be back," Tommy says.

"Somebody else you know just said that a couple of minutes ago," Victor says.

The night goes well, and Millie and I chat up a storm between my drink creations. I share everything with her, the call from Lillian before we left, how wonderful the visit was with my sister, how Tommy was full of surprises—both good; elaborating about Shannon, and bad; not elaborating about his almost choking me to death—and the excitement of the morning shuttle ride. She hangs on my every word, savoring her gin martinis. But she has an odd look about her as she nudges me into a more detailed conversation involving our shuttle "exit."

She says, "Kitty, dear, I'm a little confused about what happened on the limo or whatever it was you were riding. Was it the guy in the sweatshirt who threatened you or the businessman in the gray suit with the weird eyes?"

"I can't tell you," I reply as I place of couple of drinks on Jeannie's tray. "Everything happened so fast. The more I think about it, the guy in the sweatshirt was just changing seats. But that man in the business suit scared me to death." I then told Millie I'd seen him at the gate before we boarded and then after we landed, along with the same man who was with him both times. "The man with eyes that reminded me of death looked right at me and Tommy, and then reached around for what I have to believe was a weapon. Tommy has a different take. He says the guy in the sweatshirt was maybe looking to rob us, and the guy in the gray suit was just standing up to stretch and decided to scratch his back. Whatever, we weren't hurt."

"That's so frightening. I'm glad neither of those two men in the gray suits hurt you."

Mike comes to pick up Millie and she once again tells me how pleased she is that Tommy and I weren't harmed by the encounter in the shuttle. I thank her, but as I watch her hanging on Mike's arm as she walks out, it hits me that there's something off about what Millie said to me. I don't know what it is, but I'm sure I'll think of it later, and I pass it off to the fatigue I'm now feeling. The night wraps up nicely and the doors close at one sharp. We all gather in The Pit and kick off our shoes and relax.

Robert, who verges on being silly gay, swings over the back of the sofa and slides down to sit next to Phillip, who moves over a little to accommodate him.

"I have a problem, everybody, and I don't know what to do about it," Robert announces. "Wait till you hear this."

We all give him our undivided attention, since we know we're going to get a good laugh.

"I served a couple tonight who just got engaged. The guy wanted the ring put on the stem of a rose that I was to present to his Sheila with the dessert. You know, on one of those little tea roses that I place on the side of her ice cream thingy. Well, that's not important. Everything goes great, but when he leaves he touches my arm and makes a point of telling me that my tip is under the plate. Which is odd because he tipped me on a credit card. So I go back to the table and under his plate is this." He holds up a folded piece of paper, which he waves around.

"Christ, the anxiety's killing me," Polly hoots. "What the hell does it say, Sugar?"

Robert clears his throat in dramatic fashion and reads the note as if he's reporting the news. "'I think you're fabulous. Call me.' And here's his number."

Phillip slaps Robert's knee. "You go, boyfriend! Damn, that never happens to me."

"Be serious now. Whatever do you think this means?"

"He wants you—bad," Phillip says, taking a sip of wine.

"But ... but he just proposed to someone. And it was a ... female."

"You certain it was a woman?" Phillip quips.

"Looked like one." Robert looks away and knits his brow in confused thought. "But, gee, I don't know, do I?"

We're all giggling, and Polly taps her glass for order. "Now just wait a Dixie minute, y'all. Maybe he just wanted to tell you that the service was great and to call him so he could thank you over the phone. Or maybe he wants you to work an engagement party or even the wedding?"

"It's probably very sensible," Jeannie says. "I wouldn't hesitate to call him if I were you."

Phillip rubs his narrow chin and shakes his head. "What do you think, Tommy?"

"Oh, no, you don't. I'm not getting involved in this. Ask Chris, he's in charge now." Tommy gestures at Chris, who's sitting on a section of hearth that extends to the side of the fireplace. "See, Chris, this is the shit you have to put up with around here."

Robert is scratching his head, as if this is what he's supposed to do for effect. "What if I call and *she* answers? I can't just say, 'Your man left me a note to call him.'"

"No, that would not be a good idea, Robert," Chris says and laughs. "I have no idea what to tell you, except if a woman answers, hang up— and fast." Everyone laughs at that remark.

"As I think about this further, I would call," Phillip says. "I'd offer my professional services, and see what he says then. If he says, 'Yes, I want you to serve a party,' or whatever, then you know. Or if he says just, 'I want you,' then—" he rolls his eyes—"take a chance on an Indian blanket."

"Ah, I love this place." Jeannie says and roars along with the rest of us. Except for poor Robert, who looks as befuddled as ever.

"Oh, by the way," Christine says and chugs the last of a glass of beer, "She Who Does Not Dance came in for a drink a few nights ago."

I feel Tommy tense up beside me. He says, "What the hell, Christine, did you serve her?"

"This *is* still a public bar, isn't it?" She forces a laugh but then sees how serious Tommy is and continues with a straight face. "I didn't know exactly how you two parted. I mean, we all saw her here with Dr. Vassar the other night, so I assumed you two had smoked the peace pipe. She was fine. Seemed almost human, smiling and making small talk."

"Small talk with whom?" I ask. "Was Millie here?"

"No, Millie didn't come in all the time you were gone. Wow, did the atmosphere in this room just change or what? Did I say something wrong?" She takes a big swallow of her beer. "It all seemed very innocent. She asked about you guys and said she stopped in to wish you well, that she was worried Kitty might have misunderstood her motives."

I shake my head in disgust, not at Christine but at Lillian's continued deceit. I can see that Tommy's just as pissed as I am. He's rubbing his hands over his eyes, as if trying to wipe her away.

"Did she say anything else?" Tommy asks Christine.

"She said she didn't know you guys went away, asked if I knew where you went, which I didn't, wanted to know when you would be back, and I told her three days ago. I didn't know you were going to stay two extra days, wherever it was you went—"

"San Francisco," I tell Christine as well as everyone else, "to see my sister." I hand her another beer I just poured into a glass. "I know this has turned into an interrogation, but do you mind telling me whatever else you might remember she said?"

Christine takes a pull from her beer, the same as a man might. "Said she wanted to come by and work things out with you and Tommy. She didn't want any hard feelings and wanted to be friends with both of you."

I bristle, "Just for the record, Christine, I'm not a friend of Lillian's, and she *did* know we were away, just not where, so her visit here was with malicious intent, I can assure you."

"Well, it didn't smack of anything underhanded. She was genuinely nice. We had a normal conversation about business and Christmas and all that stuff. In all honesty, Kitty, I thought she was sincerely trying to make amends with you. There's nothing worse than a sudden breakup. But when the finality of it reality hits, most people try to get past the pain and get on with their lives. I thought she was really trying to make amends. Sorry."

I can't find fault with Christine for her ignorance, but I certainly can blame Lillian for continuing to weave her web of deceit. "There's no such thing as making amends with Lillian," I say with disgust. Tommy stands and raises his hand to take over for me.

"I know her all too well," he says, now in his usual stance as if making a Deal, "and she's a snake in every way. I'm counting on everyone here to respect our privacy and keep Lillian away from us. We ended badly, and she's still scheming. And it sounds like as much as ever."

Christine shakes her head. "I'm really sorry."

"We're not blaming you," Tommy assures her. I do the same, going over to her and whispering in her ear and giving her a big hug.

Polly rises from the sofa and faces Tommy and me, as we're standing next to one another. "Now that we're aware of the situation, y'all can count on us to dig the moat." She raises her fist high over her head. "One for all, and all for one. The battle lines are drawn.

The seriousness of the conversation puts a damper on further Pit activity, but it's getting late and we are all ready to break up anyway. Tommy and I collapse into bed, utterly exhausted both physically and emotionally. He kisses me softly and says nothing. I'm convinced he's very concerned about Lillian's visit here while we were gone. I am as well, now certain he grossly misjudged or misrepresented his assurance that everything would *pass*. I'm so tired I don't even remember saying goodnight, but along about dawn he awakens me and we make hard, passionate love like we have no tomorrows.

The next day we don't move until well after noon, and upon waking I know he hasn't let go of me all night, as the sheets are twisted around the two of us and we are virtually tied together as one.

Chapter 23

NEW YEAR'S EVE ARRIVES and The House staff and its patrons are rapt with anticipation. People have either finished their meal and are filing into the lounge to assure a good seat or they are virtually blown in by the frigid night to welcome in 1999.

Pauley appears at seven-thirty and bops over to my bar for a drink and a chat before he begins what will be his longest session of the year at The House. The mood is electric, and the night is already flying along. As always, when I'm this busy I lose track of time. Tommy comes to the bar for a round of drinks, and I see his Grand Marnier included, so I know he's been invited to sit at someone's table.

I miss Millie, but she and Dr. Vassar will be attending the party at The Country Club. She would rather be here at The House, especially if Lillian is over there competing for her husband, but this is one time she has little choice except to keep a stiff upper lip and endure the evening.

Roy McGrath, of all the people I didn't expect to see tonight, shows up and he looks wonderful ... and sober. He orders a club soda and lime and beams when I tell him how much he's been missed. Tommy drifts up behind him on his way to the dining room and gives him a big greeting and says, "Roy, you have no idea what you missed while you were gone." Then he winks at me and adds, "Kitty and I got engaged."

Roy stands and congratulates us both with bear hugs. "I wish you two every happiness, of course, but I secretly wish I were the one who was marrying Kitty. I never stopped thinking about her while I've been away, but without the hooch I'm stronger and better now than I've ever been."

Tommy slaps him on the back and says, "The important thing is that you're back home with us. Not a week's gone by that your name hasn't been mentioned in some way or another." Roy beams at the perceived compliment. Tommy leaves, chuckling so loud I can hear him above the din.

Before I know it, midnight is nearly upon us—and the countdown begins. Now I work ultrafast, popping the corks on champagne bottles and filling the flutes on the trays I've set up at the service bar. There is room enough for six trays, each holding a dozen flutes. When I finish, Tommy sneaks up from behind and slips his arms around me. I smile wide and lean back against him. "Happy New Year, Sweetheart," I say as whirl around and kiss him.

He rocks me gently, barely grazing my face with his. "Do you realize this is the first time I get to kiss you for real on New Year's Eve?"

"Meaning what?" I snap my head back. "All those past years were bogus kisses? And French jobs at that?"

"You've no idea what was going on with me all those years. New Year's Eve was the one time I could hold you in my arms and kiss you passionately and have it all be okay. My God, I wanted you so bad, and you'd kid around about it, and afterwards I would walk away so conflicted."

"And here I thought you were just a cool Joe who could not have cared less."

"Oh, I cared. I waited all year for that kiss." He pinches my behind, and it make me giggle.. "And now I wonder why I wasted so much time. I love you, Kitten, Happy New Year." He kisses me deeply, and I don't care who might be watching. But when he pulls away I feel like crying. So I cling to him, overcome by love.

He rubs my back and kisses my neck. "My precious Katherine," he whispers and ambles off.

Soon the party poppers explode like firecrackers as 1999 is welcomed in, and we're in full party mode. Christine takes the bar from me so I can have some champagne, and wish everyone I run into a Happy New Year.

Of course, all the men want to dance with me. It's like I'm this untouchable Barbie Doll all year long, but for one night, for a few minutes, I'm available for "touching." I thought I might have a problem with Roy, and he's the third person I dance with, but once Pauley's song is over he bids me and everyone else a good night. I've felt sorry for Roy before, but I this time I almost grab him by the arms and pull him back to the party. But I exercise my better judgment and let him move on without adding to what must be considerable anguish on his part.

I dance with all four of my beer men, and a few other guys, including Ray, who misses his Mildred, as do I. What I'm happiest about is that Pauley keeps each song short. He's a smart old coot who's been to a lot of rodeos of his own, I'm learning.

Tommy's dancing with his faithful following and having fun. Chris whisks me away after I finish dancing with a fellow I barely know from the bar and says, "I just must have one dance with the best and most beautiful bartender in the East. Okay, East, West, North, and South." He then blinks twice, his beautiful mouth comes open, and his perfectly straight jawline drops. "Don't look now, Kitty, but isn't that Lillian sitting at the far end of the bar?" He turns me around where I can look over his shoulder, and sure enough Christine is setting a Manhattan in front of Lillian.

"Oh, dear God," I mutter with disgust. "One look at Lillian in this lounge is all Tommy needs. It will spoil everything for him tonight."

Tommy is off flitting from table to table, chatting with everyone, unaware Vampira is in the building. I've never seen him look so happy. He's crazy with merrymaking and whips me away from a dance partner and cuts up with me to everyone's delight. We run through some well-practiced prattle that always draws laughter from patrons and rowdy comments from staff. At the end he bends me over and plants a full kiss on my lips and proclaims to everyone that I'm the light in his world.

Happy as I am on the outside, my stomach is roiling at the thought of Lillian sitting at my bar. But when I glance in her direction, her glass is half-full and her barstool is empty. I catch sight of a mink I recognize as hers as she rounds the corner to leave. She is clearly rushing off, and I sink against Tommy in relief. He never saw her here; but she certainly saw us, and that makes me smile.

New Year's Day slips on like a pair of comfortable old slippers, and Tommy and I share a quiet morning. We sip hot coffee on the veranda, wrapped up together in his quilt, the harsh weather outside not bothering us in the least. Tommy pulls me close. "We're invited to Polly's at noon for the football games, and she said she was going to tape the parade from earlier if we want to watch it. This is a play day. Then we can start to nest. I have no clue about how this is done. I'll give you my credit card, and you go and shop and make a home for us." Tommy looks extremely cute as he's going on about whatever it is he's going on about. He continues, "I'm very new at this. You might not believe me, but I've never lived with a woman before on what could be called a serious basis, or even had a sister to harass me, so is it any wonder that everything you do intrigues me?" He tousles my hair. "So whenever I'm ignorant, you'll have to put me in my place."

"Mmm, I love it when you give me carte blanche to do that."

"What? Shop or put me in my place?"

"Both," I answer. "Here's what I'd like to do. Tomorrow, after work, we spend the night at my humble little abode. I have a few more boxes to pack up and get ready for the move. What time did you say Bruno and Victor were coming over with the truck in the morning?"

"Around nine."

"We'll get all my stuff to your place, then I'll see what else we need. I have a suspicion it won't wear the numbers off your credit card." Tommy doesn't say anything but I have to believe he likes hearing that. Who wouldn't?

The New Year's Day party at Polly's is homey and sweet and the laughs are abundant, but we are exhausted and beg off as soon as the second football game ends. We hardly remember falling into bed and I sleep through the night. Tommy tells me he did as well.

Tommy and I eat our breakfast in the dining room, in a little patch of warm winter sunshine, read the paper, and enjoy the scent of the Christmas tree. We hate to see it come down, but it will be history in another day. After breakfast, Tommy puts Mr. Bug in a little basket behind his bicycle seat and takes off for the dog park in town.

While he and Bug are gone, I settle into my yoga routine, peacefully meditating in the sunshine in the dining room and listening to classical music. Life is good.

Later, we sit and read and chat about the new rules that Chris has told Tommy about. As we all predicted, drinks on the house are discontinued. Even Bruno and Victor must run a tab. It's long overdue. The House needs to tighten up financially.

The new blood pumping into the House's old veins is exciting. Up in the office, we look at the plans for the landscaping that's to begin in March or as soon as the weather breaks. Of course, I have my own ideas. Bruno is right, however, as I, too, hate to see our baseball field gone forever. Then I think about how long it's been since we've played a game and I laugh.

The new, expanded staff will host lunches, and now there's talk in earnest of adding a daytime chef. We already have a booking for luncheons on the lawn in June, complete with outdoor chamber music. More bartenders will be hired, and I'll be responsible for the main bar as well as the satellite bars for luncheons and private parties.

By complete happenstance, tomorrow is the last day of my apartment lease, and since we recruited Bruno and his truck, with Victor's help, to move me into The House, Tommy and I decide to sleep over at my apartment so we can get an early start.

Pulling at me is my sentimentality in wanting to spend one last night at my place before closing this chapter of my life forever. I genuinely hate to see my place go. I have lived there a long time, with so many pleasant memories, but it will be a happy lonesome as I start my life over with Tommy in my beautiful new home at The House.

This afternoon, while we dress for work, I find a couple of old photo albums of Tom and his family. He sits with me for a few moments, pointing out his mom and dad, his uncles, his grandparents in Italy. The other album is about his military years.

"Holy crap, Tommy, look at you in your dress blues. How incredibly handsome you are. You could have been a model for the Marine recruiting poster."

"Don't be ridiculous. Come on, let's go downstairs and get to work." He pauses and stares at the albums. "Take those with you tonight when we go over to your place, and I'll tell you about more of the pictures." I nod and stack them one atop the other.

This evening everything at The House runs like clockwork. Since it's a post-holiday night, business is brisk in the lounge but slow in the dining room.

Mildred is seeing Ray on what she refers to as a serious basis, and I will no longer have to call her son to take her home. I wonder what she has told him about Ray. Whatever it is, I'm sure Mike appreciates that his mother is well cared for. I guess John Vassar is happy that Millie is occupied. Some people, especially the very rich and the very powerful, have remarkably lenient family values. But it's not just someone like John Vassar. Look at Eleanor Roosevelt. It's impossible to gauge what one person will let another get away with if there's value to be had all around.

This night, even though it moves like a well-oiled machine, yawns on. Two couples hold up the bar until after closing time. Tommy and I were hoping for an early out, but true to the nature of the lounge business there is always someone who wants to close the bar, as if it were a rite of passage of some sort. After the "just one last drink" couples leave, I hurriedly count my empty bottles and wash down the back bar and polish the front bar. Tommy takes my cash drawer upstairs to the office to count the receipts. The phone rings, but there's no one at the end. Probably someone looking for one of the couples who just left.

We change clothes, I load my arms down with the photo albums, and Tommy takes Mr. Bug out to the car.

At my apartment, I make chicken sandwiches and open a bottle Pinot Grigio I was given as a gift so long ago that I don't remember who it came from. We toast to my last night here before curling around each other like stray cats.

The neighborhood is busy tonight despite the early-morning hour. Cars rush down my street, tires squealing, and the neighbors call a loud farewell to some departing guests, A cop chases someone or perhaps it's fire engines that wail mournfully into the night. I'm almost asleep when two people shout at one another on the corner, and when they quiet down I hear a faraway dog barking continuously as a lament to his lonely existence.

"How the hell do you sleep here?" Tommy asks as he pulls a pillow over his ears. "It's after two o'clock in the morning and its goddamn Grand Central Station. I miss the quiet boonies."

"And this coming from a man who grew up in New York City?"

"Point taken." He pulls the pillow tighter to his ears.

I lift one end of the pillow from Tommy's ear and kiss the lobe. "You get used to it. I don't generally hear the noise around here anymore, but it does sound like there's more going on than normal."

Mr. Bug raises his little head and makes a cute "O" with his mouth. He howls, and soon I hear a second set of sirens his ears have picked up before mine.

* * *

Those sirens in the night portend a change to everything Tommy and I and all our family at The House hold dear. Yet while the fire is all-consuming from a material perspective, our souls remain intact, and we rise like a phoenix from the ashes to greet an uncertain dawn—and we survive.

PART IV

"FROM THE ASHES"

Chapter 24

THE DAY AFTER THE big fight between Troy and Tommy, while the two men bare their cuts and bruises, we all feel beaten as well. Our House family all gather at my place. We barely fit in my small digs, so they take it upon themselves to push furniture around. They have brought food and beer, and Victor starts preparing a special soup he guarantees will soothe Tommy's sore gut.

Chris calls to see how Tommy is doing, and we invite him over as well. He might be new, but he's already one of us, and comes bearing a large bottle of Grand Marnier. "Nothing helps to heal more," he says pointing to the bottle, and this gets even Tommy to smile.

Tommy gets up from his sofa, no small task in his condition, and in front of everyone tells Bruno he's truly sorry for taking a swing at him, and especially for connecting.

"Defalco, I'm going to tell you this one last time, you and I are far too old for this dance any more. Our body parts are going to hurt more and the pain will last longer. You're a fucking lunatic when you get cranked up, and you know it. I would never deny you the right to knock someone into tomorrow land if they need it, but you've got to know when to quit. I have two words for you, my friend, 'anger management.'" Bruno looks at Tommy sternly and pats his cheek, the one that's not red and swelled up like a muffin. "One day I won't be around to haul your ass out of trouble, and you'll be in a heap of deep shit." He groans. "And that day's here I'm afraid."

Tommy manages to gives him a hug. "Thanks, buddy."

"Lemme go and get me drink," Bruno says, and he waits until Tommy can push himself away.

"Holy crapoly, Tommy," Polly says when she sees him wincing as he staggers back to his spot on the couch. "I never thought I'd ever see you get the bad end of a fight, but you sure in hell did this time, Sugar. I'd strongly suggest you find another way to show your disapproval of things." She laughs, and Tommy in turn tries to laugh with her. But he winces again, as either his jaw or his ribs are bothering him.

The discussion turns to Troy, and that he was out of line, not only regarding the fight but with his overall behavior after the fire as well. Tommy then shocks me by defending Troy, saying he's young and stressed to the max. He wants to patch things up with Troy as soon as possible, as they've been such good friends for so long. This reaction really has me shaking my head.

Victor shakes his head right along with me. "You can't be friends with a cokehead. They can't see reality. I wasn't there, but swinging a bat at someone's gut that hard is dirty pool any way you look at it. Hell, this wasn't a fight between strangers over a carjacking somewhere in New York City. This was a pissed-off kinda fight. And any fight with someone strung out on drugs is a bad thing. He could have killed you."

Tommy again comes to Troy's defense. "He wouldn't have used that tree limb if I hadn't scared him so bad."

"He was high, Tommy," Jeannie says We all know that. You called him out for what he was doing to himself. Why are you still defending him? Isn't that enabling in the worst way?"

Tommy says nothing, appearing lost in his thoughts.

"Well, shit," Christine says, "what the hell do we all do now?"

"I think we should open our own place," Polly says. "We certainly have the staff."

"Except most of us have to find work immediately," Jeannie says. "This would drastically cut down on our involvement with any plans for starting a new place."

"Jeannie's right," Chris says. "Any way you look at the situation, it's all about money." He glances at Tommy, who gives him an almost imperceptible shift of his eyes, which I can't read. "And unless someone can fund the entire amount, or can collateralize the whole note, it's virtually impossible to borrow the money to start a restaurant. And before anyone asks, the risk for rebuilding an established restaurant—and it returning to what it once was—is enormous. And the cold, hard fact is that it costs twice as much or more to furnish a restaurant like The Carriage House than it did, say, even twenty years ago. We're talking *a lot* of money. Something much smaller might be possible to swing from personal assets, but it wouldn't be anything like what was just lost. I'm sorry, but that's the way it is."

Most heads in the room are low, mine as well. Polly asks him, "What about you? You just barely started this job. Where will you go now?"

"I think I'm going to hit Atlantic City and see if I like it there. It's where I was heading if Troy hadn't hired me. High-end hotels and casinos. My resumes are still in place. I'm used to resort and hotel work. They have a fast turnover, so I'll probably land a position pretty quickly. Trump just opened a new hotel casino. The place is hot. Might be appropriate for a lot of you." He points toward Tommy and me. "With your management talent and maitre d' skills, and Kitty's bar abilities, you guys would fit right in." He raises his voice. "It might be something for all of you to think about, and it's fairly close by. When I get hired, and I'm saying it this way because I'm confident it will happen, I'll certainly do whatever I can for each one of you."

"Atlantic City." Christine wrinkles her nose. "Not for me. Nope, I'll stay around here. This is home to me."

"It's not for everyone," Chris admits. "Casino work is fast and my friends who are in it say it can be damn political at times—and at all levels. But the money can be very good."

"I can see me in Atlantic City," Bruno says. "There's always openings for good chefs, so maybe I'll go. Good thought, Chris. Thanks."

Chris says, "Polly, the servers down there can make out like bandits." He gives her a wink, and I smile to myself.

"I think Cheryl and me will go back to New York City," Victor says, getting up for another beer. "My uncle has a decent Italian restaurant there. We may go up and help him out for a while. He's been asking us for years."

Phillip shares that he and Barry have long talked about what they might do *after* life at The House. He says they've planned to live somewhere close to the Main Line outside of Philadelphia and open a little specialty shop that offers a combination of fine wines and floral arrangements. Maybe a mail-order business also, which is the rage now.

"Wow, now that's a great concept," always-positive Jeannie says. "You guys will land on your feet, I'm sure of it."

Phillip gives her a hug. "It's something we've been planning on doing for years. Sadly, losing The House opens the window for us to attempt to do this now." He sighs. "In life, one thing you can always count on is change."

Tommy says, "My guess is that the news about the insurance is already out. It's the information that most inquiring ears on the grapevine will want to hear. I think job offers will be out there for me, but it's the slow time and that might be a problem. Now's not the ideal time of year for a guy like me to look for work."

"Do you think Lillian will give you a recommendation?" Bruno asks.

Tommy replies to the obviously sarcastic remark with raised eyebrows and a shrug.

Jeannie says, "Speaking of good old Lillian, did you guys have the local news on this morning and see her and John Vassar talking about how sad they were to hear about The House burning down? They said we were such excellent competition, and they wanted to offer a reward fund to find out who started the fire."

I give Jeannie my most perplexed look.

"I know," Jeannie says. "It was almost like they wanted people to see that they were innocent of torching the competition."

Tommy furrows his brow. "We didn't see the news today but it's very odd that John would expose himself publicly like that. He's a very private person. He's seen at The Country Club when he's in the area, and that's about it."

Phillip says, "It does seem that showing up on the local news so soon after the fire makes them look a bit suspicious."

Tommy says nothing, but the skin on his forehead is so tight his brain has to be hurting.

When the beer is gone, and the late afternoon sun spills its last dollops of golden light across my apartment's hardwood floor, we agree to meet up later at the Brass Rail for a bite to eat.

As I clean up the dishes, Tommy says, "Let's go over to The House and look around before it gets dark. Maybe my bike made it through. I kind of feel drawn to go there."

"Me too. I want to see what's left of six years of my life." I drive because Tommy says it hurts for him to move his arms. I'm getting worried he's injured a lot worse than he's letting on. If this continues tomorrow, he's going to the hospital whether he wants to or not.

It's a strange feeling driving into the parking lot that we both took for granted for so long. Long yellow ribbons of caution tape stretch around the site. What remains of The House looks like the result of a bomb blast and not a fire. I reach for Tommy's hand and we sit in the car, just staring at The House's foundation, both of us losing track of time—or not caring.

The sun is starting to set, and winter twilight comes on fast, so we get out and hold hands as we approach the edge of what had been an outer wall to The House. So many shapes seem to appear in front of me, only to morph into a pile of ashes that still holds some warmth yet could not look any colder. It's so damn eerie, and I've never wanted to cry as bad as I want to right now. But somehow I'm able to control my sorrow.

We make our way around to the back, where Bruno's beloved baseball field sits, and to where the shed once stood. Tommy carefully steps over the burned debris and finds his bike melted into a clump of metal. "Ah, well. It was a damn hot fire. I figured it was gone."

I wander out to the tree where we used to sit for so many hours, talking about what I thought mattered. He leans against it and holds out his hands for me. I come close and we stroke each other gently. He says, "Do you have any idea how I cherished those nights with you? How much I loved you, wanted you, and how I had to push you away?"

"I wish you hadn't," I tell him. "I wish we had the memories of all the time we lost."

"I don't know. I think maybe it made us that much closer. I feel as if I've known you forever." He kisses my neck. "We shared some deep things that, maybe if we were a couple back then, we would have hesitated to tell each other. Do you know what I mean, Kitty? I think we have so much more than most other couples, all because our friendship came first. We never feel a need to lecture, or change each other, or berate each other, even though we argue constantly. We accept each other and give each other space. I love that about us. I love that we can tell each other anything and not fear blame or judgment."

"With that said, Tommy, I hope you take Bruno's advice and get some help controlling your temper."

"I know I'm an asshole about fighting. I know how concerned you and my friends are for me." He sighs and holds me closer. "I just have so much trouble controlling myself, when that inner trigger goes off, and I'm blind with rage. I know do need to get some help, and I promise you, I will."

"Tommy, there's one thing, and it's as big as a mountain, but what's going to happen to us now? The service side of food and beverage is all we know. Restaurants and bars. Suppose we get bored with each other, suppose we can't find work together and life pulls us onto different paths? It happens all the time to couples professing to be madly in love. Who are we without The House? Who the hell are we with just each other and nothing else around us? For the first time in my entire life, I'm honestly afraid of the future." I still refuse to cry but my insides feel like a river is raging within me.

"Baby, don't," he says softly. "You're depressed and so am I. We shouldn't have come back here. Let's go, it's getting dark, and this place is making us both uncomfortable."

We walk around the pile of ashes, and I get the strangest feeling that stops me cold. Tommy is standing still as well. It's as if there is a message we need to hear. My first thought is that it's a warning. I sense it again and Tommy whispers, "Did you feel that?"

I nod with a shudder. It's as though a dark secret is rising from a burnt throat, crying out a death rattle. I say, my voice cracking, "A mortal monster burned The House down. That's what we're being told."

"But why?" Tommy asks. Of course I have no answer, and we hurry off.

Back at my apartment, we curl up quietly on the sofa. "Are you still depressed?" I ask him.

He looks at me seriously. "More than you, if you can believe that. The House fire took me down with it. I felt it suck all of my energy out of me." He places his hand on my neck and massages it. "Do you really think that could happen to us, Kit? What you said back there?"

"I feel sad, really sad. I'm uncertain and worried for us. Maybe all of this has caught up with me."

He starts to get up. I help him because he winces. "We need to get out of here," he tells me, giving me a hint of a smile. "I don't want both of us feeling like this. Let's go out get a drink and something to eat. It's almost dinnertime anyway."

"Are you sure your stomach can handle it?"

"I'll be fine, Sweetie. I just can't stay here, doing nothing. And when was the last Friday night we weren't working?"

"This is exactly what I was talking about, my love."

"We'll weather this," he says, but his weary tone reveals his true feelings. Yet somehow I feel wisps of fear dancing around us, like snow-flakes blown against a frosty window. I want to throw myself into

Tommy, climb into his heart where it is safe, funny, and warm with love. Then just as fast the mood leaves me, and now I'm not just scared of the future, I'm terrified of what it might bring.

Chapter 25

POLLY IS SITTING BETWEEN Chris and Bruno, and she waves to us to join them at the bar.

We take our seats, after gathering and sowing seeds of greeting to a dozen or so people we know at the Brass Rail. I bask in the comforting glow that only a familiar bar and its regular crowd can provide.

"Wow, this is a rose between two thorns," Tommy addresses Polly as he carefully slides himself onto the stool next to Chris. We have a drink, and order dinner at the bar. We chat easily as we eat. When dinner is about over, I catch Chris and Polly playing footsies, so it's clear they'd like to get going. I get up to go to the powder room, and this allows our little party to break up, as Bruno bids us a goodnight and Polly and Chris do as well. I come back, and just as Tommy and I are about to leave, Millie comes in with all her normal fanfare, which increases when she spots us. We tell her we're on the way out, but she will have no part of it and demands we join her for a drink. Even Tommy, sore body and all, cannot refuse her. She settles onto the barstool between us.

I go into detail with Jim, the Brass Rail's bartender, on exactly how to make Millie's martinis, and she gives me a grateful pat on the arm as soon as she takes a sip of the first offering.

"Glad you like it," I say to her, then in a stern voice I add, "Now make this your nightly haunt so we always know where to find you."

She takes another sip of her drink but seems deep in thought, which is so unlike her, and she says, "It's so good to see you both. How are things going?" She pauses again. "By the looks of Tommy's face, I'd say not too well."

Tommy fills her in on the fight between him and Troy, and he tells her the truth about the insurance. The only thing he leaves out is Troy's apparent heavy drug use.

"It's so unfortunate about the insurance, but never should that have happened. Troy made a colossal mistake. Never burn your bridges, especially in anger. But he's a user, so go figure. What was he on, cocaine? Speed?"

I'm shocked, since this is the one issue Tommy didn't discuss. "How do you know about that, Millie?"

"Oh, please. Troy is an open book. Lillian too. You know it; who doesn't know it? I might not be a bartender and see this all the time, but I wasn't born yesterday, and I have a sixth sense about drug use." She squares up with Tommy. "You were pretty handy with drugs in Nam, were you not, Tom?"

Tommy nods and shifts uncomfortably. "Yeah, I was, Millie, but not anymore." She still holds his gaze, then smiles sadly as she gently touches Tommy's puffed and nicked-up face.

"You're far too beautiful a man for this." She studies both of us for a moment and changes the subject. "You kids look so tired. I can't imagine why." She winks. "In the past month, you have lived a year's worth of events. In all honesty, I'm worried about you two."

"Well, we're a little worried about us too," I say, propping up my chin with my hand. We've had enough to drink to be mellow, and it feels lovely to wind down.

"We want to find jobs so we can work together," Tommy tells Millie. "But it won't be easy."

"It'll be damn near impossible," Millie says so loud and fast that it startles me. She takes out a cigarette and Tommy lights it for her, using a book of Brass Rail matches wedged in place on the side of the ashtray. "Suppose just one of you finds work? What will the other do? You both are such workaholics. I wonder if either one of you could sit home for even one week by yourself."

I sigh. "You know us well, Millie. We were so damn restless tonight we had to come here. It's been two days since The House burned and we already have cabin fever."

Tommy shares with her that his life at The House was so perfect for him, and that it'll be an enormous undertaking for him to live and feel comfortable someplace else, even with the woman he adores. He's says he's anxious now that there's no work to keep him grounded. He adds, "I never thought past The House, and now I feel lost. I'll figure it out, but at this minute I haven't got a clue."

Millie puts out her cigarette, of which she's taken only a few drags, and pushes the ashtray away, followed by her drink. "Not mixed as well or as cold as yours, Kitty." A cocktail waitress comes by, and she orders another while Tommy and I both ask for coffee. I walk up to Jim and tell him to add more olives to Millie's drink and to shake it a bit longer. He rolls his eyes but nods.

Our coffee and Jim's second attempt at a Kitty-quality martini are served. Millie takes a sip, and her brief sigh tells me that Jim will still need a bit more training. She makes small talk, then says, "Tommy, Kitty, I've watched you two very closely for eight years. There's no doubt in my mind that you cherish each other in every way, but you don't have a clue of who you are to each other without your tuxedos on and the distractions and interactions caused by the people around you."

I'm dumbfounded that she could know what I'd just been talking about with Tommy.

She continues, "Tommy fell in love with a classy bartender, and you fell in love with a debonair manager. You've shared places deep within your hearts, I don't doubt that, and your devotion, as I said before, is evident. But unless you can tolerate being totally bored when you're with each other, how can you truly be comfortable with your relationship? With the loss of The House you were suddenly set adrift, alone in your own little raft."

"If you're trying to cheer us up Millie, it's not working," I tell her.

"I don't mean to depress you, but I do mean to teach you something. I'm an alcoholic. I know it and I don't care, even if it ultimately kills me. I've been in this routine my whole married life and have no desire to change. I drink to avoid feeling lonely. That's what I do. But I wasn't always like this. I was in love once and had a bright future. It was quite the happy, busy, full life, and I loved being rich. However, the social life was what we based our relationship on, nothing else. I was John Vassar's trophy wife, and I enabled him to climb the social ladder, but when he got to the top rung there wasn't room for me. It was agony to be abandoned."

Tommy appears to be in a trance, but he nods when the server asks if he'd like more coffee. I lean in closer to Millie to catch her every word.

"The bar scene is a seductive mistress," she says after taking several sips of her martini in succession. "It will draw you in until there's nothing else you would rather do than come to your favorite watering hole every might and socialize. Soon you start to identify with it all. It makes you feel like you belong to one big family. In a sense, you do, but you're still alone at closing time. The booze, which seems to help you think clearer, help you cope better, help you laugh louder, help you feel more deeply, in truth does just the opposite. It will even lull you into thinking that life is okay. But, as we all know, it's a lie."

Tommy listens intently, not saying anything. Millie reaches to each side and covers our hands. "I want you kids to make it, but I'm here to tell you from experience, it's easy to lose yourselves in business when you also work together—and in turn lose your heart."

"Millie, I never want to lose this woman. She's my life. But I hear what you are saying, and it's scaring the hell out of me. But the bar and restaurant business is who we are."

"I'm not saying that's a dreadful thing. I'm just saying that you must put some dimension into your lives. Don't be content to be just what you've been for years. And, most important, you both need a life outside the bar and restaurant business."

I cradle my coffee cup, wishing I might find an answer somewhere in the residue of what's left, but it's like dark mud, the same as I feel inside at the moment. "Like Tommy said, we don't know anything else."

"Life has already shown you how easily everything you hold dear can change and be taken away in a blink. Or, over time you might see yourself in the mirror and realize you're not the most exciting bartender anymore, or that Tommy, God forbid, has an accident and can no longer manage a restaurant. There's one constant that you both must have in order to survive what life throws at you from here on, and that constant must be each other and nothing else."

Tommy sighs and says, "Well, we certainly have enough around us here as a reminder of all that you are saying. We'll have a lot of time together looking for work."

"That's exactly what I mean is wrong with your thinking, and I see it in both of you." Tommy lights a cigarette for her and Millie takes a deep drag and lets the next words spiral from her lips as she exhales the smoke. "This is a perfect time for you two to get away for a few weeks. I want you to go my place in Palm Beach. Have a pre-honeymoon, so to speak; enjoy being alone. It's a lousy time to look for work anyway. Meet me here tomorrow night, and I'll give you directions and the other information you'll need. I want you to leave the day after tomorrow, all right?"

We are struck silent for a minute. "I don't think we can afford to do this," Tommy says, echoing what I'm thinking.

Millie takes a checkbook from her purse and begins writing a check. "I want you to go out and buy decent clothes, and a lot of them, either here or down in Florida. And get a couple of fashionable suits. You'll need them to find work. You too, Kitty, buy some business wear. I'm calling Jorge, my houseman, and telling him you two will be staying for a while. I'm hoping you and Tom will become close friends with Jorge and his wife, Carmella. I'm counting on it."

"Are you sure about this?" I ask, stunned to the point of being euphoric.

"I'm as certain as I can be. And I want you to drive, not fly, and meander along the way until you run out of things to say to each other. Literally."

She hands Tommy the check and her eyes softly glow. "Take it, I have lots. Money does me no good whatsoever anymore, other than knowing it makes life easier for those I care about. I love you, my dears. Be happy, learn about things that matter between you and be always in love. Don't let life take that away from you like a thief in the night. If that happens, trust me, you will wonder where it went and never get it back."

"Millie, this is a lot of money, we don't know what to say." Tommy says as he shows me the check and meets my eyes.

"I draw in a sharp breath when I see the amount she has written. "Oh, Millie, are you sure?"

"You will need adequate funds to enjoy Palm Beach, believe me." She laughs.

I give her a long hug, and she pats my arm. "You have provided me with years of fun and the best of care. It's the very least I can do for you and Tommy."

I glance at the check again and say, "I can't thank you enough for your generosity, but it almost seems like you want to get us out of town." I laugh but I mean every word.

Millie orders another martini, which being her third will be her last. She's been drinking fast, and when it arrives I'm glad she takes only one small sip. "Dear girl, you've always had good intuition. I want to do a little digging into what really happened to The House, and I don't want you two here while I'm doing it."

We both put our cups down and stare at her. "Now that's pretty damn vague," I say seriously.

"I found it a little too pat that my husband and Lillian were shedding tears on TV when they talked about the fire. I thought he was already in Barbados with her. I also think it's about time I look into John's implant business, something I should have done long ago."

That Millie would reveal this "family matter," and almost cavalierly, has me come up in my chair. Tommy leans into her and what he says next is like a message in a spy movie: "Millie, I don't want you to do anything about checking into John's medical business. You must promise me that you won't go investigating. Look into the fire all you want, but please let the other go."

Millie's eyes narrow and she points her cigarette at Tommy, as if she's got him in her sights and is drawing a bead on him, ready to squeeze the trigger at any moment. "You know something about all of this, don't you, Thomas? John's business, I mean?"

Tommy jaw muscles twitch, his eyes steel on Millie's. "He can be a dangerous man, even when he's not threatened. But I have to think you know that better than I. As for his implant operation, it has a hollow floor. I just don't know where—and don't want to. I'm begging you not to go looking for trouble."

"I just found it … and it's all around you." She snatches Tommy's hand. "I always suspected you knew more about his business matters, and if I think this, so does John." Even though now well into her third martini, her eyes have a razor sharpness to them.

"I don't know anything more than—"

"You listen to me, both of you, and you do *exactly* as I say. By tomorrow afternoon, I want you out of this town. Leave as soon as you are packed. Say nothing to anyone, especially your House family. Once you're away from here you can take your time. But get to my villa in Palm Beach. It's the last place he will look for you. I will join you shortly, but you must not worry about me. I know exactly what I'm doing. Do you hear me?" Millie's tone is deadly serious, which is a first in all the years I've known her. "If my instinct is correct, you are in danger, my dears." She frowns. "I never should have let it get this far."

"What do you mean?" I ask, more than a little bewildered.

"I'll explain everything to you later. For now, go back to your apartment and pack. You might even want to leave first thing in the morning. Take your car and not Tommy's." She writes on a napkin and hands it to me. "Here's the address and the phone number at my villa. Remember, the majordomo's name is Jorge and his wife is Carmella. They will be expecting you. Now go."

We say little on the short drive home. My thoughts dance around what Millie has said.

I've harbored thoughts that Lillian was the one to worry about, assuming she will do anything to get Tommy back, but now I wonder how her romance with John Vassar fits into the puzzle. But there are other issues as well that have me horribly at odds. Tommy used the words, "hollow floor," which sounds like an intelligence phrase, and I'm still not over the conversation with Millie when she literally grilled me about what happened during the shuttle ride in San Francisco. I still can't figure out what it was that she'd said, but something was not right—and it's not going away. I must put this together before it drives me crazy.

We do as Millie suggested and pack. I leave a check for a month's rent plus ten percent on my kitchen table, which is agreed upon with my landlord, whom I called once we got in. He offered the same rent if I signed a new lease for a year, but I explained that I'd likely have to move to find work, so this was best. I call Jeannie and ask if we can leave Mr. Bug for a somewhat extended period, and she acts delighted. I follow Millie's advice and don't tell her where we're going, and she doesn't even ask but hints that maybe we're off to be married someplace and honeymooning. I can only laugh shallowly, wishing it were true.

The forecast is for snow all day tomorrow, so we lie in bed and ponder the weather.

"I wonder why we can't fly," I say, not relishing driving any distance in a snowstorm.

"No, the deal is that we take your car, and that's what we'll do. She wants us to meander along and be bored with each other. Remember?" Tommy's sudden assertive attitude about this trip has me befuddled, but what else is new?

"Why my car?" I ask.

"She probably thinks we can pack more in it, and she'd be right.

With mine being a two-seater and with not much of a trunk, your little wagon is better."

"It's still small." He gives me *his* look, so I change the subject.

"I'm excited about getting there. Balmy breezes, palm trees, the ocean, the beach."

"I'll have to buy a Speedo. All Italian men wear Speedos."

"Not *my* Italian man," I say, snuggling closer to him.

"Hmm, I love the sound of *my.*"

"Then I'll make sure you hear it a lot."

He traces my face with his fingers and toys with the curls in my hair.

"Did you call Molly and tell her about any of this?" he asks.

"No. She'd be begging me to come out to the coast to be near her. She'd probably give us the money to live until we found work, but I wouldn't want that and I didn't think you would either." *Should I have asked him? Millie's right, as usual. I know virtually nothing about how Tommy really feels about anything.*

He says, "I was thinking of Shannon. How her parents' lives revolve around her. How content Dan and Molly seem to be."

"That's because they're both on heavy Prozac." I laugh. "What? Are you pining away to be a father?"

"Me? Of course not. I'm way too old."

"You're not too old. You're forty-five. You'd be fifty-five when your child is ten, sixty-five when he or she is twenty, and a perfect age for grandkids at seventy-five. Age isn't like it used to be. Hell, seventy is the new fifty. Look at you. You're forty-five but act like a twelve-year-old most of the time." I kiss his forehead. While I'm doing so I examine his cheek and jaw. The redness remains but the swelling seems to have gone down, and Tommy appeared to get into bed with little discomfort. Then I thought about the car. I'd have to drive, since Tommy is hurt, so maybe that's why Millie said we should take my Subaru. But Tommy's condition didn't seem to have any influence on Millie's remark, as it sounded like she'd made the decision without considering his injuries, one way or the other. She simply did not want us traveling in his car, period.

Tommy gets my mind off my latest conundrum when he asks me, "Do you ever worry that maybe your biological clock is ticking away? Maybe one day you'll regret not having a kid."

I arch an eyebrow at him and hold it. "Why would I want to have a kid? I have a kid: *you*. What's this about? Do you want to have a baby?"

"It would add dimension to our lives maybe. Millie said we need dimension."

I shoot upright as if stung by a bee. "Are you out of your freakin' mind? Let me refresh your memory, just in case certain recent events have perhaps slipped off into Neverneverland. We have no jobs, no home to speak of, no clue about the future, and we don't even know if we can stay in the same room together with nothing to do except have sex and eat. And you want to have a baby because it might add dimension to our lives? This is right up there with, 'Let's get married. It might be kind of fun.'"

He smiles sheepishly. "I was just asking because I want you to be happy, that's all."

"I *am* happy. You fill my life with everything I'll ever need. You okay with that?" He gives me a stupid grin and I kiss him. "We can go visit Shannon anytime you need a kid fix."

As sore as his body must be, he manages to make love to me. When we finish, we get laughing over the silliest things. I do love this man. And it's during these moments that I can't imagine anything happening to ever destroy our world.

Chapter 26

THE NEXT MORNING, AFTER coffee and a couple of stale biscuits, we leave around seven, drop off Mr. Bug with Jeannie, who greets us at her door as bleary eyed as we are, and I drive five hours. We beat most of the snow, and Tommy says his ribs are feeling better, so he takes over the wheel after we eat a quick lunch at a roadside diner. I fall happily asleep, listening to him sing along to a James Taylor tape.

I wake up, sensing the car has stopped, and I blink sleepily at the dimly lit surroundings. I check my watch. My God, I've slept all afternoon.

We're at a gas station/convenience store that's not part of a chain. I wander into the building. After asking about the restroom I'm handed a large wood dowel with the words Ladies' Room scribbled in black Magic Marker and a key bolted to it. I'd like to see someone try to walk off with this monstrosity.

The toilet area, consisting of a commode with awful smells coming from it, and a filthy sink with wet paper of all sorts on the floor around it, is disgusting and then some. A broken mirror, with a phone number clearly written in lipstick, adds to the effect. I make sure not to touch anything, and I pee standing over the toilet, a technique all girls learn at a tender age from their mothers when a public restroom is the only choice.

"Be careful not to drizzle on the seat," my mother would say, no matter how awful the conditions, adding, "You must always be a lady."

Apparently the brave females who ventured into this pigsty before me had not come by the benefit of a similar upbringing.

There are no paper towels nor any soap in their respective dispensers, which of course are broken open, so I rinse my hands under a thin trickle of cold water, using the sides of my jeans as a towel. I return the key to the store attendant and find Tommy outside pumping gas. I sneak up behind and start to put my arms around him. The split-second I touch him he jumps as if a flash of lightning hit nearby. Then he whirls around, the same menacing look on his face as when he almost choked me to death. But I catch a break. He slaps his hand to his chest and avoids hitting me.

"Jesus, Kit, please don't ever come up behind me like that again. I tend to act first and think later, especially in a place like this."

He's of course right. And considering what happened in San Francisco, I should have used better judgment all around. He pulls me into him, and he's shaking, so there's no doubt I startled him. I apologize and he holds me. I hear the nozzle click just as a dark-colored sedan pulls in to some shadows near the store, and the vehicle's headlights are turned off. I don't know why this particular vehicle interests me, but I look at it curiously from over Tommy's shoulder. What I observe next is what doesn't happen—as no one gets out of the car.

"Again, I'm sorry, Sweetheart," I say and kiss him softly, wanting to leave right away. "Let's find a motel. If we don't, I'll make love to you right here, right now."

"Here, at this dump of a gas station?" He chuckles. "It would be quite a show for those people in that car back there."

"You noticed the car too?"

"You're getting spooked about everything. Look around. It's the only other car here."

We both glance toward the car, and the moment we do the headlights come on and the car pulls out onto the road.

"That's still creepy," I say half to myself. "The car came in and just left. No one got out."

Tommy gets behind the wheel and says, "They probably didn't like the looks of the place." But he adds upon driving away, "I got to admit, this is one strange little gas station. Something straight out of Stephen King."

I decide I've overreacted again. "I guess King has to get his ideas from somewhere. Probably stopped here once too." We both laugh but I'm still unnerved.

We spend considerable time searching for a motel that is halfway decent, when we come to a Holiday Lodge sign. The room isn't gigantic but it's clean and there are extra pillows in the closet, as well as more towels. It feels fabulous to relax, and I'm happy to be in new surroundings. Because of the late hour we checked in, the room choices were few and we settled for a unit with two queen beds. Tommy snatches the bedspreads and tosses them in the corner. He says they are never washed. I think he's right about that, but I also think he's being a bit dramatic.

He falls on the bed closest to him and not me. He burns tonight, and just the thought of him fills me with excitement.

"Come over here," he says.

I play the imp. "You come over *here*. I don't have to obey you." He gets into the game immediately.

"Don't be so damn annoying. Now get over here."

"No way." I sit on the other bed. "You come over here."

"Why do you have to be such a pain in the ass? Why can't you just be warm and sweet and come when I call you? One day, if you continually ignore and defy me, you may get run over by a bus, and then how will you feel?"

"Huh? Run over by a bus, say you? Where do you get these ideas?" I giggle. "I'm not your dog, and you're no longer my boss. Any other man would already be over here on my bed, slobbering and pawing at me."

"Aw, come on, Kit. I asked you first."

"Good Lord, you're such a child."

I stand up on my bed and slowly undress, studying his changing expression at each garment I remove. When I'm down to my bra and panties he begins to frown.

"Are you going to come over here to this bed, young lady, or do I have to come and get you?"

"What makes you think you could possibly catch me? I'm way younger and way faster than you. Catch me? I think not. How dare you even think you could?"

His jaw is tight and twitching, and my suspicion is that he's feeling no pain in his face as I sashay like a lioness in front of him. I flip on the radio on the nightstand. As on key, the music is perfect for a slow strip-tease and I dance like a sultry, flickering flame for him. I do erotic moves that I'd never even dreamt of doing for anyone before, and he watches me intently.

"Jesus, you're hot," he seems to be saying more to himself than to me.

I never thought dancing like this would be such a turn-on, but I'm literally feeling my own body heat the more I move for him. I never considered that strippers get excited by their own moves, but I can now believe it happens. He reaches for me but I manage to avoid him.

Three times he attempts to take me down, and in each instance I wiggle away from him and rotate my hips seductively between two chairs in the corner before coming back his way. I move as though I'm making love to one man and then the other. When he can take it no longer, he grabs me with such force that he knocks the lone picture off the wall, and we crash to the floor right along with it. Nothing breaks, meaning neither us nor the cheap frame on the even cheaper print, and he throws me down hard on the bed and pins me to it. Some women think a man's strength is just for talking points, but Tommy's physicality is pure sexuality that drives me insane.

The sex this night, which I can describe best as making love during a powerful storm, delights us. We both say it reminds us of one of our favorite song lyrics, Elton John's "Laughing like children, living like lovers, rolling like thunder under the covers."

I have never known anyone like Tommy when it comes to love-making. He's so utterly unselfish, slowing and waiting to find out where I'm "at," asking what I need and what I'd like. He gets supreme pleasure from my getting the most from him. He makes love like the tango; deliberate and graceful, but also passionately rough. The sex between us gets loud, as we reach our "time," but we learn our ecstasy is not as popular with the occupants in the room next door to us, who bang on the walls. We ignore this at first, as their timing could not be worse, but when we are finished we hear an old woman yell, "Quiet down or you're gonna give Charlie a heart attack. And I can't drive back to Wisconsin by myself."

We look at each other with the same "Oh, shit" expression and crack up. Tommy tells me breathlessly, "Now, *this* is what motel sex is all about."

The next morning we're up early, checking the hallway before leaving the room, which we race out of quickly to avoid any chance of coming in contact with Charlie and potentially exacerbating his fragile heart condition.

We eat a huge breakfast, and Tommy agrees to take the first shift driving. On the way to my car, out of the corner of my eye I spot the sedan that was at the gas station the night before. I'm to the point of walking over to it and introducing myself to whoever is inside. Of course, I could be mistaken about this being the same vehicle. It was dark. So I pass on the idea.

Tommy asks me what's wrong, and when I mention the car he repeats that the San Francisco trip has made me squirrely about everything. But he consents to spending a few moments studying the vehicle. He says he'll drive around the motel and come up behind the car so I can at least get its plate number, if that will make me happy. But when he does this the car is gone, so all we can do is get on the Interstate.

When I take my turn driving, Tommy doesn't say much, acting tense, nervous and irritable. I want to say something but remember Millie's advice. These last couple of days are indeed the most time Tommy and I have ever spent together, and I'm learning to leave him alone, because I, too, like my "space" as the kids call it. Whatever the name, it's real. And Millie is damn smart.

While I drive, Tommy reads a local paper he picked up at the motel on the way out. I don't know how he can do it and not get carsick. But he makes me stop routinely so he can take a pill, which he explains is why he doesn't get motion sickness. Once again, I'm learning as I'm going. But he's giving me short answers to anything I ask him, and he seems acutely anxious. I'm guessing part of this is due to boredom. I've seen this side of him sometimes at The House. Those were the nights that I just steered clear of him until he smoothed out, so this behavior doesn't throw me too much. But after another hour passes, I've have enough.

"You seem a little cranky," I say as I park at the pumps of another gas station that would provide Stephen King with material. For starters, the attendant I meet inside the building I enter to buy some snacks and drinks could be the twin of the banjo player in *Deliverance*. I pay the guy and don't even think about asking to use the restroom.

"I'm just having an off day," Tommy says after I get back in the car. "All this riding and driving is getting to me."

We reach Jacksonville that night, and he seems intent on finding a motel with a bar and restaurant because he wants a meal with drinks. We find something called The Thunderbird Inn that advertises both.

We check in but want a drink before anything else. We settle down on the barstools, and Tommy orders a double Dewar's and I order a Jack Daniel's and ginger, not the usual drinks for either of us—but these are unusual times.

The lounge is typical for a roadside motel, with multicolored over-head lighting dimly illuminating the bar. However, there is a rather large dance floor and a stage. It's only a little past seven, and the marquee at the entrance read that live music starts at nine, so we have plenty of time to enjoy our drinks before dinner. But when we go into the restaurant, we see a "Closed for Remodeling" sign. Tommy is pissed and raises his voice to the guy at the front desk, but he's told we can order a simple meal at the bar. So, we return, have to find different seats since ours are taken, and we order hamburgers and fries. Exactly what Tommy didn't want, so he's now sullen and agitated at everything.

After dinner I go to the Ladies' Room, and on my return I find Tommy and the bartender engaged in deep conversation. I bop up to my barstool, smiling at them, praying that Tommy's mood isn't going to get him into another altercation. Instead, the bartender and Tommy shake hands and he excuses himself and rushes to the Men's Room. My thought is that he's having "bathroom issues" and that the bartender has perhaps given him something for this. All of us in the bar business carry over-the-counter products, like Imodium, for our personal use. I just hope it's nothing worse that's bothering Tommy.

The band has just started and they don't sound too bad. They bar has filled up with people, some travelers, but mostly locals, I guess.

I wait nervously for several minutes until he returns. He smiles as he rubs my back and leans in close to me, making my lack of availability clear for any man who might be curious. He's now upbeat and wants to dance. I have no idea how he can possibly be interested in anything but sleep, as we've just started on our forth drink. I agree even though I'm considering that Tommy must be in pain somewhere every time he moves.

Halfway through the song, I feel a familiar light-headiness that I know from past experiences will put the room in full spin if I don't sit down. There's not a feeling I hate more than I try to sleep after drinking too much and this night falls into that category. I push Tommy from me, and return to my barstool. He follows me, and before he can ask I tell him what's happening to me. I order a straight ginger ale, and as soon as I gulp it down I signal for another. The bartender, whose name I learn is Kent, brings me munchies without my asking, and I tip him five on the spot.

The opposite of the way I feel, Tommy has kicked into high gear and is chatting up everyone at the bar. The band takes a break, and I tell him I'm cooked and going to the room; he can stay if he wants, but I'm definitely leaving. He's forgotten about our suitcases, and I forgo reminding him that they're still in the car. I don't care, I just want to get into bed.

He says he'll finish his drink, and be along to the room shortly. I fumble the room key into to the second floor door lock and settle into the room in a whirlwind of stumbles and grabs, and leave a trail of clothes from the dresser to the bed.

Fortunately, I'm not spinning, and I instantly fall asleep. I've no idea what time it is when Tommy comes into the room, but he wakes me up to cuddle. I want no part of anything except sleep, and I pass out again.

That morning, traffic noise from the nearby Interstate rouses me. Light is now coming from around the sides of the plastic drapes covering the room's large window. My head is pounding, and I'm way too hot. I drop out of bed and shuffle off to the bathroom. I hate being hungover. I decide to brush my teeth, take two aspirins and enjoy a long shower. Thankfully I see our suitcases which Tommy had brought up sometime last night and I rummage through mine and find what I need. Soon I'm under the showerhead and the hot water feels marvelous.

Tommy sneaks into the back of the shower tub with me and gives me a sheepish grin. I don't move out of my heavenly hot rain that's dancing a healing jig on my head and shoulders.

"So tell me again why we drank so much last night?" I mutter as I look at him, only one of my eyes open and that just barely.

He chuckles and begins to soap me up with what soon becomes sweet lather. "Are you going to use up all the hot water before you allow me in?"

He sounds fresh as a daisy, as if he's slept for ten hours. "Motel rooms don't have individual water heaters," I tell him before realizing he's just trying to be funny. Then I groan and move a little to the side, but he maneuvers me out of the way and steals all the shower spray. However, he kisses away all my disapproval and we wash each other thoroughly and pat each other dry, of course managing to turn this into a carnal encounter of the most enjoyable kind.

After dressing, we grab a coffee and get on our way, skipping breakfast for a change. My stomach isn't ready for anything solid yet, and I have to think Tommy's isn't any more receptive. He offers to drive, which works for me and I soon fall asleep.

By noon we're in Central Florida, and the weather's warm and soothing. I feel better already. The farther we go the warmer it gets, and it does wonders for our moods. Tommy is back to his funny, chatty self, and this makes me feel better, as well. If I could just bottle this and pour it on him whenever he gets in one of fits of bad humor. *But is there a big enough bottle?*

Our map tells us we are no more than 80 miles from the Okeechobee Boulevard exit in West Palm Beach that will allow us to take the bridge to Palm Beach. Just as I smile to myself that we are almost there, the skies open up. There's considerable flooding, I hear sirens, and Interstate traffic is stopped on both sides. When the weather clears and the traffic begins to move again, we've sat in one place for three hours.

If Millie wanted us to be together for extended periods, bored out of our minds, she got her wish. We're both grumpy and need to pee. He's so sullen that we switch seats, climbing over each other from inside the car—no small task in a Subaru—and I take over the driving. His facial expressions during our acrobatics show me that he's far from over the beating he took from Troy. Why this man wanted to dance last night, I'll never know.

The line of traffic stops and starts and we idle seemingly forever. Tommy is fidgety and quietly brooding. A signpost reads that the Fort Pierce exit is one mile ahead, and another sign indicates all sorts of fast-food joints, trucks stops, and regular gas stations. Being the devil-may-care person I am, I start to creep onto the shoulder of the road. I figure I'll just shoot on down the collar on the right until I get to the exit, and get the flock out of this traffic.

Tommy comes alive, as if stung by a bee, shouting, "What the hell are you doing?"

"I'm getting out of this traffic," I tell him. "I'm just scooting on down to the next exit."

"You can't do that."

"Of course, I can. I'm doing it."

"It's against the law."

"There's no law that says I can't drive on the shoulder of a road."

"Yes, there is. You can't travel on the shoulder."

"Well, I am. Sit still and be good." I naturally say all of this in a way that I hope he'll take as funny—with me just being me. But he reaches over and grabs hold of the wheel.

"What is your problem?" I snap at him, genuinely getting mad now.

"Don't do this. Stay put in the lane we're in. We don't need the cops stopping us."

"What cops? And who cares about them? I'm the queen of avoiding tickets. I'm a woman who cries." I'm half-smiling until I see he's looking serious, so I ask, "What the hell is going on with you?"

"I just don't want us to get pulled over. I don't like cops, okay?"

"I don't like cops either. But trust me, we'll be fine."

"No, goddamn it, we won't be fine. Now stay in the fucking lane behind traffic until you can exit legally. If you don't do this, Kitty, I'll be really annoyed. Mad even."

"I already *am* annoyed and mad. So leave me the fuck alone so I can drive." I slap his hands away from the wheel, and this was no love tap I gave him.

He growls, "You know how I lose it when I get upset. If we get stopped by the cops, I'll get angry and they'll beat the crap out of me and throw me in jail."

I burst out laughing. "What is *wrong* with you? Where does all your paranoid shit come from? I'm the one who's been constantly looking over my shoulder."

His features are so taut, which makes me laugh even harder. "Why in hell would they throw you in jail? Why would you lose your temper over something stupid that I did anyway? I'll take care of my own problems, thank you, and handle things if we get stopped. My God, you're so strange sometimes."

"No way we can take the chance. I hate cops. They're unpredictable. They could make our lives a living hell. We're out of state, and they look for people like us."

"People like us? Two adults driving a goddamn ten-year-old Subaru station wagon, and we both have to pee out our ears, which is what I'd tell the cop. Seriously, why on earth would they be suspicious of us? Why are you so freaked out?"

"I'd get upset and the cop would handcuff me." He shrugs and looks away. "It's a phobia I have."

"Of getting handcuffed?" I pucker my lips. "There goes *that* bedroom game." He's still not lightening up. "You're serious, aren't you?"

"Yes, I am. Maybe it's a throwback to my days in New York when I was a kid. I just don't want anything to do with the police. So drive carefully and don't take chances." He looks at me and takes my hand. "Please, no more of this. We'll be out of this in a few minutes."

I sigh and get back in line. "Jesus, this is another thing I'm learning about you. Do you want to tell me what happened back in New York?"

"No," he says brusquely.

Fortunately, as Tommy predicted, our line of cars starts to move more rapidly. I reach over and pat his knee. "I'll be your Joan of Arc, Thomas, Baby. I'll protect you from all law enforcement evils. I get along famously with police officers, so not to worry, my big unruly juvenile delinquent."

There's still a trace of concern in his eyes, but I don't care. We're finally at the exit, and ten minutes later, after we've both hit the restroom, all's well in Tommy's kingdom once more. Now I just want to get to Millie's Villa as fast as I can.

Tommy drifts off to sleep, not knowing that once traffic clears I book ninety all the way down the Interstate to West Palm Beach.

PART V

"THE ILLUSION OF PARADISE"

Chapter 27

WE GET TO THE ISLAND of Palm Beach late in the afternoon and in a short while find ourselves before an immense iron gate at the address Millie gave us, where we key in the numbers she provided. The gate opens, and we turn onto a long pearl-white driveway hemmed on both sides by palm trees and flowering tropical shrubs of every description. The drive ends in a circle around a pink-and-white fountain in front of a Mediterranean ranch-style villa with a red terracotta barrel-tile roof.

An archway with Spanish columns covers a brick walkway to the house. The main entranceway in front to the villa's massive front doors is covered with vibrant trumpet vines, bougainvillea, and birds of paradise and their combined scents are completely intoxicating. And if this isn't idyllic enough, perfectly manicured palmetto palms and luscious green plants blend with a thick carpet of verdant grass that stretches around both sides of the house.

"Holy crap," I whisper to Tommy, as if louder words might disturb the surreal calm we've just stepped into. "'Just a little winter getaway,' is what Millie called this place."

I key in another code written on the note I'm holding and the front door opens. I stand dumbstruck, and Tommy as well, with his eyes wide, exclaiming, "Wow!"

The foyer flooring is laid out in a gorgeous mosaic of tiles, of course in a Spanish motif. Two identical lion's-head fountains carved from blue marble are mounted to our left and right, each facing the other. The trickling voices of their waters welcome us as the gentle splashes seem to dance in the golden rays of sunlight that pour down from a domed skylight.

Stepping from the foyer, we stand overlooking a massive sunken living room, with walls that seem to breathe through pink-brick-and-sand-tint inlays. The ceiling is a neutral shade of natural wood.

Directly in front of us, the ocean glistens behind a floor-to-ceiling sliding-glass wall that runs the entire length of the living room. The room opens onto a pink- and sand-colored patio dotted with cocktail tables displaying the same mosaic designs as in the foyer. I can't resist walking outside, where the patio drops down a level to a crystal-clear aquamarine swimming pool surrounded with grotto rocks, with a waterfall on one side that creates soothing, bubbling sounds.

I explore a bit more, and beyond the pool, on the next level down, are red bricks supporting a hot tub large enough to seat a baseball team; this area also surrounded by lush tropical foliage.

Natural stone steps invite a short walk over plush grass to a private ocean beach. Five giant palm trees give shade to anyone wishing a break from working on a tan, and there is an array of beach chairs set out for relaxing in the sea breezes close to the water.

As I'm scanning the two-story wings on each side of the main structure, wondering just how many bedrooms this house contains, a voice comes from behind us, and Tommy and I both jump a little.

"Oh, I am so sorry. Welcome, Kitty and Thomas. I've been expecting you. My name is Jorge Vasquez. I am the Vassars' houseman and personal slave." He laughs and we shake hands. Jorge is my age, or so I think, and he owns a cultured, liquid delivery that plays well with his Hispanic accent. He's dressed in white dress slacks and an elegant European-cut patterned shirt with an open collar. He is a handsome man in every respect, with deep, honey-glow skin and dark eyes that smile. My first impression is that he looks just like one of those jockeys who are interviewed after winning the Kentucky Derby. "I apologize for not being here when you arrived, but my wife is very pregnant, and I was with her when you drove up and could not leave her just then."

"This house and grounds are nothing short of magical," I say.

"I'm glad you approve. Come, let me get you settled in." He gestures to the right. "Over here, beyond the kitchen, and down this hallway, are the private rooms of Dr. and Mrs. Vassar and their son Michael. All of that is closed up now, but over here—" he points to the left—"is all yours."

He takes us back through the living room and down a tiled hallway in the left wing. We come to a set of carved oak doors that open to reveal a bedroom that's larger than my entire apartment. It's decorated in dazzling summer whites and butter yellows, with rich blue appointments. A ridiculously large four-poster bed faces a set of windowed doors with electrically controlled drapes, which open to the sea. I would expect to see this suite in Town & Country magazine.

I wave my arms and laugh. "Now, this looks like Mildred!"

"Yes," Jorge says. "This is Mrs. V's favorite room, and she often stays in here rather than in the master-bedroom suite. She says that the overall house is too masculine for her. She also loves the Florida sunlight and the openness this room provides her."

He throws open another set of doors, providing a private entrance to the pool, which is now "resting" in the early twilight and glowing from within like a turquoise jewel. Soft amber lighting illuminates the nearby alcoves.

Tommy gasps. "This is like the most exotic five-star resort in the world." He's stayed in many such places with Lillian, so I'm certain his remark is without exaggeration.

Jorge smiles. "Yes, it is a truly impressive house. It is one of the older ones here in Palm Beach, built by the famous Addison Mizner. In the 1930s, he designed a great many of the lavish mansions on this island. He was uncommonly quirky for his time, and most loved for his interpretation of Moorish-Mediterranean architecture, even though he did ruffle the feathers of the purists of the day. As well as what we now refer to as the Vassar Villa, he built Mar-a-Lago for Marjorie Meriwether Post, and the estate home the Kennedys called 'The Winter White House.' The list goes on and on. But I won't bore you with any more of my prattle. You will learn the local history on your own as you become familiar with the area."

Tommy glances at me and then asks Jorge, "Does Dr. Vassar come here often?" I remember Millie telling us that this would be the last place her husband would think to look for us. But now I wonder about this, and I'm glad Tommy asked the question.

Jorge hesitates just enough to make me believe he has to consider his response. "Dr. Vassar used to entertain here quite often. Half-dozen or so formal gatherings during the season and numerous smaller parties at other times throughout the year. But this all stopped about three years ago, and he hasn't been here since. Mrs. V and her son still come down several times a year by themselves, but they don't stay very long, and never winter here like they used to. I'm only telling you all this because Mrs. V told me you know all about her and the doctor. She also said that Kitty is her best friend, and from her I am to keep no secrets. But, as you can imagine, I'd prefer you hear everything about family matters from her." He makes a slight bow.

Tommy nods and I say, "Millie, ah, Mrs. V, is precious in every way to me and Tommy. But I had the same curiosity about the doctor." I change the subject. "Do you and your wife live here in the house?"

"On the far side of the residence is the three-room suite Carmella and I call home. We really don't think of the mansion as anything but a beautiful building we are paid to see maintained. All the primary work is done on a strict schedule by crews I manage. They come in from the outside on various schedules, and none live here at the house or at what used to be the maids' residence that's off from the front and hidden by trees. Of course we have armed security at night that patrols the area, and whenever I have a crew coming, such as the maids or gardeners, I'll leave you a message so you won't be surprised." He turns on a lamp that resembles a seahorse, which sits on a nightstand next to an enormous closet I've only caught a glimpse of through a slightly open door. "Just press the blue button on any phone you see in the house or outside it, and I will be at your beck and call."

Jorge then explained that there are a great many wonderful establishments in Palm Beach to dine and relax with a beverage, but that he will be more than happy to prepare whatever foods or beverages we wish. We can either leave a note in the kitchen or call him. To continue this fairytale, he adds, "I refresh the flowers and fruit daily, and place appetizers around the pool bar at cocktail time. But that can be anytime, if you just tell me."

He brings out two terrycloth robes from the closet and lays them on the bed for us. "No one will do any housekeeping in your room, only my wife. You cannot miss her because she is very pregnant with our first child, and of course extremely beautiful." We all smile. "She normally works around the property with me, making certain the crews do their jobs, but now I allow her only to make the beds and dust." He shrugs and laughs. "She says she has to do something."

"I don't want to put you out for meals," I say. "This is all too much, and the least we can do is find our own food." I have to laugh at my remark. Like we'd have to forage for a meal in Palm Beach. Jorge comes to my aid.

"Whatever, your wish, but I must tell you that Mrs. V has given me absolute instructions to make your visit here perfect in every way, I think you will find me a willing and fair chef." He smiles. "Carmella and I generally come into the main house at nine every morning. But let us know the night before, and we will have breakfast ready at whatever time you desire. Or you can call us in the morning."

"You are too good to be true," I say.

He laughs. "I know you two must be tired and hungry. How about some dinner? Whatever you'd like. Steaks? Seafood? Pasta?" He disappears around the corner to a wet bar by the pool and prepares two snifters of Grand Marnier in the time it takes to blink. "Mrs. V has the bar stocked with many pleasures, and I believe this is your spirit of choice.

But always help yourself to whatever you desire should I not be around—or you don't want me in the vicinity." He gives his idea of a wicked grin, which is more like the way a gentle mouse would look at a piece of cheese.

"Jorge," I say, "you are in a class by yourself," and we toast him.

He says, "Enjoy. Relax. I tell you what, I have two beautiful filets that I will grill up for you, make a nice salad, parsley potatoes, and serve a nice merlot from the doctor's private stock. Medium-rare okay for the steaks?" We nod. "Carmella baked bread this morning. I've already sampled it too many times. It is excellent."

"I won't lie, we *are* famished, and steaks sound wonderful. Tommy?"

He nods and puts his hand out to Jorge. They shake again and Tommy says, "This is way too much for me to comprehend right now. We didn't anticipate anyone to wait on us. It's not often that I'm at a loss for words, but I am right now. Thank you."

"Change out of your stuffy, northern clothes, and take a nice swim or jump in the hot tub. Or take a walk on the beach. I will serve dinner at seven o'clock, so you have almost two hours to get settled in and unwind. The beach is ours, meaning it's private for our use only, but I would caution you to go naked only after dark." He laughs. "People still stroll through every so often, looking for shells and whatever. Outside of that, do as you wish. I am blind as well as mute." He smiles like a little mouse.

"Oh, yes, one more thing. Mrs. V told me she will be calling to welcome you herself. There is a phone behind this bar—" he points below to where we can't see—"and a portable phone will ring poolside, as well. You may answer either." Before we can say anything he waves and hurries off.

We stand silently with our drinks. We're overwhelmed with Jorge's exuberant energy and he raises wide smiles from both of us. Tommy blinks several times and shakes his head furiously. "What the hell just happened here? He's like a Mexican Leprechaun."

My eyebrows have been raised in surprise for so long that I think they may be stuck that way forever. I answer him with a string of giggles.

I see our bedroom now lighted in beautiful earth tones, and all is like a dream: the warm, salty sea breezes engaging the white lacey curtains in a sultry dance, the rustling of the palm fronds whispering a gentle hello, the rhythm of the waves caressing the beach and promising to awaken our souls if we'll just allow it to do so. And now "Summer Wind" fills the air, playing through outdoor speakers I can't see in the night.

Tommy springs to life. He picks me up and swings me around, his pain from the fight obviously now just a memory. He kisses me and says, "I think we must've died on the way down here, and this is Heaven. Did you imagine any of this when Millie talked about her little villa?"

"You make me laugh." I kiss him back. "I knew the Vassars were rich, but nothing like this. I can't wait to sink into that hot tub."

As we change into our bathing suits, Tommy calls from the bathroom, "You swim?"

"A little."

"Good. Because I would hate to drown you right off the bat." He sweeps me up and runs out to the pool. I'm screaming as he jumps in, with me in his arms. "Tommy, *no!*"

Jorge comes from the house, laughing and carrying a platter of appetizers. "I can see I am going to have my hands full with you two. You guys spell trouble." His laugh fills the air.

He gets our drinks from the wet bar and moves them to the edge of the pool for us. Leaving, he shakes his head as he calls over his shoulder, "I hope you like the rat pack music of Sinatra and Martin."

"Jorge, this is great," Tommy says. "Sinatra is my man. All Music is my friend."

The water temperature is ideal, and we hold each other close as we float around. "Tommy, how perfect is this? How wonderful. I love you, Sweetheart."

He takes off swimming. I'm not at all surprised to see how beautifully he moves through the water, with long, powerful strokes, his body sleek like a porpoise's. He's as at home in the water as he is on dry land, a true man for all seasons.

I can swim exceptionally well myself, and I manage to match his pace.

For no explainable reason, I reach a level of happiness I've never felt with him before. We're not in tuxes, we're not working together, and we're not surrounded with distractions and people. It's just Tommy and me, alone, swimming in paradise. Maybe we're getting the first part "right" of what Millie said would be necessary for us to make it as a couple.

After several laps we stop at the end of the pool. We're both breathing hard, and he says, "I'm impressed. Matter of fact, damn impressed, Kitten."

"Just a little something else you didn't know about me." I hop out.

We take our drinks and step down a level to the hot tub, which is gurgling in its deep-blue light as if in happy slumber. "This is so surreal," he whispers as we sit, folded into each other, drinking our golden liqueur, feeling the warmth within and around us.

The phone rings, but neither of us spot the physical unit. Jorge comes to the rescue, carrying a portable phone, and he hands it to us in the tub and hurries off.

It's Millie. "Hello, my darlings. You've met my precious Jorge. Isn't he just a prince? I insist that you become great friends, and I mean that." She's excited that we are already in the hot tub and awaiting dinner. Of course, we're both gushing compliments, Tommy and I talking over each other into the phone. She tells us there's a foot of snow at home, and that we left at just the right time. Then there's a pause and her tone becomes somber.

"I have some news that affects both of you, and I don't know which one more. I'm glad you're both sitting down—"

"Millie, what's wrong?" I ask, not having a clue as to what could affect both of us.

"Lillian is dead."

"What!" Tommy shouts. I can't tell if he's pleased, distraught, or shocked. For me, I'm stunned.

I ask cautiously, "Do you know what happened?"

"Last night, she overdosed. At least that's the first indication. One of her employees found her in her office at The Country Club this morning.

She didn't go home last night, and a half-empty bottle of vodka was found next to her and a syringe was still stuck in her arm. A person I know with the police said there were enough drugs still on her desk to kill an elephant."

An unsettling thought hits me. "You said indication. I get the impression you're not so sure it was suicide?"

"Don't know, my dear. But John's nowhere around, and he can't be reached by phone. So there could be a lot more to this. Is Tommy still there?"

Tommy says, "Yes."

"I hope I get this right. Michael wanted me to tell you that he went to John's personal computer in his office and removed you as the driver."

Tommy makes a face but says politely, "I don't understand what he could be talking about."

"Damn it, I knew I'd screw this up. He said he took you off the driver?"

"Mike took me off the hard drive?"

"Yes! Yes, that's it. My Mike is a wiz at this computer stuff. It's all Greek to me. Now there's apparently no connection between you and John anywhere outside of your employment at The Country Club."

Tommy collapses against the back tiles of the hot tub. His relief is contagious, and I squeal with happiness, mine of course because there's no more Lillian to contend with.

"Tell Mike I owe him, big time," Tommy says. "But why did he do this?"

"Because I'm going to the police with everything on John's international drug ring. You think I didn't know anything about this, after all these years? I'll tell you about everything that takes place when we get together. What's important is that you're not on any of the computer material. Oh, and Mike said he removed this driver thing, so you really are a ghost."

"I, ah ... I really don't know what to say."

"Then I'll say it for you: What John was holding over you all these years is now gone."

So it was John who had Tommy all wrapped up in a nice little ball, not Lillian. Yet I have to believe they were both in cahoots in every way, and my Tommy was just their pawn.

"We wish you were here, Millie," I say to her, breathing a sigh of relief for Tommy.

"I'll be there soon enough, along with Michael, but I still have some business to tie up. For now, my dears, this is your time. Do your homework. Be alone and learn about each other. We'll all get together soon. Just know that for now I'll be there in spirit. In the meantime, if you should need me for anything, just call." She sniffles. "I love you both. Goodbye now."

Tommy tells her, "We love you too, Millie. Thank you so much for all this. This trip is the highlight of my life. Kitty's nodding her agreement. We'll never forget this wonderful gift. We will always be so grateful to you, and me to Mike. But we're especially thankful for you." He hangs up and looks at me quizzically.

"What is it?" I ask.

He frowns mildly. "I don't know. It's nothing. Just Millie, I guess. You know how she can—"

"She said something to me when she was asking me about our shuttle escape that still has me bugged. But I'll figure it out before it's too late."

"Before what's too late?"

"I'm sorry, I meant before it doesn't matter anymore." *But I meant it exactly as I said it.* So much of this is very wrong. I should be elated that Lillian's dead, but it's like it didn't happen. And Tommy seemed horribly distraught at the news—and having to catch himself.

"How do you feel, now that Lillian's dead?" I venture to ask him.

"Not believing it. Of course, Millie wouldn't lie."

"She's so hard to read," I say. "So alone in her millions. Or hundreds of millions it looks like. Of course it has to be unimaginably hard for her turn on Dr. Vassar, but it seems odd she'd wait until Lillian is dead. What would that matter? I wish I knew what was going on."

"I worry about her going after her husband's business dealings," Tommy says. "I know how mob bosses operate, even though this may be a little different. She has to be very crafty to orchestrate his arrest and not implicate herself. It can be very dangerous cutting the head off a poisonous snake. The head can still inject venom an hour after it's dead."

"If anyone has the grit to do it, Millie can. I'm sure Mike will advise her, and she'll have the best legal team money could buy."

"Let's hope it's enough."

We soon get too warm in the hot tub and hit the pool again to cool off. Wrapping ourselves in the robes afterwards, we lie together on a double lounge chair, holding hands until Jorge tells us dinner will be ready in fifteen minutes. We hurry back to our room, take super-quick showers, and are at the dining-room table just as he's opening and decanting a bottle of red wine with the flair of a seasoned wine steward like Phillip.

The dinner is fabulous, the steak well marbled and then cooked to melt-in-your-mouth perfection, and Carmella's bread is fabulous, and we tell him so. He beams and promises to let her know of our pleasure. He says she is now rested and will greet us tomorrow at breakfast.

There are fruit tarts of a half-dozen varieties for dessert, and fresh coffee. After clearing the dishes, and showing us how to operate the entertainment center in the den, a room adjacent to the living room, and opposite the hallway to our suite, Jorge says that he's going to retire.

We finish the last of the wine, and although it is still early for bar night owls like Tommy and me, we can't wait to fall into bed.

Jorge has turned down our bed and left a note explaining how to operate the air conditioning, but we opt to leave the windows open so we can hear the ocean. As has been the precursor of my falling asleep of late, my mind is racing in complete contradiction to my exhausted physical self. It went right by me when Millie said she was going to expose Dr. Vassar's international drug ring. I let that get confused with international implant ring. Tommy has always denied that John Vassar had anything to do with illegal drugs. But I always found this suspect, and not just because Lillian acted stoned most of the time. And regardless of how confused Tommy might be at a comment Millie's made to him, I'm still rolling the shuttle story around in my head, trying to isolate the piece I'm missing that has me going batty.

However, even with all that's going on inside and around me, in a few minutes I'm sound asleep, adrift in a huge bed of crisp yellow sheets, white eyelet spreads, and deep-blue pillows, with the melodic voice of the sea singing its love songs through the gently swaying palms.

Chapter 28

I AWAKEN SOMETIME BEFORE dawn to find Tommy is gone. *Jesus, not fucking again.* I literally crawl on all fours to the edge to the bed wondering why people need such a prodigious field to sleep in. This bed could sleep half the staff at The House. I catch myself. The House is past tense. I throw on the robe and walk outside.

The chilled, damp dawn air lies in silence between the gentle breaking waves, just like the pause separating one's breaths.

The dark-gray predawn light prevents me from spotting Tommy anywhere along the nearby beach.

I walk down the steps and across the thick, wet carpet of grass to the soft sand, now cool to the foot. I venture out a little way toward the ocean and scan up and down the coastline. Nothing resembles a person. I briskly return to the lower level and sit on the edge of the hot tub, no longer gurgling and illuminated and seductively inviting. I find this a strange predicament to find myself in—since even in these palatial surroundings I could not be more isolated and alone.

I'm sitting for just a few minutes when dawn begins to scratch long pink lines in the skin of a gray sky. It always amazes me how quickly day "begins" once it gets started. Within minutes, dark, sinister-appearing shapes brighten into familiar things and the ocean changes color.

I gather my courage again, and this time I walk all the way down to water's edge. The gentle waves nibble at my toes, and I find I'm smiling despite my concern for Tommy. Then I see him in the distance; a small running dot moving in my direction. Relieved and upset with myself for thinking ill of him, I amble back to the little grove of palm trees to wait for him.

I've never been up close and personal with a palm tree before, so I allow my curiosity to take in every inch of what I can see: its funny, ringed bark and how it can grow in a sway; its ever-moving fronds quivering in the slightest of air currents. My prize is a fallen coconut I find peeking out from behind the largest of the trees. I pick it up like a just-discovered treasure. Wow, I'm a wench marooned on a desert island. Or I'm a Spanish explorer—all because I found this "astonishing" coconut.

Tommy's walking, hands on hips, catching his breath from his run. He does not see me in the early morning haze. He stretches, and as always I admire his strong body. How he keeps it to all muscle and no fat is something I wish I could learn. I continue to chastise myself for thinking he could lose a few pounds. He walks to the edge of the waves and pees.

I saunter up alongside him. "*Piss in the Ocean?* I'm pretty sure that's a card game I used to play as a kid. However, I see you give it literal connotation." I continue my intellectual discourse. "I'm sure this could also paint you a portrait of the meaning of life, and how insufficient your existence is in the vast expanse of creation unless, of course, you believe within your prodigious ego that your minuscule liquid contribution is realistically making a difference."

"You're a pretty deep philosopher so early in the morning, aren't you? He looks over his shoulder and smiles. "Hello, Sweetheart."

"I was worried, scared even, when I couldn't find you. You ever think about leaving a note?"

"I'm sorry, Kitten. I should have left you one. We went to bed so damn early last night that I was wide awake before dawn. So I went for a run." He gives me a peck on the lips. "Come with me next time." He catches my disdainful look. "You don't run?"

"I have never seen anyone smiling while running. You're on your own, my love," I want him to recognize that I'm still an adventuresome spirit. "Come, see what I found." I run up to "my" palm tree and pick up "my" coconut. "Look, a real coconut. I bet there's milk inside." I shake it to my ear.

He chuckles and looks fondly at me, and I'm again taken with him. So handsome, with his hands low on his hips, the salt-and-pepper chest hair that trickles down the middle of his stomach—and below his waist. His muscular legs and powerful thighs.

I lean back against the palm tree and let my robe fall open, allowing him to gaze at my nakedness. I give him my most sensuous Hollywood pose, even parting my legs just so.

It requires only a moment before he shakes his head. "If you only knew what goes on inside me when you pull shit like this. It's a wonder I don't pass out right now from every drop of blood rushing all at once from my north to my south." He presses me back against the gentle bend of the palm tree and we manage to kiss until we're both out of breath. His hands are warm against my cool skin, and I wrap my legs around his waist. He glances around the vacant beach.

I kiss him quickly on the neck and then lick his earlobe. "Don't tell me my old hippie lover is concerned that someone might catch him in the act." I add a snicker for good measure.

He's now breathing more heavily than when he'd just finished running, "I don't want to appear rude." We walk back to the mansion where I carefully place my cherished coconut by the private entrance to our suite. We take a long shower together and crawl back into bed to get a little more rest before starting what we believe will be a busy, fun-filled day.

The surf starts to build; it grows as the temperature rises. Soon, however, this becomes academic, since a stiff wind kicks up and makes the ocean's gentle patter turn into a roar. Just as I'm about to close my eyes to get what I'm certain will amount to a few minutes' sleep at best, classical music starts to dance on the new breeze frolics that through our open windows, and I see movement around the pool.

We hear the hot tub start and watch as two tables are rolled in and set up by a twenty-something man and woman, both with blond hair, great tans, and athletic-looking. "Good morning," Jorge says as we emerge from our room. "I trust you slept well?"

"Peacefully as in an angel's arms," I tell him, and Tommy agrees.

Jorge nods and grins. "That is because angels live here at this villa, and I'm quite serious about that."

Carmella pads over and stands, smiling wide, beside him. She is indeed beautiful, and her large belly makes it clear it has to be her and no other.

"This is my wife and love of my life, Carmella. And this is our son, Emilio, who's just not here yet." Jorge pats her round tummy.

"Aha, you took a peek and know it's a boy," I say.

"Si, es nino—se Emilio," she answers, smiling as proudly as is humanly possible. We go through the introductions and small talk. I hug Carmella, and tell her that I am excited about her baby. She giggles and says, "Mucho gracias."

Jorge says, "Are you ready for a lovely massage?"

Our beaming, surprised faces give him the answer.

"I called them last evening when I saw how tired you both looked. Every day should start with a massage." Jorge gives Tommy a sly wink. "Especially when one may have some sore spots that need healing."

Tommy looks at him and Jorge smiles. "Mrs V told me you had a little accident before you left New York."

Tommy caves with a laugh. "My God, is there nothing Millie hasn't told you about us?"

Jorge smiles broadly. "Details make for great service," he says with a wave and turns to bustle off. "Breakfast with be served in about an hour "Enjoy!"

We drop our robes and position our bodies on the tables under the softest sheets I've ever felt against my skin, and for an hour we're transported to another dimension, with aromatherapy oils complementing the most heavenly massage imaginable. Afterwards we feel completely satisfied. Tommy offer them a tip but they graciously refuse it, saying they are well compensated for their services. They remind us that we *are* guests. I tell Tommy under my breath." So this is the flip side of service. I can get really use to this."

He chuckles and says, "After all the service we've given to others, I think we deserve this."

Jorge and Carmella serve us a breakfast with enough food to feed a half-dozen hungry soldiers. Afterwards, Jorge laughs at me and my excitement over the coconut and brings a machete to open it for us. He gives the coconut a whack and hands me a hairy little sphere from inside the pod that looks like a miniature bowling ball. He expertly chops one end open so as not to spill the contents and offers me the milk.

"Wow, I'm pretty impressed," I say. I take a small sip of the murky grayish liquid and scream, "Ugh, this tastes terrible!"

Jorge nods and guffaws. "Coconut milk is definitely an acquired taste. But coconut meat, now, it is delicious. I will grate some for you tonight and make a dessert with it."

An hour later we are leaving the villa, and I have a pocketbook full of notes on where to go and what to do once we get to where we're going.

The Island of Palm Beach is only sixteen miles long. We discover that we can take a tour of Worth Avenue for an hour, led by one of the area's top historians. We learn all about "The Gilded Age of the '20s, '30s, and '40s," and how Henry Flagler and John D. Rockefeller started it all.

Tommy's a man on a mission when it comes to absorbing history. He's engrossed in everything our guide says about The Everglades Club, and how it was built on a dirt road in 1918, unfathomable by today's standards, and that The Sailfish Club followed in 1925, bringing wealthy businessmen to this tropical paradise.

He's profoundly interested in Addison Mizner, whom Jorge had told us built Mildred's masterpiece along with so many others. Tommy wants to see The Boca Raton Club with its Cloister Inn and other monuments to his brilliance and vision. But it was Palm Beach that held court to the Vanderbilts, and names like Hutton, Post, Phipps, Dodge, Guest and Du Pont.

Tommy wanders around the museum we come to, lingering in long study of a single old photograph of Palm Beach's most notable women and men, the true old money who pulled it all together.

We stroll the four blocks of Worth Avenue, with its rows of shops catering to the fabulously affluent, before I drive him all over the island, looking at the mansions and elegant properties that are accessible without breaking and entering. We wind up at The Breakers Hotel for lunch. Jorge told us that Tommy would need a jacket to enter the lobby, and a blue blazer of Michael's fits him like a glove, so we walk around like royalty. Albeit I am woefully underdressed, but why should an obvious baroness care about the pompous silliness of elegant habiliment for a noon repast?

After a lingering lunch that the baroness found divine, we take in the grounds, as if just one of many such haunts we visit routinely on our worldly tours. Tommy plays the role to the hilt, posturing himself as if he has come home. I give him a gentle poke on the arm and remind him that our bank account would need a whole lot more zeros at the end of it —a whole lot more—to get anyone in these digs to even raise an eyebrow.

The Breakers is like a palace, where iconic movie stars like Cary Grant and Gary Cooper were frequent visitors, and we enjoy exploring the hotel as if we are two stowaway kids just set free. I see excitement in his eyes about being amid this wealth in Florida. No, not Florida; to be precise, *this* Florida. He wants to be here in Palm Beach. And Millie has made it possible so he can let his imagination overwhelm his reality, and I must admit that I find myself getting caught up in it too at times.

We are going to buy a bottle of Champagne and sit under an umbrella by the pool, but since the skies are clear and the sun is brilliant, we decide to go back to Vassar Villa and relax with cocktails by the pool.

266

It's not exactly like we're taking a second seat, even in comparison to a place as venerable as The Breakers.

We change into our swimwear and enjoy a lovely afternoon. We absolutely refuse to have Jorge cook for us tonight, and I can tell he's happy he can be with Carmella.

The evening is warm and romantic, and we find a fabulous restaurant for dinner, Taboo, which makes the most fabulous brandy Alexanders I've ever tasted, mine included. The bartender, Randy, fills the shaker with three giant scoops of real ice cream for each drink. I had one before dinner and one afterwards instead of dessert, and if I lived in Palm Beach I'd weigh 200 pounds. After discussing a chateaubriand that Tommy admits was every bit as good as The House's, causing both of us to pause and tear up for a moment, we decide to go back to the beach at the villa and walk in the moonlight.

As one looks toward the ocean from the Villa, the shoreline is wide and open to the right. Off to the left, however, the beach curves around to form a small secluded cove with high dunes and dense foliage closing off most of it and definitely discouraging anyone from trying to access the area from the rear, even by tank. We nestle ourselves in a little clearing and make the sweetest love imaginable. We don't have a care in the world, and we also don't have a clue that we are being watched, and have been all night.

Chapter 29

WHEN I WAKE UP the next morning Tommy is again out running. I wait to shower with him, and we share a superb breakfast of strawberry crepes —of course made with Grand Marnier. We drive around and see some new and now old "by one day" sights, and then take a unanimous vote to chill out on the beach for the rest of the day. We are still not quite caught up from all the driving to get to Palm Beach, and we're also coming to grips with the reality of being allowed into this paradise.

Jorge has read our minds, which he does often it seems, because we find a stack of beach towels and several tubes of sunscreen in various strengths on the steps leading down to the beach. We see that he's also moved two beach chairs to water's edge and set up an umbrella for us. He's provided a large cooler and a radio, as well.

"Man, this guy is good," Tommy says as he opens the cooler and finds a six-pack of beer, premixed margaritas, and a bottle of Chardonnay. Of course, there are glasses. "This would be a good job for us, don't you think?"

I wrinkle my nose. "I think it would be very lonely. We need people around us to create excitement, not to mention that our boss might well be a miserable sonofabitch like John Vassar. You saw some of those people who formed the backbone of Palm Beach aristocracy. From Flagler to Rockefeller and in-between, these people weren't known as anything but ruthless in everything they did. Imagine being the help and having to put up with their whims?"

"Well, they weren't all priggish snobs, and some had the time of their lives. You don't need a bad attitude to be rich. In order to live well, it's not a requirement that a person has to be a jerk. We know some very well off people, and I wouldn't hesitate to work for any one of them. They're not all are bastards like John Vassar."

"Agreed," I say. "But just for the record, I'd like to be on *this* side of wealthy. You could come and work for me, if you so desire." I turn and look at him over my lowered sunglasses.

Tommy chuckles, "And you could work under me, anytime."

"I believe I already do that, my sweet. The pay isn't great but the benefits are splendid."

The beach is once again perfect, and we stretch out side by side to soak up the rays. He lathers me up with sunscreen. Otherwise, as fair as I am, I'll burn to a crisp. He brags that he never burns. He adds that it's because he's an Italian. His comment is met with a handful of thrown sand as I chide him. "You play that Italian card way too much."

We drink a margarita apiece as we languish on the soft cushions, drugged by the deep heat, the hot but comfortable sand at our feet, the smell of the sea, the rhythmic, soft hissing of gentle waves lapping the shore. It's all pure seduction.

"That's it for me," Tommy says after a half-hour or so, getting up and walking to the surf. "Coming?"

"Yep, I'm fried."

The ocean feels cold, but as we swim out farther it becomes exhilarating. I can clearly see all the way to sandy bottom, and I observe little fishes darting here and there below our legs. There's something profoundly spiritual about being in the ocean, floating in The Mother's salty womb, combined with the heartbeat of the surf and the oxygen that's paramount to what's alive in nature.

We share no words but enjoy each other at the level of deep gazes and soft kisses and gentle fondling. After a while we break away, swimming, diving under the waves, and body surfing to shore like two kids. We repeat the process until we are wrinkled and waterlogged. We flop into the beach chairs and bring out the margaritas, which of course Jorge has replenished. And now that he knows we like them, he even chilled glasses in ice and has included lime and salt to enhance the premixed concoction that wasn't half bad out of the bottle to begin with.

"Amazing," Tommy says, pouring out the perfect drinks as we stretch out under the umbrella. He lies back in the lounge chair and takes a long sip of his margarita. "We need to discuss what the hell we are going to do when we get home. The bills aren't going to stop. Not that I have any huge bills." Tommy chuckles but I don't know how he can. "I have about $8,000 in my checking account, $1,200 in savings, and around $20,000 in stocks that I've played with over the years. I never really planned on creating a future for two. I thought I'd be a bachelor for life, or marry someone rich, like Lillian. You're not rich, are you?" He peeps at me over his glass.

I choke in mid-swallow at the mention of Lillian's name, and I have to recover before I can say, "I used to be rich, but not anymore. The pay of a bartender isn't the road to becoming wealthy, as I'm sure you well know. Like you, I never planned on anyone in my life but me. I have two grand in checking and what the hell is savings? I pay my bills as they come in, from my weekly tips." I run my tongue around the rim of the glass and taste the salt, and only then do I take a long sip. The blend is powerful, and I'm an experienced drinker. It's obvious that Jorge also made these margaritas with Grand Marnier and not Cointreau or some other liqueur, and he's got the mix down pat. I want to know the exact measurements. I didn't believe I could learn a thing new about bartending, but last evening's brandy Alexanders and these margaritas prove there's always something to pick up, as bartending is indeed a craft.

"Do you want to try Atlantic City?" he asks.

"I don't know. Bartending in a casino would certainly be busy, but … well, I'm just not sure."

"What about here?"

"Much as I'd love the lifestyle, it's a case of affording it. We're fish out of water here, and we wouldn't last a month on what we have financially. No, we need to go home and use Florida as a goal to strive for. We have friends and support at home but not a soul here." I place my leg over his so I know I have his undivided attention. "Tommy, I don't understand something." He raises his eyebrows. "Your reaction after Millie told us that Lillian was dead seemed to be little more than passing surprise. It's like she never existed. I won't tell you I'm not happy she's no longer around to plague us, but I don't understand how you can be so indifferent."

He shifts so my leg falls from his, and his face gets as gray as the cloud that just appeared overhead to block out the sunlight. He doesn't say anything but looks up at the sky. When the sun peeks through again, he says, "Lillian and I had a very complex relationship. And before you ask, a lot of it involved John. But I never ran drugs for John or handled anything other than delivering documents. Now, if there were checks in those bundles, so be it. And there could have been wire-transfer documentation for off-shore accounts, and these also had to be hand-delivered; again, so be it."

"What's this got to do with Lillian?"

"Let's just say she was a lot smarter than someone who just ran a golf and tennis club." He takes a slurping sip of his margarita. "Maybe 'smarter' isn't the right word, but she definitely knew a lot more about money than the average person in business, is what I'm saying. Do you know her background before she bought The Country Club?" I shake my head. "She was the president of a bank. And she wasn't just the president, she owned it one hundred percent. Sold it for six-and-a-half million. It's where she got the money for The Club, which she bought for cash. And when she ran the bank, she paid herself a half-million a year and saved most of it. Lillian had a lot of issues, I'm the first to admit this, but she was brilliant with money. Why do you think John hooked up with her?"

"I guess I should be impressed, but I'm not. None of this tells me why her death didn't seem to surprise you beyond asking rather indifferently how it happened."

"Because I thought it would be me, instead. Now, please don't ask me anything else about Lillian."

"So you think she was killed, don't you?"

"You're asking me."

"So, goddamn it, tell me.

He stares out into the ocean, but for a only a few seconds. "Millie said something that got me thinking that Lillian was killed. She didn't drink vodka."

I should have picked up on that as well, since her drink was a Manhattan, and nothing else, which means that if she was killed, it was by someone other than John Vassar himself, as he surely knew what she drank. In this regard, the murder was sloppy and now I, too, am certain she was killed.

I sit in this glorious setting, thinking about vicious-bitch Lillian, and for the first time ever I feel sorry for her. All her money and power, and she dies like a common crook.

Tommy brings me out of my melancholy stupor. "Bruno said he'd look around for us in Atlantic City, and Chris said we could earn considerable money in the right place. Maybe we should do that, stash away the chips and plan on Florida in the future." I chuckle warmly at him. "Dearest, we have been here a day and a half. And I've got a feeling Florida in the summer may be hell for northerners like us who like the cold. To quote Shakespeare, 'All that glisters is not gold.'"

"Merchant of Venice," he quickly says, quite proud of himself.

"Very astute, my impulsive child, and you didn't try to improperly correct me with 'glitters.' And you now know everything I learned in the two years I went to college."

"I didn't know you went to college?"

"Well, I did. Tell you about it sometime. But, back to the present. We are paupers in a rich man's, or I should say woman's, playground. Life's an illusion, at least most of the time—and a place like this can definitely influence just about any fantasy—so we can't be hasty in whatever we decide."

"We can be just as poor here as at home. But you are right, Kitten, if it wasn't for Millie, we wouldn't be here at all."

He pours the last of the margarita mix and says to me, "If this is Millie's idea of the school of hard knocks for learning to be alone with each other, I think we're passing with flying colors."

We take another swim and walk the beach for a while, hand in hand. I find two beautiful shells, and we poke curiously at a horseshoe crab that washes ashore right in front of us. When we get back to our beach, he sits in the surf and pulls me down between his knees, wrapping his arms around me, nuzzling my neck.

I playfully ask him a question that came to me from out of nowhere. "So, Mr. Thomas Defalco, you're forty-five, and I thought I had good sex my whole life, but I discovered I was wrong after that night with you in The Pit. I'm going to tell you right now that I'll never answer what I'm asking you, but how old were you when you first had sex?"

"With myself or somebody else?" I've heard the line before, so I give him a bored look.

"I was fifteen."

"Fifteen? What on earth could you have at fifteen?"

"A hard on, for one thing." He laughs loud.

I reach around a slap him. "Be serious. Who on earth could you have sex with at fifteen? A cheerleader wannabe who was out to get back at the world because she didn't make the squad?"

"No, a woman forty years old, and her name was Alice Fisher. She lived three doors up from us, in Queens. Alice used to break in all the young boys in the neighborhood."

"You've got to be joking. What about Child Protective Services or whatever it's called?"

"Never had such a thing, at least that any of us ever knew about. And before you draw conclusions about her being fat and ugly with warts on her nose, she was the most beautiful woman I'd ever seen at the time.

Smart and sexy, with a great body too. She'd get one of us boys to help her in with groceries or to do some maintenance work for her, and she'd pay us with sexual favors. Her husband was killed in the war, and she lived in her house alone."

"You sure you're not making this up?"

"Not at all. And you asked, so I'll finish. She taught us the finer things about sex. Specifically, how to be gentle and the ways of pleasing a woman. She taught us to have the girl come first because girls take longer, and we should be grateful that they wanted us at all." He laughs. "She was amazing. She must have had every kid I knew who was mature, but we really respected her and never joked about her."

"Yeah, but kids always talk, and today the adults go to jail. More females all the time."

"Here's the thing. Lots of stuff was suspected, but everyone knew that when the first guy talked, it would mean she would no longer be available. But more important, the kid who told would be killed by the others. Alice was like a goddess to us, and she had a way of making it all right, a passage into manhood, something you needed to know how to do correctly. She taught us all about birth control, too, and of course about VD. Regardless, the boys always had to wear protection, and I'm serious."

"I'm still amazed she wasn't busted."

"My guess is she was always in that business, and probably did most of the kids' fathers in their day. So they figured it was a good thing for their sons to learn from her rather than from some schoolgirl who could get pregnant because she or the boy didn't know any better. Every so often the cops would come by and question some of us, but we took a sacred oath never to tell." He pauses and hugs me. "Anyway, she died of leukemia a year later, when I was sixteen. Her funeral was packed with young men who had fallen madly in love with her, including me. You might think it odd to hear me say this, but she was a classy woman."

"Wow That's quite a story. No wonder you are such a considerate lover. Seems to me your neighborhood should erect a monument to her."

Tommy says, "I'm amazed that I never told you about Alice Fisher, as close as we've been. And I won't ask about your first time, because you already told me ages ago."

"I did?" I ponder my memory.

"You and Polly had us all in stitches one night in the Pit when you discussed your first boyfriends." He puts his glass in the cooler.

"Oh, yeah," I say, but my mood suddenly changes.

A heavy sadness settles in me. I turn our easy conversation around as quickly as a sailboat tacks around meet to a sudden change in the wind. "I was very young then, Tommy. Stupid and young and aggressive is a bad combination. I thought I knew everything and that I was bulletproof. Nothing bad could ever happen to me. Hell, I was from a rich family. But the days that were fun and wonderful soon became devastatingly difficult. I put a terrible strain on my parents. I've told you about a lot of it."

"But you were passionate about what you thought was right. You wanted change because you believed the world needed it." Tommy smoothes the hair back that the wind is blowing into my face. "We all did things when we were young that could be viewed as stupid, danger-ous, and hurtful. That's what *young* is mostly about. Everyone has degrees of regret. That's the process of growing up."

"So things change you forever," I say quietly. My lower lip starts quivering, something it's not done for years.

His face deepens into concern, and he searches my face. I avoid his eyes, and he gently brings me back to his. "Kitten, you know we're a safe harbor for each other. There's nothing you can't share with me."

The tide's coming in and the waves swirl around me, offering to cleanse me of previously unspeakable burdens. He removes the swirls of hair that a new wind has blown across my face.

"What is it, Sweetie. You can tell me anything, you know that by now."

I take a deep breath, but the words hang in my throat until I can finally blurt, "I had an abortion at eighteen."

275

"Oh, Kitten." He looks at me with such profound concern that I start to cry.

"I was so afraid, and I didn't know what to do. I had just started college, and I was there only a few months. I was staying off campus with a bunch of kids I didn't know. My father would have killed me, or the news might have killed him. He had a bad heart. Our fights alone put him in danger of too much stress. He had paid for my entire college education, and my whole future was now turned to shit because I got pregnant by someone at a stupid party, and I never saw the guy again."

"You don't need to go through this for me." Tommy says gently.

"No, I want to get this out." I swallow hard and continue. "Back then a girl had to be twenty-one for a legal abortion or have parental consent, and being Catholic that would have been totally out of the question. So some kids told me where to go, and I had it done. I bled so badly, there was a time when I thought I was going to die. Yet I couldn't tell anyone what was wrong. It was a different world back then."

He nods and kisses my forehead, drawing me closer to him.

"I got through it with my belief that the soul doesn't enter a body until that first breath is gasped. Like when God breathed life into Adam. And that is what I believed then and what I believe to this day. But when I finally did go to a gynecologist for a checkup and told him that I'd had an abortion, he read me the riot act. He was some sort of religious zealot, but he also told me that my uterus was so torn up that I should forget about ever having children. So I did forget about it. After that, I never felt worthy of having children anyway. I also hardly ever had a period, so I stopped taking the pill. I've stayed as far away from serious relationships as I could so I would never have to reveal this secret to anyone. Now I'm telling you."

"Oh, my sweet baby girl," he whispers as he brings my head to his chest. He lets me cry while he talks to me. "You did what you needed to do, at the time. You thought that abortion was your only option, and in your heart it was. You had no other choice under the circumstances. No one should judge you for doing what you did. But you're a damned harsh judge of yourself, you know that?" He takes some sea water and washes away my tears.

"I'm so very sorry you had to live in torment all these years, I'm no stranger to self-condemnation." He pauses." Since you shared your innermost secret with me, I'm going to tell you something I've never uttered to another living soul."

I raise my head to look at him and his eyes have a depth to them that seems bottomless. He mouths words that barely come out as a whisper from his lips: "I killed a baby once. We went into a village that was ravaged by the Viet Cong. Everyone was dead but this one little infant lying next to his dead mother. He was naked and maybe a year old. He was burned badly and pretty mangled, but he heard me approach. He turned his head and looked at me, and then he did that thing babies do with their hands when they want to be picked up. He trusted me to pick him up and comfort him. He was looking at me when I shot him, yet he saw right through me."

I feel the emotion rise in him, and his throat closes so no more words come for a moment. He struggles as if he can't breathe, but he continues, "And I ask myself every day and night what kind of man would do that? My anger and shame sank me deep into drugs to keep that vision under control. It was the single most horrible thing I did over there, of so many that trashed my faith in God and of myself as a human being. I was so ashamed and still am. I couldn't even tell the therapists at the hospital about it because it was so intensely personal. I swear, you're the only one who knows this."

I sit up and hold his face in my hands. "That baby was suffering and near death. What kind of man were you, you ask? A compassionate man. You did the compassionate thing. An honorable Marine stops the suffering."

"That would be fine, but goddamn it, Kitty, I didn't feel compassion. I didn't feel anything. That's what happened to me over there. I just stopped feeling. I did what I thought needed to be done at the time, but it has tormented me every day of my life." His beautiful eyes are now craters of woe. "At the time, you also did what you had to do." He is about to burst into tears.

"I could have had the baby and put it up for adoption," I say.

"And I could have called a corpsman, but I took the easy way out."

We both ponder the checkmate of the moment. I gather my emotions and say, "Sometimes we do things in life that screw us up. We took the path we felt we had to take, period. You thought that child would have a horrible life if he survived, of which the odds were slim and none. Everyone, if honest, has a story like ours. Maybe not as intense, but in its way just as burdensome. You and I are good people, and that's what matters in God's eyes. I have to believe this to survive, and you must too. And I'm not eighteen and you're not in Nam anymore."

We look at each other a long time, with the rising surf thundering around us.

"I was wrong about how I feel about you, Kitty. I told you once I could never love you more. But I was wrong about that. My love for you is infinite."

I whisper to him wearily as I rest my forehead against his, "I want to give all this pain to the sea. I want to wash it all away." I pull him to his feet. The tide comes in and churns heavily around us. I hold out my hand to him "Come here, love." He laces his fingers with mine, and for a moment we stand in silence.

He glances at the sky and back to me and says softly, "I just want that baby to forgive me. I need his forgiveness to set me free. That's all."

"Then just ask," I say gently. "But, more important, you need to forgive yourself. I need to forgive myself. I'm strong enough to do it, now that I've told you. You are too, Tommy. Sharing this dark pain is the first step. Are you ready?" The silence is sacred. He's far away somewhere in his mind. Deep grief is splashed across his face, and he shakes his head. "I just can't let him go. I wish I could—but I can't."

His eyes beg me for an answer, but all I see are his tears, so I tell him softly, "Forgiveness *is* letting go. You have already let that baby go by sharing him with me."

"I did?" is all he can manage through his sobs.

"Yes, my love. You gave him to me. I took him into my heart so you can free your own heart. He's in a place where he has already forgiven you. Now you can let it all go."

He covers his eyes with his hands and his whole body shakes. I reach out and touch him, and he desperately pulls me to him. There are no words to explain what I'm feeling, but I sense how deeply he's moved.

"Let's release our babies and forgive who we are," I say, taking his hand and coaxing him into the welcoming waves.

We swim out together underwater, and when we return to shore he scoops me up in his arms and kisses me all over my face, his eyes shining. "I feel baptized somehow. How do you possess such wisdom? How did you know just then what to say about forgiveness?"

The answer I give him surprises me as well. "They were whispered through me by an angel."

Chapter 30

I WAKE UP DURING the night and reach over for Tommy, once again finding him gone. I've been through this enough that I now fall quickly back to sleep. When I open my eyes in the morning he is sitting on the side of the bed, fully dressed, just staring at me.

"What are you doing, Sweetheart?" I ask as I wipe the sleep from my eyes.

"Just looking at you—and how beautiful you are."

I smile up at him; my handsome Tommy. He places his hand around the back of my neck and kisses me gently.

"Kitty, you need to know something. I've tried so many times to tell you this but I just can't find the words. I have talked to Jorge about this, and he will stay here with you and comfort you, but I need to leave. I just can't do this anymore."

Jorge is standing beside him and says, "Tommy needs to do this. I'm so sorry, but as he says I will be here for you."

I can now see clearly, and Tommy's eyes are glassy and bloodshot. He tells me, "Millie wanted us to find each other's secrets. Well, this is mine. I'm living a lie, Kitty. I'll always love you—but I love someone else more. I've tried to forget her, tried to get her out of my system, but my feelings for her are too powerful me to ignore. This woman and I have a long history together, and I need her more than I ever imagined. I should have told you earlier." He pauses and glances away. "I wanted it work out for you and me, but she dominates my every thought and I can't escape how

I feel. I hope you'll understand in time that I never meant to hurt you. But I need to leave now. She's standing by the pool, waiting for me to go with her to the airport. I'm sorry, but she's the real deal breaker."

"What the hell are you talking about?" I'm straining to grasp what he's saying. Indeed, there's a woman by the pool, standing next to Tommy's suitcase. She's dressed in a gorgeous all-white business suit, and she has beautifully styled whitish hair, with blond highlighting that shimmers in the sunlight. I start to laugh, guessing this is some sort of game. But his mien doesn't change, and I soon come to the realization this is no joke.

Horrified at the prospect of his leaving me, I yell, "You can't go! For God's sake, we love each other!" I reach out to grab him and he shakes me hard.

"You don't know anything about me. I love this woman. She will always be in my life. So you need to get over it." I slap his face and his nose begins to bleed. He's shaking me as the blood flies from his nostrils and I hear, "Stop it, Kitty. It's all right." It's only then that I wake up.

"Whoa, Baby," I hear him say as I'm sitting up in bed and he has me by my shoulders. It's not quite dawn yet. "It was just a bad dream, Sweetie. Wake up. Look at me. Everything is okay now. I'm here, and you're safe." His voice is like liquid valium, as it soothes me immediately.

"Oh, dear God, that was a dream?" I am sweating and shaking all over.

He pulls me close. "Yes, just a dream. You're safe and all's well. It's all good." He kisses my face and strokes my hair. I cling to him, unable to quit crying.

"Awww, my precious Kitten." I love when he says that, but now the words make me cry harder. "That must have been some dream." He turns on the lamp closest to me. "You look terrified."

"It was so real. So frightfully real."

"The bad ones usually are. Do you want to tell me about it?"

My words come in a rush as I explain what I recall. He shakes his head repeatedly and then chuckles, which I don't appreciate. I let him know and he says, "I'm not making light of your dream, but I assure you I'm not going anywhere, especially with a white-haired woman. Has my first love come to claim me? Do you think it was poor Alice Fisher?"

"Did she have white hair?" I ask, which is about the dumbest thing I've ever said.

"She would be pretty old now, so I guess she'd have white hair." He chuckles again, but this time I'm not upset. I even smile to myself at how a person's mind can capture what can seem like the most insignificant details from some event and turn them into the focus of a dream—or nightmare.

"Your bopping me in the nose and giving me a nosebleed isn't surprising, considering the way some of our battles go." I start to laugh now. "I'm going to tell you a story," he says, turning out the light and snuggling with me under the covers.

"When I was a little boy and I'd have a terrible dream that would scare me, my father, Antonio, would put me on his lap. He would hug and kiss me awake, and then he'd say in Italian, 'Tomaso.' He called me Tomaso. 'Tomaso, it's time for you to become a warrior. You know these evil dreams are just stories in your mind. And you've got the power to change any story from bad to good. I know what a brave boy you are, and I see you as a gallant knight, riding your horse and swinging your sword overhead, ready to slay all these dragons in your dreams. You know how fierce dream dragons can be? They can take any form they want. But you know their game. So here's the deal.'

"By the way, if you ever wondered where that phrase came from, I picked it up from my father. He said it all the time, along with other Italian men in the neighborhood. So he'd say, 'Tomaso, here's the deal. You go back into that dream and become the warrior who changes the story so it all comes out the way you want it to. Always remember, you're the dreamer—not the dream. You have the power to change everything, while dragons in dreams have no power at all.'"

I hug Tommy. "What a beautiful story. Your father must have been a wonderful man and loved you very much."

"He did. Antonio Michele was a good man in every way, and he wanted me to be a loving father just like him one day. I'd name my son after him, if I had one. I guess I let him down, big time." He sighs and displays the saddest smile I believe I've ever seen on anyone's face, but it gradually goes away and he's back to his normal self.

"Now, young lady, here's the deal. It's time you return to that dream and kick some serious butt. First, tear into that old white-haired bitch and tell her I'm your *forever* man, and to get herself back to wherever she came from. Then tell me to cut out my dumb shit and climb into this bed and make love to you long and proper or you'll bloody something worse than my nose." He has me laughing now, and his eyes are twinkling. "As I think about it, I guess I have no other option than to do just that right now." He rolls over and kisses me. "See how you have the power to change anything?" He climbs on top of me and spreads my legs with his knees. "And it's my loving duty to appease you in every way possible. It's a hard job, but I guess this is in my deal." He smiles wickedly.

We make wonderful love until the sun is pouring through the glass French doors. We open the drapes completely and find Jorge poolside, setting out a tray of coffee and pastries.

We shower quickly and greet a day that hits us like the air from a blast furnace when we slide open the glass doors that allow us private access to the pool.

"Whew, it's going to be hot today," I say to Jorge as Tommy and I sit in chairs on either side of an umbrella anchored to a table.

We tell Jorge that we'll be gone all day and probably won't be home for dinner. We plan to go south on A1A to Ft Lauderdale and maybe try to make it all the way to Miami.

The day is crystal clear, and the ocean stretches out hypnotically while the Intracoastal Waterway to our right gives us some great views of what serious money buys in terms of real estate. We stop often so I can take pictures of everything from mansions to street scenes I find of interest. I also take photos of Tommy, capturing his subtle expressions, the sparkle in his eyes, the comical looks he gives me when the mood strikes him.

Our first "official" stop is Boca Raton, and we stroll around the pink and white main plaza off Federal Highway, which sports an enormous number of fine restaurants and top-name stores. Tommy is over the moon about this place.

At one shop he purchases a beautiful blue suit made of the finest Italian silk, which is similar to the one he lost in the fire, along with a fabulous tie. He also picks out a pair of Italian loafers and a matching belt. I buy a sweet sundress, with shoes and a purse to match. I also buy a giant floppy sun hat that shades me all over. He gets to giggling over the hat so ridiculously long and loud that I have to smack him to shut him up.

He also buys a pair of light yellow slacks, already hemmed to his length, and a polo shirt with pastel stripes. A cool-looking, sky-blue sport coat that fits him like a second skin makes the outfit incredible. We look like Florida natives now—if not even the scions of old money.

There's a poster on the square advertising Sunday's match at The Royal Palm Polo Club, and we agree that we *must* attend. We promise ourselves to wear our new outfits while we saunter the grounds, sampling fine wine and chatting with the upper crust.

Our next stop is The Boca Raton Club, which our tour guide in Palm Beach told us was another lasting tribute to Addison Mizner's brilliance. We tell the gatekeeper we are guests of Mildred Vassar, and after making a phone call and checking our driver's licenses, he smiles and waves us through. We idle the car through the beautiful grounds and park down by the marina.

"Look, Tommy," I bubble. "This little rowboat is for sale, and check out the name." I lace my arm in his as Tommy is adjusting his sunglasses to protect his eyes from the glare caused by sunlight bouncing off the water. As we come nearer the boat, I add, "Actually, as I consider this vessel further, I would want something a little bigger."

A beautiful pleasure boat with a fly bridge is moored snugly in slip twelve, with a For Sale sign affixed to one window. The name *Katherine's Obsession* stops Tommy in his tracks.

"Well, I guess I'll relent if there's nothing close by that's any better," I say. "Go ahead and sign your name to a check. Just leave the amount open and place it on the windshield."

But Tommy isn't laughing. He stares at the lettering and turns his head to the sky.

"Hey," I say and give him a gentle poke, "let's go and have some lunch." But he's deep in thought and offers no response.

I poke him again. "Hello, Earth to Tommy."

"Let's go on board," he says.

"What on earth is wrong with you.. We can't just go on this man's boat, or yacht—or whatever it is."

"Yes, we can. We're interested parties."

"The hell we are." I laugh and pull him away.

"Come on."

Before I can offer my rebuttal, he places me over the railing and I either step onto the deck or into the ocean. I say, "Jesus Christ, Tommy, this could have alarms all over it."

But he's not paying any attention to me, and I blindly follow him into the main salon. The wood is dark mahogany, and everything smells of class and money. As we explore, we discover this yacht has a large, elaborate stateroom, two guest bedrooms and two other smaller sleeping areas for families or crew, a cozy den area with a wet bar, four lavatories and three with shower stalls, and a galley that's as big as the kitchen in my apartment—and a hundred times better appointed, with full-size appliances that are top of the line. Located on the fly bridge, *Katherine's Obsession* has a hot tub that's large enough to seat eight. And the helm boasts gleaming instrumentation with power-operated seats wrapped in deep, butter-colored leather. I sit in one and melt into it.

The outside deck contains cabinets to store fishing gear, along with several live wells, and there's a waterskiing platform that could be also be used for sunbathing. Holy crap, what's left? Tommy pulls open a door to reveal two engines that appear the size of something on a jet, and I can only imagine their power—and what it would cost to operate these behemoths.

Leaflets listing the yacht's specs are spread out on the largest table on the main deck. It's a 75-foot motor yacht with less than 400 hours on it, built in 1987, and the asking price is … I can't stop seeing the zeros, as there are six with a number in front. And the first number is not a one.

"We're going. Now!" I pull him onto the outer deck, my anxiety level on overload.

He reluctantly hangs behind like a spoiled kid but he brightens up at seeing the architecture of the palatial main structure and the splendor of these beautiful grounds when he takes it all in from our vantage point at the marina.

The interior of The Boca Raton Club is breathtaking, with numerous gold and pink ballrooms and a lobby that is the embodiment of Mediterranean and Moroccan influences. There are colonnades with arches everywhere. We walk by a room two maids are entering and see a giant parlor palm inside. We ask and are told that each room is graced by a similar tree.

The mention of Mildred Vassar's name brings wide smiles and abundant nods from the staff. They seat us at a window table overlooking Tommy's yacht. He's obviously enjoying acting rich and important. And when he's in this mood he's such a delight in every way. Our lunch is of epic proportions, and we enjoy it immensely. We also learn that our money is no good at The Boca Raton Club, as Millie has ordered that our bill be assigned to her standing account.

Outside, and just beyond our range of vision, two men lean against the dock piling. One takes off his sunglasses and cleans the lens. His black, empty eyes squint against the glaring sun just as a gust of wind snaps his coat jacket back to reveal a long-barreled gun.

Chapter 31

WE DRIVE SOUTH TO Fort Lauderdale. Once there, we take a water taxi tour on the Intracoastal Waterway and I photograph some the most beautiful houses I've ever seen, as well as "complementary" yachts snuggled against nearby seawalls. We see sailboats that could make it all the way across the Atlantic to Europe, as well as colorful catamarans owned by rich tycoons; many of these million-dollar-plus crafts are used solely for racing.

I nearly lose my hat in a sudden gust of wind, and Tommy makes a funny, heroic save that almost takes him overboard. Two other couples are on the taxi with us, and Tommy's chivalrous effort makes us all laugh. It breaks the ice, and the six of us have a grand time together.

We get a tip from one couple about a Polynesian restaurant in Ft. Lauderdale. It's a place with leis, drinks in coconuts, and a fire-dance show, so we decide to go there for dinner.

Women in grass skirts welcome us and place incredibly fragrant leis around our necks. Then we are swept away by a heavily tanned, almost-naked young man who takes us through a jungle to an outside tiki bar. Tommy orders us a specialty drink that comes in a glass bucket with two straws. It's the most lethal drink I've ever consumed. I think the bartender just empties entire bottles of booze into this one concoction. It's called Passion Punch, but it should be renamed Date Rape Serum. I stagger to our table in the restaurant, and by the time our dinner is served I'm so pickled I can hardly sit up to eat it.

Tommy on the other hand is quite sober, although he matched me sip for sip. Come to think of it, I have never seen Tommy over the line. Tipsy, yes, but never drunk. This is puzzling because we drink a lot. I know my limit, and I generally stick to it—except on nights like this one —but I've seen Tommy often go beyond me by a mile and develop nothing more than a red face. Amazing.

The show starts with these skinny guys dancing around with practically nothing on and twirling fire sticks. I'm literally lying on the table—my chin is in my hand, but my elbow just won't stay upright, so my head slides forward until my face is virtually inches from my plate. Tommy gives me a smug sniff and shakes his head.

"I can't believe you're such a lightweight," he says, with a laugh I find to be downright mean. "You're sloppy drunk, you know that?" I give him what I hope is my best smile, and he laughs so hard he chokes.

The show thankfully ends, and he pays the tab and manages to get me to my feet and wipe the food off my lei. The latter two actions are accomplished in one move. His powerful arm, wrapped around my waist, allows me to leave with some semblance of dignity. We have to walk on a wooden dock, past some boats moored to it, to get to the parking lot. This makes the task of making it to my car all the more difficult, as the slats are easy to trip over, and I do a great job of almost pulling Tommy down with me several times.

When we get almost free of the dock, Tommy stops our progress and asks if I'm all right. I say "shertainly." It sounded all right to me.

"Stand right here while I find the keys in your purse," he tells me.

I nod, hand him my purse, and walk directly off the side of the dock.

"Sweet Jesus," I hear him say as he grabs for me.

He manages to take hold of the back of my blouse as I go over, but it pops all the buttons in front and slips easily off my arms. Tommy is now standing on the dock with my blouse dangling from his right hand and displaying a wide-eyed, Mr. Bug look. He peers down into the water at me. "Holy shit, Kitty. Don't drown, for God's sake." A man in the parking lot who sees me go in runs over to help, but I'm happily paddling around in a little circle like an orphaned duckling, giggling all the while.

"There are steps on the end of the dock," the man says as he points. "If you can get her to swim over there, she can climb out."

"Sweetheart, swim over to these steps," Tommy says. "Here, over here, not that way," but of course I don't listen.

Meanwhile, the people on one of the luxurious yachts we just walked past have a party going on, and a dozen or so people are all on one side of the deck, watching me. They put a swim ladder over the side and encourage me to climb aboard.

On the dock, people start to gather to see who drowned. Tommy, still clutching my blouse in one hand, starts waving it around like flag. He tells me over and over to get to the steps, but I just giggle and thrash my way over to the ladder on the party boat. I hear Tommy bellow, "Kitty, get your goddamned, drunken, Irish ass over here, *now!*"

I climb unsteadily up the ladder to the yacht's main deck, and a man suavely wraps a towel around me. It's praiseworthy that I wore my prettiest lacey bra for all to see.

The man holding me in the towel is amazingly handsome, and I drink in his dark, tanned face and piercing blue eyes as he smiles warmly at me. He rubs the towel on my back to help me dry off. I bat my eyes at him and say I'm grateful.

Someone on the boat calls out to Tommy, "You need to chill, my man. Come aboard and claim this beautiful, wayward woman."

Everyone is laughing at me, and a woman in a string bikini offers to make me some coffee.

Tommy comes aboard, and true to his unflappable style, he's smiling and shaking his head, which is a relief to me.

"My fiancée can be more than annoying and quite a handful at times," he tells another scantily clad woman, who is offering him a drink. He declines with a cordial smile as he wraps his arm around my waist. He gives me a hard little shake to let me know, even though he's smiling, he's furious with me. He gets me off to the side and puts me into my shirt. But when he tries to button it, of course there are no buttons.

"Well, screw it. Just leave the goddamn thing open." He frowns. "You've got to start listening to me. When I tell you to do something, you should do it and not defy me, young lady. What did I tell you about the bus?"

"Da bus? I didn't see da bus. Was there a bus? What bus?" I begin to sway in the breeze that's blowing across the open deck. He closes his eyes, and I believe I detect the sound of chuckling coming from deep inside him.

This party is filled with bright, thirty-something people, all drinking, laughing and smoking weed, so we immediately feel at home. They seem genuinely delighted to have us aboard. I guess they consider us ship-wrecked souls saved from the ravages of the sea.

Tommy agrees to a drink just as someone comes with coffee for me. We're soon sitting on the back deck of this magnificent yacht, now quite sheltered from the dock and its potential for disaster.

We smell pot wafting from somewhere and a young woman offers a half-smoked joint.

Tommy takes a toke but says I shouldn't partake, saying it probably would put me to sleep, and he doesn't want to have to throw me over his shoulder to get me to the car.

"So stay here and party with us," the handsome man who rescued me walks up and says. He introduces himself as Pete. "We're going to cast off and cruise the Intracoastal in a minute. You're welcome to come with us."

Everyone around us agrees that we should join the party, but Tommy says we need to get home.

"I'll bet she had one of those killer drinks they serve in the coconut mugs, didn't she?" a guy asks. He appears a bit younger than rest of the crowd, and I manage to tell him our drink came in a big, damn tub.

"You guys must be tourists," he says as if he's making a startling revelation.

Tommy politely tells a short story about losing the restaurant in a fire and that we're now unemployed and visiting South Florida as the guests of a wealthy friend. He shares snippets of our lives while I, on the other hand, am passing out.

Pete looks at me as my eyes are closing and says to Tommy, "She doesn't need coffee, she needs a line. Does she indulge?"

Tommy says no, I don't do coke, but Pete pours a little line of white powder on the back of his hand anyway and holds it under my nose. "Wake up, beautiful lady, and sniff a little of this. It'll bring you right around, and I promise you'll feel much better."

I open my eyes to find his hand in my face. "What is that, coke? No thank you." I rest my head against Tommy's shoulder. Tommy politely pushes his hand away and reminds him again that I don't do coke.

Even in my drunken state, I hear Pete offer it to Tommy, who says, "It's not to go to waste," and I see him casually snort the line up one nostril and then the other. His eyes immediately start to water, and his face flushes a deep crimson.

"Whew, this is excellent shit." Tommy laughs and shakes his head. "Thank you, my man."

"We sail with only the best," Pete says, patting Tommy on the back.

I'm struggling with what I just heard and saw, and I'm so upset that I force myself to hear everything around me.

Soon Tommy is flying high and he's the brightest star aboard the yacht, in virtual heaven with his new friends. We cast off and the humongous yacht purrs to life and gently moves out into the canal and then on to the Intracoastal. It slowly and effortlessly slices through the still waters and past the twinkling houses that in the distance look like constellations, each different from the other. There's smooth jazz playing in the background, and I'm about to pass out when I hear Pete and Tommy talking.

"Will she be okay back there?" Pete asks Tommy, then as a serious aside, "She doesn't puke, does she?"

"Kitty? Naw, she'll just sleep this off. She's cool."

I'm lying on a lounge chair in the very back of the yacht, and Tommy covers me with an afghan some kind soul just brought me. Then he goes off to party in the front of the boat with the others.

I'm gratefully alone. What no one is aware of is that I stand up and puke neatly and unnoticed off the rear of the boat, and go back to sleep. I can't remember when I've been so wasted. It's not a pleasant feeling and provides one of those "I'm never going to drink again" pledges, which usually come up short after two days at the most.

I wake up some time later to Tommy's lips on my neck, and I smile. But upon opening my eyes, I see that it's Pete. Almost immediately I hear Tommy behind him hollering, "Yo! What the fuck are you doing, man?" He angrily grabs Pete by the back of his shoulders and jerks him off me. I sit up, startled. Pete raises both palms to Tommy in apology.

"Sorry, man," Pete says. "It's the ecstasy. No harm, Tom. It's cool. I'm sorry."

Tommy blessedly releases him and asks me if I'm okay. I nod.

Pete runs his hand through his hair and says, "We're ready to wrap this up, anyway. We'll be back at the dock in a few minutes. Really, Tom, I'm sorry." Then he mutters, "Damn Ecstasy," as if that is the only reason why he came onto me. I thank God Tommy let him go and didn't fly off in one of his rages.

Tommy sits down next to me. I ask what time it is, and he tells me it's well after three.

"Holy shit," I whisper. "I'm so sorry. Are you still mad at me for playing around in the water?"

He unfolds his hands, which are clenched tightly between his knees, I assume so he wouldn't kill Pete, and pulls me to him, "No, Sweetheart, I'm mad at myself. I should have just taken you off this damn boat. We should never have stayed." He brushes the hair away from my face and can't resist a small, sympathetic smile. "You certainly look like hell, my pet."

"I feel a lot worse than that, believe me. I can't remember when I've felt this horrible or got this drunk."

As we make our way down the metal gangway to the dock, Pete smiles sheepishly from the helm and says it was nice meeting us. We say goodbye and carefully plan our movement down to the parking lot.

"Now you walk on this side of me, away from open water," Tommy says and grins. I offer him a brief smile, but I'm far from interested in humor of any kind, as now I've got another issue with him that will have to be discussed once we're both sober. My suspicion is that this talk won't go well.

Chapter 32

WE GET INTO THE car and he pulls out onto the street, heading north. I narrow my eyes at the vacant roadway as we cruise up A1A toward Palm Beach. My mind is clearing, and I remember Tommy snorting a line of coke as casually as if sipping Grand Marnier. I want what I say next to sound calm and relaxed even though there's fire in my eyes. I take a deep breath. "Tommy, you told me you don't use cocaine."

"I'm sorry, Kitten. We should have just left right away. I shouldn't have done that line, but it wouldn't have been cool to leave right then. It's considered not polite to blow and go."

He takes my hand. "Baby, this was just an ill-timed deal. Everyone does coke these days. You're a bartender, you know that. Actually, I'm amazed after all those years behind the bar that you *don't* do coke. It's no big thing. It just happened. I couldn't refuse it after he lined me."

I do know how common coke is, and that it's used by all sorts of people, especially at a bar since it tends to neutralize the effects of alcohol. But this doesn't justify its use in my mind, and I let him know. "You told me you just smoked pot, and had a couple of routine prescriptions that sometimes foul you up. You never mentioned coke."

I get a chill. I tell myself that I've never seen Tommy really drunk. He's always up and cheerful, energized and funny, poised and confident. But he hardly sleeps either; sometimes up before me or going to bed after me. His explosive temper, irritability, mood swings and control issues, along with his irresponsible thinking at times, has me thinking about

Lillian's words: "Tommy needs me, and he will always come back to me." And then what Troy said at the fight, as if he and Tommy used drugs together—and routinely. At the time, I assumed it was just Troy's way of venting his anger about the fire. But was he telling the truth? and Lillian too?

"Damn it, damn it, damn it," I repeat under my breath as I look out of the car window.

I'm too spent physically to go after this issue right now, as my head is pounding and I feel nauseous again. Even though there are few cars on A1A at this hour of the morning, there are plenty of stoplights and we have to go through a half-dozen or more towns, some of which have low speed limits, and the last thing Tommy can afford is to get stopped, so it takes over an hour and a half before we reach the villa's gate.

We hardly speak at all during the entire ride back, but Tommy checks on me often and strokes my face lovingly, asking me how I'm feeling. But I know him, and behind his smile is a rising concern. He is all too aware he's created a firestorm he's going to have one hell of a time putting out, if it can be extinguished at all.

Regardless of my still-inebriated condition and my exhaustion, I cannot fall asleep. I stand in the steaming shower and try to let the water calm my troubled mind. Perhaps I'm overthinking this. So what, he snorted a line of cocaine? He said it was because he had to, and I know how people can be around drugs. You've got to be on the same page or they get suspicious, assuming you're a cop.

Each time I believe I've got everything perfectly sorted out, I get a cold, sick feeling. I climb into bed and sleep uneasily until late morning. Tommy is standing at the foot of the bed when I wake up. My guess is that he has never closed his eyes throughout the entire night.

He moves to sit on the bed, caressing me awake. "Hello, my love. I brought you coffee."

I smile weakly and shake my head no to the coffee. I climb out of bed and use the bathroom and brush my teeth. When I come out, he's naked and lying on the bed.

"I hope you don't mind, but I just had to tell Jorge about your dip in the drink last night, excuse the double pun." He starts to laugh and rolls onto his back, chuckling. "We had a good laugh at your expense, and I'm sorry about that. I love you so much. Do you know that?"

He holds out a hand to me to come to him, but I dress instead, ignoring his nakedness, which is almost impossible to do.

I say as I tighten my belt, "Never again will I drink anything out of a tub the size of a bushel basket with flowers floating in it."

"You were simply amazing to watch, trying to eat your dinner as sloshed as you were. Oh, those flowers were from your lei." He bursts out laughing, sounding silly and not natural. "I'm sorry. But you've got to admit, it is pretty funny." I glare at him. "Kitten, I'm not making fun of you, you know that, right? I'm sorry about the whole night."

"I'm just very hungover, so I'm not in the mood for anything but drying out."

He catches my hand and pulls me over and down on the bed with him. He studies my face a moment then kisses me. I don't return the fervor. He pauses a moment, then sighs and stands.

"Jorge has something for you to eat, if you want. I thought maybe we'd see the Everglades. Jorge says an airboat is the only way to do this. He's given me the directions. That is, of course, if you want to go."

"I'm sick as a dog, and you want me to perch like a hood ornament in the blazing sun on a wooden chair in front of a roaring fan—with a decimal level of five thousand—that's mounted on a boat that races like hell through a swamp. I'll get back to you on that." I let my eyes gently close. My head is pounding and I'm ready to throw up at any second.

I keep my eyes closed and the room starts to spin, which generally signals I'd better find a toilet, but I sit up on the edge of the bed, trying to shake this funk I'm in and hoping my head will clear. Blessedly, in a minute my nausea subsides, but I cannot shake the vision of Tommy smoothly taking in that line, saying how excellent the "shit" was, as if he had done it thousands of times. But something is wrong with this story. He has none of the telltale physical signs: no flared nostrils and no constant sniffling. If he did coke, even on occasion, the sniffling would be evident—it's impossible to conceal. What am I missing?

Mad as I am about the drug issue, I fight to put a name on what's bothering me most, but I must: betrayal. I take a deep breath and wonder how I will play the cards I've been dealt. For eight years I have trusted Tommy one hundred percent, and until now I've never found him to have lied to me once, nor betrayed our friendship. I remember our conversation when we agreed that dishonesty would be our only nemesis. And what about his other admissions of late? How could anything be more gut-wrenching than to admit to shooting a baby? This man has always been the one constant in my life, and I love him enormously, so I need to be so careful with this. Still, I have to know, even if it means the end of us as a couple.

I go out to the pool. He's sitting at a table, and I sit across from him and he pours me a cup of coffee so fresh I can practically smell the beans roasting. Tommy looks rested and happy despite his being up all night, as I'm certain he's not had a minute's sleep.

My sexy Italian has started on a deep tan that brings out his golden eyes. I never get tired of looking at him. I'm so grateful for our easy laughter, shared jokes and open displays of affection. So many couples we know have lost their humor and all sense of intimacy. I cherish him in so many ways and pray I'm terribly wrong about our mutual trust having dropped by the wayside—the one aspect of our relationship that can never waiver.

He sits back in the chair, his fingers over his lips as he talks. But mostly we eat in silence.

"Okay, Kitten," he says softly, removing his hand from his face. "This isn't our style, so let's have it." He waits and I say nothing, so he volunteers, "It's about the coke, isn't it?"

"Hell, yes, it's about the coke," I say, all the air suddenly sucked from my lungs. "You lied to me, and I'm outraged that you have betrayed our deal to always be truthful with each other, to never conceal something that could harm us. And now ... now I see you casually using coke, and

I'm so damn afraid that what Lillian said was true. She said you would always come back to her because she had something you had to have. I stupidly thought it was sex. Damn, how naïve could I be? It was drugs. Fucking dope. I don't know what kind, but you're an addict."

He leans forward and reaches for my hand, which I pull back.

"Damn it, I'm telling you the truth, I'm not a user," he screams, then calms down as he continues, "I'm not addicted to drugs. I have perfect control over everything I take. I don't do hard drugs anymore but occasionally I smoke a little pot, and rarely a line of coke. That's all. I don't want this to be a huge thing between us—because it's not. I take a little coke now and then for recreational purposes only, just for a lift, a little energy boost to get me though the tight spots. Last night was wrong, but it's over and done with, okay? You're so precious to me, Kitten, and I never want to fill you with fear or doubt about us."

"It would seem that in all the times we discussed your past drug use, you told the truth. But you never said anything about still using coke. Ever."

He sighs, and I can tell he's highly agitated but forcing himself to remain calm on the outside: the always-in-control Tommy Defalco—until he goes through the roof. "I hardly ever do coke. It's just one of those things I didn't think was important to discuss. Last night was a stupid act of bad judgment. My God, if I was using coke regularly I'd be sniffling my brains out. And does my nose look like a cokehead's?"

"Tommy, it would break my heart to find out, after all these years, that the man I fell in love with isn't who I think he is. You, more than most, know what drugs do to people." I hold his eyes with mine. "You know as well as I that coke is nothing to play with. It will mess up your heart, especially if you drink along with it. Please, for us; no, for you, please ... no more. And if a *party* calls for its use, we leave."

He touches my face and nods, and for now this issue is closed. I believe him. I've got no reason not to trust what he says. He reconsiders, thank God, the airboat ride in the Everglades because of my hangover, and we decide to lie low and maybe go dancing later this evening—if my head will allow it.

Complying with Millie's wishes, we have started to develop a solid friendship with Jorge and Carmella. But this would have happened without our being asked, as we found them to be delightful people. One night after dinner, Tommy caught Jorge by the arm and said, "We appreciate all that you and Carmella do for us, but we don't expect for you to cater to us like we're special. We're working people, just like both of you, in the service industry. Well, we *were* working; now we're unemployed." Tommy grinned, and Jorge agreed that from then on we would all be on first name basis.

We like the both very much and find them to be charming as well as funny. Many hours are spent chatting and sharing our stories but they hold their personal stories close. We get a sense that Mille played an important part in their lives and they don't tell and we don't press.

Today, we relax with Jorge and Carmella, and in the evening we go out with them to dinner at one of their favorite places. It is small, intimate, out of the way, and we have a scrumptious Mexican dinner. Jorge drove, so he takes us back to the villa and Tommy and I go to a nightclub recommended by him and Carmella. I drink ginger ale all evening, and it feels heavenly to be in Tommy's arms again and dancing with him, the second-best thing he does.

Sunday comes, and when we mention the Polo match to Jorge, he demands that we attend. He shares with us that he once worked for a top polo club, managing the stables and training the horses. We beg him to come with us but he declines. I wear my very Palm Beach sundress and wide, floppy sun hat, and Tommy wears the killer outfit he bought in Boca. We spend the afternoon doing what all decent Palm Beach people do at a polo match, which is wandering around aimlessly with a glass of wine in one hand and looking distinguished. We're good at pretending to know what's going on amidst thundering hooves and handsome, exquisitely fit, middle-aged riders. However, I must admit that I took a step backwards when a damsel in no form of distress appealed to me to please tell her what chukker it was? I had to give a lot of thought to "chukker," as I thought I misheard her at first, but I eventually said, "The second." She threw up her nose and said, "I thought it was the third. Oh, well, it's so easy to lose count of these things," and walked off—aimlessly.

I must admit that we look as if we belong here, and it's fun to see people's heads turn and whisper behind their hands as their eyes follow us around. We play our parts to perfection, nodding and pointing at the horses, and talking seriously about absolutely nothing. I did learn, however, that a "chukker" is a period of play lasting seven minutes long and a game consists of six of these. I asked a little kid, who couldn't tell me enough about this horribly boring game, saved only by the hilariously activity of all of the spectators flooding the field at half time to stomp down the divots caused by the horses' hooves. It's a tradition performed to assure a smooth playing area from goal post to goal post. We laugh until tears form, watching well-dressed men aggressively replace clods of turf and stamping them flat like little boys in a mud puddle. Equally funny are the women, tottering about on the grass and making their own holes with their expensive high heels.

But Tommy loves this game—or I should say the spectacle. He can't get enough of acting important and all-knowing, so we share little looks between us to let the other know what we are thinking—supposedly. Behind the guile of a thick Italian accent, he introduces himself to others as Dr. Alessandro Ferrari, and flaunts me as his wife, Christina. I actually like the ring the name has to it. Christina Ferrari, kind of a high-class stripper or woman wrestler. Or the latest makeup from L'Oreal. Think I'll keep the name for whenever I'm having a bad day.

We leave, with Tommy waving to someone in the crowd he doesn't know, and leisurely drive around, laughing until our sides hurt as we enjoy the afterglow. We take a back road until we find ourselves in complete wilderness. We drive down other roads that just end, or they are suddenly covered with sand that's rather deep. We stop just before venturing too far on one such sandy road, at a spot where it's quiet with not a breath of air stirring. Spanish moss hangs from the trees, and towering palms seem to have pulled themselves up tall, with the clusters of coconuts under their fronds keeping them balanced.

"This is exotic back here," I say to Tommy. "It's exciting, desolate, mysterious, and dangerous. Good stuff for a mystery novel. And yet we can't be five miles from some of the most expensive real estate in America."

"Yes, and this looks like great snake country too," Tommy offers quickly. "Let's head back to the villa."

"No. Let's keep going. This is fun."

"No. We're leaving." He turns my car around and drives fairly fast.

"Are we in some sort of hurry?" I ask, really confused by his sudden mood swing, which this time comes totally out of nowhere.

He snaps at me, "I just want to get back. I'm tired of being out here. Okay?"

"Okay."

My car's air conditioner has gotten a good workout in South Florida, but it still works fine. Yet his face is flushed and he's perspiring heavily.

"Now it's my turn. What's wrong with you?" I gently stroke his neck and shoulder.

He reaches up and takes my hand in his and rests it on his leg and smiles thinly. "I'm okay."

"You seem moody."

He slams on the brakes and glares at me. "Jesus Christ, I'm fine, okay? Stop with the questions. I've just had enough of driving, and I have a headache."

I take my hand from his leg. "Do you want me to drive?"

"Stop it, damn it. Can we just ride back in peace and quiet?"

The rest of the way back is all quiet and no peace, at least for me. He says nothing and neither do I. He does look as though he's in pain, so I suspect he does have a wicked headache, but how quickly it came on puzzles me, as well as why it would cause such a drastic change in him. Nothing like this happened on the way down to Florida, nor has he acted like this in all the time I've known him.

I guess this is one of those "learning" things Millie warned us about.

We get to see crummy moods and rude behavior, both ways. And now as I'm thinking about it, at work I've seen him go in and out of his little snits, and we all learned it's wise to let him be, as they generally pass quickly. Lord knows, I've had my fair share of bad moments as well—and mine tend to linger.

It makes me a little sad that we can't be the perfect couple, but life doesn't work that way for anyone. Even Tommy Defalco and Katherine Cunningham have to face up to that.

Back at the villa, he goes directly into the house, leaving me in the car. I shake it off and use the walkway on the side of the mansion to go for a stroll on the beach.

I feel happy, the wind tickling my long bare legs with my dress, my hair blowing freely, my floppy hat dangling from one hand, my shoes in the other. I stop and breathe in the salty, clean air. I love this place.

When I get back, and Jorge is tidying up the pool area. I swagger up the steps to the hot tub and flaunt the image I'm now portraying, acting not unlike Katherine Hepburn in "The Philadelphia Story." I feel rich and entitled, and I love it.

Chapter 33

"HELLO JORGE." I SAY, smiling.

Jorge looks up from his work and smiles back at me. "Hey, Kitty, did you enjoy your walk? It looks as if it did you good. You have that marvelous Floridian glow."

"Thank you. I love this place." I sigh with contentment and then ask, "Have you seen my bad news bear?"

"Tommy went to the store for something and said he'd be back in a minute. How would you like a nice, frosty gin and tonic with a succulent slice of fresh lime handpicked from our own trees?"

"You have lime trees?"

"We do. Lemon also. Come see."

I follow Jorge into the kitchen, weaving through the pantry and storage rooms to the backyard. He opens the screen door and we step out to an expansive garden. Before me, a cornucopia of tomatoes, peppers, squash, melons, beans and various lettuces seemingly stretch all the way to the now setting sun. There are also trees bursting with limes, lemons, and grapefruits. Carmella pops up from within the garden with a handful of onions. She waves hello and I call back to her, "How are you and little Emilio feeling today?"

"Pretty good, but I think Emilio and I are both tired of this present arrangement. He is ready to come out into the world and I'm ready to help him." She laughs and Jorge is beaming. "Any day now."

"Oh my God!" I exclaim as I take in the mass of the garden. "Look at all this."

Jorge sweeps his arm around." We take care of all of this, with some outside help, of course. What we don't use we give to the free co-op for the under privileged. It is one of Mrs. V's projects that she learned from her beloved pelicans."

"Pelicans?" I ask, more than a little puzzled. "You mean the sea birds?"

"Pelicans are Mrs. V's favorite bird. She finances a sanctuary nearby to assure their safety. She loves that pelicans sometimes share their nest, even feeding the other birds from their pouched beaks. She relates to their generosity of service to other, and Mrs. V is a profoundly generous person."

"That she is, Jorge."

"There is a folk belief that pelicans protect fishermen and sailors. They are said to guide those lost at sea to safety, and if the sea claims a life, the pelican will scoop up the soul in his large beak and carry it majestically home to the Great Spirit."

"What a great story," I say, remembering that Millie sometimes wears a beautiful gold broach of a pelican. I chastise myself for never asking about it.

A loud buzzer sounds that makes me jump, and Jorge laughs. "It lets us know that someone has arrived. Must be Tommy back from his errand. I'll go and tell him where we are while Mel shows you around the garden."

Jorge returns with Tommy in tow, who is smiling widely at the bountiful garden. He winks at me and touches my arm, which I snatch away from him.

"How's your *headache*?" I ask him with cool indifference. I feel like being a little bitchy, just because. I know he catches it because he smiles cautiously, saying his head is better.

"How nice," I say, brushing past him and tossing a Gloria Swanson look. He gets it that I am more than annoyed and I ask, "Where were you?"

"I went out to get something for my head. I looked for you to go with me, but you were out walking."

"Jorge would have given you something to relieve your aching head."

He takes my shoulders and turns me towards him. "Kitty, I apologize for being such as ass this afternoon on the way home. I'm so—"

"I don't care if you get into a lousy mood now and then, just don't make me feel as if it's my fault. When we were at The House, I didn't have to deal with your temper tantrums. I had the luxury of walking away and going back to my work. But, Tommy, hear me well, if you crash on me one more time, I'm going to be really angry." He looks so apologetic that I cave and add a soft, "Okay?" at the end of my elaborate speech. I hate myself when I do that. He nods and kisses my hands.

Carmella finishes picking the onions and walks us cheerfully around the garden pointing out this and that vegetable. She is so heavy with child that I wonder how on earth she keeps going. If it were me, I'd opt for reclining in a hammock for the whole nine months.

Farther up on the lawn and past a few massive palm trees, I see a beautiful patio that graces the side of a monumental gold and white wing on the mansion. Carmella notices my curiosity and says, "That's the Vassars' private quarters. Their side of the house is as big as the whole villa. You must see the ballroom. It's magnificent."

Jorge addresses Tommy, "Millie phoned earlier today and asked me to give you something. It's in her study, so as long as you are both here, lets walk up and I'll show you some more of the residence."

We walk over the shaded lawn under the most beautiful palm trees I have ever seen and climb old stone steps that led onto a marble patio. Another set of stone steps descend from the other side of the patio to a series of reflection pools. Jorge unlocks giant glass French doors and we enter an enormous gold and white room with a white rug and French provincial furniture. A huge glistening chandelier hangs magnificently in the middle of the room over a polished dance floor. Ceiling to floor mirrors tucked into gilded arches grace the wall to the right, and to the left matching windows enable dreamy gazes to the garden pools. The feeling is surreal and peaceful. There is a gleaming baby grand piano sitting in one corner of the room and a large mirrored bar in the other. Throughout the room, comfortable sofas and chairs team up with ornate tables. Tommy and I stand open mouthed as we take in the sight.

"This is what Mrs. V calls the back room. This is where they entertain most of the time. This room has its own private entrance, separate from the main house. Usually they have a small orchestra come in, and the affairs are quite festive. The guests love to wander around the reflecting pools. But every once in a while someone will fall in, and we have to fish the person out and fan him—or *her*—dry." Jorge waves his hands in a la-de-da motion and Carmella giggles.

This gives me a sense of how they feel about tending to the ultrarich, and it reminds me of how the staff at The House would respond. Suddenly I'm very homesick, but I can't wait to open up to Jorge and Mel, and them to us, and share stories that only "the help" can tell.

We leave the ballroom and walk down a lavish hallway past a dozen or so closed doors until Jorge stops and announcing Millie's study. The room is sweet and homey with none of the pretentious formality that we have just seen. One wall is completely covered with old photographs and framed certificates I don't remotely claim to understand. Her desk sits to the side of a window that looks out over a small secluded outdoor courtyard and fountain. Over her desk is a large oil painting of two pelicans sitting on a dock at sunset. It seems to mesmerize Tommy.

We look over the numerous photographs of Millie as a little girl, Millie as a beautiful teenager with her wide, trusting eyes and impish grin, and her wedding pictures.

"Oh, look at this," Tommy says softly as he points to a photo of Millie as a bride. Her beauty is deeply compelling; truly a trophy bride as she once described herself. John Vassar stands close beside her, and they look happy and very much in love. I remember her wistful words to us: "I was once in love as you are now."

There are multiple photos of Millie riding gaited horses, and Jorge shares that she was an avid equestrian.

"She also raised champion dogs," he says as he straightens a photo of a substantial kennel housing terriers and Great Danes. Her dogs won many Best in Show and Best in Breed awards at prestigious shows like Morris and Essex, and Montgomery and Westminster in Manhattan. They were all shown by the best handlers in the country, but to Millie's credit she knew her dogs as well as she knew her horses.

There are photos of Millie and John with citations signifying around-the-world cruises, and pictures of elaborate parties where they were among the rich and famous, each photo portraying a happy couple lost in the good life. There are also scores of photos of their son, Mike, from babyhood to adulthood. After taking in all of this history, I realize how little Tommy and I know about Millie.

Jorge opens Millie's desk drawer and the first thing we see is a large pistol which shocks me and causes Tommy's brow to crest. Jorge sees our surprised expressions and quickly explains the gun by saying, "Mrs. V believes one can never be too careful and to always expect the unexpected. I might add, she is an excellent shot." That she has a gun in her desk drawer in her private quarters might mean, besides the obvious intruder possibility, that perhaps she felt she needed protection from the one closest to her—namely John.

Jorge takes a velvet box from the back of the drawer and presents it to Tommy.

"What is this?" Tommy asks as he pulls a gold-chained medallion from the box. I move in closer to see for myself. The medallion is beautifully inscribed with what seems to be Latin on one side, and on the other is the image of Michael, the archangel.

"Is this a religious medal?" I ask.

"Not in the sense you may think. Millie is Jewish, and not very religious, but she holds great faith and respect for this angel, Michael. As the story goes, Millie found this medal in an antique shop many years ago when she was a young wife. She was drawn to it because of the mysterious inscription and how powerful this angel appeared. The shop owner told her about Michael the Archangel and how he was the one to ask to cut through the barriers blocking the happiness to life. He was the one to bring courage to fight personal battles and win out over them. He is brave, strong, and yet compassionate—and his miracles are many. All you have to do is ask for his help and he will never fail you."

"I don't understand—" I say, but Jorge cuts me off and continues.

"This happened in a time when she and Dr. Vassar were not getting along. He started to have affairs that Millie knew about and was staying away longer on his business trips. She had lost two babies and was seriously depressed, and so she drank to hide her sadness. By her own admission, she was on the verge of suicide. She was so unhappy that she felt no way out, then she found this medallion and started to ask this angel for help."

Carmella picks up the story from Jorge, choosing her words carefully in English: "Millie believed with all her heart that Michael would hear her prayers and give her the courage to survive her unhappiness. Soon after, she discovered she was pregnant. The pregnancy was riddled with problems but she swears it was through Michael's help that she stopped drinking and smoking. Michael showed her how to live a healthy lifestyle that helped her to deliver a beautiful baby boy who she named Michael gratitude."

Jorge finishes the story: "Of course, raising a teenager alone, and living with Dr. Vassar's infidelities, took its toll on her and soon she was back drinking and smoking." Jorge grows serious and his voice deepens as if he was speaking from a personal experience. "But I am here to tell you, there is power in this Michael."

"I believe in angels," I say absently to no one in particular. "I just never think about them, but I believe they are real. I believe they are God's messengers sent to help mankind with all sorts of things."

Tommy puts his arm around me and looks at Jorge and lifts the medal. "So, why do you think she gave this to me?"

Jorge shrugs and says, "Perhaps she thinks you need Michael's help somewhere in your life."

We walk back onto the patio, and Jorge locks the doors after us as Tommy puts the medallion around his neck. He turns to Jorge. "Please tell Millie when you talk to her next that I'm truly humbled by this gift. It's beautiful, and I'll honor her wishes and wear it always."

Jorge smiles and exchanges glances with me. "Tell her yourself. She'll be here tomorrow in time for lunch."

Chapter 34

I FALL ASLEEP TO THE distant grumblings of thunder only to awaken from a flash of lightning and an immediate blast that sounds like a bomb going off. Rain and wind batter the glass doors and windows, and this gigantic fortress of a bedroom now seems fragile and vulnerable.

I reach for Tommy. Of course he's not there, so I sit up and pull the covers around me. The storm is clawing at the doors and windows like a savage, furious beast and I call out Tommy's name. I don't receive a reply, but why should I expect anything else? So I click on the light, only to find that the power is out. Surely on a property this grand there must be a backup generator. I wait expectantly, but even after several minutes the power remains off.

It's not long before I'm lonely and terrified—and a little girl again. As the wind hammers the walls and the rain bangs on the windows, I weep and ask aloud, "Where is he? Could he be out for a run and caught in this storm?" My tears translate to anger and frustration as another brilliant, blue-white talon slashes across the sky and its mate shakes the windows, this time driving me clear under the covers. I've never felt so alone and afraid yet worried and angry as well.

I fumble around the nightstand for my watch. I can read the fluorescent dial in the dark. It's 4:20. Worry finally drives me from the bed, and I gather up my clothes from the day before. I need to find Tommy, even if it means going out into this horrible storm.

I open the bedroom door and walk outside and under the colonnade.

I call his name, looking out over the patio, the pool, the hot tub; everywhere I can see as the storm rages around me.

I hear a noise and spin around. Tommy is sitting in the dark by the door. "Holy crap!" I shout at him, my heart racing.

There's another lightning blast and crash of thunder. He looks ghostly in the unnatural white light of the flash.

"Tommy, why didn't you answer me? Shit, you scared the hell out of me! What're you doing out here?" He doesn't answer any of my questions, which frightens me even more than what's going on with the storm.

"Baby, it's okay," he says as if in a trance. "I just couldn't sleep, so I decided to come out here, sit quietly and watch the storm. Go back to bed, Sweetie."

"I don't want to go back to bed without you." I start to cry. "I was so damn worried about you."

"I don't understand. What's the problem?"

"Do you really have to ask? I hate not having you with me all night."

"I can't sleep sometimes. Then I do better when I'm alone."

"You need to be alone and away from me all night—every night? Jesus, Tommy."

I go back to bed and sob into my pillow as the storm continues to rage around me. Tommy doesn't come to comfort me, and I realize he's stoned. Twenty minutes later the power comes back, and it's not long before Tommy climbs into bed and reaches for me. I crawl as far away from him as I can, and in this bed an elephant could fit between us. For the first time ever, the unthinkable is happening. I don't want Tommy to touch me. Despite how upset I am, I fall into a deep sleep.

The day breaks cloudy but storm-free when I wake up. Tommy is sleeping deeply, and I lie there looking at him for a long time. His handsome face is so peaceful now, but I see a difference since we've been together, and essentially by ourselves. He's endured too much stress too fast: the ended romance with Lillian, the fire, then Lillian's death, regardless of its cause, and all the traveling. But I, too, have experienced enormous pressure, yet I coped with it while it's obvious he hasn't.

My most immediate concern is where he got the drugs last night. I would have smelled pot in the alcove where he sat strung out, but there was not the slightest scent. He doesn't have coke, of this I'm pretty sure, but he's definitely taking something. And if Tommy is addicted to drugs, then he's been lying to me, and this is the one deal he cannot break and expect our relationship to survive. I've analyzed every way I can, and my opinion is that he's in denial—and in his mind guiltless.

He rolls over, opens his eyes, stretches and smiles at me. "Good morning, Sweetheart," he softly purrs as he rubs my arm. I look at him with a steady, intense gaze. I cannot let this go one minute longer.

"You were stoned last night."

He rubs his eyes. "Oh, no kidding. I took something to help me sleep, and on top of all the wine we drank earlier, it totally zoned me out."

"Did you not know that I cried last night? That I needed you desperately during the storm, and you completely ignored me? Do you have any idea how that hurt me?" I keep my voice even and determined. I'm not going to come unglued—or give up discussing this.

He rises up on one elbow. "I didn't know. I'm very sorry."

"How could you not know? I stood in front of you, sobbing, and you said nothing to me when I called your name. You sat like a statue. You were so stoned you had no idea I was even there."

"I told you, that sleeping aid on top of what we drank whacked me out." He turns away but quickly faces me again. "When I did come to bed, I remember you pulling away from me. *That* I do remember."

He must think I'm either a fool or will accept anything he says, since we didn't drink more than three beers apiece at dinner with Carmella and Jorge, who don't drink, and wound up talking with them for a couple of hours over coffee. We look hard at each other for a moment and I begin to cry, but he has no idea what is really causing these tears. He says, "Kitten, please don't cry. I can't breathe when you cry. It tears my heart out." I let him pull me against him because I'm so afraid of losing him, not because I buy his story. He whispers, "Forgive me."

No, forgive me. "Why are you having so much trouble sleeping? It seems like every night you're gone at some point during the night, and always before I wake up."

"I run most mornings, you know that."

"Yes, I do. But not during the night, and you've not been yourself lately. This frightens me."

He sighs and glances around anxiously. "I don't know how to answer that, other than maybe I'm finally coming down from all the shit we've been through recently, and my habits are all screwed up." He takes one hand in both of his. "I don't want to wake you, so I just get up, but I do know I need more sleep. That's why I took the pills last night. Didn't put me to sleep, though, just stoned me out."

He goes the bathroom, takes a shower and shaves. When he comes back to bed he wants me, and right or wrong I welcome him passionately. In truth, he's all I have right now, and I need him no less than the air I breathe. Regardless, I don't want to feel what I felt last night, ever again.

The day wears a dismal, gray cloak against the wind. The palm trees brace against strong gusts that send sheets of rain in waves across the beach. Tommy seems fine mentally even though he looks a bit ragged—for him. We have breakfast in the kitchen with Mel and Jorge. Then Jorge asks if we have any plans, and we say no, especially with the weather's being what it is, so he suggests we spend some time in the den, a room we've not stepped foot in except once.

"Would either of you like to read the local newspaper?" Jorge asks as he strips off the plastic protective cover. I nod and he hands it to me. I notice other several papers, still in their wrappers, on a table next to a sofa that could seat a dozen couples without anyone's bumping knees.

"You don't read the paper?" I ask Jorge.

"The newspaper is something I hardly ever read," he replies. "Weeks can go by, and the papers usually just pile up." He gives me a pained look. "I get all the grim news I need off the TV. When I do read the paper, I generally only look at the sports page, for polo scores and things."

"You told us you worked at a polo club."

"Did you like the match?" he asks me, arching one of his thin eyebrows.

"I'm not going to lie, no. But I enjoyed the excitement and the people."

He smiles knowingly, as if my answer is what he expected. "Before this job, all my life I worked with horses at racetracks and later polo clubs all over Florida. But when the Vassars asked me to come to work here, I couldn't refuse, and I mean that, as Carmella and I bank every penny we are paid. But I miss the horses. Maybe get my son interested—if Carmella will ever hurry up and have him." He chuckles.

"Seems like quite a switch to go from horse training to becoming the manager of an estate like this," I say, not expecting anything except a laugh, but Jorge surprises me.

"There's actually quite a bit of a story to this. But it's for another time. For now, I have to get the house ready for Mrs. V and Michael when he arrives tomorrow. My wife needs to rest today, so I will have double duty." He laughs.

"Can we help?" I ask.

"Thanks but no. I have extra help coming in. Although Mel and I handle all of Mrs. V's personal services, she considers us family and wants our company as much as she can."

"I can relate to that," I say with a chuckle. "Millie always said the staff of the House were like her children. She insisted on service, but never held her position over any of us."

Tommy and I go back to our suite. I'm far from through with him, but I've gone as far as I can for now. I open the drapes, and the sky has started to clear and a stiff, cool breeze is blowing away the angry gray clouds that remain from the early morning storm. The day promises to be sunny but not nearly as warm as the past week. I brought the newspaper with me, and Tommy reads it under the colonnade leading from our private entrance to the pool. I fall asleep and its Tommy who awakens me and says that Jorge just alerted him that Millie is on her way from the airport. He also told Tommy that Michael decided, at the last minute, to stay in New York.

I shower and put on my new outfit, and Tommy and I are standing in the living room waiting for Millie. It's half-past noon, so she's running a little late. Jorge has the house alive with music and fragrant from fresh flowers set out everywhere in gorgeous vases. He's placed a banquet table out on the veranda, with gazpacho, strawberry, kiwi and pine nut salad, slices of rare roast beef, and freshly baked bread. I didn't see how Jorge could possibly have done all this by himself when I notice a man in a uniform setting more flowers outside and two other men bringing out food. Carmella seems to be supervising, and she and Jorge have changed into their staff uniforms. However, even with this extra help, it's Carmella who stands ready with an ice-cold martini on a silver tray as Jorge opens the door to welcome Millie.

Millie turns before entering to address the limo driver, who has brought her suitcases to the front door: "Goodbye, Reggie, and thank you. I'll call when I'm ready to fly out. You're simply a prince." She hands him some bills, and before Jorge can secure the suitcases, Millie hugs him tightly and then lifts the martini off Carmella's tray and kisses the woman's cheeks. "Oh, how I missed you two. You both look marvelous." She sips her martini and sets it on a table in the foyer as Jorge leaves with her huge suitcases. She takes Carmella's hand and holds her away as she inspects her. "Ah, look how you've grown, my dear. How many months are we?"

Carmella proclaims, "Actually, any day now."

Millie throws her arms around her. "Oh, I can't wait. My life needs a baby in it."

She spots Tommy and me standing in the living room and rushes toward us. After all sorts of hugs and kisses and a few heartfelt tears on my part, Tommy and I thank her for the best time of our lives, and I begin to tell her everything I can think of that's great about the Vassar Villa when Jorge returns and halts my effusive but most-justified praise.

Millie takes off the jacket she's wearing, and we all go outside. Jorge makes us fresh drinks, and one of the men who is helping with the food offers us hors d'oeuvres from a silver tray that's shining so brightly in the sunlight that it blinds me and I have to look away.

Millie comments on how beautiful everything is and how wonderfully the meal is being presented, then she frowns and says to Jorge, "I don't see places for you and Carmella."

Jorge raises his eyebrows as if searching for an answer, but Millie is way ahead of him. "My dears, I understand that we do have guests, but Kitty and Tom are hardly the usual snobs who pop in here. I assume you are all good friends by now, or at least I sincerely hope this is the case, so go change out of your uniforms and get comfortable and come dine with us. You know we always eat together when I come here alone. We are *all* family. I won't have it any other way. We are *all* at home with one another."

This "lunch" takes hours, and we all talk casually among ourselves about many disparate topics, everything from the polo match to the weather in New York to Lillian's death, the last something I had to listen to no matter how much I hoped I'd be in the bathroom when the topic was being discussed. Millie tells us that the police are not ready to call it a homicide, and I mention that Lillian wasn't a vodka drinker. She rolls her eyes and says that the police know this but don't consider it a significant detail, likewise that Lillian didn't have any old needle marks on her arm, something I of course knew nothing about. The more Millie discusses the death, the more obvious it is to me that whoever did this has a very long reach—and is pulling the strings concerning the investigation.

She also tells us that her husband, after the TV interview with Lillian at his side, is nowhere to be seen. She tells us that she's been in touch with the FBI about John's business activities, and he's now wanted for questioning—and perhaps the interest is encouraging his absence. She's been told an indictment is in the works, but that it will take time. And naturally it will help immensely if John Vassar can be questioned. However, it's not easy to pin down a billionaire, and this is the first time I get an idea of just how much money the Vassars control.

Carmella reaches over and squeezes Millie's hand. "But are you safe, Millie. Are you protected?"

It's the first time I heard Carmella address Millie by her first name, and it surprises me a little, but hearing how easily all this news is shared with them, it reminds me that they are more than employees—and more than casual friends as well.

Millie answers Carmella's question, saying she's in no danger and that no harm will come to her or any of us. *But how can she be so sure? With someone as powerful as John Vassar, is this really true?*

They continue discussing personal matters, even the villa's yearly household budget, which is so ridiculous it makes me laugh, as it's more than I've made in the past five years as a bartender. The conversation even turns to us—how are Tommy and I enjoying our newfound together-ness? It's all very surreal, and uncomfortable at times, but Millie chats on like there is no such thing as a secret or a taboo subject. She openly lays her life bare, as if a gift to us. I'm finding this strange, but Millie has always had the capacity to tie things up in neat little bundles, and I'm confident there will be light at the end of this tunnel, even if it's a long one.

It's late afternoon, and the bright sun is nodding off, to be replaced by its shadowy self as it rolls slowly into the horizon. It's hard to believe we have sat talking, drinking and eating at this elaborate smorgasbord for so many hours.

Tommy, for one of the few times since I've known him, has remained relatively silent, but when there's a rather long lull in the conversation he takes the opportunity to thank Millie for the medallion and inquires about it. Millie pushes away from the table and settles against the back of her chair. She nods to Jorge. "Do you want the stage to tell the story, or shall I?" It almost seems to me this was planned; with Millie waiting all along for Tommy to ask about the medallion.

"It will be my honor, actually, *our* honor, Mrs. V, to share this story." Jorge takes his wife's hand and she smiles lovingly at him. He kisses her and turns to me and Tommy.

"You see, I worked for a top polo club for many years. Mrs. V liked to walk around the stables and see the horses up close. We became friends, and many afternoons during her stays in Florida she would come and talk to me and visit with the horses.

"Carmella and I were young and just married. Mrs. V would give me money to use for our well-being, but I would spend it on drugs. We were deep in debt and every penny I made went into drugs, and I blamed Carmella for squandering our money. Drugs changed me to an ill-tempered and mean person.

"I became extremely addicted to cocaine, but I was in such denial that I thought I was handling it well. The truth was just the opposite. Cocaine was destroying me and my life. I used to tell Carmella and my friends that I could quit anytime, but I am here to tell you that there is no such thing. Not one person I know who does drugs can stop. Every time I would cut back or try to stop, my body rebelled all the harder. Then I realized I wasn't going to quit, and I couldn't stop if I wanted to."

"You seem so very far from the type of person to be on drugs," I say.

"I don't think there is a *type* who can't be on drugs. I was fired from the polo club where I worked for years, all because of my drug use."

"I don't understand," I say, the pain in Jorge's eyes evident.

"I gave all of the horses in my boss's polo string a heart medication that was supposed to be for just one horse. I mixed it in with the daily vitamins, and the combination killed most of them and sickened the rest. I didn't do this on purpose, but it cost me my reputation and I can never again work with horses for anyone."

"How horrible," I say, wishing I'd not uttered this out loud.

"It gets worse. Soon after, I was arrested and did time for possession and assault." He takes Carmella's hands in his, and she kisses them. His voice cracks at what he says next: "I caused my beloved wife to lose a baby. She was screaming when they put me into restraints. And yet, even after that, I still went back to using—and I discovered crack.

"I would die if I continued, and soon. For many days Carmella waited until Mrs. V showed up at the polo grounds. When she did, Carmella told her about what had happened to me. Mildred Vassar hired an investigator who found me passed out in a crack house, and she put me into rehab that same day. Before I went in, she placed the medallion Tommy is wearing around my neck and told me about her angel. Every time I wanted to walk away, every time I was so sick I thought I'd die, every time I cursed Mildred Vassar's existence for calling me out, I grabbed this medal and asked for this angel's help. I was there for a little over eight months. No thirty-day executive cure for me. Mildred Vassar paid for everything. She took Carmella on as her personal maid, and when I was well she hired me. We have been here ever since. I have been in recovery twelve years. And, yes, Mrs. V did make me an offer I couldn't refuse, because I'd be dead by now if I'd refused her help."

I see Tommy put his hand over the medallion that now lies against his chest. But then he takes it from under his shirt and holds it in both hands. Jorge nods to him and continues, "I could not believe that drugs had a hold on me. I believed coke to be perfectly safe, and that it made my life smoother and me more confident. But it also filled my head with unrealistic goals, and I made poor decisions. I took other drugs to round out my existence, until I could not stop the merry-go-round. Then, the Jorge I knew disappeared, seemingly overnight. I started to look and feel sick, the cops were everywhere in my constant state of paranoia, my heart was physically exploding, and I didn't know it—or care.

"Today, Carmella and I are happier than we have ever been. All those other days are just a memory for us now. And I owe Mildred Vassar everything. I love her more than I can ever express in words. She saved my life, the love of my wife, and my soul for me."

The silence that follows Jorge's story is palpable, and Millie slowly leans forward and clasps her hands together on the table in front of her.

Her voice is soft but definite. "So, Tommy, this is why you have the medallion. Today, you stop the drugs."

Chapter 35

TOMMY JERKS UPRIGHT FROM the slouch he is in and unfolds his arms. "Why would you say that? What's this about?

"It's about you, Thomas, and your addiction to drugs."

Tommy grimaces and sets his jaw defiantly. "I don't do drugs anything like what you're assuming, Millie. Yes, I was hooked on opiates while in Vietnam, but I take only what I need now." He clinches his fists, and he raises his voice and looks around as if someone is coming for him. "What the hell is going on here?"

I'm shell-shocked by the bomb Millie has dropped. I stare open-eyed at the developing drama as Millie stands up and leans over the table to face him. "You may think you have kicked what you call opiates, but you couldn't have been in a relationship with Lillian and John and not be involved in drugs. What do you think was in those documents you delivered and picked up?"

"They sure as hell weren't drugs."

"No, they weren't, but they contained the formulas for all sorts of synthetic drugs he was having made outside the country. His entire game was to keep ahead of the FDA. Once a drug was found to be illegal, he'd have one of his scientists make up another. And the crazy part about all of this, my dear, is that his implant business is legit and only getting bigger. He doesn't need drugs to support his lifestyle, but he's now consumed by greed, and whoever happens to be his latest mistress."

Tommy turns to me and says, "Kitty, you know me. Outside of

occasional weed, have you ever seen me do hard drugs?" Right after the words leave his mouth, his eyes show me he knows he has made a mistake.

"What about the coke you snorted at the party the other night?" I answer dryly.

"Damn it, I explained all that to you. Jesus Christ, I defy anyone to find drugs on me other than what's prescribed to help me sleep and alleviate anxiety." He gives Millie a harsh glare. "I don't need this, especially from you. I ask you, do I look like a drug addict? Do I have any symptoms that peg me as a user?"

Millie comes back at him in a calm, direct voice: "Thomas, you look to me like a drunk who prides himself on not drinking for months after a binge and calls himself sober, but he always has a bottle stashed some-place in his house. You're one of those people who use just enough to keep you going, but not enough to give your secret away, somewhat like a functioning alcoholic. Don't forget, I know all about this because I am one. It's too late for me but not for you." She smacks her lips together. "I love you, and I need you clean and sober."

"You don't know anything about me," Tommy roars at Millie as he stands up.

Millie roars back at him, and every bit as loud, "I know *everything* about you. I married a man *exactly* like you. No one knew what he was mining under his façade. He was warm, loving, fun, and ambitious and geared for success, but like you he harbored a horrible secret that lay hidden under his denial. He didn't look like a drug addict either, yet our whole life together was dependent on his pills and recreational drugs. I loved him until there was nothing left of the man I knew. No, he wasn't a lie-in-the-gutter down-and-outer, but he fooled us all with his creative uses of illegal substances. I never wanted to believe what was right in front of my nose. Just as Kitty makes excuses for you in her mind even now. She gives you the benefit of every doubt. Then she rescues you and enables you, the same as I did for John for so many years. The only difference between John and you is that he had loads of money and built an empire around drugs. You, on the other hand, have the proverbial monkey on your back." She points her finger at Tommy. "Free yourself or it will kill you and destroy this woman who loves you."

Tommy reminds me of an animal whose paw is caught in a trap. He keeps one hand on the table and paces back and forth. When he finally stops, he places both hands on the table, as if he's suddenly in control. Millie turns to me and says, "Kitty, go and bring me Tom's prescriptions. I want to see them."

I rush off and Tommy yells over his shoulder, "Yes, let's put an end to this before I really lose it. My three bottles of pills are on the dresser."

There's a nervousness about him that is making me sick to my stomach. I grab the three bottles off the dresser. Just before I leave, something makes me stop and think. I run my hands over his clothes and into each pocket. I search all the compartments in his suitcase and even his small shaving bag. I find nothing. I sit on the side of the bed, cautiously relieved, then my eyes rest on another bag he carries for just toiletries. I reach inside and it's shallower than it appears on the outside. So I feel around underneath and discover a lower compartment that's kept shut by Velcro. I pull it open it and three bottles of pills fall out, each in a different color. Oh, and a small, clear Baggie holding a powdery substance.

Numb and in shock, I fall onto the bed. I'm hurt and beyond furious that he has betrayed me for all these years—and lies to me even now. I run back to the veranda and throw the pills and the Baggie on the table in front of him. Then I barrel into him, my emotions thundering in my head like a thousand wild horses, and I beat on his chest as hard as I can with my fists, spitting as I scream, "You sonofabitch. No wonder you were a little panicked about cops stopping us on the way down here. I don't know what these pills are, but you have some powder, and I'm sure it's not Sweet'n Low. How dare you put me at risk for a bust at this level. You lying bastard."

Millie holds up her hand. "That's enough, Kitty, I know you're angry and hurt, but this is a healing, not a punishment. Let there be no blame or judgment, just what is."

Beads of sweat have formed on Tommy's upper lip and across his brow. His face is drawn tight, anxiety sweeping across it. "Kitty, I can explain—"

"You go to hell, Tommy."

He reaches out to me and I slap his hand away. He pulls it back as if it stings and says, "We're good, you and me. We're tight, best friends. Remember, we got a deal. We're friends, no matter what."

"No, Tommy. There's no deal between us anymore. These drugs and your lies are the deal breakers. You could've told me any number of times that you were struggling with drugs, and I would have helped you through it—for us." I hold up the Baggie and shake it at him. "But you chose this."

"I—"

I begin to cry hard and my wailing interrupts him as I shriek, "This was right in front of me. I feel so stupid for not seeing it. That nightmare I had the other night is real. The drugs are the white-haired woman you love more than me. Get help in rehab now or snort your life up your nose and lose everything you love. The choice is yours. Let Millie help you heal your life, or live without the one person who would have loved you unconditionally if you had just told the truth."

Millie says flatly, "She's right, you know? You have a choice. You have so much good about you that you need to make the effort to save yourself. You've been in rehab before, so you know the score. You can get clean, but like with Jorge—who's already agreed to sponsor you by the way—it's not going to be a thirty-day-and-out program. I will take a while to get this—"

Tommy screams, "For the love of God, I'm no drug addict. I have perfect control over what I use and when, and what I do is no one's business but my own. I don't know where all of this is coming from. I never expected to be on trial here, and I don't deserve to be humiliated. Fuck this, I'm out of here."

We hear some commotion and turn to see John Vassar casually strolling out to where we are sitting on the veranda. He's followed by two men, one with a pistol pointed at Tommy and the other with a similar gun aimed in our direction.

"Well, how convenient is this?" John croons as he motions his men into position. "All my pigeons in one place. It just doesn't get any better than this, does it?"

Millie shakes her head at her husband. "For God's sake, you fool, what is this? We have all sorts of staff running around the house."

"Not anymore. I sent the kitchen help home, and the guy you had cleaning or whatever is going to have one hell of a headache when he wakes up."

"You're cra—"

"Shut up, Mildred. You've said quite enough for a lifetime recently. Really dumb move, by the way, throwing me under the bus to the Feds. But now you've bitten off way too much of the hand that feeds and bejewels you." He snarls. "It's going to my pleasure to send you off to hell, you drunken old sot."

John Vassar addresses the rest of us. "Everyone get over there to right, against that wall. Defalco, get over here with Mildred. I want to see your faces when my loyal housekeepers and Kitty all die together." And just to Tommy, "I had different plans for Kitty, but what the hell, I haven't got enough time to do it right."

"John, don't do this," Millie says. I've never once seen her nervous, but her voice is quaking.

Tommy starts to walk slowly past us when Carmella suddenly screams out in pain and doubles over. Her water has broken and she wails out again just as Tommy crosses in front of me. He glances over his shoulder and our eyes meet for a split second, and I'm instantly looking into the fire-stoked face of that young warrior in Nam. The same look in the picture that fascinated me now becomes flesh and blood. Tommy leaps through the air, utters an indescribable scream, and grabs the gunman nearest him by the head and breaks his neck in one fast twist. Before the other man can react, he kicks him in the face with such force that the blow sends him sprawling. The man loses the grip on his gun, and Tommy kicks him again the face, this time knocking him senseless.

As if this were one continual dance move, Tommy spins around to John Vassar and has him by the throat, his face inches from the doctor's. Tommy's eyes appear strangely serene as he picks up a carving knife from the table. He lowers himself to his knees, taking John with him, the butcher knife now under the doctor's chin. The blade is pressed so firmly that rivulets of blood trace down his neck. John Vassar has the look of a man gazing at his own death.

A voice booms out of nowhere; it's deep and commanding: "Defalco, stand down." We look around and see men with guns everywhere. Again, the voice booms, demanding, "Goddamnit, I said stand down." All guns are trained on Tommy. There's complete silence except for Carmella, who's whimpering as she's being shielded by Jorge. Tommy's head moves around in short jerks, stopping in one spot as we hear the voice still again: "Defalco, drop the knife and stand down."

Tommy slowly gets to his feet, and a man with eyes as dark and endless as a moonless night lowers his gun and slips the knife from Tommy's hand. It's the same man who has scared me so many times.

"It's done, Mr. Defalco," he says as two men fit John Vassar with handcuffs while a gunmen is wrestled to his feet. I hear a man, who's kneeling over the other gunman, saying he'll need an ambulance, and another person telling him that one has already been called for Carmella.

The man who seems in control holds out his hand to Tommy. "Do I know you?" Tommy asks as he takes the man's hand.

The man says, "I'm the FBI Special Agent in Charge, Jack Collins. No, Mr. Defalco, you don't know me. But I know all about you. Semper Fi."

"You were there? Nam, I mean?" Tommy asks.

"I was in Nam just about the same time as you. Long Binh. At least that's where I started from. We were all a little crazy then." Agent Collins takes in everything with one sweeping glance and stops on John Vassar.

"Of course, some of us were crazier than others." He gives Tommy a hard glare. "Are you all right, Defalco?"

Tommy rubs his face and seems to take in what's around him. "Did I kill anyone?"

"Damn near. We think you broke one man's neck, but he's alive. Probably wishes he weren't about now. He's a hit man we've been after for a long time." He points. "That fellow over there has a busted jaw, thanks to you, and Dr. John Vassar… I think you've only murdered his pride. But even his billions can't get him out of this one."

Tommy nods and turns to me. I rush into his arms. Two paramedics are tending to Carmella and getting her onto a stretcher. Millie is with another EMT but she seems more concerned about Carmella than anything, and she's demanding to go with her and Jorge to the hospital.

I say to Agent Collins, "You've given me many sleepless nights. All along, I had this feeling you were after us."

"In many ways, that's true. We had a tip that John Vassar was after Mr. Defalco. And we needed him alive because we believed he was the best way we could ultimately take Dr. Vassar down. Of course, we had no idea it would end like this. We've been on this case for quite some time, but Vassar has always eluded us. His operation is huge, so capturing him is a big win for us. And no matter what else he's charged with—because of what happened here—he'll stand trial for attempted murder, conspiracy to commit murder, kidnapping, and assault and battery."

"But how did you know to start tailing us, or whatever you call it?" I ask.

"After the fire, Mrs. Vassar put the wheels in motion to have her husband arrested. She was surprised to know that we'd been on his trail for years. She also wanted to make sure you two were protected. We've had a team, including me, following Mr. Defalco and you from the time you got on the plane to San Francisco, thinking Dr. Vassar might send someone to harm you. We foiled several attempts on Mr. Defalco's life during the past ten days, and we apprehended the man on the shuttle in San Francisco, who was intending to kill both of you."

"That man in the hooded sweatshirt on the airport limo?"

"We took him into custody, and a lead he provided was instrumental in breaking the code to Vassar's business. As it turned out, many of Vassar's people jumped ship when they found out about our investigation. We knew that Vassar would come out of hiding at some point to deal with his wife, but we sweetened the pot a little when we let slip through the grapevine that she was helping you. We knew Vassar would put two and two together and know she would keep you here. It was just a matter of waiting until she decided to visit. Dr. Vassar doesn't want anything to do with New York State since his girlfriend met her demise there, so here was the perfect place for him to ambush all of you. The sonofabitch has a helluva network. If I told you how he got here, you'd never believe it. Regardless, we were fairly confident Dr. Vassar would follow Mrs. Vassar. And we were right. Unfortunately, the timing wasn't exact."

I keep staring at this man with eyes like dark pits and he smiles at me. "Really, Ms. Cunningham, I *am* one of the good guys."

I smile back. "You don't exactly look like a good guy, is all."

"Yeah, I get that a lot. My eyes have never shown much emotion. Lucky for me, my wife thinks they're sexy." I peer at him and he asks, "Do I still scare you, Ms. Cunningham?"

"No, sir, but I just figured out something that's been bugging me for weeks, and it's all because of that gray suit you wear."

"Our uniform, so to speak. We alternate with blue."

"It's the gray. Millie kind of interrogated me after the shuttle incident, and she asked me about the man in the gray suit who I said had 'hollowed-out eyes.' Sorry. Anyhow, at that time I'd never told her you were wearing a gray suit. It wasn't until *later* in the conversation that I mentioned this, but I could never remember the sequence of that discussion until now. Crazy the way the mind works. I probably never would have figured it out if you weren't standing right in front of me—in a gray suit."

He nods and smiles but turns very serious as he picks up the powdery substance in the Baggie and the three bottles of colored pills and says to Tommy, "We're going to take all of this along, with the assumption that you'll be getting the help you need. Do we understand each other?" He raises his eyebrows at Tommy.

Tommy nods. "Yes, agreed ... gratefully agreed, sir."

"Then we won't be bothering you again." He takes a step but stops and turns back. "Oh, and Tom, get some help with that anger issue of yours too. The sooner the better. Then come see us if you need a job. I've already got a file on you, and there's a spot in the Bureau for a man like you, trained in martial arts. I'm dead serious." Collins smiles in a way I deem honorable and walks off.

Tommy and I say nothing as we rush through the house in time to hear Millie arguing with the same paramedic who was with her out back: "This is perfectly asinine. I'm not going to lie down on a stretcher and be taken to a hospital when I'm absolutely fine and can get there on my own, if I needed to go and I clearly do not. All I want is to ride along with Jorge and Carmella, so I can see this baby born."

A young paramedic argues with her, "Mrs. Vassar, please. You've had a tremendous shock to your system. Please let us check you out."

"Oh, shock my ass. You must think I'm some frail old bag who walks malls to keep her heart going. I tell you, I have never felt more alive than I do at this moment. Now let's get this show on the road."

She sees us and gushes, "Oh, my dear Tommy, you were outstanding. You're my hero. I never saw such moves. All you needed were wings to be my angel."

"Millie," Tommy says quietly, "I could have killed someone."

"Well, you didn't, did you? That's not to say they didn't deserve it. They were going to kill us, so—"

"Why, Millie, I've never known you to be so bloodthirsty," I say and add a little sly grin.

"I'm not," she replies in a huff. "I'm just ... well, a realist. And John Vassar will now get what he deserves. I couldn't be happier that this whole sordid affair is finally over and done with. Now, can we please get to the hospital so Emilio can come into this world with his godmother nearby?"

"He's the real hero," I say. "He announced his arrival at just the right time."

Tommy takes Millie by the arm and gently pulls her to him. "Millie, can you ever forgive me?"

Millie searches his face. "For what, Thomas? For following the blueprint of your life thus far?" She laughs. "Oh my dear, it's all in the game of life. There's nothing you could ever do that would beg my forgiveness. I love you so much. Now, go and do the right thing. Check into rehab, clean up your act, and for God's sake, marry our Kitty."

Tommy squeezes my hand and hugs Millie with his free arm. "I will, I promise. Thank you, Millie.

"You need to thank my son, Michael. He didn't come down here because he coordinated everything with the FBI and helped them track that stupid submarine John uses when he's in a pinch. Have to admit, of all the things I didn't know about, that was on the top of the list. But Michael found some invoices from a few years ago and put it all together."

I say with a smile, "A submarine … now *that is* creative. No wonder he went undetected for so many years."

The moment Millie leaves, Tommy turns to me and breaks down, so we go inside the house and sit in the living room. He collapses into a crouching position and I curl around him. "Who am I? Who the hell am I … that I can do what I do to people? The drugs temper my emotional pain, that's why I take them. But the hurt always returns in one form or another. Oh, God, I need help."

I hold his head and whisper to him, "Tommy, I don't think you ever healed from Nam. Maybe you never will completely, but now you have the opportunity to truly forget the past and go through the entire recovery process. And I'll be right there with you, Sweetheart, whether it takes weeks or months or years."

He wipes his face with his hands. "I didn't lie to you, I lied to myself. I really didn't think I was addicted to drugs. I've lived in denial for such a long time, but I always thought I was true to us. I felt I was telling the truth. My God, I would be dust without you in my life … without a life to look forward to … together."

"Don't …" I put my finger over his lips. "Don't say anymore, Tommy. This is all part of our life's plan that Millie was telling us about. We've come this far, be grateful that we have a tomorrow to take one more step toward. If we do it right, our love can carry us through this. Come on, we have a baby to welcome into this world."

Chapter 36

EMILIO SANCHEZ VASQUEZ ARRIVES perfectly healthy despite the fact he's only 5 pounds 6 ounces, and at the perfect time of 8:42 in the evening. Because he is a little on the small side, he's kept in an incubator for four hours, so it's not until two in the morning that we can all traipse into the room and see Carmella and son. Tommy and I stay just long enough to get a glimpse of the baby and to smile at Carmella and to hug Jorge.

During the first twelve hours after a birth, the hospital's policy allows for only a few people in the room at a time, and mostly just family, but Millie is having none of this. She has a "meet and greet" session going on all morning, and many of the villa's outside help stop by to ogle the new arrival. Everyone wears a surgical mask, and there's no touching, even by Tommy and me.

Speaking Spanish to Jorge's and Carmella's family as they arrive, and having everyone laugh when she has a word or two mixed up, Millie's the life of the birthing party. We're exhausted from the drama of the day before and haven't slept, but Millie is fresh, riding the excitement as if she's atop a wild horse she has no intention of taming.

We sit in the waiting area outside the maternity ward until things quiet down later in the morning. Then we go in to visit again, this time so we can have a few words in private with Jorge and Carmella. They weep when they see us, and there are few words said, just deep feelings all around. We get to see little Emilio before the nurse rolls him back to the nursery.

Tommy is amazed by how small the baby is and whispers with amazement, "He could fit in the palm of my hand."

"Yes," Jorge says. "But look how he punches the air and kicks his feet. He's a fighter, this one. So alive, he is." He beams so wide it's a wonder his face doesn't explode.

Carmella laughs. "Yes, better he kicks and punches now that he is out. I lived for months with him fighting inside me."

Millie breezes in and announces that she's going back to the villa to catch some sleep. She already has a car waiting and says, "Michael is due in this afternoon, and I suspect he will be full of drama, so we need to clear up everything by having a little *sit down* together. And—" she takes Carmella and Jorge by the hand— "I have a service coming in to clean all day tomorrow so we can entertain later this week." We all look at her in amazement. "What?" she crows. "This is celebration week! I want everyone around me. I want a party, and, by God, I'm going to have one."

Tommy turns to her and says, "I'm afraid I won't be there. If Jorge can get me admitted in the rehab center today, I want to go." He smiles softly and Millie's eyes fill with tears.

"The sooner you begin treatment, the sooner you can come home, Thomas. It goes without saying, for what you did in saving my life and the lives of Jorge and Carmella, you and Kitty can live at the villa for as long as you want." And to me, "Kitty, come home after you say goodbye, and get some sleep. Later, join Michael and me for dinner out. I don't want you to be alone, and we can discuss the things my son will want to hear from someone other than me." She shakes her head in disgust. "He simply won't believe that John was going to kill me."

Then, in a flurry of waves and blown kisses, Millie walks briskly down the hall, stopping to hug nurses and even an orderly.

I've been floating on streams of consequences, seemingly for weeks that have really been just days. I'm spent and tired and inwardly absent from any true feelings, suddenly robotic in my words and actions. My essence is gone, and I'm null and void in any connection with my life. All I know is, I am saying goodbye to my Tommy in the hospital parking lot while Jorge waits for him in his car. I have never had such mixed emotions about anything, and my stomach is so tight I'm cramping and the pain is getting worse.

Jorge and I talked earlier while Tommy caught some sleep in the waiting room in the maternity ward. He told me that the rehab facility is very nice and not more an hour's drive south of the villa, in Lauderdale Lakes, just north of Ft. Lauderdale. Tommy will receive the best care available. He also says that the program demands there be no outside contact with Tommy for quite a while, so I will have to be patient.

Tommy and I say a simple, strange goodbye, as if both of our hearts are compromised by too much information from recent events. I go first: "My heart is breaking to let you go," I say in a strained voice. "But I hope you know this is the bravest thing you've ever done, even more than risking your life to save all of us."

He takes me in his arms. "Kitten, I honestly didn't think I was addicted, but every day I think about drugs. And I'm tired, Baby. Tired and ashamed. I'm ready to let go. The hardest part will be to straighten out this violent behavior of mine. I kept the experience of killing that baby in Nam hidden from everyone. But since sharing that secret with you, I think this is a step in the right direction. I can tell the doctors now, and get the right kind of counseling." His eyes look like blots of brown oil paint. "The sooner … I do this … the sooner I can get home to you." He smiles and kisses me through our mixed tears. "Then … the sooner I can make you my wife. That is … if you'll still want me."

I have no words, and I honestly don't believe he is expecting any, and of all the difficult experiences of late, letting go of Tommy's hand is the hardest. Then I have to watch Jorge drive him away, and now I'm totally alone in a sea of cars. I find mine and start the engine, but before I can fathom where I'm going and why, I break down into screaming, violent sobs. I vent all of my anger, fear, shock, disgust and frustration by beating on the steering wheel with both hands.

I scream a prayer in gibberish and wail through my loneliness and despair. I don't know how many minutes have passed, maybe even an hour, until I pull slowly away from the parking lot and out onto the street and head east toward the ocean, my one sure way of finding the villa. There is a dull drumming in my ears, and I'm beyond caring that I'm barely going faster than an idle speed. Cars are honking all around me as I look beyond a stop sign to a small abbey tucked behind a pink cement wall lined with palm trees.

I park my car and walk down a white stone path to the quaint chapel. I pass through the open oak door and see two monks arranging the altar. They turn to me, surprise evident on their faces, and I collapse to the floor and into the arms of yet another miracle.

I spend the next three hours pouring out my life and my heart to these two men of God, who listen with sympathy and patience to all that I tell them. They bless me and pray with me and wash my soul with reason, hope, and, yes, even humor. By the time I leave I feel refreshed and connected, with the promise of new friends and new outlooks. They invite me to Mass the next Sunday. I say maybe. I just didn't want to make a commitment I might not fulfill. But I will come back to this church before I leave South Florida.

I reach home after becoming hopelessly lost, which I thought would be impossible. I was on Bayview, which I mistook for A1A, and when I finally arrive at the villa I am reintroduced to Rosa, Carmella's mother, whom I met briefly at the hospital. She says she's often hired by Mrs. V to fill in for Jorge and her daughter, and, of course, she will be staying to help care for the baby during the early days.

Blessedly, Millie is sound asleep, so she has no idea I am this tardy. Rosa says she has been touching up the house here and there, and offers me a bite to eat. Even though I'm starving, I tell her I'm going to bed. I don't know if she's aware of what occurred the day before on the veranda, but I certainly don't feel it's my place to tell her.

She already has the big bed turned down for me, and soft music is playing. A cup of tea is sitting on a nightstand, along with some pastry. I devour the rolls and drink all the tea before sliding between the crisp sheets. Then it hits me that Tommy has been to the room and has taken his suitcase and his old and new clothes. I scurry around the room and find the compartment ripped from the bag where he concealed his drugs. He has made a circle with a Velcro strap and placed a note within it. I'm so nervous that I tear the paper before I can get it read, and then my hand is shaking so hard that I can hardly put it behind my driver's license in my purse. It's Tommy's tears that have soaked "I Love You, Kitten" that have made me so emotional.

Exhausted as I am, I have trouble falling asleep. But when I do, I sleep straight through until noon the next day, missing Michael's arrival and the dinner plans Millie had planned for us the previous evening.

Rosa greets me with a knock on my door and a smile. I sit up in bed and look at the time. "Oh, my gosh, did I really sleep this long?" I remark more to myself than to her.

"Mrs. V told me to let you sleep as long as you wanted. She and Michael went out this morning. They will be gone for most of the day, but she left me instructions to pamper you until you can't stand it anymore." She laughs. "You deserve it." She turns on the shower and fluffs out a terrycloth robe for me and sets it on the bed.

"Brunch is waiting poolside. And whenever you are ready, I give a better massage than that sexy boy and pretty girl the Vassars use." She hesitates. "Mrs. V also said for me to tell you to stay out of your head and keep into your dreams, whatever that means." She gives me a motherly look and a shrug. "Me, I would have just said, 'Don't worry.'"

Rosa leaves, and I feel wonderfully rested and self-assured. There's not a hint of concern for Tommy; not the loneliness I thought I would feel waking up without him. It's as if, overnight, my life finally fell into a place of perfect order. I know Tommy is being taking care of. There are no more unsettling questions nibbling at the edges of my mind. We're all safe from John Vassar and possible harm, and I'm in the arms of extreme luxury. So, for now, life can get no better.

I take a long shower to wash away the mental ashes from the day before and put on my bikini, which I have to admit I can still fill in spectacular fashion. As I step outside, the warm Florida sun flashes in my eyes and makes me squint. Then I see a woman in the hot tub, wearing a wide-brimmed hat like the one I own, sipping a cocktail. She turns and lowers her sunglasses at my approach. "Jesus Christmas, I'd be as pickled as a fritter in moonshine if I had to wait any longer for you to get your fair behind out of bed."

For a moment we don't say anything but just gawk at one another. She sees I'm stunned into silence and fills the pause, "So, how are you, really? And before you lie, Millie told me all about Tommy. Best thing for him. Sweet Cakes, we all knew but no one wanted to tell you. Lord knows, we all tried. Specially Jeannie. She really loves you."

Her eyes brim with tears, as do mine. We come together in an embrace and cry softly together. Then she holds me away and I cry and blurt, "Polly, when and how on earth did you get here? You don't know how overjoyed I am to see you." Now I really start to bawl.

"Millie called me and asked if I could catch the same flight Michael was on. Seems Millie wanted me down here with y'all. Course I said, ' Hell, yeah.' I came with only my toothbrush, bathing suit and two pairs of clean undies. It's all I had time to grab." I revel in how wonderful she is as she giggles sweetly and waves a hand around. "Damn, Sweetie, girl could get to like this place. I honestly didn't believe a castle like this existed in real life, let alone that I'd ever get to set foot in one. Kinda always thought this stuff was only in fairy tales."

"I feel the same. Every day is a dream, and I have to pinch myself." I'm about to ask about what, if anything, has gone on with the investigation into the fire at The House when Rosa serves us berry crepes topped with fresh cream, and eggs with Canadian bacon. I can now say "brunch" like I'm accustomed to it, and I laugh at my foolishness. But I'm so hungry, regardless of how I want to designate the meal, that I ask Rosa if she has anything else I can eat. She brings me two baked crescent rolls stuffed with chicken salad, which I also devour like a hungry lioness.

And now that my tummy is hurting it's so full, Polly and I chatter away like two teenagers just back from first dates. We carry on like this until it's time to get serious, and I ask her, "How is Michael taking everything?"

"We talked all the way down on the plane, and his only concern was for his mama and y'all. Mike and his daddy grew apart from the time he was a young boy. Dr. Vassar was always aloof when he was home, so even as a kid Mike knew something was up with his daddy, which is why he feels so devoted to Millie. Years ago, he set himself up as her guardian protector, as if Millie ever needed one." We laugh. "Mike's always been kind of *away from us* at The House, so none of us ever got to know him, but I can tell you from the three hours I spent sitting next to him on that airplane, he's one smart cookie."

"Did he think John was capable of cold-blooded murder, especially Millie?"

"He was, and is, totally shocked that his daddy was personally capable of murdering anyone, but even more so that Millie was a target. That's what he's agonizing over now. He says he feels a level of betrayal he can't put into words. He has lots of anger to cope with."

We swim a little while in the pool, then I decide to take Polly out to see a smidgeon of Palm Beach. When we return, we stroll into the main house to overhear Millie talking on the phone: "Well, you're damn right it's a scandal, and probably one of the biggest in Palm Beach in decades. That's why I'm calling you. I'm hosting a Scandal Party this weekend, and you must come." On her next phone call:

"Hell, yes, of course it's in bad taste. What could be more decadent than flaunting your dirty laundry in the faces of those who think they're talking behind your back and revealing secrets they don't know a damn thing about? It'll be delicious. Trust me, it will be an affair to remember. Will you come?" And on the next call:

"Indeed, wear something scandalous if you want. And, yes, you may leave your underwear at home if that's your desire. Just be sure to attend." Millie roars with laughter, "All right, see you Saturday, Edith. Oh, and Edith, please extend an invitation to your transvestite friend. Yes, Fiona. I adore her. Or him ... whatever. Tell Fiona to bring a couple of friends. I want this party to be way over the top. Yes, by all means tell everyone it's to be a Scandal Party to end all. Goodbye now."

Polly and I look at each other and then at Millie. I've never seen so her happy. Mike enters the room and immediately comes over to hug me.

He's smiling, and I feel a bit awkward and say, "Mike, I just don't know what to say. I—"

"How about a simple hello? I can't handle anything more than that right now." We both offer a guarded laugh and spend a moment looking at one another.

I tell him softly, "You saved our lives, Mike. A hello is hardly enough. We're so grateful to you and your quick thinking."

Mike smiles and kisses my cheek. "Kitty, Baby, there are no words that need to be spoken between hearts. And as I understand it, Tommy's the one to thank or all of you might not be here. The FBI arrived, but it sounds like they were a little late. Now, if we could just talk Mom out of this party." He laughs heartily and this makes me very happy.

"Yeah, well, good luck with that," I say and roll my eyes. "Polly and I are going to do a little shopping before the stores close. We won't be long."

"Great," Mike says, "When you come back maybe we'll take the yacht out for a while. I need some sea air to clear my head. I've got the boat moored on the Intracoastal, and it's beautiful at night. How about seven, seven-thirty?"

Polly looks as if she is going to explode and gushes, "Yes, Mike, that would be fabulous." Then she grabs my arm and squeezes it, whispering as we walk off, "They have a *yacht*." I won't tell her that I've already been on the Intracoastal at night, as I don't want to discuss anything about my maiden voyage.

Taking Polly shopping and sightseeing does wonders for me. There's something magical about shopping with a girlfriend. After walking Worth Avenue and getting Polly a cute sundress and deck shoes, we discuss deep topics over a brandy Alexander at Taboo, which my new bartender friend, Randy, again makes to perfection.

She catches me up on the comings and goings of The House family. Chris has been hired to manage a casino hotel in Atlantic City. She tells me he'll start in a couple of weeks. Bruno is looking for work in Atlantic City and has some leads. Jeannie caught on at the Brass Rail, along with Christine. I'm not at all surprised about Jeannie, as I feel about her as she does about me, and I've got to talk to her about Mr. Bug, hoping she'll keep him, as having the dog around would constantly remind me of Tommy, and I couldn't handle it. I'm a little surprised that Christine was hired by the Rail. I'm probably wrong to feel this way, but I'll always have a hard time excusing the way she seemed to constantly defend Lillian. Phillip and Barry are working on their future plans and don't seem too concerned one way or the other. Robert hasn't found a job yet, but rumor has it that the engaged fellow might hire him for some sort of permanent work. Now that's one scenario I'd like to follow up on. Victor and Cheryl left for New York the day after we left for Florida, and Polly assumes they are going to work in the family restaurant.

"My God, Polly, our lives have all changed in such a short time." I sigh. "You haven't mentioned Chris and you. Are you still the item of the century?"

She dips her straw in her brandy Alexander and slides her tongue down it, slurping all the way. "No, Kit. Chris and I broke up. We're still friends, but he doesn't have a place in his heart for me. He loves someone who is unavailable, and he can't get away from her. He's lost, lost, lost. I tried to start a relationship with him because he's a fabulous guy, deep and sensitive and not all business when he lets his hair down. I guess I fell in love with him a little, but it wasn't to be." She gives me a cockeyed glance and I pull her head around to me. Our eyes lock, and it feels like my heart stops beating.

"Surely it's not me?"

Polly nods. "But he knows the score with you and Tommy. Still."

"Well, to be honest, maybe I did lead him on a bit. I'm embarrassed to say I enjoyed his advances. He's so different from Tommy." I look away but come right back to Polly. "I'm going to tell you the truth, now and then I do think about Chris. Does that make me a bad person?"

"Hell, no. It makes you human. Tommy has had Lillian and so many others you've known about, yet you managed to set all this aside. You have an amazing relationship, based on a friendship that eventually led to real love, but I think deep down inside you harbored certain doubts about him."

"You just told me I had it all figured out. Or at least kind of—then you took it all away." I laugh hollowly, not at all clear what she's getting at.

"I know you better than anyone, Sis. I know you love Tommy, and have for a long, long time, but you've been blind to his drug use. And now you're found out about it and his real involvement with Lillian, not to mention John Vassar. Chris considers you the love of his life—and you got away. Maybe someday you might feel something stronger for him. Who knows?"

I put my head in my hands. "Polly, I don't honestly know what I feel anymore. I've loved Tommy for years, you're right. And I've done this with blinders on. I never figured out what Lillian had over him. Hell, I thought it was sex. I'm such a fool about things I should know." I smile wanly. "Maybe Chris *was* one of those things." I shake my head. "I'll just never know."

She questions me from under raised eyebrows and I shrug the silent answer, then she says, "I need to tell you something at the risk of ruining the surprise—which it will. Millie has everyone from The House who she could get ahold of flying in for her party on Saturday." She gives me a golly-shucks grin. "And Chris will be here too, not that you'd be interested, of course."

Chapter 37

MONEY CERTAINLY HAS ITS benefits. Millie gets a party in place that would take The House a month to orchestrate, and I thought we knew what we were doing as well as anyone. Food, music and entertainment materialize at the snap of a finger. Vassar Villa is infused with out-of-state guests filling the many bedrooms and giving everything a resort aura. Rosa and two other family members I've just met hover around everyone like bees pollinating flowers, acceding to each visitor's every wish. Jorge routinely checks in on everything, but Carmella is now home and he spends the bulk of the time he'd normally allot to villa functions with her and Emilio instead.

Millie has allocated the suites next to mine for The House gang, and I can't wait to see my dear friends. As it ends up, Bruno must decline because he's starting his first week as a chef at a casino. Jeannie, conversely, is able to attend only because Christine has offered to stay back and work at the Brass Rail in her absence, so I guess I'm going to have to lighten up on my negative feelings for her. Phillip and Barry will be here with bells on, literally. And then there's Chris. Anyone else from our group was either unavailable or Millie couldn't find them, although at the last minute she was able to contact Victor, who is coming without his wife, as she'd found a job.

My heart vacillates between extreme sadness at not having Tommy at this party to blessed peace in knowing he's safe and starting the healing process. Millie keeps my spirits up as she tells me, "I know how much you long for him, my dear, but hold him in your thoughts and see him growing stronger each day, because he is. I promise you that."

Even with her pep talk, however, it just doesn't seem right that this frivolity is unfolding on the heels of what happened on the veranda, but Millie will not see the gala as anything but a joyous release. And it's not long before I'm caught up in her wave of excitement.

Seeing my friends from The House walking through the airport make me cry and laugh at the same time. Polly and I get warm, long hugs from Jeannie, Chris, Victor, Phillip and Barry. For the next few hours, after they get over the shellshock of the ultrarich life at the Vassar Villa, we talk nonstop. I get tender support from everyone regarding Tommy's plight, and all sorts of advice. I feel their love and concern, and I have immense gratitude for their standing behind Tommy. Chris is especially sweet and funny. However, if I'm to believe Polly, and I have no reason to think otherwise, Chris is experiencing difficulty controlling his emotions. I'll see how everything goes, and maybe I'll have a heart-to-heart with him before he leaves.

The party is, in one word, incredibly outrageous. Okay, that's two words, because there can't be one without the other when anything involves Mildred Vassar.

Millie has indeed opened her heart and home to throngs of people from all walks of life. She floats from room to room in a long rhinestone-studded dress that catches the lights like a disco ball. The staff is dressed in sharply pressed linen uniforms, and each member freely gives smiles along with exceptional service.

The bar is an array of rainbow liquors for creating dazzling mixed drinks of every description. Yes, even I'm impressed. There's a twelve-person orchestra set up around Millie's white concert grand piano in the white and gold ballroom. Positioned strategically on the lawns and around the reflecting pools, mimes, jugglers doing magic, and jesters blasting long flames of orange fire from their mouths entertain anyone walking by. In one corner of the lawn, and situated within my favorite little cove of palms, a blackjack table and a roulette wheel are set up, and beautiful girls in dazzling costumes deal the cards and spin the wheel and drop the little ball.

The entertainment reporter from The Palm Beach Post and her assistant can't do enough interviews, and a few well-known paparazzi peruse the guests list and then attack their prey like circling sharks, taking photographs to sell to the highest bidder. None of the guests seem to care, and only Millie and Michael are aware of who's really noteworthy. So far it's civil and no photog has been asked to leave.

Polly, Jeannie, Chris and I stand on a little spot on the lawn next to one of the reflecting pools and observe Phillip and Barry conversing with people of all persuasions in the crowd, clearly loving the interaction and the festivities.

Chris laughs as he shakes his head. "Look at those two. Could they be more at home with all of this? Ten will get you twenty they never leave Florida."

"What the hell," Jeannie blurts. "*I* may never leave Florida."

Polly snatches a champagne flute from a tray that seems to pass by on its own. "Y'all, I vote for every one of us staying. Tommy will need us when he gets out, and Kitty will always need her family around her." Everyone toasts the suggestion and Chris puts his arm around me.

"You're a strong gal, Ms. Kitty Cunningham. How you weathered this nightmare is beyond me. I have nothing but the highest respect for you." He pauses, and this has me a bit nervous about what he's going to say next, but he surprises me with, "And respect for Tommy for having the grit to accept what he's doing now. He's quite the man. You two are an amazing couple. I wish nothing but happiness for both of you when all this settles down."

His genuine concern and friendship touch me. I catch Polly looking at us, and this makes me a bit self-conscious. She must sense this because she raises her glass and toasts: "Here's to the love between each and every one of us, for all the right reasons to fill all our life's seasons. We *are* family—forever." She smiles and winks at me. "I love you, Sis."

As the evening settles into a calmer pace, the orchestra is playing soft music and our conversation turns to Tommy and the funny and often wild times we shared at The House. Before long I'm laughing so hard my side hurts, and Phillip and Barry encourage everyone to dance on the floor at the same time, saying that Tommy would have loved it. I agree, so we do, and we drink and laugh; and, yes, even cry a little. I don't know what I would be feeling at this party without my friends around me.

Millie is like a feather in the wind, and I notice how Mike follows her around, keeping her rock steady when the breezes get too intense, since not everyone at the party is on board with this open display of sheer honesty. Some murmur under the sabal palms and behind their own palms while their fingers cover their traitorous faces. But Millie is undaunted, fielding questions to some often quite personal issues with poise and humor. However, Millie is Millie, and she takes a few untoward criticisms from some haughty guests with a little less than grace and ease, requiring Mike to step in and smooth out any ruffled feathers. Everyone always seem to laugh in the end, with Millie's outbursts of course the loudest.

The festivities bring in the dawn, and at seven in the morning a breakfast fit for the first-cabin patrons on a cruise ship appears over a long string of patio tables. Those who have demonstrated the ability to truly party hardy relax like family members and sober up to become their refined selves again.

Jorge sits for a time with us and remarks, "The night was a huge success. No one fell into the reflecting pools except the jester." He laughs. "That put his flame out." Then Jorge says he has to get back to Carmella and the baby. He leaves us with, "This party was perfect, as Emilio would have kept me up anyhow."

The next two days are comfortable and uplifting. Mike, Millie, Jorge, and even Carmella and Emilio spend time poolside with our gang from The House.

Mike takes everyone from The House out on his yacht, *Million Dollar Baby*, and we cruise to Ft Lauderdale and back. The trip is a far cry from my excursion with Pete. We do this the next day as well, and spend both evenings dining at an exceptionally fine restaurant, once at Stan's on the Intracoastal in Ft. Lauderdale, and the second evening at Busch's on Ocean Avenue between West Palm and Delray Beach. Mike can only dock the boat nearby, as the restaurant isn't on the water, and we're required to walk a couple of blocks, but meeting and then observing the two bartenders at Busch's, Liam and Jerry, work their magic makes the jaunt worthwhile. What pros. The restaurant, known for its great lobster, serves this heavenly entrée with pasta. Pasta and lobster? Well, odd as it might sound, the combo is terrific, and I order straight spaghetti with meat sauce that is fabulous.

I do believe that Phillip and Barry have forgotten all about The Main Line in Philly and want a life in Florida, as all they talk about is finding a storefront they can rent somewhere in Palm Beach. This might be a big bite, but I have a suspicion they have the resources—or can come up with what's necessary. The rest of us smile at their dreams and conjure up a few of our own, which we freely express. During one of our side trips, we go to The Boca Raton Club and walk down to the marina where Tommy and I saw *Katherine's Obsession*. The motor yacht is gone, but I have everyone in stitches telling them how Tommy and I sneaked on board as if ready to write a check.

Day three brings tears and goodbyes as I say farewell to everyone but Polly, who will stay a few more days with me. Jeannie has agreed to adopt Mr. Bug, and I kind of got the impression she wasn't going to give him back to me if I asked. Phillip and Barry are going to stay on, as they've already developed a friendship with another couple who will be helping them fulfill their dream of opening a shop that caters to wine connoisseurs as well as those who appreciate high-end floral arrangements. Could there be a better location than Palm Beach, Florida?

Chris's and my parting is not nearly as difficult as I imagined. He's been amazingly good about not getting all over me, and when we have talked he's let me control the conversations. However, he does hold me for a very long time when we are alone in the house just before a limo is to take him to the airport. He searches my face before asking if I'm sure I'll be okay. It's obvious he's having a hard time leaving me, but he's not making me uncomfortable, which I didn't think would be the case. It's not to say that my love and concern for Tommy has diminished in any way whatsoever, and Chris seems to accept the way I feel about Tommy, but his honest concern for me touches my heart—and deeply. Honestly, I hate to see him go.

That night, I dream of Tommy and me somewhere in the future, and I awaken with a smile and a sense of well-being. I tell Polly about it at the breakfast we share together by the pool. I look at my stomach and think I've gained an inch with all the rich food this past couple of weeks. She says we'll both need to work out double if we have any more of Randy's brandy Alexanders at Taboo.

I giggle as I relate the dream, which is still is fresh in my mind: "Tommy and I are at a lake in Maine and we have an eight-year-old son. He's a real pistol, just like his dad. Yet Tommy thinks the boy is just like me and—" I stop talking, feeling strange all of a sudden; something warm gliding through my body and up my back.

"You okay, Sis?" Polly asks, leaning toward me and placing her hand on my arm.

"I'm, ah … fine. I just had the oddest sensation when I was talking about that boy. It's weird, though, he had a girl's name. Yeah, it was Michele, one of Tommy's father's names." I shake my head and my hair flies around. "Wow, that was all strange—and topped off by that feeling I just had." I shake my head again.

Polly bites a piece of bacon in half and says with a laugh, "Maybe you're pregnant. Y'all been going at it like two minks on the moss for months."

I lose my smile. "I was told years ago by a gynecologist that I can't get pregnant. My uterus is too messed up, and I haven't had a period since forever. I told Tommy I couldn't have kids and he was okay with that. He said he didn't want a family either, but I feel bad because I think he, deep down, wants kids. The way he acted around my little niece in San Francisco left no doubt he'd be a great dad too."

"Well, Sis, miracles happen."

We spend the rest of the day hanging out with Millie and Mike, sunning ourselves and taking long walks on the beach. I tell Millie that I need to go home soon and take care of some things, pay bills and what-ever. She convinces me to forget the apartment and move into the villa with her. She invites Polly to do the same, but Polly doesn't want to give up her house just yet. She says that maybe later she and Jeannie might find a place together here in Florida, but not just yet. I respect Polly for her maturity and also her integrity, as most anyone on this planet would jump at the chance to live at the villa, even if the stay ended up being short-term. Every day on the grounds is a day in paradise, so who could argue with that?

Later that evening, Millie sends Jorge, Carmella and Rosa out to a fancy place for dinner while Polly and I babysit tiny Emilio. I hold him for hours, stroking his soft cheeks and living the dream that I had about Tommy's son. For the first time ever I long for a child: Tommy's child.

The next morning brings rain and Polly and I stand drinking our coffee and looking out of the sliding doors at the wind-driven, turbulent surf. Jorge was called to the rehab earlier, which I couldn't understand since Tommy is not allowed to have visitors, and it's only been little over a week that he's been in treatment. However, Jorge didn't seem too worried, so I shrugged it off.

Rosa cooks breakfast for us as Emilio coos and gurgles from a port-able bassinet and gazes thoughtfully, I have to think, at the dancing chickens moving on a plastic rod above his head. Mike has left to meet with someone about a real-estate deal, and Millie, as is her custom, is sleeping in.

Later, I'm in my suite with Polly drinking coffee when Rosa knocks on the door and asks if I can come meet with Jorge, who is back from the rehab center. His shirt is soaked from the rain, and I notice that Carmella and Emilio are not in the breakfast area. My first thought is that something happened to her or the baby, and I'm about to burst from fear. It's then I notice a policeman who's been standing off to the side of the big kitchen, and he steps forward with his eyes on me. I'm so nervous that my skin is prickling all over; once more I'm thinking only the worst regarding Carmella or Emilio. The coffee mug I'm holding slips from my fingers and shatters at my feet on the tile floor.

"What is it?" hearing my voice sound much louder than normal. "You're all looking at me." Polly reaches for my arm.

"Ms. Cunningham," the officer takes off his hat and begins, "there was a disturbance at the rehab facility in Lauderdale Lakes early this morning. Mr. Defalco, who is listed in the records as your fiancé, was in an altercation with a patient with a violent criminal history. This man was in lockdown, but somehow he overpowered two orderlies and took a young woman hostage in the lunchroom." The cop halts his speech, and his Adam's apple looks as though it's about to pop out of his throat. "Mr. Defalco was in the kitchen at the time, with three other people. He tried to normalize the situation, and he almost succeeded, but I'm sorry to inform you that Mr. Defalco was killed while making a valiant attempt to save the woman. He was shot by mistake when he was trying to get to the other man. It was a horrible accident, and the perpetrator was ultimately shot and killed by the police unit I … I was with on the scene. I want you to know that Mr. Defalco saved that woman's life, as she would have been stabbed to death before the perpetrator could have been subdued. This won't make you feel any better right now, but Thomas Defalco died a hero."

The officer is choked up during the entire time he tells me all this, but the words mean nothing to me after I hear: "Mr. Defalco was killed."

I remember the floor disappearing under my feet and an unnatural sound escaping from my throat.

When I come to, I'm lying on the bed in my suite and Millie is sitting next to me, rubbing my arms as if trying to get life back into them and me. She looks so old I hardly recognize her. Her blond hair is in total disarray and she wears no makeup, her face an emotionally torn picture. The sliding doors are open to let fresh air into the room, and a nurse or some such medical person is now putting on a blood-pressure cuff on me.

Mike is back, and he's saying something to other people I don't know who are standing in the room. I see Millie clamp her hands over her mouth and turn away, collapsing into Mike's arms. I feel Polly holding and talking to me, but I don't know what she's saying. I see Jorge taking over for Polly and holding my hands to get my attention. Everyone wants to say something to me, but I hear nothing and I pass out again.

All I remember clearly about that entire morning, after I come to for a second time, is telling Polly that I need to see Tommy, and her nodding and saying she'd drive.

Epilog

THE SAND IS SUGAR-SOFT on my bare feet as I walk into the sunlight that splashes a long shadow behind me. I'm wearing a breezy yellow and white sundress that flows around the calves of my legs as I move, making me feel ultrafeminine. I take off my wide-brimmed sun hat and shake my long red curls loose. The morning is Florida perfect, with a low, whispering surf gently slapping at the beach.

Polly says I look like a model, and that cheers me up enormously. It's just what I need to hear. She scuffs along beside me in her sandals, the open toes making her push a little too deeply into the sand. "Wait just a piddlin' pea hen minute. I have to take off these damn clodhoppers." She leans on the arm of a handsome Latino man, about ten years her junior, who flashes a wide white smile at her but gives me a "wondering" look.

I stop what has been a deliberate stroll. "Polly, did you ever stop and consider that Pablo here, who loves you beyond Hell and back, rarely understands a single thing you say to him?"

She laughs and says, "Doesn't have to. We're happy as is." She sighs and says to me, "Damn, Kitty, has it really been six years ago today? It seems as fresh in my mind as if it were yesterday. I miss him so much sometimes, same as I do all those years at The House."

We walk on together and the tears under my sunglasses are making it hard for me to see through them. "Tommy is always with me in my heart. I especially feel him all around me today. I think he would be happy and laughing with all of us right now, don't you?"

Polly can't answer and turns away so I won't see her crying. I remember that horrific day at the villa when the news of his death was delivered by the cop who I later learn was the one who shot Tommy by accident. He quit the force but I had nothing to do with his decision, and no charges were pressed. Still, he couldn't do his job with Tommy's death always hanging over him. He wrote me a letter saying this, and I will always respect his honesty and his courage for coming out to the villa and facing me.

I remember clutching Polly's hand when we arrived at the morgue, and Millie's using her influence to get the authorities to let me view Tommy's body. It was him, yet it wasn't. I recall how peaceful he looked. I remained calm, resolved, teary but controlled, curious even. It's strange how one's thoughts twist and turn when looking into the face of a loved one who's been stolen by untimely death. It was as if, any second, Tommy would open his eyes and give me that sexy grin and I'd hear his deep chuckle.

Then it hit me that he would never again call me Kitten or passionately dash me around a dance floor, and that I would never see tears stream down his cheeks as he listened to opera. I touched his cold face, another reminder that he had changed, and I thought about his fast and fierce temper, and what he'd said about that fateful day he pulled the trigger and a soldier's job was no longer a soldier's job. Even though I might have shown him the way to forgive himself for that awful act, he could never forget what the war had made him.

Tommy was a complicated man whose light balanced his dark with the same intensity. I stood there with him a long time after Polly and Millie left the room. It was quiet and cold, the odor of disinfectant and steel all around me. It was quite clear to me that Tommy wasn't there, not at all. The man who lived in that body was gone, and that body no longer held an open hand for me to cling to.

I had him cremated, as he had no immediate family to request anything different, and for more nights than I cared to count I sat with his ashes in an urn in my suite in dark silence without anyone else around. I talked to him like a madwoman, and I cried like a child when he didn't answer. I would take the note from my wallet and let my tears blend in with his words "I Love You, Kitten," until one day the paper dissolved in my hands.

Then, one morning when the sun was uncommonly bright and a warm sea breeze was playing tag with the palm fronds, I got up and unceremoniously walked to the beach, to the exact spot where we had shared our souls' secrets, and I released him into the surf. I watched the gray-white dust come and go with each wave until the water rolled clear. I cried out my last goodbye.

Today, the dawn has broken just as morning broke on that day so many long years ago. I sigh deeply and look across the beautiful, shining ocean and out to the horizon.

"Well, Tommy," I say, as if he were standing there beside me, "see how much my life changes with every passing year? But what never changes is my loving memory of you. Millie wishes she could be here as well, to bless you this day, but her knees just can't take walking in the sand anymore. It probably takes everything out of her to admit that, but you know how she is." I laugh.

I listen to the singing of the ocean for a little while, remembering Tommy and me swimming like fishes through the waves. Then I reach down and take the hand of a small child from Chris's grip and walk her to the water's edge. Chris hands her a wreath of brilliant flowers, and she gingerly wades out with him past the short breaking waves and places this ring of my love on a swell. She giggles and jumps up into his arms with a squeal and he nods to her lovingly. "What do you want to say, Katherine Millicent Michele?"

She looks out at the bobbing wreath, her bright green eyes sparkling and her dark reddish curls blowing softly around her face. She asks Chris a question in a voice like tinkling chimes, and he smiles and assures her that what she asked would be appropriate. Little Katherine Millicent Michelle kisses her palm and throws the smooch to the sea and says, "I love you, Daddy." Then to Chris, "Thank you for letting me say that, Dad."

Chris kisses her and brings her to my side. He kisses my cheek and looks out to the waves and says, "Tommy, every year I promise to keep your family safe. And that promise will stand forever."

"Tommy," I say through fresh tears, "I wish you had lived long enough to know I was pregnant. We scored yet another miracle, but every day together was another miracle, wasn't it?" I cannot help but smile. "I dreamed once we had a son, but Kathy popped out instead. She has your sense of humor and my stubbornness, but you must have known, when you picked Chris for me so many years ago, that he would pull my world together someday. He's a wonderful husband and a great father to your daughter. Thank you, Tomaso. Be at peace and know all is well."

We turn around and walk, with our daughter between us, to where Polly and Pablo wait arm in arm. Bruno embraces me, as well as Jeannie and Christine. Phillip and Barry help Jorge pass out the champagne and Carmella brings Emilio to play with our little girl and build sand castles and tease each other relentlessly. Maybe they will end up loving each other like Tommy and me someday.

We toast to our friends—our forever family—and start back to the villa. Millie waves from the pool area, where she was able to get a good view of the ceremony with her friend, Ray, from the days at The House. She raises a martini glass and calls to us, "My God, it's almost noon, and, damn it, that must mean cocktail hour someplace."

We get to the veranda and everyone is chatting merrily as they take their places around a table laden with food. I turn and search for Tommy's wreath. It's now a mere dot, but floating beside it are two pelicans, and that makes me smile.

*************THE END*************

About the Author

Photo by Linda Kramer

SUZANNE J WARFIELD lives on a small farm in east-central Pennsylvania. She is a retired fine dining bartender as well as equine professional. She has also been a professional show dog handler and a AKC Breeder of Merit of fine Japanese Chin. She now owns and operates a small, posh boarding kennel and spends her free time writing.

70328103R00199

Made in the USA
Middletown, DE
12 April 2018